Inertial Catalyst

Archeons, book 5

by James L. Steele

Inertial Catalyst (Archeons, book 5)
Copyright © 2021 by James L. Steele

This is a work of fiction. All characters and events are products of the author's imagination. Any resemblance to real persons or events is coincidence. Human readers are advised not to lick, chew, or swallow any meteorites, no matter how tasty they may appear.

Cover art by **Valentinapaz**, Valentinapaz.com

Editing by **Alex Phengsavath**, polyglotprose.blogspot.com/

Published by KTM Publishing

Print edition set in Fanwood, Exo, and Playfair Display, all royalty-free typefaces

Print edition ISBN: 978-1-7322824-4-5

Portland

I

It was the nicest city Nipe had ever been to. She and Ekal had been living here since the convention five months ago, and she still marveled at it. They had been to cities in which the people guarded themselves against the Relians, and they had been to cities where the people welcomed them with eager scents. Portland, Oregon, was perhaps the friendliest of them all, and she had been fortunate enough to find a compatible human here.

No matter where they went, people in Portland were so eager to talk. It wasn't unlike being in the contacted universe again, even with the twinge of fear in some people's scents. It couldn't be helped, as the idea of alien life was still new to them, but it had been so refreshing to find so many people curious and eager to get to know them.

Nipe sat next to Veronica. The fox wore a loose-fitting shirt and a pair of shorts, both black. The shorts she understood, but she did not have visible breasts unless she had a child on the way, so she still couldn't figure out the purpose of the shirt, and why male foxes weren't expected to wear one.

Ekal, her raptor, stood on the other side of the woman who had taken them in, watching her drink. Nipe's tail wagged. The human body was still a great mystery to them. Their immune system was barely developed compared to a

Relian's, and by extension their bodies seemed entirely unaware of substances it should eject. Poisons, toxins, pathogens—it assimilated them all instead of kicking them out.

Alcohol was one substance the human body should have known not to tolerate. Veronica was fond of the stuff. She liked the hard drinks, the light drinks, the mixed drinks, everything except wine. Right now she was drinking vodka mixed with some sort of flavored syrup while chatting up the bartender.

Ekal had tried some the first time Veronica had brought her here, and the reptile's body had rejected the alcohol minutes after she swallowed. In human society, it was rather poor taste to vomit in the street, but the bathrooms here were too small for a theropod. She had been the butt of every joke in every bar in the city since, but playfulness came from their scents, so they had accepted her unusual limit in good humor. Ekal suspected seeing a predatory reptile humiliated in this way helped a prey species feel more comfortable around her. People often called her a dinosaur, quoting lines from *Jurassic Park*, and she took it in stride, but she wished humans had a better frame of reference for her species than the velociraptors in a monster movie.

Nipe never became intoxicated. Her body filtered out the alcohol immediately. She had infinite tolerance and thus equal fame in the city. She only drank to be part of the company Veronica kept, and to experience the taste of substances that did not exist anywhere else in the universe, contacted or otherwise.

Veronica was talking to the bartender and a couple others about the movies. People still raved about *Men in Black*, still laughed at *Batman and Robin* and *The Lost World*. They had a new movie to laugh at, *Spawn*, and the jokes flowed like the beer from the tap. Right now they were talking about *Gattaca*, which was still in theaters, and a welcome change of pace.

Ekal and Nipe laughed at all movies, and they never tired of telling people how cinema looked from their point of view. They could see the spaces between the frames of film, as well as the zipping of the electron gun on a television. Everything sounded forced and fake. None of the characters had a scent, so the emotions and situations on display felt hollow. The audio always sounded clipped above and below, making every line of dialogue feel as if it came from a far distant place. Many of the people in Portland seemed interested in knowing what aliens thought of movies and TV, but most considered it a fleeting curiosity. They didn't want to know why it was so easy to trick the human mind through acting, but next to impossible to trick a Relian.

Veronica got up from the bar and mingled with the crowd for a while. She sat down at a table with a bunch of her other friends, cradling her drink. Ekal and Nipe followed. The fox sat next to her, snatched someone else's drink from his hand, and swallowed half of it. One of Veronica's friends beckoned Nipe to sit in his lap. She switched places and plopped down. Justin was his name. Ekal scented him from across the table and confirmed the alcohol had gone straight to his crotch, as it always did. Justin had slept with Nipe several times, and his scent was still good, so she allowed him to be close to her fox.

The story of Ekal and Nipe's planet being destroyed, and the two of them were there to witness the antisphere tearing it apart as they fled through a portal to another planet and were trapped there for years until the Archeons Rive and Deka found them, had long ceased to be interesting to the bar crowd. Even the more immediate parts about the Relians seeking a new home here on Earth, and how the conventions were meant to help raptors and foxes find suitable humans to live with so they wouldn't be settled in some district of one major city. The Relians found it rather telling that Veronica's circle of friends chatted about the movies instead of something real which happened to the entire known universe.

Space Jam came up once, and that led to television shows for children. *Power Rangers* generated almost as many jokes as *Spawn*. One woman cleared space to speak and told everyone about her little girl being so into *Ren and Stimpy* it was scary. Another man at the table brought up his kids being obsessed with *Pinky and the Brain*, but he didn't mind, since he recorded it and watched it while the kids weren't around.

"Why don't you watch it with them?" Veronica asked.

"The last thing they want to do is watch their favorite show with their father!" he said.

Everyone laughed, took a drink to that.

Justin held Nipe at the waist, felt under her shirt. Nipe moved with him, grinding against his hard-on, which was not obvious visually, but he smelled aroused, which encouraged Nipe to grind harder.

This was a near-weekly ritual. She and Ekal suspected Justin had a thing for fur, and that he would have come to live with Veronica just to be around Nipe if he could, but Ekal wouldn't allow it. The man was good for sex, but not for a companion, and she had told him that more than once, both while he had been sober and drunk. He seemed to understand, though Ekal could tell he did not really believe her.

Nipe reclined against his chest, felt behind his ear, rubbing that spot that drove him wild. The others at the table were still talking about kids these days and the TV they watched. This gradually slid into the music they listened to. Veronica had no husband or children, but she listened to the others at the table talk about what was going on at home.

Justin's scent was now so strong it was all Ekal could smell. Nipe knew it was there, too, and that it affected her mood. On most planets in the contacted universe, it was perfectly acceptable to have sex with a Relian canine in public, even if sex was not a public act within the native culture. Here on Earth, humans considered sex something that must remain out of sight and preferably out of hearing and smelling range of anyone else, even with a fox.

Nipe rose from Justin's lap, wagging her tail. Justin adjusted himself and rose from his seat as he followed Nipe to the back of the bar. Ekal tapped Veronica on the shoulder. The human turned and noticed Justin following a red and white tail. She smiled, raised her glass, then turned back to the group.

Ekal walked after Justin just as Nipe opened the bar's rear door. The human was already undoing his belt. He pushed open the door with his free hand. The raptor held it open with her neck and stepped outside. It was cold out here, and a back ally in autumn was usually the last place anyone would want to have sex, but Justin liked that Nipe kept him warm.

The fox was already against the wall, shorts pulled down. Justin pulled it out, clearly having planned this, as he wore no underwear. He held Nipe and kissed her on the neck, burying his face in her fur as the cold wind blew through the ally. Nipe pushed backwards with her hips, telling him to hurry up. Justin felt under her shirt with both hands. Nipe wasn't sure why; she had no tits to grope, but he seemed to like the nipples under the fur. Nipe pushed her hips back into his a few times. Finally he angled himself and slipped in. Nipe felt instantly relieved. She had been eager for days.

Ekal stood just four feet away and watched. The first time she had done this, Justin had been spooked and almost couldn't keep it up, but he had come to understand who Ekal was to Nipe, and that nothing happened to the fox without her raptor there to make sure she was all right. After the third time, Justin accepted it as part of the deal, and now he barely noticed the theropod watching them at all. Sometimes he made passes at Ekal when he was drunk enough, but the raptor remained untouchable.

Nipe braced herself against the wall. She'd been told this was one of the dirtiest places one could do it in human society, but human references didn't matter much to her. Justin laughed about it. He would rather take her home, but Nipe never seemed interested in taking it somewhere else, so he had followed her lead. She seemed happy to keep their relationship within the realm of bar-buddies, so this was the best place to do it.

Ekal smelled something on the other side of the ally. She turned and scented it harder. A car had parked in the ally, blocking it off. Someone stood in front of it, holding a gun.

"Nipe," she said. "Something's wrong."

Still moaning from Justin's last thrust, Nipe looked in the direction Ekal was facing.

A shot fired. Ekal flinched and screeched but did not fall. She looked back at herself. Feathers stuck out of her thigh. She looked back up the ally. The man was still there, reloading the gun.

Justin pulled out and stuffed himself back in his pants as he nudged Nipe toward the door. Two more shots fired. One hit Justin in the leg, and the other hit Nipe's torso. Other shots hit the wall and bounced off the door. The first man ran up the ally, and five more sets of footsteps trotted up the other side. Someone inside the bar pulled the door shut and held it. Justin yanked on the door, banging on it and shouting.

Ekal snarled and screeched at the men and women approaching. She ran around Nipe and Justin and stood between them and the approaching humans. The people wore large coats and ski masks, far too much for the weather, but not entirely out of place either. They slowed their approach, all eyes on the reptile.

She began to feel numb. The sensation began at her hip and worked its way up her spine. Her legs began to wobble, and she turned to Justin. He was sliding down the door, slack-jawed and dreamy-eyed. Nipe had fallen on top of him, eyes already closed.

Ekal managed to stay upright and lunged at the attackers. They leaned backwards as a group, holding position twenty feet away. She turned to the lone man on the other side of the ally, the one who had shot her. He stood fifty feet away, aiming his gun at her again. She opened her mouth and screeched at him.

Another shot. This one hit her in the chest, and now the numb feeling spread from that point. She lost control of her legs and collapsed to the dirty asphalt, which emboldened the people in the other group. They ran along the wall straight to Nipe. Three of them picked her up, and they carried her down the ally to one of the cars.

Ekal screeched and tried to stand, but she was moving in slow motion.

The man who had shot her twice strolled up and stood over her. His coat was thick, and his orange ski mask did not obscure his contemptuous scent. He knelt closer, looking her in the eye.

"Don't take it personally. This isn't about you or her. It's about all of you."

Ekal wanted that scent rotting in her stomach. She raised her leg, flexed her killing claw, and slashed the man across the shin. Her claw struck bone. Ekal smelled blood. The man cursed and fell to his hands and knees. Ekal pulled herself across the asphalt, moving in slow motion toward him. A few men and one women were running up the ally from the car, shouting to him.

The man on the ground crawled and turned toward the car he came from. Even drugged up and mostly numb, Ekal was faster. She caught up to him and reached for his face. A claw slid through his skin easily and struck solid bone. He wailed and writhed as she gripped him. Ekal crawled up the rest of the way, opening her mouth. The others had caught up to him and were now piling on top of her. She felt another needle pierce her scales, and now she felt entirely disconnected from herself. The asphalt didn't feel like anything. Air felt like water.

Someone was pulling his mask off, and another person was pulling him away from Ekal's hand. The mask fell free and dangled from her claws, and they dragged him away, screaming. She had pierced his left eye, and blood was everywhere. They hoisted him up to his feet, grabbed his gun, and walked him to the car. Ekal's hand fell. Her vision felt numb as well, and she slipped away. She felt someone running back and kicking her a few times, and then the ally fell still.

2

The spacetime sphere opened in the alley at six o'clock in the morning, and Secretary Rhine and the tan and grey raptor stepped through. It closed behind them, and Rive's nose took him immediately to the blood on the asphalt, individual splatters marked by plastic cones with numbered pieces of paper taped to them.

On the other side of the alley, a uniformed police officer ducked under the crime scene tape and approached them. CJ turned to face him, briefcase in one hand, faxed documents in the other.

"Lieutenant Slim?" she called.

"Ms. Rhine, Archeon Rive. Nice to meet both of you. I'm sorry it has to be like this."

CJ met him halfway and shook hands.

"I read your reports," she said. "Have you checked all the hospitals?"

"I had a couple officers blanketing the area, checking all ERs and clinics. Nobody's reported any eye injuries yet."

CJ walked to where half-metal theropod was scenting.

"We got statements from everyone in the bar," the lieutenant continued. "The blood we collected is being analyzed. Ekal, the raptor, worked with the boys to produce a composite image of the guy she wounded. We have the darts they used."

"Yes, darts, lieutenant?"

"Full of morphine."

They stopped in front of the cones. Rive sniffed around, crouched low.

"Morphine is a controlled substance," CJ said. "Only hospitals have it."

The lieutenant nodded. "We're looking at employees of nearby hospitals, trying to find a match to the sketch. No fingerprints were recovered. Everyone at the bar checks out as a regular."

"Your report said someone held the exit door closed from the inside. Did anyone see someone come in and leave in a hurry, or without buying a drink or talking to anyone?"

"Nobody noticed. No one saw the cars either. The crime was very quiet. If not for Ekal wounding one of the suspects, we might not have anything to go on at all. Chief called you here because he thought you'd want to be in the loop. Any talents this guy can bring to the team would be a help."

Rive turned to him, rising to full height. "Ekal already told you what she knew from his scent, did she not?"

"Yeah. White male, late thirties, brown hair, brown eyes. Describes half the people in the city."

"Not his appearance, his scent."

"Scent testimony isn't exactly evidence, Mr. Rive."

"A wound like that would need to be treated right away," CJ said. "He must be in a hospital by now. Are you sure nobody's found anything?"

"So far, nobody has called."

"Is there a chance hospital staff are covering for him? If they got morphine from a hospital, it makes sense they'd give him care under the radar."

"Somebody would notice. Let me take you to the station. You can interview Ekal and Veronica and look over the evidence. You'll meet the people working on this case."

He turned and led them down the alley to a patrol car blocking it.

Rive walked by the officer's side. "Has anyone asked why these people would want to kidnap a fox?"

"Sure we have. Until we know who these people are, it's all wild guesses ranging from a prostitution ring to illegal fur trading."

"Ekal testified the man she wounded told her not to take it personally. That this was about all of us. She thought he was referring to all Relians."

"Any idea what it means?" Lt. Slim said.

"One."

"What's your hunch?" CJ asked.

"I need to be sure I have all the information before I say."

Rive ducked under the crime scene tape, CJ and the officer two steps behind him.

3

Nipe woke up in a large room, cold, thirsty, head swimming. Her clothes were missing. She rose from the concrete floor, scenting the dusty air.

She was in a cage. The vertical bars reminded her of prison cells she had seen in movies and television shows. Four walls of bars enclosed within a larger room of concrete and steel. The bars ended in a drop ceiling with a hatch built into it. She walked up to the bars, which looked pristine.

"Hello?"

Her voice echoed. She smelled nothing alive in here. The vent blew warm air inside. Electricity hummed. She turned around and faced the rear wall. A tripod stood outside the bars, a camcorder mounted on it, plugged in, red light visible on top.

She heard footsteps overhead. Loud, angry voices shouted above the drop ceiling, and the sound of a dog snarling and barking.

Sounds of metal clanging.

Sounds of cursing and snarling.

The hatch in the ceiling opened, and something lowered into Nipe's cage.

"What's going on? Where am I? Ekal! Ekal!"

A large dog kennel attached to a thick rope descended. The door of the kennel was attached to a string leading out of the hatch. The kennel lowered all the way, and now Nipe saw the rottweiler inside. The dog had bite marks up and down her muzzle, some of her fur was missing, and she smelled starved and terrified. At the sight of Nipe, the dog snarled.

Nipe backed away. The kennel touched the concrete, the rope attached to the gate yanked upwards, and the door opened. The dog bolted out of the kennel.

Nipe screamed, dropping to all fours and dashing along the wall. The dog veered for her. The cage was only large enough for her to run three strides in any direction, so she leaped at the bars and tried to climb them. The dog latched onto her tail and shook it. Nipe fell to the concrete and landed on the dog. She lunged for Nipe's arm and clamped down. Nipe bared her teeth and growled at the dog, reaching for the neck.

Now she was speaking the dog's language. The rottweiler let go of the fox and backed away, displaying her teeth. Nipe rolled to all four legs and snarled back. The dog barked at her, fur raised. Nipe raised her fur and barked louder. The rottweiler growled and circled her. She was starving, and she smelled like she had been through a lifetime of this and was alive today only because she had climbed over the dead bodies of everyone she had ever met. Her scent filled Nipe from head to tail. She knew what the dog understood, and there was only one way out of this.

Nipe leaped at the dog. The rottweiler snarled and then clamped Nipe's muzzle. She reached under the dog's jaw with a hand and clawed downwards. It forced the dog's mouth open for a split second, then she held the dog's muzzle between her jaws. Nipe's bite was stronger, and seconds later the rottweiler dropped to the concrete, whining in agony.

Her first thought was that she had shown this dog who was dominant, so she could let go. Her second thought was this dog would wait until Nipe's back was turned and then leap on her and go for the throat.

That rottweiler scent... She hated it. It was a threat to her life, and she had to get rid of it or it would destroy her.

She squeezed as hard as she could. Something cracked in the dog's muzzle, and she urinated on herself. Nipe opened her mouth up and dove for the throat. She tore it free as she jumped away.

Nipe sat on the concrete, back against the bars. She smelled new scents outside the cage and whipped around to face them. Three men and two women stood against the far wall on the other side of the bars. She recognized their scents. She rose to her hind legs and held the bars, still snarling as the flesh and fur worked their way down her throat.

"Where am I?"

Nobody answered.

"What are you doing?!"

They smiled. One of them broke away and stood by the tripod. He removed the camera and walked around the cage, watching the view screen.

"Do you have any idea what almost happened?!" Nipe screamed. "Where's Ekal? Where's my raptor? Do you know what happens to me if she's not around?!"

One of the men smiled, his scent full of disgust.

Nipe snarled and pounded on the bars. She gnawed one of them and then howled at the men and women. She screamed at the man holding the camera.

"I'm prone to reverting! Do you know what that means?! Have you ever seen a fox revert?! I need Ekal! I'll kill all of you if she's not here! I can't stop myself!"

The man holding the camera clearly wanted to get closer to Nipe's face, but he remained just out of reach.

4

Ekal paced the police interview room, her scent as panicked as her breathing. Veronica sat in one of the chairs, hand on her forehead, eyes closed. The clock on the wall read nine a.m. Rive followed Ekal with his eyes as she paced the length of the room. The other officers didn't want to be in the same room with her right now, and they didn't know how Veronica could be so comfortable with a dinosaur pacing like a caged lion. CJ watched through the small two-way mirror, standing beside lieutenant Slim.

"I didn't smell anyone at the bar who hadn't been there before," Ekal was saying.

"Was it routine to go to the back alley with Justin?" Rive asked.

"It happened almost every week. Nipe never wanted to wait. Nobody minded what they were doing."

"Somebody knew you three would be out there. Do you know of anyone who would want to take her away, or why?"

"I don't know! Rive, if she's alone for just a few—"

"That's why you're coming with us while the secretary and I help the police find your fox. If Nipe has reverted, it should be you who brings her back."

Veronica raised her head from her hands. "Why would they do this? Where would they take her?"

"I will look into that. I have a few ideas."

"What?" Veronica asked.

Rive turned and addressed the mirror. "The kidnappers would have to know a fox can revert to her old ways if separated from her raptor too long. They would have taken her somewhere they believe could hold a fox. I want to look at public records of building sales and leases. I also want you to expand your search to hospitals out of the city and state. Partner with other districts and have them visit their hospitals. Anywhere within a reasonable distance for an injury of that type. I have good reason to believe the kidnapper's intent is to force Nipe to revert."

"Force her?" Lt. Slim said to CJ. "What on Earth for?"

Rive walked to the door and opened it. Ekal followed him. Veronica rose from the seat, still holding her head. The metal raptor rounded the corner and looked directly at Lt. Slim.

"What makes you so sure of the motive?" asked the officer.

"You wouldn't believe me if I told you the truth, so I will say I was privy to a conversation that prepared me for this. Please expand your hospital search. Tell me, officer, if you had to keep a violent animal penned up, where would you go?"

"Plenty of buildings in town it could be done."

"Give me addresses, and I will need sales records for the previous six months."

"Whoa, Mr. Rive, that kind of thing takes weeks to collect and authorize."

"Why?"

"It's police work."

"A reverted fox is more dangerous than an earthquake. This is not some missing persons case you're dealing with. People will die if Ekal doesn't find her fox, and that is not a threat."

Lieutenant Slim did not look as moved as he should have been. "I'll see what I can do."

Rive stepped up to him. "If we have to, we will scent the whole city on foot until we find her."

The lieutenant nodded and yawned. Rive huffed as he walked by him, Ekal following just behind. CJ turned and ran to catch up.

"What conversation are you talking about?"

"The one that happened just before Deka, Sonjaa, and Kylac left Earth. I heard a man talking about something like this happening. I believe this is deliberate."

They turned a corner. CJ was having a difficult time keeping up with the raptors.

5

Nipe shivered in the corner of the cage. She wasn't cold, but the smell of blood was starting to make her feel good. She fought it by conjuring memories of Ekal's scent to force her lower mind back where it belonged.

She had killed three more dogs over the previous day. All of them had been lowered into her cage via the kennel. Occasionally the hatch opened and water poured from the ceiling. It was the only drink she had besides the blood of the dogs. After the first day, she realized no food was coming; the dogs were meant to be her food. She loathed it, but she relented. Their meat was sour from months of fear and rage. She hoped it would always repulse her.

Occasionally, men and women stood behind the bars and observed her. Sometimes someone picked up the camera and recorded her from different angles. The men and women on the other side of the bars never spoke to her.

It had been hours since the last dog dropped. She could hear them upstairs, snarling at each other, barking, wrestling for dominance. She counted at least six sets of paws above her. She hated the noises they made. She was starting to hate their scents, which made her shiver even more. The last few times she had reverted, it happened so fast there had been no time to think about it. This time it was happening slowly, and she felt herself coming closer and closer to the abyss—plenty of time to ponder what was about to happen.

A man opened the door and stepped into room on the other side of the bars. He had a hose. He turned on the nozzle and washed the blood out of the cage, as well as the panic scat and Nipe's urine and bodily waste. His face was neutral, but his scent was full of terror. He had probably drawn the short straw today, so he got this job.

"You know what's happening, don't you?"

The man pretended not to hear her.

"Please don't do this to me. Once I fall off the edge, you can't bring me back. Only a raptor can. If I get out of here, I will kill all of you, and I won't be able to stop myself. If I escape the building, I will kill anyone in scenting distance, and I won't be satisfied until everyone around me is either dead or bleeding."

The man turned away from her. He sprayed a turd out of the cage and into a hole in the wall.

Nipe stood up and held the bars. "You think these bars will hold me? I will get out."

The man turned. She gasped and held onto the bars as he raised the stream to her face. Nipe shouted as the water bored into her fur.

"Bars won't keep you safe! Nothing will! Without our raptors, foxes are the most horrifying form of life in the contacted universe! We don't sleep until everything around us is dead! I promise you'll be the first one I kill when I get out of here!"

He walked closer, holding the spray on her muzzle. Nipe held tighter, letting her arm take most of the force.

"I won't wait until you're dead to eat you! I'm starting to like the smell of blood already! It's making me happy!"

He aimed the spray back down to the floor and pushed the last of the blood and shit out of the cage. He then turned the water off and began pulling the hose back with him to the door.

Nipe sagged on the bars, panting, looking at him under her arm. "I'm not too far gone. Sex would keep me from reverting for a while. Wouldn't take much. Just undo your pants and get me through the bars. It'll help me a lot. Please..."

The man's face wrinkled. He gathered the rest of the hose and pulled it through the door, then slammed it shut.

The overhead hatch opened. Nipe slid down from the bars and stood halfway between biped and quadruped. Another dog was coming. His scent was repulsive. She wanted all those dogs over her head to bleed so they couldn't hurt her again.

6

Rive flipped through records of condemned buildings in the old parts of town. Some of the records had photographs, and he committed all of them to memory, along with addresses.

It had taken a painfully long time to acquire these records, two whole days since he first asked. He had already read through the statements of everyone at the bar on the night the kidnapping happened. Nobody had seen anything unusual. It was normally such a friendly place. Everybody knew each other, and it was so relaxed and calm there. There hadn't been any serious crime in the area in years.

In the middle of this room, Justin Isewell sat in the chair. CJ sat across the table from him, flanked by a couple deputy officers.

"Are you sure you don't remember anyone strange in the bar that night?"

"There was nobody unfamiliar that I could see. But I wasn't really watching. I was more interested in Nipe."

"I understand you two are close."

He smiled. "I'm her favorite. It's weird for me."

"Why is that, Mr. Isewell?"

"Because I'm gay."

"Oh. I see. If I may ask, how did you become involved with Nipe?"

"We met at that bar. I was curious about her. We got to talking. The longer I was with her... Caught me off guard.

I've never met a woman I wanted to get close to. Something about her. I hear foxes can do that. I've done things with her I never thought I'd do." He laughed.

CJ smiled. "Can you think of anyone who might want to hurt her?"

"Nobody. I wasn't the only guy she slept with. Everyone loved her, and I don't mean that in a dirty way."

"Were any of her other partners at the bar that night?"

"Half the men in that bar had been with her at least once. Half the women, too. She wasn't afraid to move things along. Someone knew we'd be out there. They were ready for all of us. I can't imagine anyone who had been with her being part of this. Especially if they knew Veronica. She used to be so withdrawn. She'd come out and drink, but would usually sit alone."

"Why did she sit alone?"

"Lot of breakups. Lot of disappointment. Most of it I don't even know about. Then Ekal and Nipe came along. They helped her through that. She recovered, and now she's joined up with everyone again. It's like the old Veronica is back. Haven't seen her in years."

The door opened, and lieutenant Slim poked his head in. "Madame Secretary, we have a break. A hospital."

CJ stood up. "Did you find the wounded man?"

"It's worse than that. He's in critical condition."

Rive looked up from the stack of papers. "Take us to him. Ekal and I will identify him."

"Where is he?"

"Sacramento."

"That far away?" CJ said. "Get us a map of the area. Rive can make a way much faster."

An hour later, lieutenant Slim and CJ walked through the doors of the hospital. A doctor and someone in business casual clothing leaned on the front desk. At the sight of two dinosaur-like creatures behind the humans, the two men straightened up.

Lieutenant Slim held up his badge. CJ flashed her ID as well.

"What's the story?" said the lieutenant.

The men shook hands with everyone, nodding to the raptors. The theropods bobbed necks in return.

"Came in by helicopter last night. Wouldn't say how it happened. His left eye is punctured. Apparently someone else tried to treat the wound but didn't do a good job. It's severely infected, and the infection has spread to his circulatory system. The pilot didn't know him. Was under orders to bring him here."

"Where's the pilot?"

"In the break room. Local police detained him."

"Please take me to him," said Lt. Slim. "This is Rive and Ekal. They know the man's scent, and they will tell us if it's the same man."

The doctor waved for the theropods to follow. CJ followed Rive. Lt. Slim walked with the business casual man down a different hall.

The doctor turned a few corners, opened a few doors, and then led them to an intensive care room. As soon as the raptors entered the room, they both growled.

"That's him," Ekal said.

"Is he in any shape to talk?" CJ asked the doctor.

"You can try, but keep the dinosaurs out of the room, please."

CJ stepped inside. Rive and Ekal backed away and stood in the hall.

The man in the bed had gauze over one side of his face. His leg was also bandaged and elevated. His remaining eye was closed. CJ picked up his chart. He had been admitted under the name Calvin Basil, and someone had noted that he had paid for treatment up front in cash.

CJ stood over him and cleared her throat.

"Mr. Basil."

The man opened his eye but did not speak.

CJ decided to cut straight to the chase. "I know how you were injured. You were abducting a Relian canine, and her raptor defended herself."

He closed his eye.

"The police here took your prints and faxed them to Portland. They identified you as Kevin Parson. You were part of a couple dog-fighting operations in the past, arrested in four states. Soon they will match your hair and blood to a crime scene in a back alley in Portland a few days ago. Did they tell you this wound might be fatal?"

He lay still for a moment, then he nodded.

"My name is CJ Rhine. I'm not the police. Where did they take Nipe?"

He did not speak.

"Why did they take Nipe?"

No response.

"What are you doing in Sacramento?"

He laughed weakly. "Because the nurse couldn't help me."

"What nurse?"

"She works for us on the side. Gets us our drugs. Makes it easier to deal with the dogs. If I had gone to the hospital right away, I might not be in bad shape. But... Couldn't risk it." He opened his eye. "Will you be my lawyer?"

"You might not live long enough to need one. How did you get to Sacramento in the first place?"

"He sent a chopper. I paid him cash. Hoping the cops wouldn't look this far."

"Where is Nipe? Why did you take her?"

He smiled. "You'll see."

"You know what happens if she reverts, don't you?"

"Once they have what they need, they'll abandon the place. Then you can do whatever you want with the bitch. I didn't want the job, but money talks."

"Who hired you? What job?"

"I don't know who hired me, but... he paid us a fuck-load of money... to... it."

CJ looked at his IV. The morphine drip had started.

"Thank you, Mr. Parson. I promise we'll be in touch. I hope you recover."

"Bullshiii... You wan me dead. Everyone duh...sss..."

His eye closed, and he drifted off. CJ turned and left the room, stopping in the hall. The raptors looked at her eagerly.

"We heard him," Ekal said. "What now?"

"We let the police and the doctors do their work. I hope he lives so I can send him to prison."

Lieutenant Slim was walking up the hall, notepad in hand. CJ led the way to meet up with him, and they stood off to the side as doctors and nurses passed them, doing double-takes at the raptors.

"Nothing useful," he said. "Pilot works for a private company. He was given the order to land outside of Portland, pick up a man, and fly him here. He doesn't know anything else. I got his employer's number. We'll call up the ranks, get phone records, see if we can find who paid them."

"Do whatever you need to do to tie that man to the crime scene. Rive and Ekal already identified him. He's in no shape to talk, and he's not saying much anyway."

"Did he say what they wanted with her?" Lt. Slim said.

"Only that we'll find out soon enough."

7

The dogs just kept coming. One every few hours. They seemed to have an infinite supply up there. When the hatch opened, she looked up eagerly for another scent to destroy. Dogs now cowered in front of her; they didn't even want to fight, only to escape. Nipe had torn the kennel apart when one dog refused to come out, and now they threw dogs down the hatch. Sometimes they landed without breaking any bones, sometimes they didn't. It was all the same to Nipe now. As long as their living scents were in her nose, anxiety filled her.

She tore them apart, whether the dog was moving or not. She had done this several times, and now a new dog fell from the hatch and landed on his side. He yelped and rose to his feet unharmed, snarling at Nipe.

Blood matted Nipe's fur from head to tail now. She rolled in it after every kill, getting as much on herself as possible. Blood smelled so good. It was the only thing that calmed the anxiety and made her happy.

This dog's scent filled her with rage and terror. She lunged for the dog and grabbed him by the forepaw. She chewed until something snapped. The dog limped away, tail between his legs, whimpering and leaving a trail of urine. The piss was a plea for mercy, and the dog was bleeding, so Nipe backed away and allowed him to live for now.

The side door opened. Five new scents walked in, all of them wearing ski masks. Nipe snarled at them, lunged at the bars and reached through, trying to claw them. They remained by the wall. One of them picked up the camera. He walked around, recording her from different angles. She followed this man around her cage, reaching for him, snarling and yelping. His scent was not wounded, and it made Nipe furious. She wanted it dead.

After a few minutes recording this, the man handed the camera to someone else, who turned it to the cage, while the first man stood before it.

"Just the other day she was coherent and friendly. Now look at her. Do you want this living in your neighborhood? Do you want it near your children? Do you..."

8

"*...want it serving your food, or working in your office?*"

The man on the tape was shouting over the sound of the fox in the cage in the background. CJ, Rive, half the police officers in the building, Ekal, and Veronica huddled around the tiny television. Most of the humans stood slack-jawed. The fox on the tape was drenched in blood and clawing the air through the bars, trying to reach the man narrating the scene.

"*We're sending this footage to every news outlet in the country. Someone will report it. Someone will show the world the truth of what we've let into our homes! You can't hide the truth forever!*"

Lt. Slim paused the tape.

"This was delivered to a local news station this morning. They called us as soon as they saw what was on it."

Rive turned to the other officers. "I know where they are. I want only lieutenant Slim and Secretary Rhine to accompany me and Ekal."

"How do you—?" Lt. Slim started to say.

"The interior matches a description of an abandoned factory I saw in the records. You'll want to check its history to find out who owns it. Take us there and hope we're not too late."

Rive turned and bolted out the door.

"To save her?" CJ called.

"To save the kidnappers."

9

Nipe noticed only one set of footsteps overhead. This made her feel better, but she would not feel safe until all of them were bleeding or dead.

The camera was gone. Nobody had come to hose down the cage, or bothered to clean up the blood. Nipe was aware of human scent above her and around her, and it filled her head with rage that only the smell and taste of blood would calm.

She had two crippled dogs in the cage with her. They didn't fill her with anger because they were limping and bleeding. One had been bleeding off and on for more than a day. When it stopped, she bit it again, and she felt much better when the blood flowed. They cowered every time she shifted positions and stayed on their side of the cage all the time.

The hatch opened again. Sounds of the last dog scuffling and whining and protesting filled the room. Nipe smelled humans up there—more scents that enraged her. She had to find them and destroy them before they destroyed her. She crouched under the hatch and leaped. The hatch was just barely out of reach. She landed, leaped again. The hatch came closer. A dog slid over the opening and fell through. Nipe waited for him to land on the concrete, stepped on his wounded body, then leaped again. Her head peeked above the opening, and she grabbed it with both hands.

She was in the middle of another cage made of chain link fence. The floor was slick in blood, fur, and dog feces. Several men crouched behind the fence, holding brooms, shovels, or long poles. They leaped backwards when they saw Nipe at the hole.

Nipe brought her hind legs up and leaped out of the hole straight for the shovel-holding man. She jumped on the shovel and climbed it to the man's arm and sank her teeth into it. The man howled. Nipe grabbed him and pulled him into the fence. Other men gathered around the cage and began beating her with broomsticks and shovels.

She released the man and snarled at all of them. She leaped at the fence and clamped down on the metal. The links bent and snapped. She spat out the metal. The men scrambled around the room and poured through the doorway. Nipe grabbed the metal and pulled outwards. The fence bent and twisted, and the links started to snap. The human scent became stronger than ever. Rage filled her muscles.

She bit and pulled, opening a ragged hole in the fence, and climbed through, the metal scraping her skin, gouging it deep. She rose to her hind legs and followed the scents.

Nipe found many. Some held knives. Others had guns. They couldn't use them fast enough, and she snuffed them out one by one. When the last one was dead, and their blood filled her nose, she sat down and relaxed. She smelled nothing in here that could harm her.

Her tail wagged.

10

The patrol cars pulled up to the old factory. Rive and Ekal opened the back doors and then dashed up to the entrance. It had a padlock on the front doors, and Rive and Ekal waited for the policeman to come. He carried a pair of bolt cutters. Lt. Slim clipped the locks, and Ekal threw open the doors. She caught the scent and disappeared inside.

Rive turned to CJ and the lieutenant. "We'll come back when it's safe."

The metal raptor took off after Ekal. Lt. Slim stood by the door and drew his pistol. CJ waited ten seconds, then ran in the direction Rive and Ekal had gone.

CJ followed Rive's tail around a couple corners. She passed a human body, neck torn open, blood dry. Flies covered the corpse, and they swarmed when she approached. She ignored them and followed the sound of clicking claws on old tile flooring.

She ran down a flight of steps and came to an open door just as raptor claws ceased to click. She heard growling and stopped at the doorframe. She peeked around. This basement area had prison bars running from floor to ceiling, and they formed a large cell in the center of the room. Outside the cage, on the other side of the room, stood a Relian canine.

CJ remembered Nipe from the conventions. She had spoken to her several times before she and Ekal found Veronica. Here she was now, covered in blood, hunched halfway down to all fours, snarling at Ekal. Rive crouched on the other side of the room, cutting off her retreat.

Bones, blood, and feces littered the interior of the cage. Skulls, femurs, spines. CJ recognized them as dog bones, some still slick with blood, and some had body parts attached to them.

Nipe snarled at Ekal and swiped a forelimb at her. Ekal lunged and collided with Nipe, sending her to the hard floor. The fox raised her arms and legs and raked her claws on Ekal's underbelly. The raptor was trying to lie on top of the fox, but Nipe thrashed too hard. She wiggled and rolled out from underneath the raptor, smacking her across the snout with her claws as she backed away.

She ran toward Rive. The raptor kicked her with his metal foot, throwing her against the wall. The fox snarled at him. Rive backed away and screeched at her.

Ekal grabbed the fox's neck in her jaws and picked her up. Nipe thrashed and howled. The raptor slammed her to the floor and lay on top of her before she could wiggle away. She held her head down by the neck and lay still. The fox snarled and struggled, but her limbs thrashed helplessly in the air, unable to find anything to scratch or grip. Rive ran up to her, held her wrist with one hand and the other arm in his jaws. Her legs were the only things free to move.

She lay on her fox for five solid minutes. The snarls and screams gradually yielded to calm breathing. Another minute later, CJ heard a voice she distantly recognized.

"Ekal..." Nipe said.

Rive released the fox's arms. Ekal rose, nuzzling Nipe's snout. The fox sat upright. She looked as drained as she sounded.

"Ekal," she repeated, gasping. "They had dogs. They wanted me to revert. It felt good. It felt so good..."

She pushed her muzzle into Nipe's chest. Nipe wrapped her arms around her and breathed her scent.

Rive turned around and looked at CJ through the bars.

"It's safe now. Come in."

CJ stepped into the room. "Holy mother of God."

Rive folded his hands close to his chest. "A fox without a raptor. This is what they are without us. It can be even worse. I brought back many foxes from the old ways. Before my metal, I was even more afraid than you are now."

"And they're all like this?"

"Most. Some are more prone to reverting than others. We teach our foxes how to divert these impulses into other things. The result makes them overly sexual, but it frees the higher mind to work. The instincts are never far below the surface. They can assert themselves at any time. A raptor's scent keeps their higher mind active. This is what happens when they revert."

CJ looked through the bars at Ekal and Nipe. The fox stood now, leaning on her raptor. Ekal moved, licking the fur on her neck, and Nipe limped with her.

"I killed them," she was saying. "They're all dead. All of them are here. They can't hurt me."

"It's not your fault," Ekal said, leading her around the cage. "I'm here now. I won't let you stay that way."

CJ backed away.

Rive approached her. "Remember this is what she always was. This was not too far under the surface. Same for all intelligent creatures, but Relain canines especially. Their animal nature is so close to the surface. It's why we live in pairs. Relian theropods have been helping the canines overcome these instincts for so long the raptors have developed an instinct to help foxes."

Ekal led her fox to the door. CJ held still. Nipe paused in front of CJ, scented her, reached up, licked her face, then followed her raptor up the stairs. CJ had frozen.

Rive had walked around the cage and stood in front of CJ. He nudged her with his snout. CJ unfroze and turned to the cage. She walked around it, observing it from all points in the room. She stopped at the spot where she recognized the camera had recorded Nipe. Rive still stood at the door, visible through the bars.

"The bars are new," CJ said. "Someone gave them a lot of money for this. It's too elaborate. They didn't do this for some crusade to reveal the truth, and they didn't just take the money and run. They were promised something else. They must have been. Rive, this isn't over. There's going to be a lot of questions. Maybe a trial. We won't be able to keep this out of the press."

"Will you represent her?"

"I can't. I'll be seen as too biased. And who knows how many other people they sent tapes to. Someone will leak it.

Even if we tell the whole story, people will only see that, and they will be scared out of their minds."

She took a few more steps, observing the cage. Rive followed her with his eyes from the other side of the room.

"Kevin Parson told me as soon as they got what they wanted, they'd leave. They hadn't left. What else did they want? Was the tape the whole point, or was there more?"

Rive remained where he was and spoke across the room, through the bars, over the dismembered dog remains.

"I believe capturing a reverted fox on tape was the goal."

"Why? What are they getting out of it? What was the point of this?"

"As they say here, follow the money," said the raptor. "If we're lucky, someone made a mistake, and we can find out who gave them funding to do this. Whoever wanted it done also wanted the press to have it in reserve, ready to broadcast at a moment's notice. They want the people to be outraged and scared. It will be used as an excuse for the people in government to make life for the Relians very difficult. Taking this to trial will achieve the same thing."

"What do you know, Rive?"

"I don't know anything. I've only heard rumors."

"What rumors? What are you talking about?"

"I will tell you when I know the rest of the story. As soon as Ekal and Nipe recover, I want to interview them, along with Veronica and Justin. He said some interesting things earlier, and I'd like to have them on tape."

"Interview?" She glared at him through the bars. "How can you think about interviews now? Rive, we have a nightmare of legal trouble ahead of us. We're talking murder, manslaughter, kidnapping—how are laws meant for humans supposed to apply to Relians? How far can you take self-defense before it becomes murder? Do the same limits that apply to humans also apply to Relians? Are there special provisions for foxes who revert, and will there be charges for someone who causes a fox to revert, and are foxes responsible for their actions when they do? These are questions that are going to the Supreme Court. I need to prepare cases—I need to get attorneys ready for this."

Rive bobbed from the waist. "I believe it's time to learn how the Relians and the humans they chose at the conventions are getting along. The people who paid money to have that tape made have heard, and they are scared. I am sure this incident was planned in order to draw attention away from how well things are actually going."

The raptor turned and walked through the door and up the stairs.

CJ stared through the bars. She heard police sirens in the distance. She gripped one of the bars. It was easy to imagine what Nipe had been through. All she had to do was help others feel it, too. She had already thought of three angles for Nipe's defense.

Neben

I

A sphere large enough for a Krone opened just outside the oasis. Norh stepped through into the bright daylight, and as soon as all four feet touched the sand, his wings stretched out all the way. A number of birds and mammals saw him emerge, and they took to the air or ran over to meet him.

It had been close to a year since Norh and Stephen had set foot on another planet, and the change in the air was refreshing. He noticed the radiation bombarding his scales, and again Stephen marveled that he didn't have to worry about it in this body.

The avians on this planet did not speak with their beaks, but their skulls had a resonance chamber through which they moved air back and forth. The opening was at the top of their skull, so when they spoke, they did not need to open their mouths.

The pangolin-like mammals on Neben spoke the same language as the birds, using their mouths to simulate the rushing-air noises of the birds. Some of the birds landed on Norh's back as the winged reptile walked to meet up with them. The bear-sized pangolins settled in front of him and gazed up.

"Are you looking for where it happened?" one of the mammals asked.

"Yes, the Relian Archeons. Where are they?"

The avians took to the air. The mammals turned and fell in line for a single portal at the hub. It led to a region of the planet where it was night, as it would have to be for the Relians to stand safely.

Stephen spread their wings and pulled their body straight up. He flew with the birds a great distance, a full tenth of the way around the planet. Stephen enjoyed how eager to help the Nebens always were. It was deeply rooted not just in their culture, but their instincts.

Norh touched down on the night side of the planet, scenting the air for Relians. He found them, and his nose led him across the sand. The birds landed all around and on top of him, and now their bodies glowed green in the dark with absorbed energy emanating from their feathers. Since Norh had helped them establish contact with the Eich, the birds had shown their deepest gratitude by treating him as a member of their flock, and now his body shined in their light.

The mammals who had taken a portal there had been waiting for him, and they scampered around him as he walked. Norh and Stephen listened to exactly one hundred and thirty-three people tell him fragments of the same story —one that had been going around the planet for days. The pieces added up to a linear sequence.

Two avians, Hune and Mieh, and one mammal, Ervar, were in this region at the garden when they saw something in the distance. On a planet comprised entirely of desert, a dark spot stood out, so they investigated.

As they approached, the speck of black took on the form of a canine from Rel. They recognized the ears and a tail, and it moved around like a fox as well. Ervar called out to it. Its head turned, but the thing had no depth or definition, so they could not tell if it was looking at them or away.

It lowered to a quadruped stance and seemed to move in their direction. Hune realized it was approaching and called out, banking to the side to avoid it. Mieh dove the other way, Ervar rolled across the sand, and the fox-shaped sphere landed. It had extended what appeared to be its whole arm into the sand where Ervar had been. She rolled to her feet and stared at it.

The canine thing removed its arm from the sand and turned to face her. Ervar realized it was not its arm, but its claws. They were as long as its arm.

It turned its muzzle up and noticed Mieh in the air. Its legs expanded underneath it, and it leaped high into the sky, swiping its claws at him. Mieh banked left and right and flew in circles. Its claws created a great deal of turbulence, which threw Mieh from the sky and into the sand below.

Meanwhile Hune had circled it, so now she had a clear look. It really was a moving antisphere in the shape of a fox. Its depth seemed to collapse into two dimensions no matter which angle she viewed it from. She only had a moment to observe it when it turned in her direction and lunged. She dove out of the way, and at that moment the fox-shaped antisphere seemed to become aware of where it was.

It fell from the air and sank through the sand, leaving a deep hole that went all the way to the water table. Mieh landed next to Hune and helped him to his feet. All three of them approached the hole. Moments later, it climbed back out and crouched in attack stance.

It charged and chased them one after the other. The sounds its claws made as they cut through the air and sand were terrifying, but they helped the Nebens gauge where its claws were and where they were going, as it was very hard to see the claws without a sense of depth.

The three of them became good at keeping their distance and dodging the attacks. This canine had a pattern, and they had learned it. They observed the moving antisphere closer, Mieh and Hune from the air, Ervar from the ground.

Eventually, the canine-shaped antisphere stopped attacking. It appeared to look at them. From the ground, Ervar thought it was crying in pain. Then it bent at the waist, shoving its head into its chest, folded into itself, and disappeared.

It left behind a scarred landscape and a deep hole in the sand, which Norh and Stephen were on the way to see right now. They told him Qan was sleeping some ways off and asked if he wanted them to wake her.

Norh answered for them. "No, don't wake her. I will speak to the Relians. Thank you."

Airy voices told him they had reached the place. A number of Nebens walked about. Standing out in the herd were four Relians, two raptors and two foxes. Stephen and Norh wondered if the other Nebens could see Friend.

Norh's senses took in the site as a whole. U-shaped trenches cut through the sand in all directions, footprints everywhere, those of the Nebens who had been part of the scuffle as well as canine. The mammals herded him around the trenches in the ground to the Relians. The birds on his back preened themselves, enjoying the privilege of riding a Krone. Stephen spread their wings in a smile. He felt like a member of two species at the same time, and he wished the Krone had a way to blush.

The birds and mammals around the new disaster site noticed the dragon. The birds took to the air in a wave and flocked to him. More avians landed on him. The mammals bounded through the sand, calling to him. The four Relians turned to face him and waited. Kylac's tail wagged. The raptors shared a smile.

Friend's face appeared in front of Norh's and matched his steps as he approached. "No, they can't see me, not even Qan. Don't mention me. It will make things easier."

Stephen was about to answer.

"Don't bother talking. I've already calculated every word you will ever say given any set of stimuli, but I want both of you to know how amusing it is to witness a human and a Krone sharing a body. It's entertaining. By all means, continue existing. The two of you are great inspiration in so many ways."

Friend's muzzle winked away, and now the Friend in the distance wagged his tail. Norh stood before the Relians, covered in birds with glowing feathers and surrounded by a large herd of pangolin creatures almost as a large as Relian theropods.

"Glad you're here," said Sonjaa, the raptor with green scales and yellow highlights on her hands and neck.

"Did they fill you in?" asked Deka, the dark-blue theropod with the single red stripe running up his muzzle all way down his back and ending at the tip of the tail.

"I heard the whole story on the way," Stephen said. "What did I miss while I had to make a way on my own instead of a certain someone making an instant portal for me?"

Friend grabbed his sheath and shook it at Stephen. He pretended to whisper, and the Krone heard him as if his voice grew from a seed in his ear. "You didn't ask."

Kylac's tail hung limply. His single ear remained folded against his head. "There isn't much here, but the story they tell combined with the site itself is interesting."

"Can I get a tour?"

"Gladly," Deka answered.

Friend yawned and disappeared.

The mammals dispersed so they would not disturb the site. The avians sat on Norh, giving him a pleasant glow, lighting him and the sand for several paces around. The Relians led him to one particular place.

"This is where the antifox was when the Nebens found it," Deka said.

"Antifox?" Stephen said, unfolding his wings slightly.

"Notice the sand."

Stephen lowered his neck and scented a canine paw print in the sand where Friend's old ways had been. To his surprise, he found an odor on the grains.

"I don't know that scent," Stephen said, raising his head. No matter how long he inhabited Norh's body, he still felt guilty for using Norh's voice.

"Nobody does." Deka's blue scales looked black in the light the birds gave off, and his stripe appeared yellow. "The antispheres that caused the disaster did not leave a scent behind on the land they touched."

"Any ideas?" Sonjaa asked.

Norh took control of their neck, bent down and scented the place again. "This scent is unfamiliar. Has it left behind this odor on other worlds?"

"We are told so," said Kylac. "Nobody knows what it is, or what it means. Hune, Mieh, and Ervar smelled it, too, when they were close enough."

"Could this creature from the Lake have a scent?" Norh said.

"That's our best guess," Deka answered.

He turned and led Norh away from the center, following its paw prints to a place where its claws had cut through the sand. The Krone walked alongside it, scenting it the whole way. Birds rose and took off from his back, making room for new ones to land there and cuddle up to his scales.

"There's a scent here, too." Norh scented harder. "How is this possible? The antisphere swallowed the sand it touched. The Nebens said it made noises through the air, as if it swallowed any matter it touched, so how could it leave something behind?"

"We think it means the antifox is not an antisphere," said Deka.

"It's trying to bite and scratch," Sonjaa said.

"I don't understand," said Norh. "Is there more?"

"Yes."

Deka led Stephen and Norh to the hole in the ground where it had fallen from the air. Norh bent to the ground and peered inside.

"It made a hole here, but it also floated in the air. It did not make a hole in the ground when it walked or ran. Why here?"

"It's in the Lake," Sonjaa said, hands apart. Stephen and Norh could hear her heart beating faster from here. "The laws of physics are different there. It doesn't understand that. Maybe it expected to fall through the sand, so it did."

Stephen took over their mouth. "It's still learning about its environment. So what happens to the people it touches? Qan said there were deaths."

"We're about to leave for the sites on other worlds," said Sonjaa. "We'll find out more."

"Anything to help us understand what we're dealing with."

"We know exactly what we're dealing with, Stephen," Kylac grumbled, his single ear still folded back. "Friend moved his conscious mind outside the universe, he separated his old ways from his higher mind, and now disembodied animal instincts are running around outside the universe. It feels scent anxiety, and yet it does not have a nose. It sees, and yet it has no eyes. I think it's pounding on the door of our universe, searching for sights, smells, and sounds. It doesn't sense others in the usual way anymore, but it is aware other people are here, and it reacts the only way it knows how. Our first task is to understand how it senses its environment."

More birds rose from Norh's back, and just as many new birds landed in their place. It made the area flicker in green light. Norh lay in the cold sand. The birds conversed on his back. He had been listening to them since they started landing on him, and they were talking about the new disaster and what it meant. He observed the hole and the trenches in the sand.

A few mammals and birds wandered around the site, trying to imagine how a canine made of antisphere would look. These were sight-based creatures, so they did not think in terms of scent and sound. It was hard for them to imagine something in which the dimension of depth collapsed into width and length, and yet still interacted with the universe. Norh and Stephen had a difficult enough time imagining it.

Qan's scent approached from the oasis, and Norh turned to her. In the distance he saw flashes of electricity coming from the pool. Eich were down there, talking to one another. Stephen smiled with their wings. It had been so long since he had seen the Eich, and the sparks of lightning that were their language filled with him nostalgia.

"Hello, Qan," Norh and Stephen said at the same time. They winced. Usually they could never share the same body part at the same time, so it caught both of them by surprise.

"Good to see you two again," she called as she padded across the sand. "How is home for you, Stephen, now that you're a Krone?"

Stephen smiled with their wings. "It's not really home anymore. It's familiar, but I understand what Norh means when he tells me I can't really be part of it anymore. I still talk to my sister, and she and Alex enjoy talking to me, but I can't really do anything with them. Can't take them to amusement parks, can't take them to waterfalls, like I kept promising Alex I'd do. Even the things we talk about... We're running out of things in common."

Norh took over their mouth. "Your humanity slips away little by little."

Stephen answered him. "Yes, yes, I know what you mean. All these wonderful experiences I'm having, but so what if nobody on Earth knows about them?"

Qan was shaking her head from side to side, as was the way the people of Neben laughed. The birds had also adopted this the gesture generations ago. Qan now stood in front of Norh, looking up at him.

"Listening to the two of you talk never ceases to be amusing. Did everyone fill you in?"

"Yes, we know what's happening. We want to help."

"Not sure how you can be of help," Deka said. "Not sure how any of us can. There's only one person here who can fix this, and he refuses to help at all."

Friend appeared on top of Norh's back as a caricature of a Neben bird with red and black feathers. He nestled in with the flock, feathers glowing red instead of green.

"I already told you. If my old ways find me in the Lake, I will revert out here. Destroying the universe is easy from where I am. I don't want to, but my animal nature won't hesitate. There's only one solution, and the fox who can make it happen refuses to do it."

Kylac growled. "Joining you in the Lake and sending my own instincts somewhere else just so I can fight yours somehow? That isn't a good idea. Who's going to fight mine?"

"Instead you intend to trap my old ways in this universe. It is in the Lake. It has no numbers to calculate. You will never be able to block its movements."

"If it comes to this universe, it will have numbers," Kylac said. "And if it does not, I can open an antisphere and send it somewhere else."

"No matter where you send it, it will find me. First you have to tear down the walls you built around your knowledge of the medium which exists outside the universe."

"Our solution is on the way to yours," Deka said. "We'll try it first. If it doesn't work, then we will try it your way."

"Can you teach us about the Lake?" Norh said. "Without us causing new disasters?"

"No." Kylac turned and stared at the spot where the antifox had been. "I don't think there is a way. If Friend won't do it, then I'm the only one who can fix this. It will take time to break down the barrier in my mind. Maybe with Deka here, it won't be so bad."

Friend's fur glowed brighter and brighter. The other birds noticed the red light drowning out their green dim. Finally Friend's fur glowed half as bright as the star that lit this planet during the day, which caused the birds on Norh's back to flap in place and scream and shield their eyes as they looked for the source.

"Or maybe you'll remember you don't need Deka and destroy the universe anyway," Friend said.

Kylac shuddered, looked up at the glowing foxbird atop the Krone. "I think you're due for your daily disemboweling."

Friend became a fox again, but his fur still glowed. His tail wagged and sent streaks of light high into the zenith, casting the whole region from horizon to horizon in a red glow that changed night to day. The birds and mammals on the ground looked around in wonder.

"I'll make my flesh taste like raptor meat just for you!"

A sound emerged from behind them. Deka and Kylac recognized it as the sound of matter being swallowed and falling into someplace beyond comprehension. They turned around. An antisphere in the two-dimensional shape of a Relian canine stood in the same place where the three Nebens had discovered it, a piece of nighttime that refused to be chased away by the red glow Friend had created here.

It stood on all fours, but then rose to full height. Now its hands became distinguishable from its body. Its fingers extended all the way down to its knees and ended at points. It looked around, turning in all directions, as if it did not expect to be here and had to get its bearings.

Friend disappeared. The birds resting on Norh's back took flight and circled overhead. The mammals quickly backed away from it. Deka snarled and lunged forward a few strides, splaying his claws. Sonjaa ran to his side and faced off with it. Qan huddled into the sand. Norh and Stephen began circling the antifox.

It opened its mouth and tried to scream. Nothing came out. Deka and Sonjaa screeched at it. It ignored them and ran on its hind legs straight for the retreating mammals.

It crossed the distance in three strides as its hind legs doubled in length. Its claws speared the closest mammal, and then they returned to normal size. It slashed again. Its claws cut through another mammal's chest. A second swipe severed an arm. Blood gushed out and spilled across the sand.

The antifox turned and stabbed the next closest mammal in the back. Its claws left neat holes in its back, and blood bubbled up from the intrusions. The mammal fell forward, and the antifox withdrew its claws and spun around. It slashed the next mammal downwards through the skull, claws sliding right through skin and bone with seemingly no friction. The antifox did not cut through flesh. Flesh fell into it.

Deka and Sonjaa pushed through the mammals and birds, snarling and screeching, trying to draw its attention. Stephen and Norh had circled behind it, cutting off its escape. Kylac stepped away from Qan and walked toward the antisphere shaped like a canine.

It had finally noticed Deka and Sonjaa, and it leaped away, snarling at them silently. The birds circling overhead started to dive. One swooped the antifox's head. Another dove at it. Friend's animal instincts ducked and snarled at the glowing red sky. A bird was coming down. It leaped into the air, swiped her with its claws, and severed the bird's wings. She flipped head over talons into the sand.

The antifox remained floating in the air, slashing wildly at any bird that came near. It cut off wings, necks, feet, beaks—whatever happened to be in reach. The Relians watched from the ground.

A sphere opened directly beneath the antifox. Kylac and Deka turned to Qan, who had just risen and was now watching the antifox as birds dropped left and right.

The fox seemed to realize where it was, and gravity gripped it again. It fell straight down and collided with the spacetime sphere. Qan fell clutching her skull and rolling on the ground. The portal had been cut in half, and now it closed. Kylac ran to Qan and helped her up to her feet. She was conscious but shaken.

The antifox stood on the sand, its claws now twice as long as its body. The Relians and Norh had closed in and surrounded it. The birds had retreated, and so had the mammals. Now the antifox stood with Deka and Sonjaa at the front, Kylac and Qan to one side, Norh guarding the rear.

It turned in all directions once. Twice. Norh slinked toward it, mouth open. Deka and Sonjaa screeched at it, swiping the air with their claws. Kylac left Qan's side, and stood on his hind legs, gazing into it.

The antifox screamed, and this time something did come out. The sound came not from its mouth but resonated from the entire body. It rose from a low moaning to a shrill canine shriek.

It sank down into the sand. The sand began moving like water, swirling around and into the negative fox. Deka and Sonjaa braced themselves, but the sand flowed out from underneath them without taking them with it. Kylac dropped to all fours to remain standing as the air and ground swirled and spiraled into the Lake contained within the fox. As the sand swirled from underneath them and disappeared, they descended into a pit. The antifox still resonated, still screamed. It seemed to scream louder with every grain of sand it swallowed, every molecule of air that vanished into it.

They had dropped fifty paces down. Kylac held onto Qan as they fell deeper, helping her stay upright. Sonjaa and Deka were too far apart to hold each other. None of them could see through the rushing wind and sand. Norh crouched low to the ground, observing what happened to the sand as it entered the antifox.

The pit filled in with water. Deka and Sonjaa were over their heads. Kylac and Qan paddled to stay above the surface. Norh lay up to his stomach in water.

The antifox stopped pulling in the sand and air and floated under the water, seemingly choking and gasping, trying to swim. The antifox screamed through the water as it folded into itself and disappeared.

Deka and Sonjaa kept jumping to stay above the surface. Norh and Stephen spread their wings and flapped just enough to raise themselves a pace above it. They hovered over Deka and Sonjaa and picked both of them up, one in each forelimb. He flapped harder and carried them ninety paces up and out of the pit.

He set them down on the ground and was about to fly back down for Qan and Kylac, but Neben birds had already flown down there. Moments later, they flapped back up, five each carrying Kylac and Neben's Archeon. They set the two of them down ten paces from the lip of the pit.

Pangolins bounded across the sand and nudged the Relians. Birds dove from the sky and landed on Norh's back. They tried to preen him, the only way they knew how to comfort someone.

2

The wounded and the dead lay on the sand by the oasis. Qan had only kept one oasis full in this region so the cave below would still be flooded. Eich were down in the water, shooting lightning at each other. Smaller bolts struck a few of the Nebens.

Norh lay in the pond at the oasis. He had displaced enough water to flood the sand twenty paces out, and right now he was webbed in lightning bolts as the Eich gathered around him and spoke to him at full volume. He couldn't speak back right now, but they told him everything that had happened since he had left.

Norh lowered his neck completely underwater and pressed his forehead against a crystal canine's head. It shot Norh with bolts of electricity. Other Eich paddled around in the pool, firing bolts at one another, aiming others at Norh. The Krone took the electricity with ease, but he could only speak to them in a whisper and at extremely close range.

They told him about their first experiences offworld. It hadn't been easy for them, given their special biology, but by conserving their voices, they survived out of the water for days at a time. Qan had even made ways to planets with electrified atmospheres, and they stayed there for many days at a time.

Qan had not let them leave the planet until recently, when she believed their minds had been sufficiently opened up by spending time with the avians and mammals. It was a rare moment in a species' history when its collective mind opened to a new perspective on itself. A moment when it began to understand things from the point of view of a different species and became eager to seek out such understanding.

Norh and Stephen did not expect it to happen in their lifetime, so they did not think twice about staying on Earth for the last year. Now they both regretted missing that moment.

Stephen raised their neck out of the water and looked out over the wounded.

"See Norh?" Stephen said. "It is possible for a lone species to learn."

Norh took control of their mouth. "That was never in dispute."

"You're worried it's too late for humans. Look at these guys. They were alone for thousands of years, learned to program a natural computer, figured out how to copy their neural patterns into the crystal, and now they're becoming part of the contacted universe. It's possible!"

"Even in the contacted universe, there is a great amount of debate as to how much of behavior is caused by environment and how much is genetic. No species is doomed by genetics to die in its instinctual ways, even lone species. There is a point of no return for every race. I do not yet know if humans have reached it."

"It can't be too late," Stephen said. "I'm pretty cynical, but I still don't want to believe all humans are selfish assholes. I hope Rive will do a good job taking care of everyone. Should we have stayed and helped with that?"

"Friend's old ways are adapting to their environment. They will continue to expand and grow, and the damage they cause will become larger. I believe we will be more useful here."

"Glad you think so. I'm still overwhelmed. What we're trying to do... It seems impossible."

Norh spread their wings. "After I share a few more memories, you won't even remember what that feeling is. In a way, I do not wish that to happen."

They watched the people of Neben tend to the wounded.

The quadrupeds walked around licking the wounds of the birds who had lost wings or legs. Pangolins licked one another to stop the bleeding. Other birds huddled up to the wounded for comfort, having no way to deal with wounds of this kind. The entire population of the planet had gathered to help.

People with lost limbs lay next to people with stab and slash wounds that cut through bone and muscle. Muscle, bone, and flesh were not split open. They were missing.

But the most terrifying were those who had suffered wounds to the skull. The bone was gone, but the brain seemed to be untouched, even where the claws had penetrated. Those people alternated between rambling and screaming and talking coherently and mumbling nonsense. Qan moved from person to person, trying to speak to them, but they did not seem to hear her.

Deka, Kylac, and Sonjaa sat by the pond, observing the frenzy and taking in the scents of grief and fear.

Deka watched Qan tending to one mammal who had been stabbed through the skull. Qan walked to the next person, tried to comfort him, but he mumbled gibberish and thrashed around. The next person she walked to did the same. Nobody heard her, even those who looked directly at her. They kept breaking out into fits of rambling, screaming, and crying.

Sonjaa convulsed. Deka turned to her and nuzzled her snout.

"Deka, it's happening again. I feel like I'm falling."

"Don't run from it. Analyze it. What's happening?"

The giant pangolin next to Qan fell silent. Qan hopped over to her and shook her gently with her forepaw. She pressed her forehead to the wounded mammal and cried for her.

Sonjaa shivered. She dry-heaved. She choked on imaginary vomit and rose to her feet. Deka stood with her. Sonjaa turned and walked away from the hub, into the desert. Deka followed a few strides behind her as she tried to balance on unstable legs.

"It's the Lake, isn't it?"

"Deka, please, no," she stammered as she stumbled across the sand.

He ran to catch up to her and then stood at her flank. Sonjaa tried to move on, but she stood still, panting, stomach trying to throw up.

"Sonjaa, I didn't push you before because I thought your mind would build a strong enough subconscious to handle your experience in the Lake. But it's getting worse. We can't ignore it anymore. You have to face this."

"I can't— I can't— I can't even think about it!" She doubled over, vomited acid. She hacked and coughed as she rose halfway up.

Deka wrapped his neck around hers, touched her claws with his. "What's happening to those people?"

"Don't make me do this!" She dry-heaved again.

Deka turned her around and pointed her in the direction of the wounded, Kylac sitting off to the side, overlooking them. Sonjaa tried to raise herself more, but she could only stand halfway up, still shaking.

She looked over them. "I can't... It'll happen again."

"Why are you afraid of that?"

"Because it feels the same! It happened to me before and I almost—!" Her voice cut off as her stomach heaved again. Nothing came out of her mouth this time.

She panted and shivered herself down to the sand and lay in it. Deka lay on his stomach next to her. He did not let her turn away from them.

"You need to face this."

She could not blink as she looked at them. Several people moaned and screamed and thrashed limbs. Qan ran from person to person, completely helpless to ease their pain.

"Their minds," Sonjaa began, shaking so hard she could barely speak. "They're draining. Into the..."

Deka rubbed his cheek against hers. "The Lake?"

Her entire body dry-heaved. She gasped as she found her voice again.

"That's what happened to me. I remember. Friend's first antisphere—the one that destroyed Rel. It swallowed me, too. It took me outside the universe. When I first fell into the Lake, it felt like something was..."

She stopped breathing. Sonjaa choked and gasped, but nothing happened. Deka leaned on her harder, rubbed the back of her neck up and down with his chin. Sonjaa gradually loosened up and took a breath.

"...trying... spread me out." She gasped again, and this time she inhaled. "It did... for a while. I was spread out. I panicked. If anyone could have heard me... I would have sounded like them. But I saw you, Deka. I followed you. That pulled me together."

"You can face this. You are in control."

She tried to hide her muzzle in the sand. "It's happening now! My mind is sinking! It weighs too much! It's falling out of me, just like theirs! Those people are dead! Unless they find a way to hold themselves together out there, they'll die screaming!"

She hyperventilated and vomited more acid as her body convulsed. She rolled over to her side. Deka stood and gave her room. He crouched over her and lay his neck across her abdomen. She panted for a while, gradually calming. Deka rubbed muzzles with her, feeling her claws.

Finally she looked up at him. "I'll be fine. Your fox needs you more than I do. Don't leave him for me."

"You are not taking me away from my fox. You never have."

"That's exactly what I'm doing. That's all I've done since I came back. You don't have to feel obligated to help me, too."

"I thought I'd be imposing on you if I tried to be too close. I know I can never replace your fox. It's been strange having you around for so long, without a kill to share, but I enjoy having you with me. Rupi isn't here to help you face this, but I can try."

She did not answer. Deka waited until she stopped shaking. He raised himself and gently scented her. She wasn't asleep, but she was trying. Deka climbed to his feet and turned to the Nebens. Qan was still running from person to person as they screamed and thrashed. Kylac sat overlooking the scene.

Deka trotted up to the fox. He nosed his neck.

"She said it felt as though something was spreading her out."

Kylac sighed. "She may be right. In our bodies right now, we have a brain. In effect, it holds our conscious minds here. We don't have to think about staying together. But outside the universe, whatever lies beyond it... the Lake, there is no container. A conscious mind is the only thing that can exist. Friend's old ways apparently don't just swallow matter. They also destroy the container of conscious thought."

Deka look out over the Nebens. "Any ideas for how we can prepare for this?"

"I'm afraid to have ideas."

Deka turned back and nuzzled his fox. "You can handle this. You did it once."

Kylac stared out over the wounded, eyes empty. "I miss being a Relian canine. I miss exploring the contacted universe. I miss you, Deka. I miss holding you back from running headlong into everything. I miss seeing you rolling around on the causeways of Hithe and sitting in the trees on Ixcy talking to the fish. I miss being happy. Everyone used to be happy. When I think about the future, *this* is all I see."

Deka had the feeling his touch didn't reach the fox. He rose as he looked out over the Nebens. Most of the ones who had suffered wounds to the head lay motionless and silent.

Deka turned to Sonjaa and growled. He looked out over the wounded and the dead and growled again. He sat next to Kylac and snarled with every breath as he observed. He closed his mouth and breathed through his nose.

"Kylac, I would give anything to have those years back. It hurts me to watch you living like this. After we worked so hard to help you become stable, I liked it when you started holding me back. You were always right. I was about to do something stupid, run into something without thinking. I miss laughing with you. We'll get it back. Somehow, we will."

The glow of the birds' feathers began to fade, which meant daylight was approaching. Norh was safe, but the Relians would not survive the radiation the daytime star gave off. Qan walked up to them, stopping just a pace away from him. She stared at the sand.

"I'm closing this oasis," Qan said. "How is your fox? Is Sonjaa all right?"

Deka's hands remained apart. "We have all been wounded by Friend's actions in one way or another."

She raised her eyes. "It touched a portal I had made. Everything it touches falls into the Lake. It tried to take a piece of my mind with it. I knew it would, but I had to be certain. That thing is a living antisphere. There's a way to Magor at the hub. I'll expand it so Norh and Stephen can fit through. Go there and learn all you can."

She turned to Kylac, and then looked in Sonjaa's direction. "I want to go with you, but there's nothing I can do to help. Neben can't risk losing their Archeon, especially when the Eich are just beginning to explore the contacted universe."

"I am so sorry," Deka said.

Qan turned and looked him in the eye. "Kill it. If you need me, you know where to find me."

The planet's star peeked over the horizon. Deka turned around and ran to Sonjaa. Kylac rose to his feet and walked in his footsteps. Stephen and Norh rose from the pool.

Maggie

I

James Summit and Bethany Black sat on the couch. The camcorder mounted on the tripod in front of the television pointed directly at them, a retail handheld camcorder, not the professional, bulky ones Hollywood used. CJ stood behind it, adjusting the focus.

A tape recorder stood upright on the coffee table just below the view of the camera. CJ thought it would be a good idea to record an audio-only version of the interview in case something happened to the videotape.

Rive was in the other room, talking to the Relians

She couldn't believe she was doing this. Kevin Parson had died in that Sacramento hospital, both Ekal and Nipe were under arrest for murder, and CJ had spent every day of the last two months preparing their defense attorney. Self-defense was the expected angle, especially since Mr. Parson led the team that kidnapped Nipe, but the prosecution argued that self-defense only went so far.

CJ knew if Ekal and Nipe had used a gun to defend themselves, this case would be over in a flash, but claws and teeth had been involved, so did that count as defense, and were such extreme measures needed, given that their human captors were no match for them?

CJ had been preparing people to answer these questions, expecting this to go all the way to the top of the court system. She went to bed and woke up thinking about it. It was obvious to her, but she had to make it obvious from a legal perspective.

The police had had no luck tracking down the source of Mr. Parson's funding. That building had been recently purchased by shell companies registered in Panama and the state of Delaware, and there was no information on who the actual owners were.

News outlets in seven states had received that tape, and so far the press had respected the president's request to show restraint in reporting about the Relians. The story was too big to keep hidden forever, and eventually the charges against the Relians in Portland would make headlines. CJ's head reeled at the legal trouble those men had made for everyone, but it was bound to happen sooner or later. She had hoped it would not happen on her watch, but then again, she trusted herself to handle it right.

And all Rive could think about was conducting interviews. The metal raptor had pulled her away from meetings and brought her all over the country just to record the words of the men and women who had taken Relians into their homes.

Rive went out of his way to pull CJ from the legal proceedings. After the third time, she was sure the raptor was doing it on purpose. Now was a very important time to collect these, he kept saying. CJ thought she understood what he was getting at: hearing from other people who were getting along well with the aliens might prove excellent evidence in court and deter politicians from clamoring for mandatory muzzling, or declawing, or something.

So CJ had taken frequent breaks from the case to go around the country with Rive and interview the people. Today was James Summit's and Bethany Black's turn.

"I want you to talk about what life has been like with the Relians," CJ repeated. "Mention the incident with the police if you want, but more importantly, talk about what happened afterwards."

"Right," said James. "Do we have to do all of this in one take?"

CJ smiled, straightened up. "This is supposed to be your real thoughts, not something that's been edited or censored. It's raw data for future generations to comb through and get a feel for this moment in history. Be real, and don't be afraid to tell the truth. This could be in a time capsule someday."

"Yikes," said Beth.

"You two are part of history. Speak to the people of the future. Help them understand what's happening now. Ready?"

They smiled, checked with one another, and nodded.

CJ reached over and pressed the record button on the tape player. She sat down in her chair behind the camera and pushed the button on that.

"October seventeenth, nineteen ninety-seven. I am Secretary of Relian Relations CJ Rhine here with James Summit and Bethany Black. Tell us why you went to the convention in San Diego earlier this year."

"Well, it was my idea," James said. "I wanted us to go, but her job wouldn't let her take time off."

"Figure that one out," Beth said. "Aliens from outer space are on tour in California, and my boss wouldn't let me have a day to go meet them."

"I couldn't believe it either, but I didn't want to miss it. So I went alone."

CJ crossed a leg and smiled. She'd heard variations of this story several times before. James told most of this part, how he met Sors and Prael, and his reaction when they told him they were a match. He had no idea what that meant at the time.

"You know how dogs just kinda know who's a good person and who isn't? Imagine if they could tell you flat out. So I was really worried what they'd think of Beth."

She laughed, whacked him on the leg.

Things were all right for the first couple of months, but gradually the mood in town changed. Beth took over this part of the story, the incident with the police. CJ knew it all too well, the first major problem she and Rive had resolved.

Noland, the police chief, had resigned shortly after the FBI began investigating his department. Without him, things settled down. James and Beth had been happy to return to normal life.

About two months after the police stopped their surveillance and harassment of the Relians, Beth and James began arguing. All of a sudden it seemed the smallest thing either did bothered the other.

"It was cabin fever," Beth said. "It really was, but it didn't feel like it, since we had these two with us."

"Getting out and doing other things didn't seem to help," James said. "I didn't like being with her. She didn't like being with me. It just didn't seem like this was working out anymore. Had nothing to say to each other. Nothing was fun anymore. Made everything she did so annoying."

"He complained about being out of this, or out of that, but wouldn't go out and buy it! Griped about this, whined about that, did nothing about it. I kept telling him to, and he wouldn't. Led to some stupid arguments."

"Yeah, got bad enough we talked about splitting up. Didn't seem like anything was getting better."

"And then Sors, our raptor, got up, stood between us, and declared we were a good match, so there would be no splitting up."

CJ shifted in her seat, checked the camera to see how much tape was left. James picked up where Beth left off.

"Then he told Beth I hated her mother." James laughed. "I told him not to tell her that."

Beth was smiling, looking down at her lap. "And Sors turns to James and tells him I hated all those westerns he watches."

Now James laughed. "I had no idea. She'd always watched them with me, even when she was keeping me company when I had insomnia."

"*Gunsmoke, The Rifleman,* John Wayne movies. Even *Zorro.* Never knew late night TV had so many westerns. I told Sors I hated them, but I never told James."

"And we laughed," James said. "The first laugh we'd had in a long time."

"It was like this big relief. It was only just last week he told us why he did that. He and Prael understood what the problem was. We were both pretending. Putting on masks. Afraid to be ourselves around each other. Don't know how he knew, but ever since then, he's been there. They both have. Reminding us there are no secrets. Secrets hurt relationships. Now I actually enjoy those westerns. Don't have to pretend to be interested in them anymore."

CJ checked the tape again. Still plenty of time remaining. She looked past the humans on the couch, at the Relians in the hall. CJ could tell Rive was talking to them in their native language. She listened, aggravated that no matter how much of it she heard, it only sounded like grumbles and growls to her ears.

2

The Monterey Bay Aquarium wasn't too busy this time of year, and on a weekday they had plenty of room to move around inside. CJ wished Rive would make a way to the White House so they could get back to the Portland case, but the raptor insisted they take a day to come here, since last time they had left without visiting it. CJ had neither been here nor heard about it. Rive was curious because he'd seen how the location had been used in a *Star Trek* movie and wanted to see the real place.

It was nice to walk around without anybody knowing who she was. Rive drew a lot of stares, but for the most part people focused on the marine life. CJ wondered how often Beth and James had brought Sors and Prael here.

She was glad Rive had made a way to Washington just large enough for her to deposit her briefcase at the office. She would have been too nervous carrying such an important historical document around for so long.

There was no such thing as a whale exhibit, but the aquarium had jellyfish. They stood in front of the moon jelly tank. Rive's species did not convey emotional through facial expressions, rather the way he held his hands indicated he was captivated.

"I've heard people come to aquariums to see aliens," CJ said. "Ocean life is the closest thing we had to it until you showed up. Are you interested in jellyfish?"

"I've met sentient jellyfish," Rive said without looking at her. "I came here to see the different paths life can take on different worlds."

"There are intelligent jellyfish out there?"

"Yes, and fish, and birds, and reptiles, and other life forms that do not resemble anything you know."

CJ looked at the jellyfish. The transparent life forms puckered and pulsed up and down, collided with one another, barely noticing. "How? Where is their brain?"

"They are nine hundred and forty-six times larger than this. Their brains are made up of neurons spread across the entire body. Their perception of the world around them is fascinating to comprehend. I've spoken to many in my life."

"How do you speak to a jellyfish?"

"You must learn their language, and they must learn yours. I met several who understood Relian, and I learned how they speak to one another. Twitches and flicks of the tentacles. It's a subtle language, and their bodies are so large it is difficult even for me to catch everything they say. They have an equally difficult time understanding me, watching my mouth and my throat, as they have no ears to hear. The effort is worth it. These little guys," he touched the claws of his nonmetallic hand to the glass, "show that the potential for intelligence exists in all species. Chance largely determines which ones will be able to reach it."

He turned to her. "I have wanted to come here for some time, but I did not want to without you."

CJ smiled. "Why's that?"

"It delights me to show you something new. It has been a long time since I felt that."

CJ's smile widened, and she looked at the undulating creatures in the tank. "You're a fascinating person to listen to. If you weren't a theropod made of metal fused with skin, I'd call your stories too outrageous to believe."

"I also want you to stop thinking so much about the incident in Portland."

"The future of your species is at stake," she grinned, "and all you want to do is yank me to Colorado, or Florida, or Alaska and do an interview. How can you not be worried, Rive? All the Supreme Court has to do is make one choice out of fear, and Relians will find themselves in internment camps, or in line to have their teeth and claws removed. We could be looking at the next Plessey verses Ferguson, used to justify discrimination and fear for generations. I intend to prevent that, and you don't seem concerned at all."

"I have a larger goal in mind."

"This isn't large enough?"

Rive backed away from the moon jellies and walked onward to the next tank, which contained a smaller, meaner-looking, red-colored species. In the back of her mind, CJ wondered why jellyfish did not sting one another when their tentacles brushed against each other, or became tangled with other jellyfish. Rive observed them, the faint light coming from the water reflecting off his metal, making it look so much brighter compared to his skin. He seemed to be metal standing without skin now.

"We have done eight interviews so far. Things seem to be calming down in terms of problems between the species. Our next stop should be Delaware to speak with Lucy Schrifton. I understand she has an interesting story for us."

"Have you already called her?"

"No, but I heard people in the White House commenting on what happened. It's important for us to record it on tape."

"This one in particular?"

"Yes, tomorrow I will call her and find out when we can interview them. I think we'll both be surprised."

"Why do you want to distract me from the Portland case?"

Rive clicked his claws. "Because it is not as important as you think."

"Your evasiveness is irritating. Please just tell me."

Rive turned and faced her, still holding his hands together. "I'm not certain of what's happening either, but the more interviews we do, the more confident I am. Once I'm sure, I will tell you everything. I promise. For now, I want to enjoy this world while I still can. And... I like your scent when you're not thinking about the case."

"Well when you put it that way, it makes me want to walk away from elected office."

Rive turned to the tank, holding out his hand. CJ smiled, reaching out and slipping her fingers between

Rive's. It was his metal hand, but she didn't mind because sharing a smile with an intelligent theropod was high on her list of things not many people got to do.

The jellyfish pulsed to and fro, up and down. It was so calm and quiet in this hallway. Nothing but jellyfish. Creatures who spent their whole lives drifting through the ocean, reacting to stimuli. She tried to imagine what being conscious of that kind of life would be like.

"So what do intelligent jellyfish talk about?"

"They are endlessly fascinated by the idea of dry land. Most aquatics are. Fish can at least see the surface and survive on it for brief periods. Invertebrates cannot. Just the idea that life exists above the water is incredible to them. A few I talked to were learning calculus, and the way they talked about it was so interesting. Everything in water-like terms—"

"What, calculus?"

"That's right." Rive rubbed her fingers with his claws.

"What would a jellyfish need with calculus?"

"They also know algebra, quantum mathematics, grammar of languages they are physically incapable of speaking. All the intellectual studies."

CJ laughed, then rubbed Rive's fingers. "They can't write anything down. You need graphs and paper to do that. And they don't build anything, or send rockets to the moon. Why would they need it? How would they learn it?"

Rive rubbed her fingers slowly, smiling gently, but not patronizingly. It had taken her this long to learn the difference.

"The ability to visualize and remember becomes sharper as a species matures. Having a companion race is invaluable for developing it. As for why, it helps them explain their environment. Your kind told stories and invented gods. Others sense patterns and find connections in their world. Numbers emerge from that. They then move on to finding relationships between those numbers, and thus every species invents these systems of mathematics."

CJ bumped her fingers against Rive's, simulating clicking claws together. "Well, aliens are here now. I think we're on the way."

"Some of you, definitely. Others, no."

Rive nudged her. She followed, still holding his hand. Rive walked only as fast as CJ could, still rubbing her fingers. The next tank was another species. They were so alien, and yet the alien next to her, sharing a smile with her, seemed so human. She wasn't sure when it happened, but she found herself rubbing his claws faster instead of smiling with her mouth.

Magor

I

The Relians stood on a solid platform of branches and leaves three hundred paces in the air. In the center of this platform hovered three spheres in a triangle formation. The next Magor tree over also had three spheres hovering just a claw's reach over its canopy. In the center of every treetop, between the triangle of portals, grew a large flower. Each platform was about eighty paces across, and these flat canopies stretched as far as the eye could see.

Norh stepped through the enlarged portal and stood beside the Relians. As soon as they were through, the sphere shrank back to the common size for most forms of life in the contacted universe.

The branches at the top of the tree interwove to form a tight, smooth surface, and the leaves grew horizontally against the woven branches to make it just spongy enough to be pleasant to walk upon.

A few Magora had seen them arrive and they were running across the treetops to meet them. Their plumage seemed to magnify the starlight it reflected, a survival adaptation they had developed generations ago to deter predators. Even dim light hurt the eyes when it reflected off a Magora's feathers.

From here, the Relians saw numerous offworld visitors at the hub. The wind blew the wrong way for them to scent the people on the hub, but they recognized a Jemum male, a Gelleen female, a small flock of armless theropods from Xce, among many others, all walking on the treetops, looking out over the forest that covered the entire continent. It was the only place the Magora and the Alkan could live, as it was too cold or dry elsewhere on this world.

A few rodents about half the size of a Relian popped out of portals a couple trees over. More spilled out of others and began running to meet the visitors.

Stephen watched the mammals approach. He spread his wings halfway, thinking they looked like giant hamsters with neon fur ranging from green to yellow. Just then, Norh shared his memories of this planet with the human, and now Stephen saw them as capybaras with hands that could grasp branches as well as burrow underground.

"Kawjor is below!" one of the Alkan called as she hopped from treetop to treetop, weaving through the hub. "The way is forty-six by thirteen, third way! Follow us!"

The two native languages had a universal means of navigating the trees. All directions were given relative to one particular treetop in the middle of the hub. The first number indicated forwards or backwards from that position, depending on if it was positive or negative, the second number meant left or right. Portals on this hub were always arranged three to a treetop. The first way led offworld, the second always led to another canopy, and the third to someplace on the surface.

Deka saw the portal and began nudging his way through the offworlders. Many of them greeted the Relians in their own languages, asking how the experiment was going on Earth. Sonjaa said it was still in progress but going very well. Stephen lagged behind, bouncing on the treetop, laughing with his wings. Offworlders laughed at him, asking him what was so funny.

"I've always wanted to do this!" Stephen replied. "I used to draw pictures of myself standing on clouds and treetops! I didn't know there was a real place I could do it!"

He jumped and bounced on it again and again, shaking the branches, making a few offworlders nervous.

Deka reached over and clicked Sonjaa's claws.

"Every time I forget Norh has a human being inside of him," she said, clicking his claws in return, "he reminds me."

They hopped a tiny gap and landed on the next tree. They saw a tiny sliver of the sparse, shaded forest below through the sphere, and then they walked on, chasing the tails of the flightless birds as they hopped from canopy to canopy.

The avians on this world called themselves the Magora. They were much larger than the birds on Neben, and they spoke with their vocal cords and beaks rather than sound chambers in their skulls. They were flightless, so their nesting habits seemed unsuited to this region. Hundreds of generations ago, they had nested on the ground, which left them vulnerable to predators and thieving lizards.

Before they gained intelligence, the Magora began climbing trees to escape their predators. They discovered one species that happened to make a kind of flat surface with its upper canopy, which elevated them above the ground and protected their eggs. Every Magora began climbing these trees, and as they did, they spread the pollen, pushing the trees to reproduce faster. The trees spread, and the Magora favored the tallest, widest platforms, so the they only spread the pollen of those trees. As generations passed, the trees became taller and wider.

Only the Magora's beaks could break open the branches and create a hole for themselves to climb through the canopy to safety. Male Magora had remained on the forest floor, foraging for food, climbing back up the tree every day, sticking their beaks through the hole in the canopy to pass the food to their mate, who then passed it on to their offspring when the eggs hatched.

Today the Magor trees stood high above the canopy of the forest, keeping it in the shade. The Magor trees were so numerous their individual platforms interlocked. The resulting forest below did not resemble the rainforest of Kattaaka, thick and impenetrable and dominated by giant insects. The trees kept the forest shaded, stunting its growth as a whole, which meant the vegetation underneath was sparse for a forest this size, and the animals below remained small and harmless.

Deka stepped onto another platform and walked through the way that led to the surface, recognizable because it was shaded. Sonjaa followed, Kylac at her tail. Stephen took one look at the portal and huffed at its minuscule size. He took note of where it led and searched for a gap in the trees. He found one, spread his wings, lifted off, soared high, and then dove. He folded his wings and slid through the gap, emerging into near darkness.

The forest under the Magor trees looked as though it were perpetually recovering from a fire, with no plants taller than ten paces, hardly any underbrush, and very few scents. So little light made it to the surface Stephen's eyes switched to night vision to navigate.

"I see what you mean," Stephen said. "The contacted universe is not built for people our size. Makes it difficult to be part of anything."

"I am used to making my own ways no matter where I go."

"I would this time, but it's not too far."

He banked and glided, keeping his altitude between the canopy and the tops of the lesser trees below.

The Relians had emerged some distance away, and they stood on bare dirt next to a large burrow in the ground. Alkan ran in and crawled out, chittering in their native language, retelling the story.

Deka had already deduced what they were about to say. He looked up at the underside of the platform overhead. His eyes had adjusted to the low light, so he could see the paw prints burned into the side of the tree.

The slight breeze brought the scent of Kawjor to them. His feathers glowed much brighter than the dim light that made it down this far, which made him difficult to look at him directly.

"Welcome back to the contacted universe," he said. "I hear the experiment with the lone species is going well. Any details?"

"Nothing we can speak of yet," Deka said. "Soon, we hope."

Twenty rodent-like creatures emerged from the hole and ran up to greet the approaching bird, their eyes always avoiding him. These were the Alkan, burrowing rodents who once fed on the eggs of the Magora. When the Magora stopped nesting on the ground, and their eggs were out of reach, the Alkan had searched for new sources of food. They found none on the ground, so they began climbing the trees.

This was when the Magor trees developed their tightly-woven canopies. Trees with it formed a barrier that kept the Alkan out, but trees without it allowed the Alkan to rise.

It was while trying to reach the Magora that the Alkan found something new they could eat: other birds that made nests in the lower branches. They began making their burrows in the root systems of the Magor trees, which sheltered them from predators, and their bodies changed to become tree-climbers as well. The escape from predators pushed their minds higher, and eventually they achieved consciousness.

The Magora had reached it at about the same time. The two species met on the ground, and ever since they discovered portal physics, they had maintained ways on the ground and in the trees to eliminate the arduous task of climbing up and down the trunks several times a day to feed their young and themselves. Everyone lived in the canopy now, fathers knew their children, and mothers no longer spent their whole lives on a nest. Portal physics had freed the intelligent species from their animal ways, as it did on every planet in the contacted universe.

They had reserved an entire subcontinent to the south for the Alkan's food. Dozens of species of birds nested there freely. Portals led to many of their nests so they could easily take an egg or two from each, but never the whole nest. The unintelligent birds never noticed three or four eggs missing so long as one remained.

Both intelligent species on this planet had the Magor trees to thank for pushing them to sentience. They took great care to maintain the trees and everything that supported them. The Magora pollinated them, and the Alkan killed any parasites and predators they found while hunting eggs.

Kawjor stopped in front of Deka, rubbing his vestigial forelimbs together to imitate a Relian smile. They were neither arms nor wings, but something in between which evolution had not bothered to finish. Deka, Kylac, and Sonjaa turned their eyes down to the dirt. The Magora were used to this; most people had a difficult time looking at them even in darkness.

As soon as the Archeon of Magor sat down, a Krone dropped next to the Relians, kicking up a cloud of loose dust and dead branches.

"Do you see it?" said the glowing bird.

"Friend's old ways climbed a tree?" replied the raptor.

"Friend? He is not dead?"

"Long story," Sonjaa said. "We'll tell you later. What happened?"

Kawjor turned his beak upwards.

"A few days ago, an antisphere opened in the canopy near where an offworld portal is now. Numerous people saw it, but as soon as it appeared, it rushed the group, maiming some, killing others. It then sank through the branches, ran down the trunk of the Magor and confronted a number of people on the ground. Nobody survived that encounter; we found them later, bodies cut in half or missing limbs.

"It climbed up the next Magor and attacked the people in the canopy. Many witnessed it, but all they saw was an antisphere darting from person to person. It appeared to have no form, but it moved like a living creature. Some of the people it attacked were struck in the head. They have not died, but they are not the same. Do you know anything about it?"

Sonjaa shivered. Deka heard her heart speed up.

Deka's hands sagged. "I wish we didn't."

2

Kylac sat on a rock. Above him, hundreds of circular platforms shut out the daylight. A forest of stunted trees and bushes surrounded him. Kylac's eyes and ears were aware of the depressions in the tree trunks in front of and behind him, the slight breeze making a different sound as it passed over them. Areas of the tree that had been lost to the Lake. Everything this antifox touched fell into the Lake, just like an antisphere. He was staring at the paw prints now, trying to peek at the math that explained it.

A large body approached him from behind. It lay next to him, making so little noise it seemed to have no weight at all.

"Hello Stephen, Norh."

"It came here before Neben," Norh said. "It didn't have the form of a Relian canine then. It is learning how to interact with its environment, despite being in the Lake." Stephen took over their mouth. "Now what?"

"It will keep attacking anyone it finds, trying to satisfy its impulses. It probably cannot scent anything, but it is reacting to other people as if it could. It cannot smell the blood, so it still finds no satisfaction. It also doesn't understand that the laws of physics do not apply anymore. Eventually it will learn."

"It already has."

"It's still confused. It is moving around in the Lake, jumping back and forth between it and this universe. It's still not sure how to interact with anything, but when it figures out how to satisfy its needs, nothing will be able to stop it."

"What makes you certain of that?"

"I know the old ways better than anyone. If I reverted in the Lake, that's the first thing I would want to do. Find something familiar."

Norh turned their neck to face the tree with paw prints running down it. "Do you really believe Friend separated his old ways from his higher mind? From what we have observed of their behavior, I am not convinced. Animal instincts by themselves cannot survive on their own."

"This is thrashing. It merely appears to us as an anti-sphere shaped like a fox."

Kylac smelled distant and worried. His heart pounded at a rate close to what it would be if he were running for his life. Stephen now took control of their neck and turned to the canine.

"Can we stop them?"

"I think I'm the only one who can, but first I have to re-member everything I did, and how I did it. This is bad, Stephen, and I am scared. It will require me to revert and be conscious of it the whole time. I don't want to face it again. I wanted to live the rest of my life with a subconscious."

"Does it require you to revert? Deka is here now. When you and Friend learned about the Lake, you didn't have your raptors. It will be different this time."

"Nothing will change. I will be aware of every creature in the universe. I will know their numbers. It will create scent anxiety on a scale as large as the universe. A raptor's scent can't calm that, and I don't want to... To leave Deka behind."

Stephen moved his snout next to Kylac's cheek. "I feel a lot safer with your instincts compared to Friend's. I know you can handle yours."

He bumped the fox with his nose. Kylac's tail twitched.

"Stopping Friend was the only thing that kept me from destroying everyone. The scent anxiety. Being free to act on it. I gave up being an Archeon so I'd never be tempted again."

Stephen spread their wings, shading Kylac even more. "I'm privileged to know all four Relians who saved the universe."

Kylac faced Stephen, beating his tail against the rock a couple times. "So nice to see you're not letting a Krone body go to waste. I still remember you as this jumpy, slack-jawed biped following me and Deka from world to world, trying to help us clean up after the disasters, trying so hard but usually not able to do much. Sometimes I miss that human."

Stephen's wings contracted and spread. "And you still smell like the fox who could get me in bed without even trying." He nuzzled Kylac's snout. "I miss that fox."

His tail wagged. "You do some very undignified things with that body. Very un-Krone-like things. I enjoy watching a Krone act that way. Whenever I think it's hard to believe, I just wait for you to make Norh do something he would never do." Kylac blinked a few times. "Do you... Do you ever think about that, Stephen? Your body is gone, and now you're just memories floating around in a Krone's mind. Does that really make you the same person? Do you still feel like yourself?"

Stephen tilted his head, a very human gesture. "Yeah, that can be weird. I've looked back for something that didn't make it in here. As far as I can tell, I have all my memories, so I still feel like myself. But now there are new memories. The parts of Norh's life I remember. I don't feel like I'm losing myself. I feel like I'm gaining new parts."

"Does Norh feel the same way?"

The dragon's mannerisms switched to a Krone's. "I do. It took a while for Stephen to understand I do not look down on his life. He lived a life I can never experience, and being privileged to share it with him adds to me. I am becoming someone else as well, and so far I am enjoying the new person."

"Are you two close to marrying yet?"

"We are not sure, but it will happen eventually. The longer we're together, the more comfortable I am with becoming somebody new."

"Ditto," Stephen said.

"Don't be in a hurry," Kylac said. "I will miss both of you when you're gone."

"We won't be gone. We just won't switch back and forth anymore. It will likely be the same as before."

"There's a part of me that will always miss Stephen as a human and you as a Krone. Listening to the two of you going back and forth."

"If we're right," Stephen said, "you won't even notice the difference."

Kylac's tail swished once. "I wish I could be happy both of you feel that way. I want to feel that way. I lost something, and I would do anything to get it back. This new person I've become is sad and lonely, but he's better than the monster I could be. Now I have to be the monster again. There is nothing in me but monsters. Always has been. Other foxes saw me revert, and they knew they could be one, too. Deka helped me become more than that, and now he can't help me."

Stephen nuzzled his cheek. "You tamed your inner beast once without Deka. It can only be easier now that he's here."

Kylac heard a theropod emerging from the Alkan burrow. Kylac smelled two Relian reptiles on his other side.

"What happened down there?"

Deka answered. "The bodies are the same as we saw on Neben. The people Friend's old ways touched screamed for days, and then faded away. Now there's nothing left but a mind slowly falling into the Lake."

Sonjaa was shivering and looking down at her hands. "Do you think the antifox even knows it's touching anyone?"

"I don't think it does," Kylac answered. "I hope I'm ready long before it figures that out."

A red glow popped out of the ground in front of them. The glow turned into a flame, and the flame unfolded into a fox. Friend rose to full height on his hind legs and stood before him, sheath and testicles laughably oversized.

"What's that for?" Sonjaa said, holding her hands far apart in revulsion.

Friend shook his balls at her. "Because it means nothing to me now! I have no sexual desire, and I have never been happier! It was a colossal waste of time. When I make my own universe, that's something I will do away with. No more pointless reproductive urges. It will free up the mind to do other things."

"People are dying," Deka growled. "Show some remorse."

"You like me better this way. Admit it!"

"I liked you better when you were dead."

Friend shook his junk at Deka. "I have some information I thought you might want. Seems my old ways really can trace my projections. It's darting around the whole universe, searching for a familiar environment, and me. I take a great risk every time I appear in this universe now, so I can't make any large changes. And my old ways are not just moving about at random."

"What's the pattern?" said Norh.

"Everywhere an antisphere was, everywhere a broken sphere currently is, that's where they manifest. I think they're drawn to those areas because that's where the divide between the Lake and this universe is weakest. They're trying to come back."

"How will that work?" said Deka.

"It can give itself any body it wants," Sonjaa said. "That's how I came back."

"They already are," Norh said. "On this world it was merely an antisphere. On Neben, it was a full-bodied canine."

"It's giving itself an exaggerated body!" Friend said, making his junk grow bigger. Then his whole body grew at once, up and out, until he stood as tall as one of the shaded trees.

Norh looked up at him. He smelled unnerved; very few species looked down on the Krone. Deka was not amused, and neither was Sonjaa. Kylac remained impassive. Friend paced back and forth in front of them.

"A body that allows it to fulfill its urges better! Once it figures out how to interact with this universe, it will probably give itself a hyper-sensitive nose. It already has extra long claws, and is learning how to adjust the size of its legs to chase down unfamiliar scents."

He stopped, allowing his disproportionate equipment to settle, and then shrank himself back down to normal size.

"Except it probably won't know how to recreate skin and bone. It will still resemble a piece of the Lake moving around. Eventually—"

Spacetime screamed. Friend winked out of existence just as an antisphere opened in front of the tree. The sphere collapsed into the shape of a Relian canine standing on its hind legs, claws as long as its legs. It stared at all of them.

Deka spread his claws and snarled. Norh rose to a low crouch and prepared to roar. Sonjaa crouched, killing claws rising.

The antifox screamed at them in a vocal range well beyond what a real fox was capable of. It aimed its nose up at the canopy and turned in a circle, scenting everywhere. It smelled the scents of everyone in the area, which was impossible because the wind did not go from the canopy to the ground, but it nonetheless seemed aware of the Magora and Alkan. It screamed and took off running through the shaded forest, making a sizzling sound as air fell into it.

Norh spread his wings and took off, soaring to the lone hole in the canopy overhead.

The antifox sped across the ground, screaming as it ran headlong through a tree trunk. It ascended through the forest, aiming for more trees, cutting the small ones cleanly in half. It had grown its claws and its legs to more than twice its body length and spread its arms as it approached a

Magor. It passed through, taking the trunk with it as it walked on the air into the canopy.

The scream intensified. The ground shook.

Norh slipped through the hole in the platform and rose another hundred paces over the treetops. He flapped in place, watching as the antifox bored a hole through the branches and dove for portals on the hub as the people on the treetops ran for offworld spheres.

The antifox had not stopped screaming. It ran toward the people, holding its arms out as it dashed over the treetops. Its long claws sliced people in half, severed heads, limbs, gouged into torsos, pierced portals.

The antifox seemed to lose its stance on the solid surface of the tree, and it fell straight through the branches, still moving forward. Treetops wobbled and teetered as it bored and chopped through trunk after trunk. Portals on the hub wavered and then went out. Other portals on the hub flickered, expanded, and then vanished. Norh and Stephen recognized the portals Kawjor maintained had gone out.

A few of the canopies below Norh cracked, tilted, and began sliding down. Norh looked all around. Dozens of canopies from here to the antifox were tilting to one side. People held onto each other. Others scrambled to reach the remaining portals that led offworld.

The antifox rose up above the canopy again, colliding with dozens more portals on the hub, chopping people up on the way. The sections of the Magor trees where the antifox had touched them were gone. Trees tilted. Some canopies fell straight down, smashed into the trunk, and then dropped hundreds of paces to the ground.

The antifox continued screaming as it ran through the forest, gaining speed. It left the hub and continued onward, above the canopy and below. Trees wobbled and tilted sideways in its wake. As it vanished over the horizon, its voice faded as well.

On the forest floor, the screams of offworlders and the Magora and Alkan replaced the sound of a reverted fox screaming at someone in his scenting range. The sound of trees breaking apart and crashing to the ground quickly drowned those out. The tree in front of the Relians had been cut halfway up its trunk and was tipping over. Kylac dropped to all fours and bolted around the trunk, toward another tree. Deka and Sonjaa followed.

Sonjaa turned and looked back. A glowing lump lay on the ground. Kawjor was unconscious. Sonjaa bolted back for him. She opened her mouth and clamped her jaw over the bird's neck as she slid to a stop just enough to grip him but not enough to break the skin. She flexed her thighs and lifted him. The Magor tree moaned and creaked and began to tip over. Sonjaa ran to the side, but she still didn't want to be anywhere near it when it hit the ground. Kawjor's un-conscious body dangled from her mouth, his tail and legs dragging on the ground between her feet as she ran. She was worried about tripping on something; she could break his neck if she fell now, but the tree was a bigger threat.

She darted around the trunk and set Kawjor on the op-posite side. The tree had broken through two other plat-forms above, and all of them were coming down.

Light hit the forest floor. The glare coming from Kawjor's body increased fiftyfold. Sonjaa screeched, turned her head away, and then her body turned to match.

She heard Deka approaching. He slid to a stop and stood flank to flank with her in the ribbon of light. The canopies above had either been chopped to pieces, or the trees had fallen. Light bathed the ground in the shaded for-est for the first time in millennia.

In the sky, Stephen flapped and dove as fast as he could, helping people to safety. He could tell which platforms were falling and which were still stable, and he managed to grab several dozen people at a time and carry them to stable trees. But for every dozen he managed to rescue, three dozen fell.

Stephen dove to a half-tilted platform, the people hanging on with their claws and teeth. He snatched a few from their perches and carried them to a neighboring tree. He rose to the air and dove again as he did the platform slid the rest of the way and tumbled. The people detached from it and dropped, no breath left in them to scream.

Stephen folded their wings and dove faster. Most of the people had fallen out of reach. The closest one, a bipedal reptile from the planet Luxsa, held out her hand. Stephen reached out with his. They were mere claw reaches from touching.

She hit the ground. Stephen heard her spine shatter, along with every other piece of cartridge in her boneless body.

Stephen adjusted his wings and flew horizontally, dodging debris and tree trunks. He flapped, rising into a shaft of light and dodging a falling tree trunk, and emerged from the forest. He hovered over the canopy. Stephen screamed. Norh screamed with him. Their combined voices were lost in the chaos below.

On the ground, the Relians watched light pour into the forest again. The path of destruction opened the forest in front of them. Canopy after canopy collapsed in a line leading from here to the horizon. Trees lay twisted and splintered along the forest floor. Bodies of those who had fallen from above lay strewn about.

In a few dozen more breaths, the last of the trees fell to the ground, taking their platforms with them. The screams lessened. The forest became still and bright.

3

Deka and Kylac had been here after the first disaster, the one that had started it all. This world had a different Archeon back then, an Alkan named Ichea. When the anti-sphere collided with offworld portals she maintained on Rel, it ripped her conscious mind from her body, and she did not survive.

Kawjor wasn't even an apprentice at the time. When Magor needed a new Archeon, he thought he had what it took. Deka and Kylac evaluated him and began his training. They had no time to teach him very much, but when the portals reopened, offworld Archeons arrived and began teaching him. Now he was capable of opening up to three ways at once.

He lay unconscious in the dirt, plumage blinding everyone who came to see him. During the first disaster, they had only lost portals and had to return to an older way of life, wasting enormous amounts of time climbing up and down the trees for food. This time they had lost hundreds of trees and lives.

All of the portals to the ground level of the forest had gone out when Kawjor fell unconscious. Many offworld portals had also ended. The oversized sphere on top of the tree led back down to the ground. It was the safest place in case that happened again. Norh had created the way, and the remaining people on the canopy filed down to the surface.

Kylac stood looking out over the bright forest. The ceiling was broken, and the light was an intrusion.

Deka broke away from Kawjor's side and met his fox, nudging him with his snout.

"I have to do it," said the fox. "I have to risk it. If I don't, this will happen everywhere."

"Friend has no control, but you do."

"Friend's old ways are still in the Lake. They're not here. I'm not sure if they're projecting themselves here, or if we see an antisphere because they really are here. There may not be a way to trap them on a planet. I may have to join Friend in the Lake. And somehow..." Kylac panted a few times. "Somehow I'll figure out a way to stop them. Maybe his old ways won't merge with me, maybe mine won't merge with him, and we can destroy each other's."

"Can they be destroyed?"

"Sonjaa thinks so. The Lake almost destroyed her."

"How do we interact with them? How can we find them?"

Kylac turned to him, tail twitching. "We?"

"Friend said all of us will come in contact with the Lake. Sonjaa and I are coming with you."

Kylac leaned over, nuzzled his snout, then turned back to the forest. "I don't know. I'm meditating on the Lake. I can't bring the barrier down all at once. I'll cause more disasters. I'll have to do it gradually."

"Tell me everything you can. Help me prepare for it."

"Sonjaa is the one to ask about that. She was there. She knows how it works. She just has to gather the courage to remember."

"She's talking about it at last," Deka said. "I hoped she wouldn't hide forever. Even a little information would help."

They heard a sound just to their right. It came from underneath the ribbon of light that cut through the canopy. The sound of stretching wood. They turned, and their ears focused their eyes on one of the formerly shaded trees, a species that only grew to about five paces high, with a tiny canopy covered in enormous leaves to catch as much of the dim light as possible.

It was moving. Kylac and Deka walked closer, stopping about twenty paces away from it, under the blinding curtain of light. The tree had grown an entire pace in the last fifty breaths, and it was still expanding.

They now heard more growing sounds around them and in the distance. The Magora and Alkan on the ground rose to full height and looked around. The tiny trees expanded and rose at a visible rate, reaching into the light. Ten paces high. A few dozen breaths later, they had grown to eleven. Now twelve.

Stephen and Norh gazed into the forest, captivated by the new sound rumbling through it. They approached the raptor and the fox as the tree in front of them thickened and stretched, the soil at its base turning up.

Sonjaa broke away from Kawjor's side and joined her mate. Norh arrived at the tree moments later. It was now fourteen paces high and growing fast.

The Archeons recalled the history of this planet. They did not have to remember it; it existed in the forefront of their minds, along with everything else they knew. They thought of the Magor, how the Magora gave them a reproductive advantage by selecting the tallest and largest trees with the widest platforms.

They thought now of what had happened to the forest below, how it had been gradually engulfed in shade that kept the forest from becoming thick and teeming with life. What happened to the species of plants that had been around before the Magor took over the forest?

Thousands of species died off, but a number of them survived the limited light. Most had stopped growing at a certain height and remained there, and they had been doing so for thousands of years.

Numerous plant species on other worlds stored extra energy in their roots, saving it for when nourishing light returned. It made sense something similar had evolved here as well. Not every plant tried to be the biggest and tallest;

some shrank down and waited until their neighbors fell and then grew into the gap they left behind.

The same thing was happening here, but nobody had seen a tree grow this fast before. The Archeons calculated how long these plants must have been dormant, storing up what little energy they collected from the dim light that made it through the treetops. Their root systems must have extended for thousands of paces, and now the trees were tapping into those vast reserves. By the time the daytime star set, they would be taller than the Magor. With enough light and rain, and with the new abundance of decaying plant matter to fertilize the soil, they would suck all the nutrients out of the ground, starving the Magor and ending civilization on this planet.

The Archeons looked at one another. They knew the most logical thing to do.

Norh spread his wings and took to the air. They veered to the Alkan's hunting grounds, now cut off without Kawjor's portals. There were bound to be new trees growing there, and the Krone was the only one who could reach them in time.

Sonjaa spun around and dashed for Kawjor. "Bring other Archeons here!"

People poured into the oversized portal. They fanned out on the treetop, hopping along the canopies that still stood, disappearing through offworld spheres.

Sonjaa picked up Kawjor in her jaws. She looked at Deka. Deka looked back at her. They agreed: she was not an Archeon, so she could not help them, but she could get the word out about what was happening. She ran through the portal, carrying Kawjor with her, and sped across the treetop.

Deka backed away from the growing tree to keep its top in sight. Though it was expanding, it was not branching out. It put all of its effort into enlarging the tiny cluster of enormous leaves at the top and carrying them upwards.

The raptor meditated on a way. The tree reached twenty-one paces high before he was ready to open it. A large sphere opened over the plant's growing tip. The sphere led into space, just outside the planet's atmosphere, and the tip now grew into a cold, dark vacuum.

The tree audibly slowed to a stop for a few breaths. A new sprout emerged from the bark ten paces below the leading edge. Leaves budded and unfolded. It angled into the light and began growing up to it, around the portal Deka had opened.

Deka's hands sagged. "This isn't normal for a plant. It shouldn't be able to react this quickly."

"I want to help," Kylac said. "I could open spheres over every one of those trees!"

"Don't go faster than you can handle. Other Archeons will come. We'll fix this."

Hundreds of new trees were growing all over the continent, reaching for the light to escape the bottom of a dark forest. The sounds of expansion echoed across the continent.

4

Norh dove through the hole in the canopy and collided with an expanding sapling, snapping it off midway. The top half of the trunk fell to the ground and crashed on a pile of Magor debris. Stephen leveled them off and flew them through the dim forest. Behind them, they knew, the tree would sprout a new leading edge a few breaths later and continue growing into the light.

"Times like this I wish we could make more than one way at a time!" Stephen shouted.

They followed the ribbon of light. A new tree poked out from the debris below, and they rammed into it. It bent and snapped in half under the weight of the Krone. Norh carried it a distance and then dropped it in the dark as they flew full speed across the continent.

"Can we stop it?" Stephen said.

"If enough Archeons come here, they can," Norh replied, taking control of their mouth.

"What about us?"

"We can cut the trees down to size until they make ways here."

"Can we really fight nature like this?"

"Our goal is to stop the growth so the Magora and Alkan can decide what to do about it."

"They have to stop growing at some point. Can't we remove the trees then?"

"When they reach full height, they will start spreading pollen. There's no way to tell how fast these things will reproduce. They've been waiting for this moment for thousands of years. They're taking over now while they have the chance."

"Can we get other Krone to come here and help us cut the trees down?"

"It will take too long to calculate a new way to Kronia."

Another tree faded into sight. Stephen steered them toward it.

"Besides," Norh continued, "they would not help."

"Why? Why wouldn't they help someone in need?"

They slammed into the tree, bent it in half, and snapped it two-thirds of the way down. They let the trunk drop as they sailed through the light.

"Because it's hopeless," Norh said. "You've lived enough of my memories to know. No matter how much you help people, their species speeds on toward its own destruction."

"Uncontacted races, maybe."

Norh was silent for a great distance.

"Norh? Did I say something wrong?"

The Krone was silent for a while longer, then finally he took control of their mouth. "There are many memories I have yet to share with you. One in particular I do not wish you to know. It may destroy you."

"What do you mean? How?"

"You may lose that wonderful spark of joy. I already decided it will be the last thing I share."

"Is it that bad?"

"I believe it contains what it means to be a Krone. It's what all Krone come to realize, and that's why we don't bother involving ourselves with anyone. It's what separates a young Krone from an old one."

"Worse than realizing it's all hopeless?"

"It builds on that. Stephen, give me more of your spark. Fill me with a reason to help, or I promise we will retreat to my cave and never come out again."

Stephen did not know how to do this, so he took control of their wings again and banked them side to side. Norh was trying to smile.

Up ahead, the air filled with the scents of birds. Lots of nests and eggs. Many of them broken on the ground, and still others had been dashed against the trees. Birds flew everywhere, circling above the canopy, screaming. Many had ventured back down to the forest to search for their nest.

This was the Alkan's hunting grounds. Thousands of trees reserved so the birds could nest, and so the Alkan could portal in and take their eggs. Portals had ended the need to climb trees to find food, and if this place fell to the new trees sprouting up, the Alkan would have nothing to eat.

A tree was growing out of the debris, already halfway up to the canopy. They collided with it and it snapped in half. The top collapsed, and a new sprout of leaves popped out from the side and continued growing upwards.

Stephen knew the plan, and so did Norh. They hovered under the canopy, watching the plant grow. They were calculating a way.

Stephen marveled at how fast it grew. He flew them closer and landed on the trunk. It bowed and swayed under his weight. The leading tip bent, found the light again, and grew upwards. Stephen let go, the tree straightened up, and the entire leading branch adjusted position and pointed up.

"I didn't know anything could grow that fast."

"They have been storing energy for millennia. They are using all of it right now."

"Seems a shame, ending this life. It's not doing anything wrong. We're sure they can't coexist?"

"These trees do not want coexistence."

They opened the way immediately under the tree. They captured the roots and sent them high into the sky. In mere breaths the roots would burn up in the atmosphere. The ground sank slightly into the vacuole they had made.

The tree ceased. The sound of growing stopped, and now they were aware of trees all throughout this reserve, following the path of light and debris winding through the forest.

Breaths later, a new sound came from the ground. Stephen and Norh hovered over the inert tree trunk and listened. A new sprout emerged about eight paces away from the first tree trunk. It expanded and grew at the same pace its parent had. It reached five paces high, and then its leaves sprouted. Stephen and Norh watched it for a breath.

"New plan?" said the human.

5

Twenty-one Archeons had come to Magor from just as many worlds. They stood around various trees under the bright tear in the canopy. All at once, they opened ways under the trees and sent those roots into the upper atmosphere. The trees stopped growing. Much of the forest fell silent. Deka helped create one of those spheres underground. Moments later, the ground shifted, and new sprouts surged up through the dirt a few paces away from the old trees, reaching for the light.

As one, the Archeons realized what was happening. The root systems of these trees were vast and interconnected, and they tapped into each other's systems, including the reaction to light. As long as one tree sensed light, they would all keep growing. The roots of the new trees were probably intertwined with every Magor on the continent as well. The Archeons would have to uproot the entire forest to stop them.

Meanwhile, some had already stretched halfway up to the canopy, and once they were above the Magor, they would pollinate and spread even further. The ones still in the shade might become active at any moment and start feeding on the Magor trees, if they had not already.

The Archeons did not look at one another. They did not check in with one another. Each had the same knowledge of this planet as the other, each witnessed the same thing as the others, so there was only one solution.

Archeons were creating portals to the west. When one was ready, they flooded the portal and then appeared several hundred paces away at the site of another growing tree. Everyone fanned out, following the sound to still more trees.

Some of the offworld Archeons concentrated on ways into the upper atmosphere and placed the other end over the top of the trees, cutting them off more than halfway and sending them to the upper atmosphere. The trees sprouted new leading branches and continued growing.

Other Archeons were high in the sky, hopping along the trees that were still intact, pondering the gaps in the canopy. They opened large spheres between the tops of the Magor, forming the other end deep underground to plug the light leaks.

The trees did not slow down even when encased in shadow, which reaffirmed that the new trees were connected. If their growth was this fast and invasive, nobody wanted to find out how they reproduced.

Some opened ways into space for the plant to grow into, but the tree seemed to sense an obstacle and grew around the portals. The Archeons reached the same conclusion: the trees sensed their environment at the speed an animal would.

Deka wanted to help more, but he still couldn't hold spheres open for very long, so it wouldn't be safe for him to make portals to help them move along the ground. He had to settle for following the portals others made, helping cut the tops of the trees off or make ways into the roots to slow them down.

He looked up. People were moving across the canopy, shutting out the daylight with large spheres. The ribbon of light cutting through the forest slowly zipped up, and even in the darkness the plants rose.

Someone opened two more ways, and the Archeons from the many different worlds poured in and cut the trees off further along the path. Deka made a couple spheres to sever some branches. He was glad to help, but he hated not even having the option to make permanent ways for others to use.

Deka raised his snout. He didn't smell Kylac. The fox had been keeping up with them, but sometime after the original plan to cut off the roots failed, his fox had disappeared. The most logical thing for him to do was meditate on the Lake, since he could not make portals anymore.

Deka growled at the tree in front of him, thinking both his mate and his fox were wounded and Deka couldn't help. They were reeling in anguish, and all he could do was repeat human-style platitudes.

He crouched, leaped through the air, claws fanning, and landed on the trunk of the expanding tree. He slashed it, clawed it, tore a hunk out of it with his teeth and spat it out. He pushed off and landed in attack stance, thinking about Sonjaa.

She hadn't merely been hiding from the trauma of the Lake. It had changed her, and she did not know how to handle it. Neither did Deka, as it wasn't supposed to happen this way, but her subconscious could not contain it for long, and if she didn't learn how to control it, her mind may very well fall into the abyss outside the universe.

The pieces had connected on Neben. Kylac probably didn't recognize it, but Deka understood how all three of them would come in contact with the Lake. Kylac knew he had to face the reality of entering the Lake, but Sonjaa did not. Sonjaa was just as important as Kylac, and Deka stood between the two of them. For all three of them to survive this, Deka had to push her. He didn't want to pressure her into this, knowing what it would do to her, but everything depended on it.

Deka calculated at this rate, even if nobody else off-world joined them, they would keep the trees short enough to prevent them from reaching full height and plug the light leaks long before the daytime star set.

Just as he became aware of this calculation, he smelled new people flowing in from the portals. They were putting the forest in the dark even faster. The raptor clicked his claws.

6

Stephen and Norh angled themselves to land on the tree trunk on all fours. They slammed into it with their whole body. The tree snapped close to the base and teetered to the ground.

Norh jumped off and took flight. As he did, he was ready to make a new way. He looked up, and a new sphere opened between the gaps in the trees, enrobing a circular area of forest in darkness. Despite the sudden lack of light, a new leading branch poked through the trunk and rose up.

"Norh, something weird is happening. Did you notice the last five trees had spines on them?"

"I did."

He swung their body around and tore through the forest to the next tree. The birds in the area fluttered out of his way. A few sat on their nests and huddled into them, squawking warnings at the passing Krone.

"They didn't have spines before. What's going on?"

"You already know what is happening. You do not need to ask."

"But it doesn't make sense! Trees can't adapt this quick!"

"These do. The spines cannot hurt us."

"The spines are different every time. Something weird is going on, besides the rapid growth. We've made nineteen spheres overhead—nineteen trees in darkness, but they're still growing."

"The trees are connected. They are sharing stimuli."

"Plants don't do this!"

"They most certainly can, even on your own world. Many plants display animal-like traits. One of them moved your memories into my skull after you died."

"Oh. Right. Forgot about that."

The next tree was in sight. Norh flapped their wings and banked left. Stephen adjusted their body so they would hit the tree flat on their stomach.

"How does something like this evolve? They've been in the dark for thousands of years. It's like the trees were plotting revenge."

"Perhaps they were."

Stephen and Norh noticed the tree had spines covering its trunk, and they looked different from the spines on the previous sprouts. Stephen opened their arms and legs, as if to hug the trunk, and then rammed it.

The spines slipped between their scales. Stephen reflexively let go of the tree, and they fell to the ground. Norh screamed all the way down. They landed on their back, wings spread, Norh still screaming. Stephen wrestled control of their neck from him, and he looked down their body.

They were bleeding from a thousand prickles from the chest down to their abdomen. The blood oozed between their scales—Stephen could see where the spines had entered and pried their scales loose. The blood shined bright against the dark-yellow scales of their underbelly.

Norh writhed on the ground. Stephen felt it, too. It was pain as he had never imagined before, and he had broken his arm twice. Norh ran out of breath and still tried to scream. Stephen shoved Norh aside and took control of their mouth.

"What the fuck?"

The Krone was still mindless. Stephen realized he had control of their entire body, so he rolled them over. Norh had shrunk into a quiet voice in the back of his mind, frozen in complete shock.

"Norh, are you all right?"

No answer. The Krone wasn't even trying to rise up to their mouth and speak.

"Norh! I thought nothing could pierce our scales! What happened?"

Stephen felt like Norh had curled up somewhere to cry. Stephen looked up at the growing tree. It had even more of those spines covering it now, and new ones were poking through the bark as it climbed the light.

Stephen felt the agony, too. He pushed the pain aside and flew back the way they had come. He had the feeling Norh wanted to ask what he was doing, but the Krone remained silent and hidden.

"I have a hunch."

He banked and sailed over the debris and fallen trees. He picked up speed and returned them to the tree they had just knocked over and covered in darkness. He landed at its base and looked up.

Its old spines were falling off. A large ring of needles encircled the trunk. New spines grew in their place—the same kind the other tree had, the ones Stephen would always remember as being able to penetrate Krone hide. It had been the first time Stephen had felt pain in more than a year, either internally or externally.

"This isn't just a plant. These trees can't be doing this independently. Those last five trees were defending themselves. They were trying different things on us. How did that one know its spines worked? How did it share that with the others? And... How are we going to keep the trees down to size now?"

Norh crawled up into their mouth. His voice was so small compared to Stephen's. "That... hurt."

"I don't think we can do this alone. We can only make one way at a time, and there are too many trees here. Let's make a way back to the hub and bring everyone here."

The Krone did not move to take control of anything. "Stephen... Help..."

"What?"

"I can't... Pain... I can't!" Norh opened wide and screamed again. Blood still dripped from their underside.

Stephen took the hint. He took the pain. All of it. Now Stephen wobbled on their legs and fell halfway over. Stephen gritted their teeth as he climbed back to his feet, having a difficult time moving their wings the pain was so great.

Stephen ignored it, clenched his fists, and thought of a way back to the hub. He calculated a way in the canopy, about where he determined the Archeons should be.

Norh took control of their mouth. "Thank you."

7

They had traveled more than halfway across the continent. The trees were uniformly halfway up the canopy. Fifty-seven Archeons had come to Magor from all over the contacted universe, all running along the trees, sealing off the light and making new ways across the forest floor..

Deka was among the ones on the ground far ahead of the Archeons in the canopy, helping them cut the trees down until the others arrived to block the light. He noticed the tree trunks now had spines covering them, and he wondered why they would waste valuable energy on something like that. He also noticed the trees did not grow in a straight line anymore. They snaked back and forth, turning in loops and even growing downward, which made it harder to predict where the leafy top would be and to make a way that would cut it off.

A few trees further on moved their entire trunks around. Every Archeon on the ground paused and took notice as the trunks and branches swung in erratic directions. The movement wasn't enough to prevent Deka or someone else from opening a way over the base of the tree and sending the whole thing into the upper atmosphere to burn, but watching a plant move like a tentacle in reaction to what they had been doing made everyone uneasy.

Deka ran through a new way and emerged five hundred paces further on, just in front of a new spine-covered tree twirling around. As soon as the offworlders arrived and began fanning out for any other growing trees that happened to be in the dark, the tree spat out a cloud from a few spines at its base. Deka saw what it was before it reached him, as it was so concentrated it bent the light. Pure carbon dioxide. The plant was spraying it all around itself. Every Archeon recognized it, and they backed away. The trunk continued bending back and forth as it looped and wagged its way upwards.

Deka made a sphere over the tree trunk and sent it into the stratosphere. A new sprout emerged from the base. Others had found saplings, and they kept their distance as they made spheres and cut those trees down as well.

Several Archeons made portals to the next tree, and Deka ran through one. This tree trunk was covered in spines and swinging about while it emitted carbon dioxide mixed with sulfur. Deka heard chatter from elsewhere in the forest that other trees were spraying chlorine gas, or mixtures of other chemicals.

The Archeons held position as far away as possible while still being able to calculate a portal in the area. The distance an Archeon could be from one end of the portal they opened varied from person to person, but it was never more than two hundred and eight paces. Deka could only be one hundred and forty paces away before his mind lost the calculations, and he had to move the portal closer to himself.

The plants sprayed gas at higher and higher rates. Whether the poisons killed them or not didn't matter; if the trees sensed the Archeons couldn't hurt them from a distance, it would maintain that distance. Even the Arcehons that could fly wouldn't be able to stay close long enough to make a way to cut the trees down.

These were not merely trees. This was a single organism living deep underground, as wide as the continent, something between a plant and an animal—a leftover of evolution from a time when the two biological kingdoms had been one. Now it synthesized poisons to protect itself. Next it might have the idea to transform the atmosphere of the forest and kill everything off. It still sensed light, and it was going to tear everything down to reach it. The good part was that all this extra effort on part of the plants seemed to have slowed their rate of growth.

The Archeons all reached the same conclusion. They began making ways up to the canopy. Deka watched the tree swing about, spreading the gas his direction. He backed away, climbing over part of a fallen Magor as the gas approached. A few people opened spheres, and Deka ran through one and emerged on the canopy. His eyes adjusted to the brightness of the treetop. He was too far away to make spheres now, so he followed the group. Deka disliked feeling so helpless, but if a tree came close enough, he could cut it off.

8

"Stephen," said Norh. "We can do this. Take the pain for me, and I will make the ways over the rest of the trees."

"Norh, we can only open one at time! The trees will grow over the canopy long before we finish cutting off their light! We need the Archeons to come here!"

"Just take the pain. We will finish this."

Norh took control of their body, swung around, and spread their wings.

"You know the math same as I do! It doesn't add up! We can't do this without them!"

"They're busy enough with the main path. The hunting grounds are up to us."

Norh flapped their wings and sped through the thin forest. In moments they were out of range of the portal Stephen was working on, and he lost it completely.

Stephen shouted. "Stop! Go back!"

"Keep taking the pain. I will handle the rest."

He banked, rolled, and dove back down to the ground. He leveled off and charged the tree. All Stephen could see were the spines.

"Oh my fucking God, stop! Please!"

Stephen wrestled for control of the wings, but he couldn't push Norh out of them. They rose up, spread their arms, and slammed into the tree, giving it a big hug. Several hundred needles slipped under their scales.

Stephen had no mouth, but he screamed. Norh held on until the tree trunk cracked, and then he pushed off. Blood rained from their underside. Stephen wanted to beg Norh not to do that again, but the pain was so great he couldn't displace Norh from their mouth.

The Krone turned their body around and glided through the forest to the next tree. Stephen sensed he was working on a way into the canopy to cut off the light to it.

It was in sight. Norh opened their arms and rammed the tree. Stephen huddled into himself and cried. The tree cracked and tipped over. A waterfall of blood fell from their abdomen and chest as they flew off.

Norh flapped in place for a while, then opened a way into the canopy and turned day into night. He flipped over and flew along the path of light to the next tree. The pain was so great Stephen couldn't think.

A thousand paces later, another tree came into view. It had grown more than halfway up the canopy. Norh hugged it at full speed.

They smelled gas. Chlorine, sulfur, carbon dioxide. It surrounded the tree for fifty paces. Norh's lungs burned. With Stephen busy dealing with the spines, this pain hit Norh directly. He choked and gagged and fell from the tree, landing on his side.

The Krone thrashed and rolled on the ground. Stephen still couldn't take control of anything. He wanted to beg Norh to get them out of here and let the other Archeons help; there was no way they could seal the holes and prevent the trees from growing too high now. Norh rolled around, panicking at the burning in their lungs. Stephen felt it, too, as Norh was trying to push the pain onto him.

Stephen refused. He threw the pain in their hide back to him. Norh froze up and huddled into an imaginary cave. Stephen filled their body and limped away from the base of the tree. The gas became weaker and weaker, and finally they breathed fresh air. Stephen began making a sphere.

He had the feeling Norh was miserable in their body. He took some of the pain away, gritting his teeth as he concentrated on the way through it. A moment later, Stephen took even more. Then a little more. Stephen now bore almost all of it, and yet Norh did not seem any better, still minuscule and trying to crawl back into the egg.

"You can't handle pain, can you?" Stephen said.

Norh did not rise up to answer.

"I'm taking most of it now. I only left you with the burning lungs. Admit it. We need help."

No answer.

"Let me make the way. I will take the pain again as soon as the Archeons are here. They probably got half the contacted universe working on it by now. Deal?"

Norh took control of one foreleg. He raised it to their snout and felt the muzzle Stephen inhabited. He then retreated and let Stephen make the way.

Moments later, a Krone-sized way opened up onto a canopy. Sure enough, Archeons were in the distance and approaching. Stephen walked through, spread his wings, and flew the distance to them. He landed on a treetop. The people turned and stared at him, and Stephen realized he was still bleeding from his underbelly.

"The Alkan's reserve! I'm not fast enough to make the ways to close off the rest. I need help."

The smell of surprise was even more potent than the poison gas the trees gave off. A number of them broke away, and ran for the large portal in the distance. Stephen counted fourteen Archeons up here, and they had sealed off two-thirds of the gash in the canopy. Stephen turned them around and spread their wings.

Norh surged into their body and dropped them to the leaves on their belly. Stephen wanted to stand up, but Norh resisted him. Stephen wasn't used to this. Normally when they disagreed about what to do, Norh simply allowed Stephen to take control.

"Stephen," he said. His voice was strained and small. "Give me pain. Give me all the pain you ever suffered as a human. Teach me how to handle it."

"Now? We can still help—"

"Everything!"

Stephen felt like Norh was trying to jump into him and force him to share memories. He could not, but the plea was tangible. The former human fed him every memory of pain he'd ever had. The time he broke his arm in basic training—the day he broke his other arm as a child—the head-on collision he'd been in as a teenager—falling off a bicycle and hitting his crotch on the bar—slicing his hand while working on a car—the time his neighbor's dog bit him on the forearm and latched on until he pushed his arm into her mouth and dislocated her jaw so he could escape—

Norh lost control of their urine.

Included in those memories were Stephen's way of ignoring it and still going to work, driving himself to the hospital, or sitting in class.

At the same time, Norh fed Stephen memories of the few times he had been in pain. Stephen was right. The Krone so rarely felt pain that when they did, it was an event, so they had no tolerance. He whimpered when something hurt him. He craved Stephen's memories like a starving puppy begging for milk.

In mere breaths, they had united on these experiences. Stephen no longer took all of their pain. Norh had learned how to ignore it and still function. They jointly took control of their body and unfolded their wings. Their lungs still burned as they flew toward the portal, and their underside throbbed and stung every few breaths, but now they both knew how to push past it and keep flying.

"I'm sorry, Stephen. I did not expect that. It has been centuries since anything hurt me, and it was wrong of me to push that onto you. I panicked. It will not happen again."

They felt miserable, but now they shared the burden equally. They folded their wings, sailed through the portal, and then glided ahead of the Archeons, making the next way for them.

"I don't blame you," Stephen said. "But you owe me a blowjob for that! And this one will be at the hub, in front of everybody!"

Norh laughed in midair, making them wobble.

9

The Archeons had been around most of the continent, and the ribbon of destruction that had snaked through the forest was scabbed over with portals leading underground and into space, an unbroken line of black bubbles between the green trees. Soil and subterranean insects occasionally leaked out of the portals and fell to the ground.

Friend's old ways had gone far beyond the forest, and the destruction reached out over the oceans and probably other parts of the planet, but this was the only place they had to fix the damage.

Two lines of soil-filled spheres were closing in on one another. A large plant was just thirty paces from exceeding the height of the Magor trees. A sphere opened on top of it, shutting out the light. It was the last place where light penetrated to the floor.

All across the forest, the Archeons watched and waited. The trees had created new sprouts all over the forest floor, emitting poison gas and filling the entire subcanopy with a toxic mixture of carbon dioxide, sulfur, and ammonia up to a hundred paces high down there. Only the fliers and the tree climbers dared perch themselves on high branches to watch what happened.

The invasive trees across the continent slowed to a stop. The sounds of rapid growth fell still. The gas halted, and the lesser trees were already working on filtering it from the air. The only sound now was the wind rustling the vegetation, and the birds who were trying to figure out how to get back down into the forest when the gaps were plugged with solid dirt and rock suspended in midair.

The stimulus was gone. The trees hibernated again.

The Archeons stood on treetops and cheered. The entire population of Alkan and Magora screeched and chittered at the silence of the forest. Soon they would begin talking about what to do next. They would probably wait until Kawjor recovered before deciding. They filtered through the portals and returned to the hub. The single Krone among them also returned to the hub and walked to a treetop platform that had no portals on it. He rolled to his back, doubled over, and began licking his own slit. Nobody had seen a Krone do this before, so it drew an audience.

Deka had witnessed this several times. He wondered who was blowing whom, and what the reason was this time. Clicking his claws, Deka turned and trotted away. The portals to the ground were unusable until the poison air dissipated, so he scanned the various spheres around the canopy. The treetops were deserted outside the hub.

Deka noticed a portal with a hint of red fur visible across its surface. He ducked through and emerged on a treetop halfway across the continent. His fox was sitting on the leaves, facing away from the portal. The wind blew toward the fox so he would smell whoever came through.

He heard someone else step out of the portal behind him, and Sonjaa's scent fell over him. He paused, waited for her to catch up, and nuzzled her neck. Most of the Magora and Alkan did not speak the languages of other species well enough to tell them what happened, so she had run around half the contacted universe bringing Archeons to Magor. She deserved to be part of the celebration as well. They approached Kylac together, not bothering to be quiet.

When they were ten paces away, Kylac growled, and his ear folded back.

"Are you all right?" Deka said.

Kylac growled louder. Deka was close enough to smell him, and it brought back memories of running through an antisphere labyrinth.

Deka placed a hand on Kylac's shoulder. The fox snarled. Deka rubbed his neck with his snout. Kylac kept growling. The theropod could tell by the tension in his muscles he wanted to leap up and attack, but he was holding himself down.

Sonjaa kept her distance. She looked back at the portal, listened to the sounds of celebration in the distance. Kylac was still snarling.

"It's time to come back," Deka said.

Kylac continued snarling. Deka kept touching him, forcing him to breathe his scent. Gradually, Kylac's face fell, and his voice lowered. He rose to his feet and turned to Deka. The raptor embraced him, rubbing his neck on Kylac's. The fox's scent had changed from anxious rage to anxious agony.

"Deka... I've only just started. The barrier is still there! I'm losing control now! How will I handle it when I remember everything?"

"You are better than Friend. Plus, you have a goal. You will make it work."

Kylac held Deka tighter. "What if I can't? What if lose myself? You and Sonjaa will be the first two people I kill, and then what will stop me from—?"

Deka growled at him. Kylac shrank, ear folding back and tail tucking between his legs. He held onto Deka. The raptor nuzzled him and met his eyes.

"You can handle this!" He let go of Kylac and turned to Sonjaa. "Both of you! You share the same trauma, and you will get through this!"

Sonjaa stood low. Deka nuzzled her.

"Don't ignore it. You will remember, and you will control it."

She did not make eye contact and continued shivering.

He turned to Kylac now. "The plant is dormant again. Stephen and Norh are about to celebrate with some *fireworks*."

Kylac's ear twitched at the lone English word. "What?"

Deka clicked his claws. He held Kylac around his back and led him to the portal.

10

Most of the Archeons had returned home. The ways they kept open would remain here as long as they needed to be. The Alkan and Magora huddled around Kawjor. Some people had picked him up and began carrying him to an off-world portal. The direct path to Selta was inaccessible now, so they had to take several ways across multiple worlds to reach it. As the group approached the sphere, time slowed until everyone froze in place just as they were about to enter.

Deka, Kylac, Sonjaa, and Norh turned to face the new scent among them. A Relian canine with no reproductive organs stood in the center of the treetop, leaning on the enormous flower.

Deka crouched in attack stance and raised his claws. Kylac snarled, dropping to all fours. Norh grunted and roared.

Sonjaa was already on top of the fox, cutting into his abdomen with a killing claw. Friend lay on his back, arms and legs spread apart, Sonjaa ripping his guts out with her snout. He didn't seem to run out of guts to pull out; he was a bottomless pit of entrails and organs. It took Sonjaa a few moments to realize it, then she jumped off him, the blood on her muzzle and claws suddenly gone.

As one, the others converged on Friend and ripped him apart. Norh tore off his left arm. Deka jumped on top of him and ripped off his head as Kylac tore meat from his lower limbs.

A new head appeared in place of the one Deka tore off. A new arm appeared where Norh had ripped the previous one. New meat rose up from nowhere to replace what Kylac had chewed off. Once they had calmed down, they backed away and looked at the fox. Their claws and mouths were dry, their stomachs empty.

Friend rose to his feet, fur pristine and intact. "Now that you're ready to listen, I have—"

Sonjaa silently jumped on him again, sank both killing claws into his chest and kicked backwards, tearing chunks of fur and flesh from him. She reached down and ripped his throat out, tossed the meat over the side of the tree. She casually stepped off, walked back to Deka's side and turned around, her mouth and claws blood-free again.

Friend rose to his feet, body pristine again. Deka snarled. Friend spread his arms and waited for it, but Deka did not move as he shouted.

"Your old ways almost destroyed an entire civilization, and you did nothing!"

Friend pretended to clear his throat. "I can't help. If I had made any changes to this planet, my instincts would have found me."

Deka was about to screech at him, but Norh picked up Friend and swallowed him whole. The others turned to watch as Norh gulped. They waited five breaths, and then Friend appeared next to Sonjaa. They turned to face him, backing away.

"Are you through?"

"Leave us alone before your instincts cause any more damage," Kylac said.

"I will whenever possible. No more frivolous appearances. But when you're ready to deal with them, you'll need me to lure them to you."

"Why don't you lure them into a black hole?" Stephen said, unfolding his wings and retracting them very slowly.

"Those don't exist in the Lake," said Kylac.

Friend's tail twitched. "He wasn't referring to singularities. While the rest of you waste time figuring that out, step through this way."

Friend vanished. Time wound up to a normal pace. The birds and capybaras of Magor carried their Archeon through the sphere to Selta. A Krone-sized way to Fusina opened on the edge of the treetop. Friend's muzzle appeared next to it.

"Don't take too long. My old ways might find this projection and start thrashing again. Would be a shame for all your hard work to go to waste."

"Why Fusina?" Sonjaa said.

"My old ways were just there, and they did something you'll want to see."

Deka growled and walked through. One by one they stepped into the offworld portal. It closed when Norh's tail entered.

Several Alkan on the next treetop over pondered what they should do about these plants now. They both wanted to learn more about this species of tree but could not think of a way to do it without triggering their growth reaction again. They hoped someone in the contacted universe had an idea.

Dover

I

"October twenty-eighth, nineteen ninety-seven," said a woman's voice off camera. "Secretary of Relian Relations CJ Rhine with Lucy Schrifton."

Lucy sat on the couch in her usual business attire, dressed for success, hair done professionally. In the next room, Rive was talking to Vae, the raptor, and Tema, the fox. CJ assumed he was preparing them for their interview, but she still had to wonder what they were really talking about, and why in a language no human understood.

"Please tell us why you went to the convention in Pittsburgh earlier this year."

Lucy looked down at her lap, smiling. "It was actually a risk for me. I work for a law firm, and though they claim to encourage time off, they don't. Taking vacation can end your career."

She looked up and faced CJ, who sat behind the camera.

"I knew it would be quite a drive, but I couldn't let the chance slip away. I'd heard the news, and the more I heard it, the less I believed it. Aliens are here. They're all over the world. Why isn't everyone dropping what they're doing and going to meet them? That's what I kept thinking. Why are we still arguing settlements and copyrights when we should be looking at these people? So I announced I was going to the convention to meet the aliens. I figured things would hold together for four days."

"Tell us about the convention."

"It wasn't as big as I expected. I figured aliens were here, so the place would be packed. There were a lot of people there, but it wasn't wall-to-wall. I didn't meet Vae and Tema in the meeting hall. I missed that event. I met them at the first Q&A on the second day. They caught my scent in the audience and sniffed me out. In the middle of the panel, a raptor and a fox were scenting through the audience. It was distracting, and then they stopped at me. I was on the spot, and for the first time since I set foot in university, all I wanted to do was blend in."

CJ heard claws tapping in the hallway. She kept her eyes on Lucy Schrifton so she wouldn't interrupt.

"They told me my scent was right for them. I asked them what they meant, and that's when a marine escorted me out of the room. Vae and Tema explained on the way across the convention center what the conventions were for, and... It seems weird now, agreeing to take them in having only just met them, but sometimes I wonder if people can sense this, too."

"What do you mean?"

"When I was a child, I had a lot of friends. So many friends. And a lot of other people I just didn't want to be around. Many other kids who were trying to be my friend, but I never gave them time of day, and I don't remember why. It makes me think. What if I knew those kids just weren't right for me? What if it wasn't childhood cruelty and I really could tell we just wouldn't get along? The Relians can still do that. They can just tell, but I think kids have other cues. They don't try to fake being friends with someone. They don't play politics, or I don't remember any kids who did.

"And I think that little childhood skill came back for just a moment. Talking with them on the way to fill out the papers and make it official, I knew we'd get along. There was this ease while talking to them. That's why I signed. I knew it would work out, but God, if I'd known what would happen next, I don't think I'd have done it!"

"What happened next?"

"It's a long story. The somewhat short version is Vae and Tema became curious about what I did all day at the office up in Wilmington, so I went to my boss and asked his permission to let them shadow me for a day. He said yes. He was bragging about how one of his top lawyers had a pair of aliens living with her, and he wanted them to be seen around the office, too. I think he just wanted to meet them. Vae would later tell me I smelled so nice at the convention, but quickly my scent changed when I returned to work, and she didn't like it."

"Changed in what way?" CJ prompted.

"It was the stress. I was in vacation mode at the convention. That's the person she liked. The woman who came home every night, often bringing work home with her, and went to bed thinking about the caseload... That wasn't who I was. I was on stress meds, several of them. Vae smelled how the job was changing my body. She saw the same thing I saw in the future. Heart disease, obesity, all the things associated with long-term stress. She was determined to help."

CJ hadn't noticed Rive and the Relians talking in quite some time. "Why did she help?"

"Because they're probably the best friends I've ever had. They cared about me. My scent was different, and they wanted it to be right again. I couldn't quit, she couldn't hunt, so Vae and Tema decided to be my personal assistants at work. In a few months, they had pretty much taken over the job. Oh, there's so much more to the story than that. How do I begin to tell it?"

CJ wanted the details on tape as much as Rive did. She leaned forward. "What did they do for you?"

Lucy told the long story. Vae and Tema shared the burden. Vae especially. She learned the details of each case, shadowing Lucy for weeks, learning the job. Before long, she had everyone trained to go to herself with questions instead of Lucy. She had inserted herself between Lucy and her team, and that freed Lucy to remove herself from the office. By then, Vae could call her with questions, and so long as Lucy remained away from the office, other people were convinced that she was elsewhere doing more important work.

They were right. She was at home, resting, not worrying. As Lucy relaxed, Vae and Tema started to change. Lucy couldn't catch their scents, but it was in their body language. They were stressed and tired all the time. So Lucy gave them a couple weeks off and returned to the office, and nobody asked questions. They went back and forth like this, taking two-week shifts. Things evened out for a while.

"And then we were caught. The chief executive himself came to visit me at home while Vae and Tema were in my place. I told him the truth, and I admitted I couldn't handle the job anymore. I couldn't quit though. I needed the money too much. Friends and family all told me I'd made it, that I was successful, but they didn't see the hours I put in, the worry, the medications I had to take to keep going. If I had to do it again, I wouldn't be a lawyer."

CJ smiled. She almost interjected a personal comment, but now was not the time.

"I only did it because people told me it was a great career. I could make lots of money. They were right, but you pay for it in blood. Vae recognized I was on my way to heart disease, and she took it upon herself to prevent it. Why don't we think like that? Why do people always wait until the problem is critical before fixing it? Vae and Tema didn't. They saw the early signs of the problem, and they did something about it.

"My boss allowed it to continue. Vae and Tema have no qualifications, no law degree. Everything they learned came from their time in the office. They should not be doing what they're doing, but they are. They didn't climb the corporate ladder. They pole-vaulted it. It's been a big help for me. Tema and Vae are picking up the stress in my place. My relief is their suffering. It's how the business world works. I'm not on any meds now. It's been months, and things are going strong. Hopefully nobody on the board of directors finds out. They'll use it as an excuse to fire me."

"Why would they do that?"

"Anything not normal is grounds for termination. Any signs of initiative and independence are signs that you have ambition to advance your career and won't stay in the job, so why keep you? At this point, I don't care. For the hell of it, I had a buddy of mine give Vae and Tema the bar exam. They passed. They're still not lawyers because they don't have the schooling, but they know everything they need to, and they learned it fast. I don't know what's going to happen now, but I am enjoying the relief. I've been using the free time to look at other options. Job options. I want out. There has to be something less stressful I can do with my experience."

"How would you describe your relationship with Vae and Tema?"

"That's... hard to put into words. They're like sisters, but without the aggravation. I've taken them all over the place, and they are so easy to get along with. They were right. We are perfect for each other. Even those times when we're at the office together all day and we come home at night, we never seem to get sick of each other. Funny... When I'm with people all day, I have to take time out and be by myself. Take time for myself. But I don't feel that way with them. I'm with them all the time, and I don't have that desire to get away from them. I've never felt like that before, even with the boyfriends I had when I was younger. Just wanted them to go away for a while, even when I still liked them. Not these two."

CJ checked the tape. She pointed to her bare wrist and gestured *ten minutes* with her hands.

"This has been quite a trip," Lucy continued. "I'm a much happier person now, and not just because I'm working from home half the month. I mean it's so nice to have two people living with me, and we connect so well. With teachers and classmates and coworkers, I know they're putting up with me because they want something from me, or they need me. Vae and Tema are here because they want me. They knew exactly who I was at that convention, and they didn't need to get to know me. This is... It's everything marriage is supposed to be. When you meet someone who just connects with you, and you don't have to try to make a relationship work. I almost missed that convention. I don't want to know what my life would be like now if I hadn't gone."

With six minutes of tape left, CJ shut the camera off. She reached over and hit the stop button on the tape recorder, then sat back in her chair.

"Was that good?" Lucy said.

"That was wonderful, Ms. Schrifton. And from one lawyer to another, I don't blame you for wanting to get out. I quit private practice and ran for public office."

Lucy smiled. "Never thought of that. Maybe I should run for congress."

CJ smirked. "Try governor, that way you can appoint Vae and Tema to something. First Relian public officials. No, Rive is the first. First in the state."

"Delaware is the first state," Lucy said, smiling. "It's all we've got going for us. Let's keep the tradition of firsts."

"You have tax-free shopping here. I wish we had that."

"It's so nice."

Lucy looked over CJ's shoulder. The secretary turned around in her chair. Two raptors and a fox stood at the door to the dining room, looking in. Lucy turned to CJ.

"Are we done here?"

"We are. Thank you for the interview. That was worthy of the public record."

Lucy stood and crossed the room where Rive was waiting. She leaned over, touched her neck to his in a Relian greeting, and then extended her hand. Rive shook her hand. Lucy winced at the cold, and she chatted him up in the kitchen while Vae and Tema walked in for their half of the interview. Everyone wanted to talk to the metal raptor if for no other reason than to confirm he was real.

CJ reached down picked up her briefcase and pulled out new tapes.

2

CJ had been in a hurry to return to Washington DC as soon as the interviews were finished, but as usual, Rive took her somewhere. He always made a way just large enough for her briefcase to fit through so she could drop it in the office, and then they went to the movies, something interesting in town, or just a walk around the neighborhood.

They were touring the government district on foot. For a state capital, it was tiny. The entire place consisted of just a couple city blocks and lots of green lawns spreading out the official government buildings. CJ marveled at it.

"This is it? I think Rhode Island has a bigger capital than this."

"It does," Rive said, rubbing his claws. "I like this place. It's a city, but not overwhelmingly large."

"This is laughable! Three blocks of government buildings, another three for the historic district, and that's it!"

"Why is it laughable?"

"Because there's nothing to it! Why bother with all the landmarks and historical markers? There's nothing here!"

"I read this city has about thirty thousand residents." Rive clicked his claws as he looked out over the lawn toward the tiny capital building. "You call this laughable, and yet there are many species whose population would fit in a city this size with plenty of room to spare."

"I remember you said that. I guess I needed to come here to see what that meant. An entire species... Right here, in a city this size. That is ridiculous."

"What makes you say that?"

"That's an endangered species, not a thriving culture."

"You believe a thriving culture has a large population, but a small population is dying off?"

CJ laughed. "Well, when you put it like that it sounds racist, but yes, that's how it feels."

"A symptom of an immature species that is still afraid of catastrophe wiping out the population. One that regards extinction as a threat, especially in the case of your kind, since you know you have caused the extinction of many species. Naturally, you fear it happening to you. A mature species knows the opposite is true, that a small population is a sign of a healthy society."

"I don't see how."

"Population density causes many problems on your planet. Too many people gathered in one place spreads disease, strains resources, and changes the mentality of the population. This can be observed both on the local scale and on the scale of the entire planet."

"Maybe you're onto something. Six billion people on this planet. Something has to give. Can't feed them all."

"A large population is not itself a problem. There is enough land and food and water for everyone. The primary concern is how it changes the mindset of the population. For a species of your type, the larger the population, the less the individual matters. Society begins to control the individual instead of one being able to influence it. If enough people feel lost within such a society, they will lash out against it."

"So what's the solution to that? Can't tell everyone to stop having children."

"Doing so would also be a problem. A low population is not the goal. It is an outward sign of a society's lack of a subconscious fear of extinction, or starvation, or even a latent need to leave something behind when they die to satisfy their own lack of control over their own lives. Attempting to create a low population for its own sake defeats the purpose."

"Is there any room in there for having children because they want to?"

Rive clicked his claws. "There's always room for that, but everything has an underlying reason, even if a person is not conscious of that reason. Immature species still live according to their animal nature, which becomes more and more magnified and out of control as generations pass, thus people are still caught in the struggle for survival. The urge to reproduce is an expression of this insecurity. But when a species matures, no such insecurity exists. Their basic needs are met, and there is no fear for survival. Without fear of their own demise, they do not feel an urgent need to reproduce, so the population remains low. It is something that happens on its own. Forcing it to happen would not give it the same meaning."

A few cars drove by, the drivers craning their necks out of their windows at the sight of Rive. A few pedestrians walked on the other side of the lawn. CJ noticed nobody walked on the grass here. She huffed.

"We fear extinction, so we reproduce like crazy. Sounds like something Freud would write. Six billion people, all terrified and acting out their lack of control over their own lives."

"Take away the insecurity, give people the freedom to achieve their desires, and the population will decrease. When I look at this city, and I imagine the entire species within its limits, I do not laugh. I breathe easy because I know it means they are happy."

"Isn't that why you're here? You and all the other Relians? You're going to help us with that, aren't you?"

"We are few, and there is great resistance to what we represent."

"From what I've seen, there's no resistance at all. People are getting along great with the aliens."

They had reached the corner, and they crossed the street. They did not have to wait for any cars; there was no traffic to slow them down, which amazed CJ.

"Some are. I'm sorry to say the ones who are afraid of us have far more influence than those who have embraced us. They want people to be insecure and afraid."

CJ rubbed her temple as they stepped on the curb and passed another official building.

"This really is all you think about, isn't it? Society as a whole, species as a whole."

"Not too many people are willing to listen as long as you have. I can tell you enjoy hearing it." Rive clicked his claws. "I haven't had anybody to talk to about things like this since I lost my fox. Even Deka and Kylac grow tired of it after a while. Deka was always more interested in life underwater."

CJ smiled as she reached over and held Rive's hand. Rive rubbed her fingers, walking closer to her, head touching hers. CJ had watched raptors be close by walking with their flanks touching. He couldn't do that easily with her, so this was the compromise.

"Were you always like this?" she said. "Brain moving ten miles a minute, big thoughts day and night?"

"Believe it or not, I wasn't. This only happened when I became an Archeon."

"Yes, how does that even start? How do you apply for the job?"

"If you show aptitude, someone will notice. An Archeon gives you a test. If you pass it, you move on to other tests, and before you realize it, you're an apprentice. That's what happened to me. I became an Archeon relatively late in life, and so did Friend, my fox."

"What kind of test?"

"Mental tests, mostly regarding how much information the mind can handle at once. It's a gradual process, merging the subconscious with the higher mind and becoming aware of the universe and how it truly appears. If you enjoy it, you continue. I remember making my first portal. It was a revelation unlike any other, that the mind can create connections between points in spacetime. It can hold doors open millions of light years away. Friend and I loved it. It gave our musings on quantum mechanics new depth. Deka and Kylac became Archeons years later. All four of us were apprentices at the same time, but Friend and I were further along. We began to take over the portals our mentors maintained while Deka and Kylac learned. Soon they took over the rest."

"How do you screen?"

"Screen for what?"

"Screen the bad people out. That's a lot of responsibility. It's still hard to believe. Hundreds of civilizations joined together in a community, and nobody uses spaceships. It's just a few hundred Archeons holding portals open. Are there any tests to see if someone will abuse the power?"

"Nobody would dare abuse their role as Archeon. We know what our place is, and what it means, and we are part of society, not above it. We would have to live with the consequences the same as anybody else."

"Still doesn't sound all that comforting. Civilization itself is controlled by a tiny group of people."

"Being an Archeon made me part of the universe. I was part of millions of people's lives, making life better for hundreds of worlds. That meant everything to me."

"So give it to me straight. What does it mean to be able to open portals to anywhere you want to go? How is it done? What's it like?"

Rive rubbed his claws against her fingers. "Archeons are aware of the universe as it actually is. I can perceive atoms vibrating around us, popping into and out of existence. As another example, I can sense how the orbits of the planets in your solar system create waves in spacetime, and how those waves affect the atoms inside of you. Everything the mind normally hides from us, I am aware of, and just being aware of these connections allows me to manipulate them. I find it a relaxing perspective on reality."

"So now that you don't keep any portals open anymore, what happens to you? What will you do with it?"

"Maybe I'll run for public office."

"They'd love you in California."

"What about Texas?"

Without her realizing it, they had left the government district and had entered residential. CJ paused and looked around. She laughed. Rive rubbed her fingers. They walked without care for where they were going.

Fusina

I

The portal opened on a sandy beach. Deka stepped through first, followed by Sonjaa, then Kylac, and then Stephen and Norh.

The orange star loomed large in the sky, its light overwhelming. The gravity on this world was much stronger than they were used to, and each felt oppressed by the extra weight.

Immediately the Archeons noticed the paw prints in the sand in front of them pointing inland. Deka and Kylac ran up to them and scented them. Norh and Stephen slowly approached and scented the trail as well.

Kylac faced the opposite direction. "Did it come out of the water?"

Norh and Stephen walked past them, into the waves, and stuck his neck below the surface. He remained under for about eighteen breaths, and then raised his head and walked back up the beach. Sonjaa stood with Deka and Kylac, waiting for him.

"I don't see footprints, so it didn't walk," Stephen said, lowering his head to their eye level. "On Neben, it didn't know how to handle water. Perhaps it learned here."

"It recognized the water, so it expected to drown," said the fox. "It's figuring out the laws of physics do not apply anymore. It's adapting to it."

Deka led them up the slope. They walked over the crest and entered the hub of this world on a level outcropping of rock which had been polished smooth by centuries of tides and crashing waves. A species of pink and white lichen grew on many of the rocks. Normally, portals lined this beach up and down for hundreds of paces, but only a few dozen remained. Two winked closed as they looked.

Other Archeons who had seen the destruction on Magor had closed their portals for fear of being a victim of a new disaster. Others would follow soon as they spread the word. Deka's hands sagged as he surveyed the second closing of the contacted universe. Sonjaa stopped next to him and held his claws.

Plenty of portals still led to other places on this planet. Rocky beaches, sandy ones, beaches with green water, beaches with blue water, and beaches with water so clear there seemed to be none at all.

No offworlders were here. They had all gone home when they learned of the new disaster on Magor. Even rubbing claws with Sonjaa, Deka's hands sagged thinking it was happening again: the contacted universe was closing, each planet isolating itself.

Fourteen Dasi walked between the spheres, some on four feet, others on two, some carrying seashells, others carrying armfuls of lichen. Stephen's wings stretched when he saw them. They resembled sea otters back home, but larger, about half Kylac's size, and with fur ranging from blue to green. Norh shared his memories of this world, and now Stephen knew the Dasi hunted fish and spent hours at a time floating on the surface in beds of kelp, just like the sea otters he knew.

The Dasi at the portals noticed the offworlders and ran to meet them. Many removed the lichen they had been chewing and stuck it to the spongy ground. In moments, that lichen would integrate with the vast field and replenish its supply of oxygen.

A Dasi dove into a portal that led into a deep, blue ocean. Two others dove out of portals that led into green water and rolled on the lichens. They rose to their feet, noticing the newcomers. They spat out their lichens as well and stuck it to the rock. Color began flowing back into them.

Deka and Sonjaa walked to meet everyone. The ones who had just come out of the water did not even look wet, their fur so well adapted that water did not adhere to it.

"Greetings," Sonjaa said in the whistles and high-pitched growling of their species. "We're here because something strange happened. Can anyone tell us more?"

"The Yjerm witnessed it in the ocean," said the green-furred Dasi in front of them. "A few others saw it up here when it came out. Please wait here. We will find them."

The Dasi dropped to all four feet, pulled a clump of lichen from the rocks, stuffed it in her cheek, doubled around, and trotted to a portal so blue it appeared black. She dove in and swam through the ocean on the other side.

A few others also took lichen in their mouths and padded for portals that led underwater. They dove in and wiggled away. Others walked through portals that led to other beaches.

The Relians and the Krone stood alone on the hub. Deka sat down on the lichen-covered rock bed. Sonjaa remained standing next to him. Kylac scented the area, following the pawprints in the rock through the hub. Stephen walked up to a portal that led to the bottom of a dark green ocean.

Stephen took a breath and he stuck his head and neck through. He emerged deep under the ocean on the other side of the planet. Dasi wiggled and paddled around in the dark water. They were so far down no light penetrated the surface. It would have been pitch dark here if not for the Yjerm.

Thirty-four lights shone around Stephen's head. They had noticed his arrival and swam to meet him. Norh was the only one whose body could withstand the water pressure, and even then the pressure on his eyes was so great he could only venture here for a few moments before he had to pull out.

The Yjerm so rarely had visitors other than the Dasi. Most had never seen a Krone before, and the flashes of light that composed their language were riotous and gleeful.

They swam closer. Stephen's human mind called these people angler fish, but their light lure was much more sophisticated than those primitive creatures on Earth. The Yjerm illuminated their entire bodies, and they did not simply glow but projected light all around themselves. Their collective glow brought daylight to this deep place, and now Stephen saw clearly.

Their light traveled quite far down here. Stephen saw Dasi paddling and wiggling through the water down here. His wings unfolded on the other side of the portal, thinking that his mighty Krone body could not survive down here, but these otters could. They had adapted to hunting this far down, and that's how they had met the Yjerm.

Stephen was unable to speak to them, for if he opened his mouth, the ocean would rush in at a great enough force to rupture both his esophagus and trachea. All he could do was look at them and the Dasi as they swam up to him, too, chewing lichen with their mouths closed, bubbles of carbon dioxide escaping through special membranes covering their closed nostrils.

Stephen had heard so much about the Yjerm, but could not interact with them for very long. He had spent weeks on this planet in his youth, watching them, learning their language, but unable to say anything back. He had to talk to them through another Dasi, who had developed a kind of sign language to speak to them, similar to the one offworlders used to communicate with the people of Lesa. Stephen had learned these signs, but numerous gestures required being able to swim.

The ocean on this planet was actually not that deep, but due to the high gravity, the water behaved more densely than on Earth and reached a thickness that shut out light at much shallower levels than his human mind was used to.

Then Stephen realized these memories and experiences were not his. They were Norh's. It was getting harder and harder to remember that.

His eyes began to flatten from the pressure. He pulled his neck back and emerged from the sphere. The Yjerm gathered around the portal, swimming about and looking at him. Some probably wished they could stick a limb into his world, but the lack of water pressure would kill them instantly.

Stephen looked down at the lichen he was standing on. It was special to the Dasi because it concentrated and stored oxygen in its cells. Chewing it allowed the Dasi to breathe underwater. In more primitive times, the Dasi had selected the lichen varieties with the most oxygen content, as it allowed them to stay underwater for longer and deeper hunts.

For thousands of years, that's all it had been. As they dove deeper, and their bodies adapted to greater and greater water pressures, they discovered their companion race. The Yjerm had never seen a life form like them, and could not imagine where they had come from.

The Dasi began crossbreeding the lichen for even more concentration. Now the lichen had enough oxygen in a mouthful to last a Dasi half a day under the surface. Every Dasi knew how to use it, and how to harvest it so as not to kill the plant.

Regrettably, it contained other substances that were toxic to most other species. Chewing it would make a Relian sick. Chewing it more than a few times would kill a raptor or a fox. It was plant-based, so Norh could not tolerate it at all.

The two species had learned to communicate, learned about each other's world, and portal physics emerged from this kind of understanding. The Dasi used the portals to spare themselves the long swim across the ocean to find fish, and to interact with their companion species. The Yjerm lured prey through portals positioned all over the bottom of the ocean so they would not have to waste most of their day floating still and waiting for prey to swim up to the light they made, which had freed them to explore the ocean instead of floating and waiting.

He heard Deka behind him, clicking his claws. He turned his head around and faced the raptor.

"Kylac brought me here when we were apprentices. I was on a journey to meet all the aquatic species in the contacted universe. I spent days watching the portals, catching glimpses of a life I could only imagine far down in the darkness."

Kylac was scenting the ground a short distance away. "Deka couldn't take it anymore. He had to touch one of them. He stuck an arm through the portal."

"My radius snapped instantly. Fourteen Yjerm grabbed it and shoved it back to the other side. I had a splint on it. I couldn't do anything but wait for it to heal, so I watched the Yjerm while Kylac had sex with Dasi after Dasi on top of the lichen. I remember being proud of Kylac for that. He did it on his own, without me having to prompt him."

Sonjaa reached over and shared a laugh with him. Norh's wings fluttered. Kylac stood by him, tail hanging limp.

A few dozen Dasi dove out of the underwater portals. The Relians recognized the scent of their Archeon, a Dasi with blue fur named Cilitrus. It wasn't her real name—that was made of a particular pattern of flashing light which the Yjerm had given to her at birth—but it was a name Relians could pronounce. She stood on two legs, back still curled slightly, almost as tall as Kylac now.

"Welcome! Surprising enough to see Relians again, but a Krone as well. You want to know what happened the other day."

"Did anyone see it?" Deka said.

"Everyone did. An antisphere shaped like a Relian canine swimming through the water. Swam at all depths halfway around the planet, then it came ashore and began running. Nobody saw where it went from there."

"Actually swimming?" Sonjaa said.

Kylac's ear folded back. "It's learning to interact with its environment. Did anyone see it come up for air at any point?"

"From what everyone says, no."

Deka turned, looked back over the ocean. "For it to move in the water, it must have figured out how to touch matter without pulling it into the Lake."

"And now it knows it can breathe underwater," Sonjaa said. "It's probably noticed it doesn't need to breathe at all. Once it figures out that other people can't touch it, it's over."

Cilitrus lowered herself to four legs. "I heard from other Archeons that these are Friend's old ways trapped outside the universe, and they're trying to come back. First mention of Friend and I closed most of the portals. I will close the rest if necessary."

"You should close them now," Deka said, turning back to face her. "You were lucky they didn't attack and collide with any portals. They can come back any time."

"What do you four intend to do about it?"

Kylac backed away and looked out over what was left of the hub. "I'm slowly bringing down the barrier between me and my knowledge of the Lake. Once I remember, I should be able to trap it on a planet."

"Then what?"

"That's a good question. If anyone needs me, I'll be over there. It seems deserted."

The fox walked toward a portal that led to a beach with pure, transparent water. He ducked his head and slipped through. He sat down overlooking the ocean.

Cilitrus turned back to Deka and Sonjaa. "You're going to leave him alone?"

"I can only imagine what he's going through," Deka said. "I'll give him space. I think he's the only one in the universe who stands a chance of stopping Friend's instincts."

"Are any of you hungry? The ways to carnivore hunting grounds are closed, but we can catch you some fish. And speaking of that," she chittered, laughing. "I heard you brought a human to the hunting grounds of Beslos, and he didn't enjoy the meal."

Deka and Sonjaa clicked claws. Stephen spread his wings.

"Now that you mention it," Deka said, "we haven't eaten in days. Since the ways are gone, yes, I'll eat some fish."

"Happily," Sonjaa said.

"Don't bother for me," Stephen said. "It'll only make me hungrier."

Cilitrus laughed. "We'll bring back what we can. Tell me that story. I have one for all of you as well."

She bent down, tucked a mouthful of lichen into her cheek, and then ran to the nearest underwater portal. She plunged into the dark water and swam upwards.

A portal to the hunting grounds of Beslos appeared next to that sphere. Friend faded in next to it, lacking sheath and testicles again. "All you have to do is ask. Remember, I can't read calculate what you're thinking given the situation and the evolution of your species and the history of the atoms in the universe."

"Not this time," said Deka.

"I'm here to help in whatever way I can."

"You could help by not showing your muzzle again. Every time you do, your instincts follow, so leave before they do damage here, too."

The fox morphed into a miniature Sikor, a bipedal reptile flaunting razor-sharp feathers on the arms, neck, and skull. Friend maintained his Relian fur pattern on the bare skin of the animal. "Without me, you'd have no idea where to go."

"Without you, we wouldn't need to go anywhere," Stephen said.

"I hear a distinct lack of gratitude," said the Sikor. The portal disappeared, and Friend grew and expanded into a full-sized predator looking down on the Relians. "What will it take to convince you I'm sorry? None of this was supposed to happen. If my old ways would stay outside the universe, I would reach a higher level of understanding and leave the universe forever. I had planned to come back and check in with all of you at some point to let you know that it was all worth it—that someone made it out of the universe alive before it ended."

"Just leave us alone," Sonjaa said.

"If I could do more to help, I would," Friend said as he grew even larger. His musculature became exaggerated, claws, teeth, and feathers growing to ridiculous proportions. It towered over the hub high enough to block the light of the star. "But I can't. All I want to do is leave. It shouldn't be difficult, but it is, and I am just as frustrated as all of you are. It's all I really want. Please let me leave. This is the only thing I've ever wanted since I first glimpsed a reality existing outside the univ—"

A splash hit the water behind them. The Sikor looked out over the ocean and vanished. Stephen raised his neck and looked back. Deka and Sonjaa rose, turning around as well.

The antifox floated halfway submerged a few hundred paces out to sea. It scented them from a distance. It turned around in place, scenting in all directions. It snarled at everything, its claws growing to twice the length of its body. Then it seemed to panic, forgot where it was, and sank beneath the waves. The water was dense and blue here, so they could not see what happened to it. Several breaths went by. Norh spread his wings, about to take off and dive below the waves to get a look.

The ocean swirled and pulled away, but the water itself did not appear to be moving. Spacetime moved, and it pulled the water along with it down to the bottom of the sea, stretching and funneling into a single point far below.

Sonjaa and Deka ran down the beach as the water receded from the shore and slipped below the drop-off forty paces out. Sonjaa outran Deka, reaching the cliff first. Norh had taken to the air, and he flew over the edge of the sea. Deka caught up to Sonjaa a moment later.

The water funneled into a spinning point at the bottom of the ocean not too far from the cliff wall. No drops of water fell anywhere; everything had been pulled in. The spinning point resembled an antisphere from here, but it had claws longer than its body.

They heard flopping on the lichen behind them, and they turned around at once. Three Dasi lay on the ground in front of the portals. They spat their lichen out, eyes wide with fear. A few breaths later, the last of the water was gone. From the sky, Norh and Stephen saw no water anywhere.

The portals at the hub were still there, and most of the underwater portals still led to someplace underwater, but four of them now showed an empty chasm in all directions. Deka calculated where those portals were, where the water must still be, and how far out to sea the antifox had absorbed the ocean. It had only drawn water from one fifth of it. As soon as he had made the calculations, the portals vanished.

Sonjaa ran to the nearest Dasi and nuzzled her. "Are you all right? Is there anyone else?"

The Dasi raised her head and met Sonjaa's eyes. "They're gone... They were— They stretched away... until they snapped! I was already close to the portal. It didn't catch me."

She rolled over to her back and panted.

The antifox stood far below at the bottom of the ocean floor. It had stopped spinning and now it looked up at Deka and the circling Krone. Even though it had no discernible facial features, its body language hinted it was very much intimidated by the high climb back up. It snarled at them again and scented the air. Deka had the feeling it wasn't merely scenting the surroundings, but the entire planet. It appeared satisfied, and it folded into itself and out of this universe.

Norh dove and then landed on the beach, kicking up a small hurricane of dry sand. Deka and Sonjaa looked at one another. Only part of the ocean was gone; the rest of the water was coming to fill the hole the antifox had made. The Archeons calculated how long it would take to arrive.

Sonjaa was about to stand up, but the Dasi reached up with both hands and grabbed her snout.

"There's something else down there! The Yjerm found it months ago! Text! Structures! If Cilitrus is dead, all of it will be lost when the water comes! Hurry!"

She let go of Sonjaa and rested her head on the lichen, panting. Sonjaa turned to Deka and Norh.

2

Kylac had watched the ocean retreat just moments ago, and then the portal to this beach had gone out. The wind reversed direction and rushed down into the ocean floor as he sat on the beach overlooking the empty chasm where the water used to be, his single ear folded back, thinking about the one thing he had spent more than a year avoiding.

The solution was in his head. The equations were still there, but dormant, and all he had to do was press a button in his mind, throw a few switches in the right order, and they should start working again.

He hoped he would not create an antisphere here. With a living antisphere hopping from planet to planet destroying everything it touched, Fusina did not need a second fox doing the same thing.

And yet that's exactly what he had to become. It was a scary idea, going beyond his raptor's help, contemplating something Deka's scent could not calm. He was about to revert, and being aware of the inevitable scared him even more than when it happened the first time.

Friend appeared next to him, normally proportioned and sitting, his scent calm and contented, which was everything Kylac was not. He envied that scent, even as he knew it was only there because his old ways were free to roam about on their own. Kylac did not turn to him. They both sat quietly for a few breaths. Friend broke the silence.

"My old ways took a chunk out of the ocean. Now the water is flowing into the cavity. There are exactly two hundred and thirty-one Yjerm lying on at the bottom of the dry sea. None of them are alive. Another ninety-four Dasi were in that part of the ocean at the time, and they are also at the bottom of the sea, dead. The water will reach the first area in as little as... oh, Stephen's time system is actually better to measure this. Five minutes. In his language, it's a colloquial phrase to mean no time at all. The second area is half an hour away from the water. The third area is forty minutes. The fourth is sixty-seven. The hub itself is about ninety minutes."

"And what are you going to do about it?"

"Nothing. Everyone is dead. Those who are still in the water will be caught in the turbulence, which will take months to settle, but they will live."

"You could take those people out of harm's way. You could slow time and give them a chance to find safety."

"If I change anything, my instincts will find me, and I won't be able to stop myself from destroying the universe."

"You're here now."

"I'm not doing anything they can follow."

"And how did they find you this time? Did they catch you rubbing your sheath?"

"Deka and Sonjaa don't seem to have respect for me. Hopefully this little outburst teaches them."

"They would respect you a lot more if you didn't lure your old ways to every planet we visit, or if you helped clean up the messes you make, or if you started caring about how your actions affect others. Yes, I believe we stopped respecting you when you stopped thinking about things like that."

Friend's tail wagged. "This isn't a mess, Kylac. It's only twenty percent of the ocean, and only three hundred and twenty-five intelligent lives were lost. Compared to what's going on in the universe, it's nothing."

"So you still believe they don't matter. I shouldn't be surprised. Friend, is this how you always were? Were you hiding it all these years, the whole time we were apprentices and all the times we debated the questions of quantum physics? I can barely believe you were like this the whole time, just waiting for just the right moment to show it. Someone should have noticed. Rive should have. How did you trick Rive into believing you were a stable fox?"

"You know they don't matter. You're just afraid to take on this perspective."

"Viewing the lives of everyone in the universe as irrelevant in the big scheme of things is not my idea of a good perspective. I can't believe it changed you. You must have been this way all the time. I used to look up to you. You never reverted until the disaster, and I was jealous of that. I was prone to reverting, and I wanted to be like you. I don't know who you are anymore."

"Kylac, let me refresh your memory. This planet has seven hundred and forty-five sentient life forms on it. The total population of intelligent creatures in the universe is in the quintillions, including all the uncontacted species who will perish without a single person offworld knowing who they were. Three hundred twenty-five lives are gone. Millions more if you count the non-sentient species. Objectively, it is insignificant."

"And you wonder why I don't want to be like you."

"You, Deka, and Sonjaa are the only people in the universe who ever will."

The wind slowed to a stop, and then a light breeze drifted from over the chasm, devoid of all living scents. Kylac winced.

"So what?"

Friend stood up and walked in front of Kylac, blocking his view.

"While the five of you are wasting time trying to help a few people who were just going to die of natural causes in the future anyway, I am on a mission to preserve the memory of this entire universe!"

"What are you talking about?"

Friend's ears folded back. "Sonjaa said it best on Neben. Out here, there is nothing to prevent things from spreading out. The universe is doing the same thing. Slowly, gradually, the universe is expanding because it has no container. Eventually it will spread so thin atoms will cease to exist, the barrier between this universe and the Lake will break down, and it will submerge and become part of the Lake again. I glimpsed this in the equations before, when I found the Solution. You saw it, too, I'm sure. Now I know. I have calculated the exact moment it will happen, so as far as I'm concerned, it already has."

"Don't get too excited," Kylac said.

"Three little holes cut through this fate. The only three holes that will ever appear. Including me, that's four chances for someone to get out before it ends—four chances for us to avoid oblivion. Out of the thousands of trillions of sentient life forms who will ever live and die in the entire universe, just four chances to escape. Sonjaa, Deka, you, and me. We are the only four people who will ever leave the universe. I have run the numbers over and over, and that's the objective reality. That's why I want you here with me. It's all that matters. The lives we lose on the way are absolutely unimportant."

The younger fox growled.

"I separated my old ways from my higher mind because it was the right thing to do, despite what the math indicates," Friend continued. "If someone doesn't escape this universe before it dies, we will be no better than a lone species dying off on an uncontacted planet. Imagine the whole universe meeting the fate of a lone species. Try to imagine millions of quadrillions of people dying without anyone outside of it knowing they ever lived. What if there is another layer of civilization to join, the contacted multiverse? If we don't figure out how to leave this universe, it will be as if we never existed."

Kylac growled louder, fur rising.

"Stop wasting time here," Friend said. "Stop wasting time trying to save lives. What my old ways do here means nothing."

Kylac leaped through the air and landed on Friend's chest, knocking him to the sand. When they landed, Friend did not scatter any grains. Kylac stood on his chest, snarling at an impassive canine.

"That is exactly what I don't want to become!" Kylac snarled. "If I do this, I will be tempted to think just like that! I know the math! I know they're irrelevant! I know they don't matter, and I know I will destroy them! How am I supposed to deal with your old ways?"

Despite Friend's lungs being crushed, his voice sounded perfectly normal. "Exactly. This plan of yours makes no sense, so it doesn't matter if you revert here. The damage you cause will mean nothing when the universe ends and nobody outside of it will know about it."

"Your plan makes no sense either! You have no idea how to fix this, and you don't care!"

"I care very deeply. Everything I am doing is for the good of the universe as a whole. If someone can't accept they're irrelevant, that's no fault of mine."

Kylac's snarl sank. "You'd make an excellent business-man on Earth."

He stepped off Friend and lay on the beach, facing the chasm. Friend did not get up.

"I can smell you're starting to revert right now. The equations are coming back. There is a way to activate them all at once without opening any unstable antispheres. Would you like to know how?"

"Why do you care?"

"Because it matters to you. I may be outside the universe, but I'm not a monster."

Kylac's ear flicked a few times. The smell of dead sea life wafted in the breeze.

"How?"

Friend rolled over and propped himself up on his elbows.

3

The Krone-sized sphere opened on the bottom of the dry seabed. Deka stepped out, followed by Sonjaa, and then Norh. They were about fourteen hundred paces below where the ocean portal had been, which had been eleven thousand paces below the surface. There were no cliff walls here to get a sense of how far down they were, but the extra air pressure provided all the context they needed.

They stood on a thick bed of loose soil, completely dry. This region of the seabed was flat, so they could see everything in all directions, including the approaching water in the distance. No life here. Nothing had survived.

A rumbling sound vibrated through their feet. A wall of water loomed in the distance, tall as a mountain and coming this way. Deka and Norh calculated they had just a few minutes before it arrived and crushed everything. Even the creatures adapted to life on the ocean floor would not survive that much pressure.

Norh flapped his wings and took flight. Though gravity was higher this far down, air density was also greater, which meant he was still able to take off, but he did have to move faster to stay aloft. He and Stephen flew upwards and circled the area once. They did not have to fly very high up.

Deka and Sonjaa noticed it at the same time Stephen and Norh did. Not too far from Deka's portal, a section of seabed had been cleared of silt. The theropods dashed up to it, leaving deep footprints on the way. Stephen and Norh banked and dove for it.

The silt sloped downward into the pit, and the raptors descended another forty paces. The breeze down here was strong as the air continued to fall into the hole in the ocean. Stephen and Norh landed in the middle of it, and they waited for the raptors as they sprinted into what seemed to be a city.

Carved and formed structures rose from the bedrock, not unlike the ones they had found on Neben. To their left stood a block of stone close to cubic in proportions carved out of a single rock. It had an entrance, and Deka ran up to the doorway and walked inside.

Wave patterns covered the walls. The ceiling was twice Deka's height, and it had wave carvings on it as well, some shorter than a claw's reach, others as long as the entire wall. Certain lengths repeated, which meant it had to be a language. He took a few breaths to scan each wall and the ceiling, and then he darted out the opening.

Sonjaa's tail stuck out of the structure opposite this one. Deka dashed across the bedrock and stood beside her. The wavelike text covered these walls as well. Deka memorized it, and then they ran outside.

The rumbling became stronger. The theropods sped up the avenue, poking their heads into every building. Each structure was carved from top to bottom in wavelike text. Deka memorized everything he saw and sped onward through the city. Norh and Stephen were doing the same thing on the other side.

Most of the buildings were the same size, with cubic proportions, but one structure in the middle was dome-shaped. The vibrations were twice as strong now. Deka calculated they had just enough time for one look inside, and then they would have to run for the portal. Norh and Stephen had calculated the same thing, as they were running toward the dome as well. The three of them reached the dome at the same time, and they peered into opposite entrances.

The dome was thirteen times higher than the theropods, and the interior had been covered in the same wave carvings. Under the dome's apex, a stone pedestal protruded from the floor. A portal hovered on top of it, swirling lines of purple and white projected onto its surface. Sonjaa stepped inside the dome and gazed at the sphere with her mouth open. It was certainly a spacetime sphere, and it made the entire room glow.

Deka walked inside, stood next to his mate. Norh's body was too large to fit through the entrance, so he memorized the text Deka couldn't see.

"Whose portal is that?" Stephen said.

"And where the fuck does it go?" Sonjaa said, the English curse word blending into the Relian words seamlessly.

The dome started to shake. Deka and Sonjaa turned and bolted out the entrance. Norh withdrew their neck and took flight. Deka and Sonjaa dashed down the avenue. The buildings began shaking. Deka calculated that even those solid pieces of stone would not survive the crushing wave about to hit, but the dome would, so all would not be lost.

The silt sloped upwards. Deka and Sonjaa ran up the ramp to the level platform, and they lost speed to the shifty surface. The wall of water had just reached the dome, and Deka heard the rocks shattering under the weight. The portal was in sight. Norh landed in front of it and ran through. Sonjaa and Deka ran straight through as well, and then the portal closed just a few breaths before the water crashed through the spot where it had stood.

4

Kylac clutched his skull and screamed. Friend's advice had worked. The tower of formulas he had walled off over a year ago had cranked to life as if it had never stopped. All the equations were moving, processing numbers, reminding him of everything that happened during his time with Friend. Now he remembered exactly how he did it and why. He remembered the Lake as more than just a concept. He remembered it as reality.

Kylac had been worried that remembering any one part of what he did back then would open an antisphere and destroy whatever planet he was on. The last time he had worked through these equations, that was exactly what had happened. He had opened antisphere after antisphere and destroyed multiple planets before he had a complete understanding.

Friend had given him the right prompts that triggered the equations again. Activating the equations all at once was supposed to prevent the pain and eliminate the risk.

Instead, the shock overwhelmed him. The equations cranked away—they had a life of their own. Kylac forgot how to speak. His muscles would not respond. The revelation that this universe was not real, and the real universe existed somewhere else, giving form to the familiar reality, made him remember that everything was completely pointless. Reality consisted of fake particles bouncing around, creating fake molecules, and giving rise to fake consciousness of a false universe. The real universe was not even made of atoms or matter, and his brain calculated all of that right now. It had to understand, and it would not let Kylac do anything else until it did.

The scream stuck in Kylac's throat. He lay on the sand, overlooking the spot where the ocean should have been. The wind still blew from the land and fell into the chasm. It was a warm breeze, which made Kylac all the more uncomfortable. Friend knelt in front of him. He now lacked a scent altogether, so Kylac could not tell what he was really thinking.

"Kylac, I know what you're going through. Facing reality is painful, but it will set you free."

The scream finally escaped. Kylac curled into himself as his mind processed the nature of the reality beyond reality. He shivered as the numbers began to tell him what it meant—what it had to mean, and how much of a coward he had been to hide from it.

Friend bent low, placed his muzzle next to Kylac's ear. "It's time you knew how to separate your animal instincts from your higher mind. It will be a new equation to push into that tower of yours. Once I give it to you, it will start working on its own. When you enter the Lake, it will happen automatically so you don't destroy any of the precious, pointless life that calls this place home."

He began whispering. Kylac had no choice but to take his words in. They went straight into the tower. The equation built upon what Kylac knew of the Lake now, and his mind assigned it a place.

Kylac's eyes widened. It was possible. Norh would be stunned to learn that it was possible. Sonjaa was right in that nothing in the Lake had a container; it was up to the conscious mind itself to stay together, and it would be a constant struggle to avoid being spread out so thin one could never come back coherently. Anyone could sever pieces of their own psyche and move on without them.

Friend was right. His old ways should not have done this. They were a collection of primitive impulses that should never have been able to understand where they were, let alone how to return to this universe. By the numbers, it was the perfect way to get rid of it.

Now Kylac understood how to destroy those old ways. They could never be destroyed out in the Lake, but they could be spread out far enough so they would never be able to come back. But how to interact with them without merging with them—that was one thing the equation had yet to touch on. The numbers told him how to interact with this universe, but they were still incomplete regarding objects within the Lake.

His mind built another tower with a copy of this equation as a foundation. It was happening too fast. The numbers hit him too quickly. He cried out.

Friend looked down on Kylac, tail waving.

5

The ocean floor debris had been cleared from this area as well. It had once buried the city in thirty paces of dirt. Deka wondered how they discovered them. Both cities they had visited were arranged like cross sections of a compressional wave: buildings on either side of a central street, and a dome resting in the center of that street.

They had been at the second location for just a couple minutes and already they felt the water approaching. As with the previous city, Stephen and Norh worked on the other side, memorizing all the carvings and buildings. Deka and Sonjaa were on this side, peeking in building after building, all had similar text up and down the interior.

"I haven't seen any place that looks like living areas," Sonjaa said, "or a market, or restrooms, or anything else a lone species would make."

"This can't be a lone species," said Deka, backing out of the stone cube and trotting up the avenue. "It uses portals."

"But only lone species would make something like this." She caught up to Deka and trotted by his side.

"That part doesn't make sense. How are you doing with their language?"

"No patterns yet. You?"

"Nothing. It's all these people built. Structures to house wave etchings."

"But they aren't etched," she said. "I don't see any evidence of claws or tools. It's smooth and even in every building."

"I don't understand it either, but a pattern will emerge eventually."

Sonjaa turned and ran into the next cube, which housed more carvings of different lengths, resembling a thousand variations of the English language parentheses, or braces. Deka needed six breaths to memorize the whole room, and then he backed out. Sonjaa followed him toward the dome in the center of the city.

Norh popped his head into cube after cube. Sometimes he flapped his wings. Deka hoped that meant they had realized something, as he had nothing so far, which was unusual for him. As an Archeon, he could find patterns in everything. He could decipher any written language after seeing only a few samples. He wouldn't know how to pronounce anything until he heard it spoken, but he would still know it. Sonjaa had the same talent, and yet this language eluded both of them.

The text in every building was different. The patterns repeated in small ways common to all languages, but never in a way to indicate the same information was being conveyed twice.

The rumbling of water became stronger. Deka had already moved the portal closer to them so they wouldn't have to run far this time. Norh and Stephen had reached the dome. Deka and Sonjaa had just now caught up. They dashed into the dome and halted just inside the entrance.

It was as large as the previous one, but three portals hovered in the center of this building, all equal sizes arranged in a triangle, all depicting the same purple and white colors on the other side. They swirled, casting light on the wave-writing that covered the walls and ceiling. Some of the parentheses were so large they stretched from the base of one side of the dome, across the ceiling, to the base on the other side.

"Um... guys..." Stephen mumbled.

The raptors looked at him. He was staring at the ceiling. They followed his gaze and craned their necks upward. Right above the portals was a large section of ceiling covered in smaller wave-carvings. Some sort of transparent fluid clung to it. It undulated, only the slight refractions of the light coming from the portals making it visible. In the section of ceiling the liquid clung to, the carvings were wearing out. It undulated faster. The carvings erased faster.

New wave symbols emerged from the stone where the old ones had been. As the old ones faded, the new ones took shape. Deka memorized what had been there and what replaced them.

The rumbling felt much too close now. Sonjaa tore herself away from the site and ran out the door. Deka followed. Norh pulled his neck out, folded his wings, and ran on all four legs to the portal, near the dome on this side. They were through the portal many breaths before the ocean arrived.

6

An antisphere opened over the ocean chasm. Kylac lay in the sand, trying to stop it. The Lake made perfect sense when he had trapped Friend on Reyno, but now this new equation Friend gave him threw everything off. He had to justify it. He had to incorporate it into what he already knew. It fit. It had to fit. He just had to find the right position for it. His understanding of the Lake had become unstable, and he would cause more disasters if he didn't figure it out in a hurry.

Friend held him around the shoulder. "It makes more sense if you're in the Lake."

Kylac screamed as the antisphere grew from the size of his skull to the size of his body. It was easy to imagine the antifox there, expanding itself to ridiculous proportions to satisfy its urges.

The sphere inflated at a constant rate. Kylac became aware of why it expanded: the equations showed him that it would become easier to understand the larger the space in which he worked. He projected that to its logical conclusion and yes, everything would make sense from the Lake.

The ground began to shake. Kylac closed his eyes. He couldn't believe it was happening again—he thought he was beyond this. He felt as if he had learned nothing from all those months with Friend, talking about the Lake, discussing the equations churning away in their minds. Millions of lives lost to a physics problem, and it was all they could think about. It was happening again.

Kylac opened his eyes. The growing antisphere loomed like a dark star over the chasm. The ground underneath shook and threatened to fly apart and spiral into the void.

But it wasn't really a void. It teemed with activity, form, function, maybe even life. It took a lot of effort to remember that, as right now the equations seemed to indicate the Lake was unknowable.

Friend's muzzle lowered beside Kylac's ear again.

"You know how to use the equation to move your mind to the Lake. Once you're there, all of this will make sense, and you can separate from your instincts."

Kylac panted, mesmerized by the approaching disaster. Friend was right. He knew how to do it. Releasing his conscious mind from the confines of his body would be easy now. Everything would make sense once he did.

For a moment, Kylac was going to do it just to spare these people a disaster worse than the loss of a fifth of their ocean.

Then he realized something: Friend had entered the Lake with this same information, and now his instincts were roaming free. If Kylac entered the Lake now and cut his old ways off, there may very well be two antifoxes tearing apart the universe.

"Do you need some more time to decide?" Friend said.

A sphere opened in front of Kylac. It led to Proxima, his and Deka's private world where they went to be alone with the universe. It had since been polluted by Krone semen, the scent of which Kylac used to find exotic and invigorating, but now only served as a reminder of the person he could never be again. Going there would stop the equations on this world and begin them again on Proxima.

The antisphere was close to the surface now. Pieces of the ground ripped up and flew into the dark interior.

7

There were no survivors at the bottom of the ocean. No reason to go to the third location, so Deka made a way to the fourth. This would give them more time. The rumble of the approaching water was distant and quiet for now, but it never let them forget they did not have time to explore deeply.

The raptors immediately ran for the dome. The Krone flew over their heads and landed in front of an entrance, and they stuck their neck inside. Sonjaa and Deka were only halfway there.

The cubes sped by. Deka regretted not having enough time to look inside all of them, but the wall of water was too close and they could not salvage everything. He hoped some of the structures would still be intact when the ocean settled. He thought of what was about to happen to this planet without an Archeon. They had no time to help them find and train a new one. They would have to let the contacted universe know what happened here so the Archeons could find someone. That would be difficult to do among the Yjerm.

Sonjaa was first inside the dome, Deka at her tail. Several pieces of fluid clung to the walls, erasing old markings and carving new ones. One of them was at their eye level. Sonjaa walked up to it, scented it. It smelled like water, complete with all sorts of minerals mixed in.

Deka joined her and also scented it.

Sonjaa reached out and slipped her claws into the fluid. It did not seem to react but kept pulsing and creating new symbols on the wall. She pushed her whole hand into it. Again, it did not react. She moved her hand from side to side within it, then withdrew. Her hand was not wet. Deka scented her hand. No residue.

New symbols had been carved in place of the old ones. The fluid dropped from the wall and crawled across the floor. It vanished into the lower right portal.

Stephen broke the silence. "Damn it, I wish I could fit in here!"

Deka approached the portals in the center of the dome. The white and purple light ebbed and flowed like ionized atmosphere.

"Deka," Norh said. "I will make another way just outside the entrance you came from. You have exactly eight minutes and nine seconds."

"Deka!" Sonjaa shouted.

He turned to her. She was looking into the farthest portal. A Dasi was visible in it, suspended inside the purple and white swirls.

"I'm ending the way," Deka said, crouching. "We'll be back in seven minutes."

He ran through the portal. Sonjaa followed.

As soon as he touched the portal, something slowed his momentum and then held him in place. Transparent liquid surrounded him. It was fluid, but it behaved like a gel. Deka was afraid to open his mouth, but just a few breaths after he arrived, the fluid undulated between his jaws and pushed them open. Fluid flowed into his lungs. He gagged, choked, flipped around in the substance that suspended him, and then his whole body relaxed. Sonjaa twirled beside him, just stopping her own fit of gagging. Now they both floated in an environment between liquid and solid. It vibrated against them but it did not make them wet.

"Deka..." she said. Her voice sounded different traveling through this medium instead of air.

"Yes?"

"There's Cilitrus."

He faced where she looked. Fusina's Archeon hovered in the distance, seemingly wrapped in the white and purple. Deka now realized the fluid was comprised of those two colors, but it was so sparse they were only visible at a distance.

"Cilitrus!" Deka called. His voice made visible waves in the fluid.

The Dasi paddled, turned around, then wiggled her way through the fluid to meet them. Deka and Sonjaa both wanted to meet her halfway, but their bodies did not move elegantly through whatever this was.

"Sonjaa! Deka! What happened to the ocean?!"

"Friend's old ways took a fifth of it!" Sonjaa answered.

"A wave of water is coming! Where are we? What's going on down here?"

Cilitrus swam up to them and now hung suspended in the clear liquid. "The Yjerm discovered one of these places earlier this year. We've been digging them out of the silt. It's not easy, as it's too deep even for the Yjerm to survive long. I've been studying the carvings and the portals. We've been coming here for some time."

"Where is here?" Sonjaa said.

"I don't know, but it's been so exciting! We haven't told anyone about it because we wanted to know what it was."

"Can you understand the carvings?" Deka said.

"No, and that's what was so exciting! Whoever made those ways and those carvings cannot be a lone species, but they must be radically different from us! This place is not the usual habitat for them."

"What?" Sonjaa said.

"It only extends about fifty paces in all directions, and then I can't swim any farther. This fluid is packed with oxygen, nitrogen, nutrients. You're breathing and eating it. Someone is accommodating us! This is first contact with a noncompatible species!"

She looked at each of them in turn.

"What happened up there? And where's your fox?"

Deka: "Friend's old ways took part of the ocean and every living thing in it."

"There were over three hundred people there... I closed the portals hoping to prevent any deaths."

"I don't know where Kylac is. I hope he moves away from the shore. That wave is going to slam against it soon after it reaches this city."

"It's not a city," Cilitrus said. "It's an announcement. They probably left places like this on other planets, in other oceans, waiting for someone to find them, trying to communicate."

"We have two minutes," Deka said. "We have to go."

Cilitrus turned around and faced the colors in the distance. She wiggled through the water a few strokes and stopped.

"There they are."

Deka and Sonjaa looked into the distance. They noticed wavy variations in the consistency of the liquid, which slightly distorted the colors behind it, but that was all he could see.

8

The way to safety was in his reach, but Kylac remained on the sand. The answer loomed right in front of him. The new tower would not destroy another planet. He would not enter the Lake as Friend did, with incomplete knowledge. He would not rely on Friend to help him again.

Kylac opened his mind, enduring the excruciating strain. The antisphere pulled up sections of rock and soil. If the ocean were still there, it would have begun swallowing that, too. Kylac forced himself to remember the Lake as a real place he could go, not a place he thought he knew existed. He allowed the new knowledge of the Lake to enhance his perspective on it.

As it became more real, this universe seemed less so.

Life seemed to mean less and less.

Kylac cried. He curled into himself as the ground shook. The antisphere collided with the soil and began grinding it up. Kylac allowed the Lake to become his universe.

Everything made sense. The new equations added to his knowledge of how the Lake worked. They made it more logical. The antisphere dissipated. The ground stopped shaking. Kylac stopped shivering.

He sat up. Friend stood next to the portal that led to Proxima. Kylac snarled at him as he rolled to his feet and leaped at Friend. He landed on empty beach. Friend was behind him, and the portal to Proxima was gone.

Kylac finally remembered his words. "Leave! Never talk to me again!"

"I just gave you the knowledge you need to join me."

"You knew it would do that to me! You tried to rush me! Why? Why are you here?! What do you want?!"

"I want you in the Lake. It's all that matters. I told you that."

"You almost made me destroy this planet!"

"Add one more world and a few hundred more lives to the blood on your teeth. Do you want to keep wasting time with them, or do you want to help me prevent the extinction of the universe?"

Kylac wanted to tear him apart, but he breathed slowly and calmed down. "I'll get to the Lake on my terms. Not yours."

Friend wagged his tail as he ceased to be visible.

Kylac stood on the beach and panted. The barrier had come partway down. He had closed an antisphere before it destroyed anything, but he still could not make a way. The next part of the wall covered up the equations that calculated exactly how the universe worked. When he tore that down, he would expose himself to the formulas that comprised every life form in the entire universe. He would be aware of everyone and everything that filled the universe, able to calculate their thoughts and their actions.

That's when he would be aware of their scents. His old ways would react to it, and the only thing keeping him from reverting was comparing himself to Friend. Kylac wanted to curl up and cry, but he had a wall of water to outrun. He couldn't make a way yet, so he turned around walked inland. He hoped Deka would figure out where to find him.

9

"Who do you see?" Sonjaa shouted.

Cilitrus swam farther away. She reacted as if something had just touched her.

"It's them," she said. "The people trying to make contact. I've been here a lot longer. I've seen more patterns. Maybe I've finally seen enough to recognize them. I might be ready to learn their language!"

"What are they?" Deka said.

"Fluidic life," answered the Dasi. "This fluid we're swimming in. It's not their natural environment. They made it for us. Theirs is out there. Some other liquid."

Sonjaa: "Cilitrus, make sense and make it quick! We have to go!"

"Imagine a compressional wave as a life form," the otter-like Archeon answered. "You are aware of other people in the water on other worlds, but you can't reach them. They can't see you. You're just a distortion to them. That's what they're trying to do. That's what the writing is! They've been trying to announce that they exist for centuries, at least, and I think they can only exist where the water is dense! That's why they're down here and not closer to the surface! They gave up on this world until someone uncovered the domes!"

"Fusina needs you!" Sonjaa shouted. "Come with us!"

Waves of distorted gel began enveloping Cilitrus. There were so many waves bending the liquid it was like looking at her through a rotating crystal. Deka tried to spin around, but he could not move in the gel.

"I can't tell them that!" Cilitrus shouted back. "I'll be back soon! Take care of Fusina until I—!"

Suddenly a wave gripped Deka, turned him around, and propelled him to the portal. Sonjaa also became swept up in a wave in the fluid. The shade of the dome came closer and closer, and then the wave flung Deka into the portal.

He wobbled to stay on his feet. Sonjaa splashed through a breath later. They gagged and choked, expelling gel from their lungs, making thick piles on the stone. The ground was vibrating so hard they could barely stand.

Sonjaa led the way out the entrance they had come from. The portal was on the other side of the door. As they reached it, the sound of several million tons of water hitting the roof filled the dome. Water rushed in through the far entrances. A curtain of water fell over the entrance. Sonjaa ran through it. Deka ran through as well, hit the portal, and tumbled out the other side on the beach at the hub. Norh lay a few paces from the portal. Water was gushing out of the sphere so fast it pushed Deka and Sonjaa across the beach.

The sphere closed. The water stopped. The Krone stood and walked over to them. He nudged first Sonjaa and then Deka.

"That was awesome! What did you find?"

10

Deka and Norh had calculated how large the wave would be, and how far above sea level and inland they needed to be. Everyone stood there now, on a mountaintop well away from the ocean, high enough to see the wave as it approached.

The temporary hub only had five spheres, three of Deka's, two were Norh's. They had made ways to some of the other locations around the planet. A hundred Dasi had gathered here, and several hundred more Yjerm watched through the portal. Kylac was also here. They had found him exactly where they expected him to be, and now he wanted to watch this rare event from a safe distance.

The water filled the basin, crashed against the continental shelf, rose and spilled over the shoreline. The wave uprooted trees and vegetation and filled the entire valley. The water reached the hill and climbed halfway up. The coastline became part of the ocean, and it would be until nightfall.

Fusina had lost a fifth of its water, which meant sea levels would drop by that much. The continental shelf at the hub would become the new shoreline. The water pressure would lessen, and the Archeons figured the bottom of the deepest part of the ocean would now become the preferred spot where the Yjerm would live. Anything higher would not have enough pressure for them to survive.

If Cilitrus was right, the people on that strange planet required even more pressure to survive and would not be able to come here anymore. They hoped Cilitrus would return soon, but in the meantime, Norh promised to make new spheres for them. There wouldn't be as many as before, and most would probably have to endure the long distance travel to find food, but it would make some things a little easier.

Deka lowered himself to his stomach. Kylac lay next to him, enveloping himself in Deka's scent. He had already told him how far along he was, and what Friend tried to do. Kylac never wanted to be alone again. Next time it would not be so easy to keep a clear mind.

The Dasi stood in awe at what they were seeing. Norh turned to them and explained that the ocean was still settling, and it would take an entire season for the water to find equilibrium again. In the meantime, ocean currents would be upset, weather patterns would change, millions of fish and other ocean creatures would die off. It might take a lifetime for the entire planet to find a balance again, and life on this planet would never be the same. Everyone already knew this to some degree, but facing it made them weak in the knees. Many lay down as they watched the land become ocean.

Sonjaa lay on Deka's other side, looking out over the water. "Deka, did any of their language make sense to you? I couldn't make out the text... But... I usually need to hear a language first before I figure it out, then I can attach the sounds to the..."

She began to shiver.

"...text. It's difficult to imagine. Are they physical creatures, or is Cilitrus right and waves themselves became sentient? That s... ounds..."

Deka nudged her snout as she convulsed. She hid her muzzle. Deka nudged her again.

"Sonjaa, I already know what's happening to you. You have to learn to control it."

She turned to him, still convulsing. "What's..."

Deka nuzzled her. "You don't need to think about the Lake for it to happen anymore. It happens whenever it wants. The feeling that you're falling back into it."

He turned his head to the ocean and spoke to both of them. "How did it go, Kylac?"

The fox was also shivering. "I want to sleep so badly, but I worry it would be like last time, and I won't sleep until all the equations are in place."

"So is Sonjaa. She believes if she thinks about it too hard, she will cause it to happen."

"Cause what?" Kylac asked.

"Her mind to fall into the Lake."

"Thought equals action out there. That's what the equations tell me. The most difficult part is adjusting to the idea that conscious thought is the only thing that can exist in the Lake, so how can thought exist without action if both are equal? Not understanding it meant the ways I made into the Lake were unstable. Thinking about it in part might destroy a planet."

Deka turned to the other theropod. "Sonjaa?"

She looked at him, shivering and panting.

"Can you answer that? You've been there."

She turned away. "Don't make me think about it. Please."

"It's happening on its own. If you don't make the first move, the Lake will swallow you."

She shrank into the ground. Deka nuzzled her.

"Kylac needs help, too. If you go too far, I will pull you back."

She took a few deep breaths and raised her head. She looked out over the water.

"When I was... Out there... I found you, Deka. I felt like I was caught in a dream and couldn't wake up. Images hit me, and it... it affected me less and less. Every time I saw you, I reached out to you..." She dry-heaved a few times.

Kylac looked at her from under Deka's muzzle. "You came back as different person. You changed reality to make room for yourself. Do you remember how?"

Her body forgot how to breathe. Deka leaned against her, held her hand, rubbed her claws. She clenched her hand around Deka's and faced Kylac.

"I don't know how I did that. I think... It was... I didn't have an identity anymore. I didn't know who I was. I was spread out so far. I became whatever was around me because that's all I knew. It was all I could remember."

"But the creation process," Kylac continued. "Giving yourself a place in the universe. How did it happen? There was no math for that—even when I was with Friend I hadn't worked that part out—it was one of the variables that didn't make sense. The Lake, consciousness, should not be able to interact with reality directly because particles in the Lake bounce off reality and cause subatomic particles to exist, so how were you able to interact with it at all?"

Sonjaa shivered, looking down at the thin grass. "I don't know how it works, Kylac. I never had the mind for physics and particles. I like language. It makes sense. It's a wonderful way to get to know people."

"You figured it out. You found a way to understand it."

"I did... I remembered sounds. Around Deka, the universe had a kind of harmony. A tone. I focused on that, and then... I just appeared."

"Yes!" Kylac scented in her direction. "That's how you came back. Thought became reality. You used it to hold yourself together and enter this universe. My calculations state it should be impossible, but you made it work."

"The language of the universe." She paused for several breaths. "I saw dream images of everything happening in the universe. Sometimes I focused on where Deka was, and I tried to... All of those images and sounds. They did add up to something."

"How?"

Sonjaa shivered again. "All the voices and images that hit me... They did start to make sense. It—"

She convulsed. She stopped breathing. She rolled over, choking. Her choking turned into a shriek. The shriek stretched into a howl. Deka rose to his feet and crouched over Sonjaa. He held her face still, forcing her to look at him.

"Use my voice to pull yourself back."

She stared at him, eyes emptying. She resembled one of the Nebens, mind draining out of her skull and falling into the abyss.

"Deka! I made it happen again!"

"You know how to hold yourself together. My voice is a river. Follow it."

She convulsed. Deka held her harder.

"It's going to happen whether you're ready or not. You can control it."

She held eye contact, not breathing, still draining.

"It's in your subconscious. Think about how you came back the first time. You don't have to be afraid of it because you already conquered it."

She lay still for over a minute. She began breathing again. Life flowed back into her eyes. She reached up and rested a hand on the back of Deka's neck.

"Deka, I thought about it, and it happened. I wa—"

He pressed a finger to her lips, the Earth gesture to stop talking. She fell silent. Deka let go of her muzzle and tapped her claws against his. He lay next to her and looked out over the ocean.

"Both of you did very well. We'll do this again tomorrow. You two have a lot to discuss. Sonjaa, you have much to learn in a very short time."

He turned to Kylac. The fox was glaring at Sonjaa, dry-heaving in empathy. Deka nuzzled him with his snout. He rested his head and neck on the ground. Sonjaa stretched her neck and closed her eyes, breath catching every once in a while. Kylac lay beside Deka and shivered.

Norh turned away from the Relians to the ocean and lay his neck down. The otters of Fusina dropped to sleep one by one as the ocean slowly receded. The fish watching through the portals dimmed, fading into darkness.

Columbus

I

The portal opened on green grass in the middle of a collection of apartment buildings. Secretary Rhine adjusted her coat and relaxed her grip on the briefcase. It was chilly here, so that meant they were somewhere up north. The tall buildings in the distance told her this was a major city, but she didn't recognize the skyline. Rive jumped from the portal a moment later. It closed behind him. Rive was carrying the camera equipment.

A few people were outside, but nobody had seen them arrive. CJ noticed the cars parked in the lot all had Ohio plates, but she couldn't remember who lived there.

Rive began walking to a townhouse. CJ followed him.

"What city is this? Who are we interviewing?"

Rive was clicking his claws. He hadn't stopped laughing since he told her they were leaving.

"I know we're in Ohio, but where? Cincinnati? Cleveland? Toledo?"

Rive looked back at her, still laughing. "Sometimes your lack of memory is an asset." He turned back and walked straight for the door.

"Okay, either this is really good or really bad. We are doing an interview, aren't we?"

"Yes."

"You pulled me away from a meeting to do this, so it must be a good interview."

"It will be." He clicked even louder.

Rive stopped at a door, waiting for her. CJ stepped up to the landing and stood next to him. A cold wind blew, and she hid her face from the wind. Rive did not react to it at all.

"I was in a meeting with my legal team, and the US attorney general, and the Oregon attorney general, plus two legal counsels to the Supreme Court, so I trust it will be worth it. Mildred is getting impatient. She thinks you're pulling me away every time we make progress on purpose, and I agree."

Rive now held his hands apart, but with great effort. The wind died down, and she rang the doorbell. CJ heard footsteps. She composed herself like a White House official. Rive was trying so hard to keep his hands apart, an alien's attempt to keep a straight face.

The knob turned, the door swung inward, and an orange snout met CJ's nose. Her eyes widened, and a single bead of sweat formed on her forehead. Another cold gust of wind made it fall down her face.

She would never forget those orange scales and that green, water wave pattern on top of them, and memories of all those conventions came rushing back to her. Keeping him hidden, covering for him, making sure the public did not catch wind of him. Other Relians had often told her to stop stressing about him, but she knew if anyone found out about Ratash, the press would not be able to restrain themselves and would probably frame him as a sexual predator coming to steal your daughter. Or son.

Ratash inhaled. "Nice to smell you again, Ms. Rhine. You, too, Rive."

He opened the door the rest of the way, turning around. CJ closed her eyes so she wouldn't accidentally catch a glimpse under his tail. Unlike most raptors, he often walked with his tail straight up in order to show off his slit. He was proud of how much he dripped, and he wanted everyone to see.

"Rive..." she whispered.

The metal raptor took her hand and rubbed her fingers with his claws. "No matter what they say, capture every word on tape."

"You pulled me away from the most important legal battle in my career to interview a sex-crazed raptor with a testicle fetish." She whispered through her clenched teeth. "I only just now got over the headache these two gave me!"

Rive played her fingers like wind chimes. "Hearing their happily-ever-after will keep you from getting one ever again."

He nudged her inside with his snout to her back. CJ walked in. Rive followed and shut the door. She removed her coat and hung it on the rack by the door.

"Secretary Rhine!" said a familiar voice. Malcolm Patton stood in the hallway, dressed in a yellow shirt and jeans. "Didn't think I'd ever see you again."

CJ smiled. "Nice to see you, too. It wasn't my idea to come here, but Rive has been arranging these interviews. He didn't tell me where we were going."

He walked to the living room, shook her hand. "These are the best clothes I own. Are they good enough?"

"They're fine, Mr. Patton. Honestly, I was expecting..." She could not finish.

"Expecting what?"

"Never mind."

Rive spoke from the living room couch. "She was expecting you to wear a fishnet shirt and a thong."

CJ shot him a dirty look. Rive was clicking his claws. Ratash was standing next to him, and he took Rive's hand and tapped claws with him. For the first time in more than a year, CJ found the sight of two raptors sharing a laugh disturbing.

"Ratash told me I should," Malcolm answered, "but I don't even own clothes like that. These two wanted me to go out and buy some just to see if you'd do the interview, but I'm not *that* mean."

A flush came from the bathroom, and Irus, the fox, walked from behind Malcolm. He squeezed around Malcolm, smacking his rear on the way, and joined the theropods in the living room as the metal raptor set up the equipment.

CJ covered her eyes and sighed.

2

"November seventh, nineteen ninety-seven," CJ said from off camera. "Secretary of Relian Relations CJ Rhine with Malcolm Patton. Columbus, Ohio."

She swallowed. She had opened every interview with the same question. It would look suspicious to future generations if she broke from that now.

"Please tell us why you went to the convention in Pittsburgh."

The man sitting on the couch sat in an open position, leaning back into the cushions. "I never watched the news before last year, when the aliens arrived. I listened to it on the radio, watched it at home, bought newspapers for the first time in my life. I followed everything about them for months. Then I heard they would be in Pittsburgh. That's only three hours away from me, so I took time off. I tried to get a bunch of people together and we'd all carpool there, but nobody else at work wanted to go. I thought, what the fuck?"

CJ winced, shot Malcolm a look, but he continued.

"Aliens are here! Why is nobody going to meet them? Everyone else had birthday parties or something. Fine, I went by myself, and I was the only black guy in line as far as I could see. That was kinda scary, especially in Pittsburgh, but half the time I'm the only one in clubs, too, so I'm used to it."

"And..." Again, CJ had asked everyone this question, so it would pose some pressing questions for future generations if she did not ask it now. "Tell us about the convention. And remember that people a hundred years from now will be hearing this."

Malcolm smiled. "I was in the meeting hall, and they sniffed me out. Turns out they were looking for a gay guy with a libido as big as theirs. Seems I was the biggest fag out of every con-goer in the country."

CJ heard loud clicking from the kitchen as Rive and Ratash shared riotous laughter. She kept her best disapproving-teacher look on her face as she glared at Malcolm.

"Oh, man. Those two... Yeah, I'm gay. So is Ratash. Irus is bi. Ratash stands out not just because he has orange scales, but he has a thing for mammals. Isn't attracted to his own species. Isn't even attracted to women of any species. Their scent does nothing for him. He likes mammals. Specifically, he likes balls." He laughed. "Yeah, external junk. Nothing turns him on faster, nothing gets him off like it. That's what the con was like for me. Didn't plan on getting any, but he showed me how everything works and what he can do and damn he's fucking good."

CJ opened her mouth to interject, but Malcolm kept talking.

"I learned a lot about Relians that day. The press talked about how the foxes will fuck anything and anyone they can get their hands on, but they never said a raptor would, too. Most don't, but I was lucky to meet someone who was just as horny as me. You know I whack off like ten times a day and it still wants more. Been that way since middle school. Wore out so many people, and then they show up. The things the press left out...”

He was slouching, so he sat up straight. CJ was grateful his lap was out of view of the camera.

“I found out that slit raptors have produces lube. Ratash makes enough lube for three people. So much he drips. Sometimes all day. That’s how to tell when a male raptor is horny, if you don’t have a good enough nose. See if he’s dripping. Haven’t had to buy lube all year—just stick it in his slit and you’re ready to go, and holy shit!”

He held his arm up vertically, fingers straight.

“That’s his dick. Elbow to fingertip, and about as thick, but it’s tapered and only gets that thick at the base, so you barely feel it until it’s all the way in. They call it the middle claw, and it’s a good name for it. It looks like a claw, and it gets hard but not rigid so it can bend however it needs to fit all the way in you. First time I saw it, I just stared. It was gorgeous. He knew I was the kind of person who could handle it. I smell like it. Not just gay, but someone they could get along with. A person he could build a relationship with, not a one night stand. I was all of those things. He told me the people running the conventions never thought he’d find someone like me, even the Archeons. All the marines escorting them from convention to convention said that.”

He giggled again.

“He also told me they picked those marines for the mission based on their feelings toward gays. They screened for people in the military who wouldn’t mind getting involved with the foxes, or seeing some dirty stuff happening in public places. Relians don’t think sex should only happen behind closed doors, but they respected our way of doing things. So all of those marines were either gay or bi, and Ratash had worn out a couple of them. I actually got in touch with them a few months ago, and they were so happy to hear he hadn't broken me. I outdid marines! I still laugh at that, and—"

CJ checked the tape. It had only been ten minutes. She covered her face and looked at her lap.

"His jizz is thick!" he continued. "Like toothpaste, and he produces a lot of it. It doesn't run. It sticks, and it stays there! If you were hungry before, you won't be after giving him head. It's also not sour and salty... it's kinda sweet. I don't know what's in it, but I like giving him head more than letting him fuck me. He likes to go deep but slow. Never a hard fuck with him. Irus, his fox, is the one who likes to go deep and hard, and damn, his dick is weird, too. It starts off like this." He curled his fingers to about the size of a quarter and then widened them to the width of a silver dollar. "And then swells up to this! He's huge! Not as big as Ratash, but wow. His whole dick swells up like that, and it makes me jealous every time I see it. I've taken them around town, and they've fucked with everyone I know. Most can't handle Ratash. They say he's too scary, but then I show them what that tongue can do, and they either run away or they whip it out and say me next.

"You wanna talk about trust? Try letting a guy with a hundred flesh-tearing teeth suck your dick. And then he opens wider and takes your balls in his mouth, too! Then let him caress your balls with his claws while you're trying to sleep, and he's growling at you. That's how you build trust. He said he does it to all the prey species—helps them feel more comfortable with a predator. It works. Oh, God, it works. I'm to the point where he growls at me one way and I get hard. He growls at me another way and I know he's being serious. He walks in the room, I smell him, and I get hard. I have never felt this comfortable around anyone. He has this way of making everyone feel at ease around him. And if they're not interested in him, he knows, and he doesn't push himself on them. Irus is the one who's constantly trying to get people to fuck with him. He's very good at that—I know some real church-type women who got in bed with him after just ten minutes talking to him. They both walk around with their dicks out at the clubs, and everyone is okay with it. Ratash is just standing at the bar and five people have their hands on his dick, or feeling his thighs, and he's talking to the bartender like nothing is weird. He likes it when people touch him, especially prey species. Irus pretty much has a permanent hard-on. Everyone he smells makes him hard. I've seen it. He sniffs someone and his dick peeks from his sheath. He tells me he wasn't always like that. Ratash taught him to have that reaction. He remembers when he got anxious being around other people's scents, so this is better."

He paused. CJ looked up from her hand and met his eyes. Malcolm was smiling, but perfectly serious. "And... In nonsexual terms... How would you describe your relationship with Ratash and Irus?"

Malcolm took a breath, looked down at his lap, then back up at the camera. "Ratash is like... He's like my father and my husband at the same time, but none of the creepy incest parts. Just separate the bad stuff from that and keep the good. Irus is like my brother and my husband. They're... They're easy to get along with, even when we're not fucking around. Yeah, yeah, it's not all sex. I've taken them to museums, the library—Ratash loves to read. He got me into reading. Never read a book after high school until Ratash started handing me books and telling me I needed to read this and that. So I did. And he was right. I needed to read that history on tobacco, or that political book about railroads. It was terrible, but it explained a lot."

He smiled warmly. It was a very different smile than the one he made before.

"Ratash got me off cigarettes. He read about what they were, and he pushed me to quit. I was scared. I didn't want to quit. I tried in the past and almost lost my job I was so miserable to be around. Tried all the stop-smoking aids. Nothing worked. Turns out what I needed was someone who would let me turn into the monster while I was in withdrawal. Ratash didn't want me to hide it. He wanted to know exactly what I was, and he did not think less of me. Everyone else ran away from me while I was like that, but not these two. Ratash tackled me in public when I went into a fit of rage. I screamed at him. I punched him in the face. He took it all. He wanted me to be that monster, and not having to hide it was so liberating. And I am proud to say I haven't had a cigarette since February, and I didn't gain an ounce. All because of them. They didn't just toler-ate me. They wanted me to stop killing myself. I couldn't do it on my own, but Ratash got me through it. Now... They've seen me at my worst. They didn't hate me. They weren't afraid of me. Why would they be? They have claws and teeth."

CJ hadn't felt the need to hide her eyes in several min-utes.

"Elaborate more on the tobacco. How exactly did Ratash and Irus help you quit?"

Malcolm smiled. "I warned him I turn into a dragon. He told me he gave blowjobs to two different dragons. I asked him about that. 'Since when were you interested in reptiles?' He said when a Krone is in heat, forget your pref-erence and do what they say, 'cause you'll never get the chance again! He said they make cute noises when they cum, so my dragon didn't scare him. They stayed with me. My boss allowed them to stay with me all fucking day. They never left me alone, and he told me not to hold back. So I didn't. I gave him hell. Irus, too, but mostly Ratash. He wanted to see the dragon. He wanted me to be the monster.

And I never get tired of having them around. I don't feel like I need to take time out for myself or anything. I do everything with them, and I'm not tired of having them around. I dunno. Is this love?"

CJ breathed easier for the rest of the interview.

3

Rive huddled in the kitchen with Ratash and Irus. The raptors shared a smile listening to Malcolm's interview. He was going on about their sex life, as if relieved to tell someone all about it at last. The Relians spoke in their native language, very quietly so the camera and tape recorder wouldn't pick them up.

"Happy to see you didn't break him," Rive said.

Ratash clicked claws with him. "He's unbreakable, unlike their military men."

"What have you learned?"

"It happened," Ratash said. "The emotions are the same, just as we thought. Everything I feel for Irus, I feel for Malcolm. He's become my fox, too. There's so much more I can do for him. When can we leave?"

"I've been going over the maps of all the addresses where the Relians live around the world. I'm ready to start making offworld portals. Where's the best place to make one?"

Ratash let go of Rive's fingers and led him to the back of the apartment. Irus pranced ahead of them. He threw open a door in Malcolm's bedroom. It had a large, walk-in closet, nearly empty.

"He almost never goes in here," said the fox.

"Perfect," said Rive, neck bobbing up and down in approval. "If I'm right, you'll have a way, soon." He turned to the orange and green raptor. "How have you been coping without the hunt?"

Ratash grumbled. "I thought Gaow was bad! This place wreaked my metabolism. And humans are fine with predators until we do something predatory, then they get squeamish. Definitely an uncontacted prey species. Worse. They think they're predators."

"Relief is coming."

Ratash took Rive's hand again and rubbed claws with him. "Finally, no more pads."

Rive clicked the other raptor's claws. "You still have to wear those?"

"Sometimes even at home! It's annoying. Malcolm bought me tampons once just to try them. Saturated one in forty-five minutes. Then Irus asked how many would fit in my slit, and these two started shoving them in me!"

Their claws clicked together louder.

"Eleven," said the fox, tail waving. "We stopped at eleven."

"At home I just keep a towel between my legs. In public, it's duct tape and a maxi pad. Nobody seems to notice."

Irus wrapped his arm around Ratash's neck. "That's what you think. Everyone at the clubs notices. They think it's funny, especially when they find out what his lube can do."

"Make sure you tell Secretary Rhine all about it," Rive said.

"I'm surprised she's here," said the fox. "She was so stressed trying to keep his needs hidden."

"She relaxed after you two found Malcolm," Rive said. "I hope you have at least one clean and wholesome story to tell."

"What about when I shed my fur in the spring? That was fun. Malcolm took me to the dog groomer just to see if they'd do it. He borrowed a camera and recorded it. Ratash showed her how raptors groom their foxes, and it looks so adorable on camera, thick claws being so gentle through fur.”

“Save it for last,” Rive said. “Do you have the tape?”

“Yeah, and we made sex tapes, too,” Ratash said. “Three of them.”

They clicked claws loudly. Less than half the tape was used up, so Rive figured he had plenty of time to tell them about Relian Relations.

4

The portal into the office closed. CJ walked around her desk and collapsed in the chair. She laughed as she caught her breath. Rive stood in front of the desk, regarding her, hands together in a smile. She looked at the briefcase on the desk.

As usual after an interview, Rive had opened a small way for her to leave the case with the tapes here, and they had taken a tour of the cultural district. For a major city, downtown Columbus was spacious. They had passed a lot of people who wanted to meet Rive, and the metal raptor had drawn a small a crowd.

Finally, it was late in the evening and they were home, CJ still laughing as she stared at the case.

“We can’t put this in the record.”

Rive clicked his claws. “Every word they said needs to be preserved for future generations to hear.”

She held her face. “Rive, that was the dirtiest conversation I’ve ever had in my life, and it’s on tape! It’s all people are going to listen to when these are public!”

“Real life is not G-rated, even offworld. What better way to show people the Relians are not dangerous killers? It will be an excellent counterbalance to the fear.”

CJ swiveled back and forth in her chair. "I wish I could see the jury's faces when they're deciding the Portland case and they hear character testimony like that."

"I am thinking even longer term. Future generations will remember us not as dangerous killers, but lovers. Even the reptiles."

She sat up straight and then leaned on the desk, exhausted physically and mentally.

"With a little luck, the sex will be downplayed, and the tobacco part will be enshrined in the Smithsonian."

Rive reached over, picked up a pen and a sticky note from her desk. CJ followed his hands with her eyes. Rive turned and walked to the other side of the room. He used the wall as a flat surface to write on.

"What are you doing?"

"Writing something."

"Since when do you need to write anything down?"

Rive did not answer. He wrote very slowly. Moments later, Rive heard her unlock the case and pull the tapes out.

"Rive... Something I've been meaning to ask you. Something I noticed. We've done, what, ten interviews? The humans have basically the same story. Why they went to the convention, how they met the Relians, what happened after they came home. Every time, the raptor has done something for them. Getting them off tobacco, preventing a breakup, encouraging them to quit their job and find something else. And every time, the person listens to them. It reminds me of something."

Rive had finished writing, but he remained against the wall with pen to paper. "What does it remind you of?"

"The people act very much like a fox does around their raptor. The raptor talks about the human using the same terms. My human, my fox. I was wondering if you noticed it, too."

Rive turned from the wall and returned to the desk, holding the sticky note pad up to her. CJ read it. His penmanship would rival a calligraphy teacher's. She looked at him. She read it again.

I know what's happening now, and I am ready to tell you everything. Remove your clothes and come with me. This cannot be on tape.

Rive set the pen and paper down on the desk. He had been working on this way since before they left for Ohio, and now it was ready.

A sphere opened behind Rive, occupying most of the office. CJ stood up. The raptor could tell she recognized it did not lead to anywhere on Earth. She began removing her blouse.

Rive turned around and walked through. He looked down his flank at her, waiting. CJ was practically tearing her clothes off. When she was unclothed, she spoke into the office. Rive read her lips.

"Secret Service, if you're listening, Rive is taking me someplace. I may be out of touch for a while. Please refer matters of Relian Relations to the president. Don't worry about me. I trust Rive with my life."

She walked through the portal. Rive closed it as soon as she was though.

5

Rive had told her what planet this was, but he was sure she had forgotten. She was staring in awe at everyone at the hub. There were fewer portals here than there should have been, but Rive had heard Friend's old ways had been causing enough trouble for the Archeons to isolate their worlds again.

So many people walked up to them. Reptiles, avians, creatures who did not have a parallel on Earth. Rive had translated for her, but she was overwhelmed with new sights and sensations, the knowledge she was witnessing alien civilization occupying every neuron.

Now they sat in sight of the hub but out of the way so nobody would notice them. CJ watched the people moving about. She had lost her sense of self-consciousness about her body after seeing the reproductive parts of nearly every person on the hub. After an hour of awed silence, she finally looked at Rive and spoke.

"Your fox destroyed your planet?"

"That's right."

"I don't understand how."

"We're still trying to figure that out. Imagine the universe as you know it is not real. Reality is somewhere else, causing this universe to exist. We don't have a name for this place, so Friend called it the Lake. Think of the real universe as a bubble floating on top of a body of water. Portal physics only takes us inside the bubble. The conscious mind is capable of perceiving the laws of the universe, and being aware of reality allows people like me to create connections between different points around the universe. We navigate inside the bubble by thought alone. My fox stumbled on a way to make spheres into the medium the bubble floats on, but he did not understand where he was going, so his antispheres were unstable. They destroyed everything that came near them. Toward the end, he figured out how to control them. That's when he took Kylac hostage and forced him to learn. They understood the universe so well they became able to calculate spheres instantly, and being so aware of the universe meant they also became aware of everyone inside it. This stimulated their animal instincts, and Friend would have killed every living creature in it if Sonjaa, Deka, Kylac, and I hadn't killed him."

"But you said he's not dead."

"Correct. Just before he died, he moved his conscious mind into the Lake, somehow separated his old ways from his higher mind, and now his instincts have returned, causing more destruction. Sonjaa, Kylac, and Deka left Earth to stop them."

CJ took a deep breath. "Mother of God."

"You once teased me about being so good at everything. I am an Archeon, but that does not make me perfect. I was not a very good raptor for my fox. He was stable, never reverted in his life, so I let him hunt, and I rarely said no when he wanted to mate. I wanted him to have lots of children so he could pass on his good genes. He didn't want a child. I actually had to push him to do that. Then he destroyed fifty-six planets. When he appeared to us again, on Earth, he had nothing to say to me. He wasn't interested in me. That felt like a claw to the eye. All those years together, and he says nothing."

He paused, looked out over the hub at the people vanishing through spheres. He sighed.

"Since the disaster, I have been agonizing over the questions. Were there warning signs? Did I simply miss them? Did Friend need help and I failed to recognize it? He was my fox. There must have been something I could have done. I can't think of anything. I am a Relian reptile. We're supposed to be able to help our foxes as a matter of instinct. I never had that reaction to a reverted fox, and for much of my life I felt like the biggest waste of skin among Relians. When I became an Archeon, that put my mind at ease about a lot of things. It seemed to explain why I was the way I was. Thinking back on it, it merely gave me an excuse to ignore my fox and ponder the nature of reality—the big questions concerning quantum mechanics and such. And then... I couldn't help him. I was scared again, even with my metal. I didn't have the courage to face my fox when he reverted. At the end, on the planet Reyno, I needed help to confront him, and I still feel horrible for that. I have failed as a raptor my whole life, and I have to live with it, knowing I could have prevented millions of deaths had I simply killed my fox. My ancestors did it if they had one who couldn't be tamed. I should have recognized the signs, but I was too scared, and now my fox is still out there, still killing people—other Archeons have to kill him for me. When I rejoin the contacted universe, I don't think I'll be able to face anyone. I am ashamed of what I've done. Of who I am. The one thing a Relian is supposed to do, and I needed help to do it.

"When he came back and revealed himself, I didn't want to talk to him. I had accepted he was gone, and instead of grief, I felt free. Watching how Sonjaa handled losing her fox made me question my entire life with him. He didn't want to come back to me. I didn't want him to come back. But... I did try to talk to him. While I was listening to Jeff Morton on the phone, I worked up the courage. I apologized. I asked him what went wrong. I tried to get Friend to answer me, but he wouldn't even look at me. All the evidence points to something I have not wanted to face since the first disaster. The possibility that everything he did was to get away from me. That our happy life together was a lie. An act. Was Friend faking being happy? I wasn't. I liked being with him. I never found anybody better at discussing the big ideas.

"I know now he was visiting other planets without me while I was asleep. He might have been doing it long enough to have a second life on uncontacted worlds. I think he was contemplating leaving entirely. Disappearing without a trace, going somewhere I couldn't find him, but he couldn't bring himself to do it. That's how I ended up with living metal replacing half my body. The first antisphere he opened not only tore our planet apart, it tore *me* apart.

Friend made a portal to one of those planets he had been visiting. He must have spent a lot of time there, as he knew how to tell this species of living metal to rebuild my broken body.

"After the metal brought me back to life, I had to take Friend from planet to planet while he figured out how to control the antispheres. At some point, he must have realized this knowledge of a physical existence outside the universe was the perfect excuse to leave me. He couldn't figure it out alone, so he forced Kylac to help him. He was so desperate to break out of a Relian pairing he destroyed Kylac.

"I like to think we could have worked it out, but perhaps we were both afraid of facing reality. The Relian language has no word for a raptor and a fox who don't want to be together. I think we both wanted to get away from one another, but we had no words to say it. Even in other languages, we never found those words. In Relian culture, there's just no other way for a raptor and a fox to live, but we could've tried if only he had told me he wanted something different. Maybe that's why he didn't simply close a sphere and abandon me while I was asleep. He could have, but it wasn't enough. He wanted to go somewhere I could never follow. Somewhere no one could follow. I'm tempted to think it was his canine instincts expressing themselves in a new way, but I can't ignore the possibility that this is simply who my fox is. That it's what he always wanted to do. He lashed out against a Relian life I forced him to live, and millions of people suffered and died because of it."

CJ was silent for almost a minute. Then she took Rive's hand in hers, felt his claws. "I'm so sorry. I can't think anything to say. I lost my husband to pneumonia, but that's... This is unbelievable."

Rive felt her fingers. "Working with you has been a tremendous relief. It's so wonderful to feel useful again. To connect with someone. I've been telling you the Portland case is not important. It's because we will be gone long before that case goes to trial."

"What do you mean gone? What's going on?"

"Your people want to assimilate us into your culture, but we were here to find people who can be assimilated into ours. It is far too late for us to change your society. Too many powerful people are preventing that. They have molded civilization into the shape that benefits themselves, and they will not allow us to exist unless they can make us part of that. When we first arrived, we suspected humans might trigger the same instincts a raptor has for a fox, so we tested it. We sent Relians with people to find out if it happened, and it has."

"Every time..."

"It surprised us as well, so we had to find people who were capable of living offworld in a society very different from yours. The Relians have found them. In theory, I believe the majority of the world's population is capable of adapting to life in the contacted universe. Without human authority telling them what to think and what to be afraid of, and with their basic needs met, they will be free to think for themselves, and the instinct to nurture will balance the drive to dominate. But we cannot save everybody. Now we begin the process of acclimating these people to life in the contacted universe."

"How?"

"I am working on portals that will bring them here. Their raptors will teach them how to live, and these people will be open to the change. Their first instinct is not to change others to suit their own needs. They are the people we can save."

"Save? From what?"

"From their old ways, so to speak. Normal species know they are not alone in the universe because at least two intelligent species coexist on the same world. Meeting intelligence creates a desire for understanding. They learn to overcome their primitive nature, and to transcend reality itself. Machines cannot do this. Only a conscious mind which has learned how to comprehend itself from an alien perspective can learn how to understand the universe as it is, rather than how the senses filter it to the mind. Lone species never learn how to do this because they have never been exposed to an outside perspective of themselves.

"Humanity is a lone species, and it has untamed animal instincts. Not as strong as a Relian canine's, but I notice them everywhere I go on this planet, and in everything you do. An instinct to dominate. An instinct to nurture. An instinct to compete for mates. An instinct to divide into groups and gain standing within those groups. Many others. One of the more amusing is the concept of cuteness, which is a primitive reaction to something being smaller than expected, or something nonhuman demonstrating human-like behavior. Before the conscious mind evolved, humans needed an inborn response to their own offspring so they would want to care for them. It expresses itself in numerous ways that are obvious to anyone outside your society. Without a companion species, impulses such as these have been growing out of control for generations, and they affect your society in larger and larger ways. Some cultures emphasize your impulses to nurture and cooperate, forming communal societies. Some don't seem exaggerate at all from your point of view, but the dominance instinct is beginning to take over. It is swallowing up other cultures and forcing them to become subservient to its needs. Your entire culture is built to serve it. Without a companion race to show you other perspectives on reality, this impulse will destroy your civilization. There are people we can spare from that. People who are capable of living a different way. Soon we will take those people off the planet, and humans will become part of the Relian pairing."

"It's starting now?"

"Yes, now. The people who are molding your society are already scared of us. The dominant males. Some women in there, but mostly men. They pay for politicians to be elected, people who agree with their views and do as they say, so they shape the world to their advantage. They know we cannot be persuaded to adapt to their needs, so they are about to force us. Friend showed me Deka, Kylac, and Sonjaa just before they left the planet. I overheard their host, Jeff Morton, talking on the phone to someone about contributing money to some people to create the leverage they needed to force the Relians to fall in line. The incident in Portland was their first strike against us. The press will eventually show that tape, and the media will start telling people that public opinion is turning against the Relians. They will claim that people are afraid and calling out for protection, and the people will begin to say just that. That's where you come in."

She looked at him, eyes wide and overwhelmed. She had an arm around her neck, covering her breasts. "Me?"

"Soon the news of what we are doing will get out, and a few powerful people are about to make everyone else afraid of it. They will accuse us of taking away people's freedom, and they will convince the population that we are going to abduct their children next. The people will believe it. The Relians decided you were the person who should see what's happening firsthand. Stephen once told us the individual is smart, but intelligence drops as more people gather in one place. We will never be able to convince the entire planet of our intentions, but you will be the voice of reason. The right people will listen to you, and the truth will survive."

CJ looked out at the hub again. Rive leaned on her, his flesh side. She leaned on him, wrapping an arm around

Rive's neck. He had forgotten what it was like to be close to anyone.

"I can't believe I'm hearing this."

"You've seen for yourself how the people have reacted to the Relians living with them. The raptors helped everyone become better people in some way. They will continue to do so offworld. We do it for our foxes, and we will do it for our humans, too. It's our nature."

"So you never intended to stay?"

"No. It would have been impossible for us to live in the confines of any human society."

"Everything we've done for the last year. Was it all a waste of time?"

"Definitely not. You have been an enormous help to us. And... to me."

CJ watched the people on the hub. A Host from Uiv, a quadruped resembling a furless lion, passed in front of her. She sat up and took notice of the insect with its legs buried in his skull. Her mouth dropped.

"Would you like to meet him?" Rive said.

She turned to him, her scent full of wonder and fear. Instinct and conscious thought battling it out. Rive already knew what she would say.

"May I?"

He stood, drawing her up gently with his hand. She rose with him, letting her other arm fall from her neck. Rive led her away from their hiding place and into the group of people.

"I am working on a way back to the office," he said as they approached the feline. "You will go home in a day. I will remain here, making ways for the others. In the event there is a problem and I can't make a way for everyone, we arranged a rendezvous point. They will migrate to a particular place in the country. If you need me, just slip me a note."

CJ was only half-listening. She was stricken by the feline. Rive called to him in English.

"Greetings."

The feline turned to him and answered in English, the feline and the insect alternating syllables. "Gree-tings-Rive. Who-is-this?"

CJ gasped. "You speak English?"

"Ste-phen-vis-it-ed-our-plan-et.   New-lan-gua-ges-spread-fast."

"Oh my!"

Rive rubbed his claws against her fingers.

Mero

I

The sphere opened at the first layer's hub in the valley. Norh walked through, followed by the Relians. Friend leaned against a tree as it absorbed stray electrons from the air. Norh left the way open behind them.

Deka scented the air. So did Kylac. Sonjaa looked up through the layers of atmosphere. Even from this perspective, she saw through all three. Oxygen and nitrogen at the bottom, concentrated nitrogen a few hundred paces up, and methane capping off the top layer.

Down here in the bottom layer, blue and violet curtains swirled around as the oxygen and nitrogen and all the other trace elements traded electrons. Just four hundred paces above them, the layer of nitrogen glowed purple. About eleven hundred paces above that, methane covered the planet in a thick fog of yellow. Each layer was clearly visible due to the high energy in the atmosphere, which reached all the way down to the surface of this planet.

Sonjaa turned her muzzle from the sky and scented around. The hub was empty, no people, no portals, no signs of life whatsoever.

"Where is everyone?"

"Would you like me to tell you what's going on," Friend said, "or do you still insist on doing this alone?"

"We don't need your help," Deka said, rising to full height and observing the valley.

The land between the two mountain ranges sloped upwards to the base of a mountain which rose from the second atmosphere layer and reached high into the methane. Deka expected to see people flying and walking about up there, but he saw no movement.

"This time I didn't cause what happened here," Friend continued. "My old ways came to Mero on their own."

Deka growled as he turned to the projected fox. "You know it's strange how your old ways attack everyone else, but they leave us alone. We've been in striking distance seventeen times and they have never come near us."

"You are holes in the Lake," Friend replied. "Perhaps they don't sense you."

"That must be it. We're in plain sight, it senses everyone else, our scents have been following it for nine planets, and it just happens to avoid touching us. Stop trying to help. When we need you, we'll let you know."

"Try not to die here."

Friend disappeared.

Kylac walked up next to Deka, looking at the space where Friend had been. "We really could use his help."

Deka turned to his fox. So much he wanted to say. He nuzzled Kylac on the snout instead.

Mero became still. The air shimmered silently around and above them. Norh stared at the mountain. He had already shared his memories of this planet with Stephen, and now the human felt the same way as the Krone: nervous at being grounded.

He pondered Mero's multiple atmosphere layers in which different forms of life had evolved, still thinking in terms of the measurements used on his home planet, in his native culture. The bottom-most layer only extended about eight hundred feet up, and then the oxygen dissipated into a nitrogen atmosphere. Two thousand feet above that, the nitrogen gave way to methane. Each atmosphere had its own cloud layer, all moving in different directions. The sky was made of three concentric shells rotating at forty-five degrees to one another, all of it aglow in stray electrons.

The people chose this valley as the hub because the three sentient species had first learned to interact in this very place. The valley sloped upwards gradually and crossed into the second layer. From there, the land rose into the mountain peak and entered the third layer, the only one for thousands of miles that did.

Normally portals leading to all three layers lined the hub, and each layer had its own hub, making Mero one of the only worlds in the contacted universe where species who breathed different atmospheres could meet and interact. There should have been people doing just that, but nobody was here. All Friend had told them was that his old ways had done something new and they should see it. So far, nobody could see anything.

"Did it kill everyone?" Sonjaa said.

"That's doesn't fit its pattern," said her mate.

"No scents," Kylac said. "Well, it didn't vacuum up the atmosphere or switch the layers, so it can't be too bad."

"Never say that!" Stephen yelled. "And I don't want to hear anybody say it's too quiet either! We are not redshirts!"

Norh took over control of their mouth. "That's right. We are senior staff. Nothing's allowed to happen to us because senior staff is all that matters."

Sonjaa reached over and rubbed claws with Deka. Norh had been doing this more and more, making wisecracks based on human frames of reference.

Deka began walking up the valley, ascending the gradual slope. Dozens of burrows dotted the ground, all of them unused for more than three days on this world. The Krone jumped around and dodged the curtains of blue and purple, wings flapping erratically.

"Careful, Stephen," Sonjaa said, looking down her flank at him. "The happiest character always gets killed first."

"I can't help it! This is so cool! The Northern Lights was on my list of things to see before I died, and it's so rare for it to be low enough to touch like this!"

Deka and Sonjaa shared a smile. Kylac stayed close to Deka as they passed rock outcroppings carved with glacial scars, along with plants that absorbed the stray electrons from the atmosphere and exhaled methane as a byproduct.

Most of the plants here glowed with absorbed electrons. Curtains of light often funneled into the bulbs of these plants, which grew up to ten paces tall with stems twice as thick as a sunflower's. The gigantic bulb at the top reminded Stephen of a tulip. He paused and looked into one of the bulbs as a stream of blue light fell into it.

Stephen sniffed the flower. It gave off flammable and poisonous vapors, but it looked so beautiful. His wings unfolded and stayed spread as he trotted onward, looking from left to right as more curtains fell into the flowers.

"This is just like *Star Trek*! It's the kind of colorful alien plant that only exists in clichéd sci-fi worlds! This planet should be full of humanoid aliens we can seduce! We'll be trapped here, the people will welcome us at first, and then we'll break a law, and then the people will hold us accountable, and of course punishment is death, and then we'll have to overturn their way of life and show them a better way to live! Humanity's way, of course, because humanity knows how aliens ought to live, even though we've never been to another planet!"

Norh took over their mouth. "You understand how a television series works better than reality." He called to the others. "He can recall episodes almost verbatim. He knows the characters' histories better than he knew his wife's."

Stephen took over. "It's true! I really did! She thought it was funny!"

Kylac's tail waved. Deka clicked Sonjaa's claws louder both at the sight of seeing Kylac laugh again and hearing those two go back and forth.

"Imagine if you could apply this same mental process to something of value," Norh continued. "You have the capability. You only lack the right nurturing."

"But reality is so boring! Well, it was until Kylac and Deka made a portal into my living room."

Norh shouted to the others again. "I shared my memories of this planet with him, and he still reacts like this."

The slope leveled off on a hilltop. Deka calculated they were only forty paces above sea level, and the land was still hundreds of paces away from touching the second layer of atmosphere.

"Understanding why it looks like something out of a sixties TV show makes it even better!" Stephen continued. "It means the stupidest ideas we ever had are not actually stupid! We did get some things right! Now show me the planet of sentient vegetables and living mattresses!"

"Except for the very nature of civilization, yes, you got some things right."

"Well, it was also Americans stroking their own egos during the cold war. Aliens always represented the communists, and the Federation represented the United States. We were doing everything right, and the universe would be at peace if everyone did things our way—the way of peace and cooperation and negotiation and freedom."

"By bombing Vietnam?" Norh said.

"Yes, those were bombs of peace and unity!"

Deka, Kylac, and Sonjaa stopped and turned around. Stephen and Norh were walking with fully outstretched wings, which looked undignified enough to be adorable. None of them could tell which person was in control of what part of their body.

"And don't forget the Agent Orange," continued Norh. "It's liquid freedom."

"America ejaculating orange freedom onto all of you!"

Curtains of varying tints of blue danced around Norh as he stumbled around, one wing flapping, the other rigid and straight out, bumping a large cluster of flowers, releasing clouds of methane which distorted the air around them.

"Don't make me release my nuclear freedom on all of you!"

"Bathe in it to restore a healthy glow to your skin!"

"Healthy orange glow! Available now on the Home Shopping Network—American Freedom Beauty Cream straight from the tap—call now and we'll double your order, CODs accepted—not available in stores—interplanetary shipping provided by Krone airlines. We love to fly! Flying is freedom! Do things America's way or we will make you fly!"

His wings flapped so hard he fell on his side, landing on a large patch of flowers. They released a collective puff of methane, and Norh rolled in them, wings flapping so hard they sent surrounding flowers sideways and even disturbed the aurora wafting into them.

"We will pick you up and give you freedom! We will drop you from the air as many times as it takes for you to learn to fly! Be free, little birdies! Be free to fly for us so we can take your nest! Be free as we drop you to your death! Everyone should be free! If they're not free, they will die! We're only ejaculating our beauty cream onto you to help you! You don't understand that! None of you do! Do not reject our orange freedom because we want to save you from your lack of freedom!"

Stephen or Norh started singing a medley of *America the Beautiful*, *Pop Goes the Weasel*, and the Tesra mating Call. Finally, their body ran out of breath, and they realized where they were.

Sonjaa, Deka, and Kylac stood in a semicircle around Norh's head. The Krone noticed them, apparently for the first time in quite a while. He breathed, the air slightly tainted with methane, and unfolded his wings in a smile.

"Sorry. Carried away by stream of consciousness."

The Relians could not tell if Stephen had said that or Norh.

"Keep it together," said the fox, tail waving. "And don't die before the first commercial."

The Krone rolled over and walked out of the flowers, catching his breath. "I don't know what happened."

Deka knew. Sonjaa knew. Kylac knew. They walked on ahead of the Krone.

The lack of scents in the area disturbed them. Only the electric flowers grew here. Further up ahead, electric shrubs and electric moss and electric trees that came close to crossing atmosphere layers sprouted. Most everything that grew here absorbed energy from the atmosphere and did not need to convert nutrients to sugar, or absorb light.

The electric flowers yielded to a forest of low shrubbery. Blue and purple light fell into the bushes and did not come out. The Relians fanned out between the short plants. Behind them, Norh and Stephen carefully stepped over them. They heard them apologizing whenever they bumped one.

They saw something in the distance. Deka scented it, a lone Togi male. Stephen and Norh caught the scent, too. It smelled like a Togi, but something about his scent seemed wrong.

The Togi were about half the size of a raptor, quadrupeds resembling echidnas, but with shorter spines and fur patterns that resembled the color waves flowing through the lower atmosphere as camouflage.

"Hello!" Sonjaa called in their language of grunts and low-pitched mumbles. "Where is everyone?"

The Togi were burrowers who lived in communities of up to fifty. Those communities often stayed together above ground as well, exchanging members with other burrows throughout the day as they hunted for insects and small reptiles. Foraging was rarely necessary these days, as the portals normally opened onto beaches and forests reserved for the prey they loved to eat.

This one sat alone in a clearing without bushes or trees. Blue and purple curtains drifted silently around him. The Relians approached, the Krone being careful not to step on any of the bushes.

The Togi rose to all four feet, turning around. He bared his teeth and snarled at them. It was a gesture they did not make, as they never used their teeth in self-defense. He snarled and howled at them. Their vocal cords were not suited to make this sound, but he made it. He dashed toward them, hobbling haphazardly, as if trying to rise up and run on his hind legs.

The Relians backed away. Kylac backed away so far he bumped into Norh's leg. The Togi continued running at them and snarling. It sounded comical, but nobody laughed.

Deka wanted to ask what was wrong, but he figured that would be pointless. He felt an instinctual urge to fight this creature—to fight it until that scent became calm and rational.

Sonjaa leaped in front of Deka and squared off with the Togi. As Deka predicted, the Togi reacted by snarling at her. Sonjaa did not give him a chance to attack. She lunged, killing claws down, and collided with the Togi. He slid across the dirt, reaching around and biting Sonjaa on the shoulder.

Screeching, she grabbed his snout with her hands and tossed him to the side. He landed on the dirt, flipped over and rolled belly-up against a glowing bush. Sonjaa leaped and landed on him, screeching in his face. He kicked his limbs, not quite able to reach her with his claws.

She raised a killing claw and poked him in the chest just enough for him to feel. He grumbled, snarling and flailing. He opened his mouth and bit her ankle, drawing blood.

Sonjaa clamped her mouth around the Togi's neck. She stood still for several breaths. He raked her neck again and again with all four of his feet. His claws were not sharp enough to break through Relian flesh.

She screamed with a full muzzle. She clamped down and threw him back on the ground. Still the Togi snarled at her and tried to tear her neck open. Sonjaa tensed up, about to do it again when Deka bumped her.

Her mouth popped open. Deka pulled her away from the Togi, who righted himself and charged them, bleeding and limping and obviously in a great deal of pain. Sonjaa wanted to charge him again, but as Deka pulled her away, she walked on her own, backing away from the Togi through the glowing bushes.

The Togi were not very fast runners, so the Relians had plenty of time to move away casually.

"Where is everyone else?" Kylac asked.

"Probably hiding from him!" Sonjaa answered.

"How do we make it go away?" Stephen was back far enough he didn't have to retreat.

"We find him an opponent." Deka raised his muzzle, scented the area. No other Togi scents around—exactly what he expected. "Stephen, Norh, can you see anyone else?"

Stephen raised his head and looked around. The trees obscured the view in all directions but one, and there was nothing behind them.

"None."

"Then we'll run until we find someone!"

Deka took off as the Togi reached him. Kylac and Sonjaa followed, with Stephen and Norh politely planting their feet in the dirt between the bushes. When those ended, the glowing trees began. The forest was too dense for Norh and Stephen to follow, so they spread their wings and took to the sky, flying just over the treetops as the Relians entered.

They glided over the trees, scanning the gaps for any signs of life. They banked left. Then right. Then circled once. Twice. Finally they saw another Togi wandering inside the underbrush. They circled again and landed, pushing a few trees over to make room for their body. They flapped their wings, blowing this Togi's scent in the Relians' direction.

Several hundred paces through the forest, the smell of a different Togi filled the forest, and the Relians veered into it, weaving through the trees and hopping over small plants and lizards, all glowing with electricity.

Norh felt the vibrations coming closer. He flapped his wings and raised himself out of the forest. The Relians dashed past the second Togi.

Sonjaa stopped, scented her. She snarled at her, stalked her, killing claws rising, hands fanning out. Deka slid to a stop, reversed direction, and dashed back for her. He grabbed her by the arm and yanked her away. The second Togi was in pursuit, but then she heard the first snarling and screaming at them, doubled back, and ran to intercept.

Norh circled around and then hovered in place, flapping his wings in the other direction, pushing the scent of the first Togi toward the second. Through the gaps in the trees, Norh saw the two Togi bounding toward one another, snarling and screaming in tones their bodies were not supposed to make.

They met, slashing each other with their claws, biting every part of the body they could reach. Norh watched as he flapped in place. The first Togi rolled the second one over and clamped down on one side of her throat while the second tried to slash the eyes.

The second Togi slowed. The first spiny mammal bit harder and ripped little pieces of her neck out. The second stopped moving. The other walked to the nearest tree, raised himself to his hind legs against the trunk, and scented the air. Now calm, he began foraging for food.

Norh adjusted his wings and flew over the forest to where he calculated the Relians would be at the speed and direction they were running. He dropped near a clearing twenty paces in front of them. The clearing wasn't large enough for a Krone body, so they landed in the trees with their head poking into the gap, wedging their body between several thick trunks. The Relians emerged into the clearing and slowed to a stop, out of breath, looking back as they scented the area.

"They've reverted," Norh said.

2

"The antifox figured out it can kill someone without harming the body by draining their conscious mind into the Lake," Deka began.

"Now it figured out how to imbue its own mindset onto others," concluded his fox.

"How many could there be?" Norh or Stephen said. "The total population of Togi is over seven thousand. It couldn't have gotten all of them, could it?"

"Enough to scare everyone else away," said Sonjaa, staring down at her own hand-claws, shivering.

The Relians huddled into the glowing forest. Very few curtains of aurora made it in here, as most of them had already been absorbed by the plants in the top layers of their foliage.

"What of the Yil and the Iashen?" said the Krone.

"I dread finding out what the antifox did to them," said Deka. "What worries me is that Sonjaa could not bring that one back. If Friend's old ways have injected its own impulses into others, then a raptor should have been able to."

"It means Friend's old ways are beyond a raptor's help," said the fox. "It's aware of its environment in a way that a raptor cannot tame it."

Kylac lowered his muzzle to the ground. He began to whimper. Deka leaned on him, rubbed his neck against the fox's.

"So how do we bring those people back?" Sonjaa asked, looking up from her hands. "Something must be able to reach them. Unless... Their conscious mind already drained into the Lake, and this is all that's left." She gasped. "What if that's what happened here? It recognized the people it touched drained away, so it replaced their minds with... itself."

"If that's what happened," Deka began, "then those Togi are dead, and there is no way to bring them back."

Norh tried to wiggle backwards between the trees. "Zombies! Another cliché of Hollywood, and here it is! Next we'll meet the alien equivalent of Frankenstein!" He could not move. He wiggled harder. "You mean his monster. Yeah, the monster. The air is full of electricity, so this would be the right place for it. I can hold my breath for twenty minutes. I'll explore the second layer as much as I can. Maybe I'll find someone who can give us answers." He stopped wiggling. "As soon as I get out of here!"

Sonjaa and Deka clicked claws. "There's one likely place the Togi would have fled. If the Archeon is still alive, he would have closed the portals to keep the reverted Togi from following them."

Deka began working on a portal. He turned to Kylac, who was still whimpering.

"Do you need some time alone?"

Kylac wrapped an arm around Deka's neck and clung to him. "No, I'm not ready! I'm sorry, but I can't do this yet. I know people are dying, but... That Togi... It could be me next."

Deka rubbed Kylac's neck with his claws. He turned to Sonjaa. She looked at him with her neck outstretched.

"Sonjaa?" he said. She seemed to become conscious of herself and turned away. Deka stood and faced her. "You don't have to stay over there. Kylac could use another raptor to help him through this."

She looked at the ground, panting through her nose. "No, no, that's all right. He's your fox. Not mine. It wouldn't be right. It's not right."

Norh was still trying to free himself. He could not move at all, and seeing a Krone stuck was even funnier than watching a raptor give him head.

"Will you be all right, Norh?" Deka said.

"I'm fine! I'm a Krone! I'm the most evolved species in the contacted universe! I am a mighty monster!" He had rolled over on his side and was trying to roll upright again, arms and legs flailing. "Worship me, thou primitive native! I demand virgin sacrifice or I will burn your village!"

Sonjaa turned to the Krone. She rubbed her claws.

A Relian-sized portal opened, which led to a part of the first layer on the other side of the mountain range. Deka turned to Norh.

"Meet back at the first layer's hub if anything goes wrong."

"I've seen *Sliders*!" Norh or Stephen said. "Bad things always happen when the group splits up!"

"But they always reunite just in time." Deka turned and walked through the portal.

Sonjaa and Kylac followed. The wide open plains hugged the coastline and stretched for hundreds of paces in all directions. Electric grasses and a few groupings of electric trees grew everywhere. They were on the other side of the mountains that enclosed the valley, the great peak visible in the distance but obscured by the peaks in front of it. The aurora flashed across all layers of the atmosphere. Clouds moved at forty-five degree angles to each other through each layer of the sky. The curtains of color swirled like ghosts across the level plain. Some moved out over the ocean, others came from the ocean onto the land.

It was deserted here, as well. Kylac gritted his teeth and led them further inland up the plains to their burrows.

"Why did you open the portal so far away?"

"More time to look for survivors."

"You already know something is wrong, Deka. This area is supposed to be safe from the reverted ones at the hub, so where is everyone?"

"There may be other reverted Togi. If so, there are plenty of other places they could hide."

"Makes me wonder if anyone else recognizes their behavior," Sonjaa said.

"Or if they fear it's contagious," Deka said.

Sonjaa stopped. She felt the tiny wound on her shoulder. "If I revert, you're the first person I'm eating."

Deka was about to speak when he heard flapping from above. Sonjaa heard it a breath later, and they turned their muzzles upwards. A winged reptile twice as tall as Kylac was falling through the sky straight at them. They dove out of the way in three directions, and the reptile landed in the middle. She rose to her wings and screeched at all of them, reeking of mindless rage.

The Iashen were flying reptiles who lived in the third layer of the atmosphere. They breathed methane and carbon dioxide, and their bones were hollow and connected to the respiratory system. They stored extra methane in the hollow spaces of their bones, which allowed them to hunt in the lower levels of the atmosphere. In more primitive times, they had hunted the Togi and the Yil, but when they realized they were not the only intelligent species on this planet, they began hunting other things. They used the portals for quick passage from mountaintop to mountaintop, eliminating the long flights to places they could land.

This Iash smelled as if she had come straight out of primitive times, but the wrong ones. Their instinct was to swoop down and snatch prey, not confront, but she wanted a fight. She stood on arms that folded into fleshy wings, turning around in place, snapping her snout-like beak at the Relians in turn. Deka had crouched in a defensive posture. Kylac stood on all fours, fur raised, teeth bared.

The Iash hobbled along the ground and gave chase. This was not usual behavior for them, as they were not agile on the ground, adapted to hunt exclusively from the air, but this one ran on all fours as though she had done it since hatching, and she was fast.

They only had enough air in their bones for gliding into the lower atmospheres, finding prey, an attack dive, and then a return trip back into the methane layer. She couldn't chase them for very long; running took up too much energy.

She screeched at them. Deka and Kylac looked at one another, agreeing to avoid a conflict and find the burrows. Deka turned to Sonjaa, but she had left his side. She was circling her, snarling and flashing her claws as the Iash screeched at her.

Sonjaa lunged. The Iash leaped back and stabbed with her beak. She rotated her tail, pivoted her body, and landed a quarter of the way around the winged reptile. She hobbled for Sonjaa, screeching and howling. The raptor charged her. They tumbled into one another, rolling in the dirt. Sonjaa came out on top, one killing claw aimed at her neck, the other poised over her belly. She crouched close to her and shrieked at her. The Iash flailed her wings and squawked.

Her screech lowered to a growl. She opened her mouth, wrapped her teeth around the Iash's neck, and picked her up. She threw her down in the dirt and stood over her again. The Iash squawked and screeched and beat Sonjaa with her wings. The theropod bent down and clamped her mouth around her neck. Still the Iash thrashed and screamed.

She wheezed. Her wings moved in slow motion, and then her limbs fell at her sides, limp. Sonjaa raised herself and hissed at the winged reptile. Deka ran up to her as she prodded her with her snout.

Deka bumped her flank with his muzzle. "She's dead."

She turned to Deka, scent in total disbelief. "She's can't be! She can't be—this always works!"

Deka bumped his body against hers and shoved her in the direction of the burrows. Her legs turned with her body, and she ran with him. Deka looked over the plains at a tiny speck poking up from the soil. A Togi. It disappeared down a burrow.

Kylac looked up. More Iashen flew overhead, most of them in the third layer, but a few circled in the second. Kylac dropped to all fours and ran with the theropods.

3

Norh and Stephen wiggled in place between the trees. For some reason, neither of them could decide who would control what body parts this time. Norh was moving into the lower limbs, then to the forelimbs, then the torso. Meanwhile Stephen was also trying to move into and out of those same places. Their wiggling had more to do with their struggle to agree on who controlled their body than actually trying to get out from between the trees. They flailed for a while, and then Stephen finally decided to yield entirely to Norh. They stopped moving.

"Norh?"

"I'm tired of this. Take over. You get us out."

"I just yielded to you. I'm not in control."

"Neither am I."

They lay on their side, wedged between the trees.

"Well, one of us has to take control!" Stephen said.

"Go ahead. Get us out."

Stephen filled their body and started moving. Suddenly they thrashed as random body parts started moving again.

"Norh! You said it was my turn!"

"It is! I'm not doing anything!"

"Then why are we still—?"

Their exposed wing flapped wildly, their forelimbs moved in all sorts of directions, their torso bent in every direction. It seemed to make them sink deeper into the trees.

"I don't know!" Norh said. "I'm not in any of the limbs!"

"Well, I am and I'm not telling our body to do this!"

"All right, I'm coming. I'm going to take over the forelimbs and the wings. Ready?"

Their neck was rising and swinging about.

"Yes!"

Their neck was still rising and swinging around.

"Well?" Stephen said.

"I... I was already here."

"I told you it wasn't me!"

"I don't understand. I withdrew from the limbs. I am sure I did."

"Well, this time do it so we can get out!"

They stopped moving. Stephen finally felt alone in the body. He rotated their body, stood on all four feet, moved one foot in front of the other, and walked out from between the trees. They stood halfway in the small clearing where Deka had made the portal.

"I knew it was that easy!" Stephen said. "What's wrong with us today?"

"I don't know. I was not aware of trying to move anything."

Stephen spread their wings and rose straight up through the gap in the trees. He adjusted himself and flew up the valley, up to the second layer. They began working on a breathing hole.

The landscape changed from trees and shrubs to grass. The aurora wavered and flickered around them and across the land. Stephen couldn't stop looking at it. He remembered when he was here last time the sight had not been all that moving. Ionizing particles filtered down through all layers of the atmosphere on this world, and all this was nothing more than stray electrons flying about as a result, but it looked gorgeous now. It was such a rare thing for it to be up close like this. Even though Stephen remembered flying through the ionosphere on other planets and being close to those lights, there was something special about them touching the ground.

The land sloped up, and the second layer came into view. Stephen landed as the ground rose to meet his feet, and he walked the rest of the way up. He had a way in mind and opened a portal five hundred paces away in plain sight, just large enough for him to stick his neck through, a walking goal, easily reachable.

Stephen took a deep breath, and then crested the hill. He now stood in the second layer. Instead of blue and purple, the atmosphere was a faint purple from all the stray electrons flying about. Curtains of darker and lighter violet shimmered and wavered in all directions. He walked across the land toward his portal in the distance.

Sounds were higher-pitched here because of the lower density of the nitrogen. The plants that grew here were completely different from the ones that grew in the lower layer. Most of them still absorbed stray electrons from the air, drawing a few nutrients from the soil, but these plants could uproot and move to new locations at will.

A whole different planet just a quarter mile above sea level. The genetic tree between plants and animals had never separated in the nitrogen layer, which meant the plants had animal-like traits, and the animals had plantlike traits. The flora here consumed the nitrogen in the atmosphere and gave off methane, which rose into the third layer.

Stephen looked to the left, where the mountain chain enclosed the valley. The atmosphere shimmered over there. His wings spread as he looked upon an oxygenfall, one of hundreds scattered around the planet. He remembered up in the third layer plants and animals consumed methane and exhaled oxygen. This gas fell into channels in the upper atmosphere, migrating to large shafts like the one in the distance, sinking through the layers of atmosphere and settling in the first layer, continually replenishing its oxygen. It looked like a slow motion waterfall from here, and Stephen smiled wider with his wings.

He turned his head forward and kept his breathing portal in sight as he walked across the land. It was deserted here as well. Nothing moved, and the electric plant life was indistinguishable from the animals in this layer. He recognized a few species absorbing the stray electrons in the air, growing vine-like across the ground. Other plants resembled trees, but whose roots were above ground and capable of using them for locomotion.

Several trees walked across the ground in the distance right now. They had no brain or central nervous system, merely reacted to stimuli, but they were still fascinating to watch. Truly an alien world.

Stephen opened his mouth, about to ask Norh what he thought of it, but that would waste oxygen. He closed their mouth and walked onward across the strange land full of moving plants.

He figured Norh would probably say something along the lines of it being far from unique. He had been to other planets with flora that moved even faster. Then Norh would go into a whole speech about how no matter which planet it is, life has the same goals: to survive long enough to reproduce. All species must work within their environment to do that, and individuals must meet this goal, factoring in population density and availability of food, and how hormones influence it. Norh had told him how these dynamics interact in various combinations to produce remarkably similar civilizations.

It was all predictable. Within a few hundred generations, the behavior a species adopted to adjust for environment would become instinctual. Given these two common goals, and a set of variables regarding environment, it was possible to predict what kind of civilization a species would develop.

As the environment changed, instincts often became so rooted in a species they persisted long after the need for them ended. New environmental changes meant new instincts would develop alongside the old ones, and eventually a species would become so mixed up—

Stephen froze in place, staring at the ground as flickers of aurora drifted underneath him. He couldn't feel Norh anywhere in their body, or in their mind. He didn't feel like he was imagining a conversation with Norh. He felt like he was having these thoughts. It wasn't that he was thinking for Norh, rather Norh was thinking these things at the same time Stephen did.

Quickly Stephen lifted his right foreleg. He set it down. He then lifted the left hind leg. He set it down. He was in control, but he did not feel like Norh had been displaced. He didn't feel Norh at all.

Stephen lifted his head. He was in absolute control of their body, and Norh was nowhere to be found. He couldn't feel Norh anywhere. Stephen stared at the ground again and marveled at the feeling of having the entire body to himself. Almost all of Norh's entire life was visible to him all at once. The hundreds of lone species he tried to help, the years of silent contemplation in his cave, the heat cycles he endured alone. Still a few gaps, but otherwise complete.

Stephen had opinions of some of those memories, and he could not remember if they were his opinions or Norh's.

...

Norh looked to the left, where the mountain chain enclosed the valley. The atmosphere shimmered over there. His wings spread as he looked upon an oxygenfall, one of hundreds scattered around the planet. He remembered up in the third layer plants and animals consumed methane and exhaled oxygen. This gas fell into channels in the upper atmosphere, migrating to large shafts like the one in the distance, sinking through the layers of atmosphere and settling in the first layer, continually replenishing its oxygen.

It looked like a slow motion waterfall from here, and Stephen smiled wider with his wings.

He turned his head forward and kept his breathing portal in sight as he walked across the land. It was deserted here as well. Nothing moved out here, and the electric plant life was indistinguishable from the animals in this layer. He recognized a few species absorbing the stray electrons in the air, growing vine-like across the ground. Other plants resembled trees, but whose roots were above ground and capable of walking on them.

Several trees walked across the ground in the distance right now. They had no brain or central nervous system, merely reacted to stimuli, but they were still fascinating to watch. Truly an alien world.

Norh opened his mouth, about to ask Stephen what he thought of it, but that would waste oxygen. He closed their mouth and walked onward across the strange land full of moving plants.

He figured Stephen would probably say something along the lines of it being the most incredible thing he had ever seen. Stephen said that about every planet they visited, and Norh hoped he would never stop reacting this way. The patterns life fell into were so obvious to him life ceased to be interesting. Norh had been to other planets with flora that moved even faster. Norh often reminded the human that no matter which planet it is, life had the same goals: to survive long enough to reproduce. All species must work within their environment to do that, and individuals must meet this goal, factoring in population density and availability of food, and how hormones influence it. Norh had told him how these dynamics interact in various combinations to produce remarkably similar civilizations.

It was all predictable. Within a few hundred generations, the behavior a species adopted to adjust for environment would become instinctual. Given these two common goals, and a set of variables regarding environment, it was possible to predict what kind of civilization a species would develop.

As the environment changed, instincts were often so rooted in a species that they persisted long after the need for them ended. New environmental changes meant new instincts would develop alongside the old ones, and eventually a species would become so mixed up—

Norh froze in place, staring at the ground as flickers of aurora drifted underneath him. He couldn't feel Stephen anywhere in their body, or in their mind. He didn't feel like he was imagining a conversation with Stephen. He felt like he was having these thoughts. It wasn't that he was thinking for Stephen, rather Stephen was thinking these things at the same time as Norh.

Quickly Norh lifted his right foreleg. He set it down. He then lifted the left hind leg. He set it down. He was in control, but he did not feel like Stephen was displaced. He didn't feel Stephen at all.

Norh lifted his head. He was in absolute control of their body, and Stephen was nowhere to be found. He couldn't feel Stephen anywhere. Norh stared at the ground again, marveling at the feeling of having the entire body to himself. Almost all of Stephen's entire life was visible to him all at once. The hundreds of people he had met, the years of monotonous labor, the never-ending grief for his wife. Still a few gaps, but otherwise complete.

Norh had opinions of some of those memories, and he could not remember if they were his opinions or Stephen's. He stared at the ground, exploring both his memories and the human's. The more he remembered, the less of a difference there seemed to be.

A curtain of purple shimmered past them. Norh followed it with his eyes, and then looked down his underbelly and watched it drift underneath him. He smiled with his wings. It was so beautiful. Being able to touch the Northern Lights had been another childhood fantasy of Stephen's. Fulfilling it made Norh happy. He was not used to this feeling, but it was so satisfying.

Norh noticed something behind him. It was flying toward him, making a noise its vocal cords were not supposed to make. He raised his neck. Suddenly his internal chronometer told him fifteen minutes had passed, and he had lost the breathing portal. He turned his head forward, and sure enough the sphere he had made in the distance was gone.

Norh turned his head back around and looked down his flank at the Yil. They lived at the foothills and the midlevel elevations. Plantlike insects with a body similar to a wasp, but their feet ended in tentacles that functioned as roots. They frequently planted themselves in one location for a few hours, then uprooted and flew somewhere else where the soil had better nutrients. They used their stingers and mandibles for defensive purposes. Their primary food source was nutrients in the ground, combining it with the electricity and nitrogen from the air to produce energy their bodies could use. There was still a great deal of confusion as to whether they were insects with plant traits, or plants with insect traits.

It screamed at him as it flew toward him, and Norh did not see any thought behind those eyes. Killing this individual would be no problem. Norh did not fear its stinger, as it could not penetrate a Krone's hide. Norh thought he would have to remind Stephen that their eyes were vulnerable, and these people had an instinct to attack the eyes.

...

Stephen knew he could not simply flap his wings and take off in this thin atmosphere. He turned to the left and galloped like a horse. The Yil veered to match his course, still screaming at him in its high-pitched clicks and whistles. It shouted gibberish, shrill and thoughtless.

Stephen unfolded their wings and rose into the air. He was moving fast enough to create lift now and finally he matched the speed of the Yil in pursuit. Stephen could hear those tentacle-roots causing drag, and he hoped his more streamlined body would give him an advantage.

Stephen flapped, tucked his legs as tight against his body as he could, aligned his neck with his torso—anything to help him pick up more speed. The nitrogen in the air was starting to affect him. His vision began to swim, and his wings started to tingle. Eight miles from the shaft of oxygen, and the Yil was still on their tail, stinger poised and ready to find his eyes.

Stephen kept flapping. He wanted to take a breath. Everything in his body begged him to inhale, and his muscles ached and cramped as they starved for oxygen. The shimmering air was just a few miles away. He flapped and glided through the thin nitrogen, his nose poking through hundreds of curtains of purple on the way. He saw curtains of blue within the oxygenfall, and Stephen remembered that Norh would not have been capable of resisting the pain for so long without him. He was proud of that in a way.

Two miles. The blue air looked beautiful, and that it was falling from the upper atmosphere and flowing like a slow river down into the first layer made it even more spectacular. If Stephen still had the proper glands in his eyes, he would have been brought to tears.

He felt tentacles wrapping around his tail. He felt a stinger poking his scales, searching for a vulnerable spot to pierce. The Yil crawled up his back, still poking, still probing him with its roots. One mile.

Stephen was losing altitude. His wings couldn't keep working like this. They hesitated and drooped, despite Stephen's repeated commands. The Yil had crawled up between his wings and was now probing the scales over his spine. He crawled up his back, wrapped his roots around Stephen's neck, as if trying to choke him. His scales were much stronger than the grip of a Yil's roots, so Stephen was not afraid of that yet.

The oxygenfall was so close Stephen could taste it. The different color aurora waves floating inside it were like fairies beckoning him to safety and refuge. Stephen lost more altitude, now flying just a few paces above the ground, about to tumble out of control.

The Yil climbed up the back of his head and over his crown, crawling onto his face. Stephen saw the abdomen and the stinger hovering over his right eye. Stephen stopped himself from rolling out of the sky, squeezed a few more flaps out of his wings and glided across the land. The stinger poised to sink into him as the roots wrapped tighter around his jaws. Stephen's nose broke the blue curtain, and he slipped into the shaft of descending oxygen.

He released his wings from service. It felt like they detached from his body, and he dropped like a brick and ate the dirt. He turned his neck to the side. His body followed and rolled, the Yil still clinging to Stephen's face with his roots, still screaming at him.

...

Norh rolled fifteen times before settling on his stomach. He breathed. The oxygen here was so concentrated it was almost too much, but his lungs soaked it up. He coughed. He gagged. Feeling returned to his muscles again.

The Yil clinging to his face also gagged, but for a different reason. Norh raised his forepaw and smacked it off his face. The Yil's grip had already been weakened, and it flew off his face and bounced on the ground a few times before it lay on its stomach and choked.

Norh lay still and breathed. He thought of Stephen, how he would react to this. He remembered swimming classes as a kid, how grateful he had been to take a breath. He thought of the other children in the class, how supportive they were, even the ones who bullied him outside of class. He then thought of the Army, and the training they had made him do and how unsupportive they were.

Something unclicked. He realized he did not remember that part of the Army. Stephen had told him about it, but had yet to share the memory. Norh felt Stephen occupying the left side of their body. He felt himself in the right. He raised their neck and looked to their left, as if trying to see the human.

"Stephen... Are you there?"

Control of their mouth left him. "I'm here. Was that...? Did we...?"

"We merged."

Stephen took a few deep breaths. "Oh shit. It's happening! That was... That was... It was like I was still here, and so were you, but—"

"We happened to think the same thoughts at the same time."

"Wow!" Stephen rolled them over to their back, staring up the shaft of oxygen falling from over two thousand feet up. Pure purple curtains changed to blue as they entered the shaft, and then back to violet upon exiting the other side.

"This is dangerous," Norh said. "The shock was big enough to lose the portal. We almost died out there."

"But we didn't have to waste time agreeing on what to do! We both reached the same conclusion at the same time.

Only a few memories to go. Was it scary for you? It wasn't for me. I still felt like myself."

"No. I was still myself as well."

"Well then... Norh... Will you marry me?"

Norh took a few deep breaths. He was about to answer, but he smelled something. He rolled them to their side, facing the direction of the scent. Forty-six Togi huddled close under the oxygenfall. They were walking up to Norh, chittering to them in their native language.

"Are you here to help?" most of them were saying.

Stephen took control of their mouth. "Yes, I am! Can anyone tell me what's happening?"

All forty-six individuals told him at once. Norh and Stephen counted thirty-four Yil hiding on the far side of the oxygen column. The Togi were telling him where the others had hidden, but it was too dangerous to cross the land right now.

While they were talking, Norh whispered to his left side. "I do, but not now."

Stephen raised their left hand and stroked the right side of their muzzle as the people told the story of how Togi and Yil and Iashen just started attacking them the other day.

4

Three reptiles dove at them one after the other, beaks just barely missing their heads. The first rose into the air and dove straight into Kylac's stomach, knocking him to the ground.

Deka rotated his tail, spinning around without losing any momentum, and charged the Iash that had landed on Kylac's back. Kylac wiggled and avoided the beak as it jabbed the ground left and right, and the Iash clung to him even as he rolled. Deka jumped into the reptile's side and knocked it off. He flapped his wings, righted himself, and screeched at him, hobbling up to Deka in a return charge. Deka leaped onto his chest and bowled him over, slashing him with his killing claw once. The Iash writhed and flapped on the ground, screeching. Deka jumped off and snatched Kylac up as he ran.

Sonjaa circled a grounded Iash. She flapped in front of Sonjaa, screeching at her. The raptor leaped and snapped her jaw closed over her bill. The Iash yanked backwards, flapping one wing and pushing against the ground with the other. She braced herself against Sonjaa, trying to push her away. The raptor stood her ground, then spun around twice and opened her mouth, throwing the winged reptile. The Iash tumbled over the dirt, and Sonjaa ran to catch up. She did not wait for the reptile to stop rolling; she leaped onto her back, pinning her. She crouched and clamped her jaws over her neck. The Iash flailed and beat the ground with her wings, unable to reach the theropod perched on her spine.

After a moment, the Iash sank and fell limp. Sonjaa opened her mouth and screeched at her.

Kylac had just kicked an Iash off Deka's tail. The winged reptile dropped to the ground and gasped for methane. He reached out to Kylac, still trying to fight in slow motion. The other Iashen that had attacked them also lay on the ground, suffocated and bleeding. The land fell silent except for Sonjaa yelling. Deka and Kylac turned to her as she picked up the Iash by the neck and slammed her against the ground again and again.

"This isn't you! Remember! Remember!"

Deka looked up. More Iashen circled overhead, and a few of them appeared to be diving straight for them. He dashed over to Sonjaa and collided with her flank, bumping her off the Iash. She crouched, flashing her claws and teeth at Deka.

Deka ran over to her and nudged her in the direction of the borrows.

Sonjaa screeched as she turned her head to the fallen Iashen.

Kylac ran up to her, grabbed her by the arm, and yanked her upright. Deka took her other hand and also pulled her. Two Iashen swooped at them and landed a few paces away, flashing their wings and beaks as if they had claws and teeth.

They had rolled Sonjaa up to her feet, and she ran with them to the burrow. Four Iashen had landed and were chasing them. Sonjaa slipped into the burrow. Deka and Kylac jumped in after her. Night vision took over, and now they saw the tunnels illuminated in sketches of monochrome colored with scent. Screeches and flapping and snapping beaks echoed down the tunnel for several dozen breaths, and then the Iashen flew away.

They crawled down a few curves and dropped off a small ledge into a large chamber. The scents of forty-eight Togi packed this burrow, and they all trotted up to meet them, a collective scent of horror and helplessness coming from them.

Sonjaa lay on the floor against a wall, a number of concerned Togi surrounding her, but she had covered her eyes with her hands and retreated into the egg, mumbling and crying to herself. As a group, the forty-eight individuals told them what happened.

The other day, things had been normal. Then, for no apparent reason, certain Togi just started attacking. It might have been easy to contain and isolate these individuals, but then the Iashen started swooping down and killing people.

Shortly after it started, a few of them saw the antifox speeding around, shoving its claws into people's heads. Instead of dying or bleeding, the people started behaving like reverted Relian canines, staking territory and killing anything in scenting distance. Some of the Yil reported the same thing happening in the second layer. The antifox had been speeding around the valley, stabbing everyone it could reach.

"And then it came for me," said Kiyi, the Archeon for this world. Deka and Kylac breathed easier knowing he was all right. "It squared off with me, tried to fight me. I led a bunch of people through the portal to the burrow on this side of the valley. A hoard of Togi were following us, so I closed the portals. Now we're trapped here because of the Iashen. I haven't made any more ways because I don't want the other Togi to follow me here. What's happening at the hub?"

"The Togi have become reverted Relian canines," Deka said. "Sonjaa tried to bring several of them back, but they don't respond to that."

"How is this possible?" said Kiyi.

"Friend's old ways have figured out how to drain a person's conscious mind and replace it with an unconscious one. Its own."

"Why would they do that?"

"Probably testing the limits of its environment," Kylac answered. "Regardless, they are reverted foxes."

"How do we bring them back?" said Kiyi.

Deka's hands sagged. He turned to Sonjaa. She had curled up and was whimpering. The Togi around her tried to snuggle up to her, but she limply swatted them away.

He turned back to the Togi Archeon. "I don't think there is a conscious mind in those people. All that's left is a shell acting on pure instinct."

"That walking disaster did this to a hundred people in each layer!" Kiyi shivered on four legs. "Three hundred people! What are we supposed to do about it?"

"I don't want to accept it either," Deka answered, "but it matches what we've witnessed on other worlds. For physical wounds, the parts of the body it touches fall into the Lake. For wounds to the head, the conscious mind itself falls into the Lake. Those people are copies of the antifox trying to satisfy its urges."

"Just like that? No, I refuse to believe they're dead!"

Sonjaa curled tighter into the egg. Now Deka walked up to her and knelt. He touched her muzzle with his hand. She did not reply. A moment later, she made a mournful noise nobody had ever heard a raptor make before, and they stood still and silent for a moment.

Kylac spoke in Kiyi's direction. "When Friend reverted, he was beyond a raptor bringing him back as well. His scent anxiety encompassed the entire universe, and a raptor can't counteract that. If Friend's animal nature inserted itself into those people, then they are beyond help."

Kiyi turned around and padded through the survivors. He paused halfway to the wall. "So what's the solution?"

"We go back to the hub and kill them," Kylac said. "Norh is here. He can function in the second and third layers. He's probably come to the same conclusion by now."

Kiyi faced the fox. "No... I... I can't accept this!"

"Then we'll find more evidence," Kylac said. "If we're right, the reverted ones should be easy to deal with."

Kiyi paced back and forth. Kylac repeated his proposal. Kiyi seemed beyond this possibility.

Deka was listening as he nuzzled Sonjaa's snout. He gently removed her hand from her face. She opened one eye.

"What's wrong?"

She swallowed, and then she answered in Relian. "It didn't work. I could always bring Rupi back. I... I've never..."

He rubbed muzzles with her again. "I felt the pull, too. That Togi at the hub. The instinct to help a fox, and then finding a fox beyond help. It disturbs me."

"Everyone I see here. All of them. I can't do anything. I couldn't stop Friend. I couldn't save Rupi. I can't even help these people." She covered her eyes again. "Deka, I'm useless without a fox."

"You have me."

She huffed. "All I do is take you away from your fox."

"I mean it, Sonjaa. I like having you with me. I've been wondering if we could've spent more time together instead of going to different planets once the kill was gone. We could try that."

"Try what? Being married?"

Deka rubbed his claws. "We'll be just like Penny and Jeff."

Sonjaa opened her eyes as she clicked her claws. "I *was* jealous of their marital bliss."

He bumped noses and clicked claws with her. It had been so long since they shared a laugh.

"Just because you don't have a fox doesn't mean you can't have anyone."

She held his gaze for a moment, hands slowing. "Maybe. It doesn't seem right."

The fox had finally managed to convince Kiyi to make a portal to the hub so they could observe the reverted Togi and Iashen more carefully. They would also find some Yil. If they behaved the same way no matter what, they would know for certain. The quadruped's spiked back rose and fell as he paced the burrow. Deka observed him.

"Are you all right, Kiyi?"

"This is unbelievable. I can't accept it. There must be a way to confirm."

The raptor rose from Sonjaa. "Their behavior fits the pattern."

Kiyi didn't seem to hear. He kept pacing and talking to himself.

Deka walked to Kylac, hands folded close to his chest, a polite posture when not among large predators. The fox was leaning against the dirt wall, rubbing himself, trying to elicit a reaction. The raptor bumped muzzles with him.

Kylac stared at himself. "I used to slip out of my sheath being around so many scents."

Deka rubbed his claws. "It was such a joy when that happened. I remember when you panicked when other scents were around."

"I feel dead."

"And I feel old doing all this big thinking."

The fox's tail swished once. "What big thoughts do you have now?"

"The best solution may be to shrink their territory. Push them together and force them to meet. Instinct will compel them to fight it out. With Kiyi's help, we could cover the whole hub. Norh and Stephen can do the same thing in the other layers."

"Nothing else can be done. Nothing. We can observe Relian canine instinct here, without any other variables." He met Deka's eyes. "It's just as disturbing for me to look at people who are beyond help. At the monster inside of me."

The raptor held Kylac, wrapping his neck around his shoulders. "I always brought you back."

Kylac remained rigid. "You used to be happy, too. Now all you do is fix all the broken people around you." He panted a few times. "Remember on Kronia, when you asked me what it's like to lose control?"

"You said it was the most reassuring peace you've ever felt once you satisfied the scent anxiety."

"Deka, I want that peace again. I want it so much. It would be relief from all of this. From the knowledge of what lies beyond the universe and what it means for all of us. I want the old ways to take me because it will be over. I will be at peace. I remember when sex made me feel that way. Nothing does anymore. Sometimes I think I can give the old ways a try. I want to let go. I can't think of many reasons to hold onto my higher mind."

The raptor pulled Kylac away from the wall and walked him over to Sonjaa. Deka sat next to her, and Kylac sat on his other side. He held both of them while they waited for Kiyi to make the way.

"Sonjaa, you are not pulling me away from my fox. I want you around more often. I've wanted that for years. You left because Rupi wanted to, and Kylac was pulling me somewhere else. Going separate ways after a kill was just the normal way of doing things. It doesn't have to be. Kylac, you are not broken. I like having both of you with me."

The green theropod reached over and clicked Deka's claws. "What else is there for mates to do besides share kills?"

"We could try to have eggs again. This time I'll be there every day if you want."

"I don't know about that. I think I'd rather..." Sonjaa's hands fell. She thought for a moment while Kiyi paced and mumbled to himself. "I miss learning languages. I miss being around people who don't speak my language, and I don't speak theirs. Living new cultures. Earth was wonderful while I was doing that. Then we had to be in that house listening to those rich *assholes* planning ways to enslave the contacted universe."

Deka clicked his claws. "I always loved hearing you swear. No matter what language, you make it sound beautiful. We could do that, too. Still plenty of languages I haven't learned."

"That was always something me and Rupi did. She wasn't very good with languages. She liked being among people for months, unable to speak to them or understand.

She always enjoyed getting to know a culture that way. We did that for entire years when we were younger. I think she liked it when she couldn't understand me. It always brought us closer. We found ways to understand one another. Every culture on every planet was a new life to live."

"We'll find something of our own," Deka said. "All three of us. What about you, Kylac? There's so much out there we can do. What do you want?"

Kylac leaned on Deka. "I want to be me again. I don't know who I am anymore. I lost myself."

Deka pulled them closer. "So did I. I miss running into things without thinking and hoping it works out. We got into so much trouble that way when we were little. I miss the aquatics. Chreeb... I could spend entire days listening to his voice, talking about things I would never see. All the years we spent as children, finding aquatics and getting to know them. After we kill the antifox, we'll join the contacted universe again and reclaim everything the disaster took from us. We'll make a new life out there. We'll find joy again. We'll find ourselves."

Sonjaa reached over and felt his claws. Kylac's tail swished a few times as he stared at his sheath.

5

This column of oxygen was one of the many places around the world where those in the first layer could interact with the people in the second layer. Elsewhere around the world were columns of methane rising up through the first two layers, and the Iashen could interact with the people in the two lower layers.

Stephen and Norh walked around the barrier between the two atmospheres, speaking to the Yil just on the other side of the oxygenfall. They all had the same story of being at the second layer's hub when suddenly the antifox zipped from person to person, stabbing them in the brain. The people it touched went insane and began attacking people around them, even killing them. Everyone fled for safety.

Then the portals went out. The Togi under the oxygen column were stranded here. They had tried to follow the oxygen river that hugged the mountains down to the first layer, but they found the place full of territorial Togi trying to kill them, so they had gathered here.

The Yil had also hidden from the reverted ones. Staying on the opposite side of the column was the safest place to be with the portals out.

"I have bad news," Norh said. "Those people out there are *zombies*."

The Yil and Togi stared at him. Norh then realized he had used an English word. He shook his head and corrected himself.

"They're dead. Friend's old ways put its instincts into their hollow shell. That's all they are now."

One of the Yil spoke to him through the oxygen barrier. Her voice sounded distorted. "But... My mate is out there!"

Stephen turned to her. "I'm so sorry. I watched Sonjaa try to bring a Togi back. It should have worked, but it didn't. All they know is scent anxiety. There is nothing beneath that. Friend's old ways have caused destruction and death on ten other worlds. I have been with the Relians, trying to stop them."

"So what do we do?" a male Togi said.

Norh took control of their neck and turned to them. "The solution is to push the reverted ones together to trigger their scent anxiety. They will forget everything else, even that they cannot breathe outside their layer."

"That's horrible!" said a male Yil.

"I know all of you probably lost someone close to you, but they are long gone."

Stephen and Norh spread their wings and ascended the column. The Togi and Yil looked up at him as he rose. As they gained elevation, and the mountain peak rose closer and closer to their eye level, Stephen thought of something.

"We need to be in agreement on this—"

"We need to be in agreement on this—"

They had spoken at the same time.

"Sorry, you first."

"Sorry, you first."

Stephen realized they both had come to the same conclusion. They could not speak in the upper atmosphere, so they had no other way of communicating. They did not speak again. Stephen fell into Norh's memories. He realized what Norh would want to do, and how the Krone would go about it. Norh fell into Stephen's memories, understood how he would go about doing this.

Norh and Stephen felt alone in their body. They moved as one. They thought as one. They knew what to do.

They crossed into the upper atmosphere. The trace amounts of oxygen and nitrogen in the air made thin, blue and purple curtains moving against the wind. The methane glowed slightly yellow and turned into a light haze of yellow in the upper atmosphere, but they would not dare go that high.

They reached the top of the column. The aurora outlined the river of oxygen that flowed across the interface between the second and third layers, a network of currents filled with blue and purple swirls that covered the entire upper atmosphere. All the oxygen the plants and animals in this layer exhaled fell into these arteries which merged into a column that pierced the lower layers and restored the oxygen at the surface.

They inhaled one last time, circled inside the column, and then burst into the third layer. They had to fly fast or they would drop out of the sky, so they hoped they would find someone quickly.

They flew to the mountain peak, shrouded in glowing yellow light with thin curtains of oxygen and nitrogen flowing off of it and across the top of the second layer. The mountain was in plain view now, and so was the vegetation that grew here. Vines and trees that absorbed the methane and exhaled oxygen as a byproduct. Animals that had adapted to life on mountain peaks. They resembled goats and rams. Other animals roamed the mountainside, resembling nothing on Earth. The creature that lived on sheer vertical slopes, holding on to the bare cliff face with suction-cup hooves, reminded them of a species on Naloa, which had entire continents covered in mountain peaks.

They noticed several Iashen huddled into themselves on the mountain. Their scenting range was smaller than a Togi's, being sight-based hunters, so it did not surprise them that the Iashen were relatively close. It was time to bring them together.

They swooped over the closest reptile and scooped him up. He complained and tried to stab their hand, but his beak could not pierce a Krone's scales. They banked right and flew to the next Iashen. They rolled, snatched him up in their other hand, and flew back out over the valley.

The winged reptiles in his talons squawked and complained. Stephen and Norh dove through the third layer into the second on a steep decline into the valley. They leveled off and released them into the second layer, right over a small cluster of reverted Yil. They continued diving downward and dipped into the first layer. They took a few breaths, then rolled and ascended through the second layer again. They passed over the Iashen they had dropped. Sure enough they were fighting the reverted Yil in the air. The Krone did not care who won.

They banked into the oxygen column and flew straight up to the third layer, taking one last breath, and then leveled off and veered to the mountaintop again. They searched for a more reverted reptiles. They saw two more. They adjusted their roll and flew straight for them. They decided to drop these in the first layer to keep the reverted Togi busy.

6

The methane released by the plants in the first layer rose up and collided with the bottom of the second layer then flowed like a river to columns that led up to the top layers of atmosphere, and the nitrogen settled between the first and third layers. Hundreds of rivers of methane ran along the boundary between the first and second layers, merging into columns fifty paces wide and over a thousand tall. It was easily visible by its yellow tinge and how the reduced density altered the light and sound that passed through it.

Kiyi had made the portal that brought them here, to one of the places where the bottom of the methane column touched the ground in the first layer, allowing the Togi and Iashen to interact. The Togi Archeon, Kylac, Sonjaa, and Deka stood before the column of concentrated methane and nitrogen rising up through the layers of atmosphere.

Thirty Iashen stood inside the column, looking at all of them. They had taken shelter here for protection against the reverted Iashen, as well as those in the second and first layers. One of them pointed at the mountain in the distance and the Krone flying back and forth.

"What is he doing?"

"Using their scent anxiety against them," Deka said. "Eventually only a few will be left, and they will be much easier to take down."

"Can you stop him?" said the Togi.

"Kiyi!" said Kylac. "You said you were opening a way to hub! Why did you bring us here?"

"They can't be dead! You can stop Norh! Tell him there's another way!"

"Is there?" asked an Iash.

"There must be a way to reach them!"

Deka walked up to the quadruped, placed a hand on his shoulder. "This is pointless. Sonjaa already tried to bring them back. Their minds are empty. They are already dead."

Kiyi threw his hand off and stepped into the column. The Iashen moved to make room for him.

"Stop him!" he screamed, his voice higher-pitched in the less dense atmosphere. "You're the predators! You can find a way to reach the ones the antifox touched! You can be in the lower atmospheres! Help them! Please!"

Nobody moved. Kiyi sank and couched. Several Iashen unfolded their wings and pushed him backwards. He fell over, and they rolled him out of the column. Kiyi lay on his back and gasped for air. After choking for a moment, he turned his snout and called to them.

"They're suffering, and you're hiding!"

He stood up, ran past the portal and down the steep slope away from the column of ascending methane. He jumped in place, calling upwards as loudly as he could.

Deka tucked his arms into his sides and raced for him. Kylac and Sonjaa also ran to him as the Togi jumped and shouted into the sky. Deka skidded to a stop beside him, picked him up by his shoulders, and held him up on two legs to Deka's eye level.

"All right! We'll try it here! We'll lure an Iash, and if that person doesn't behave like a reverted fox, we'll stop Norh and Stephen!"

"It will work!" screamed the Togi.

Deka let him drop, and Kiyi resumed jumping up and down and screaming at the sky. Sonjaa and Kylac joined them. The Iashen in the methane column looked on in bewilderment.

Some time later, they saw something diving at them, and they spread out to make room. He swooped the ground and flipped upwards into the air. Kiyi called and jumped around. The Relians remained still, watching as the flying reptile ascended into the third layer.

The Iash made a loop and dove down again, leveling off in the first layer and then sailing straight for Kiyi. Deka calculated the vectors and then leaped ahead of the Iash exactly where he would end up. He landed on the winged reptile and brought him to the ground. The Iash flailed wildly and screamed at them. He was on his stomach, so he could not reach Deka. Sonjaa ran around him and held a wing in her mouth. Kylac held the other wing still.

Kiyi bounded up to his face and stood just out of reach his snapping beak.

"Seeg!" he shouted. "I know you're in there! I'm an Archeon! I can sense you're still in there! Focus on me!"

The Iash flailed and screamed. Deka calculated he only had a few more breaths of methane in his bones.

Kiyi placed a paw on Seeg's beak.

"You don't know where you are or what you feel. You only react. Fight the reaction. Your mind is still there."

The Iash's thrashing became weaker. He was almost out of breath. Kiyi grabbed Seeg's head in his paws and screamed in his face.

"It's confusing—I know it is! You're better than this! I've known you since we hatched! You've been hunting me since that walking sphere attacked us! You know it's me, and you want to come back! Don't let it swallow you!"

Seeg bent his neck backwards and pecked Kiyi in the chest. He screeched at the Togi, a screech of scent anxiety, just as a reverted fox would make. He used up the last of the methane in his bones. He gasped and fell still.

Deka hopped off and crouched at the waist to be at Kiyi's eye level. "Now do you believe us? We're going back to the valley to push more reverted ones together."

Kiyi stared at the motionless Iash for a moment. "I can hear him. He's not dead. How do I help him?"

He looked up at Deka. He scented him and snarled. Then he charged. The raptor backed away just fast enough to avoid the strike. Kiyi rose to his hind legs and snarled like a Relian canine. Deka's killing claws rose.

"Deka!" Sonjaa said. She was standing behind Kiyi, looking straight at the back of his skull. "The antifox got him, too!"

Deka backed away. Sonjaa tried to crawl back into the egg while still standing. Kylac had dropped to all fours. Five Iashen dove out of the sky and swooped them. The Relians looked up the hill at the column. The portal back to the burrow was gone. Kiyi collapsed on his stomach, moaning and flailing his limbs, the stab wound in the back of head clearly visible now.

Deka shouted to the Iashen in the column. "We can save him! Keep them off us!"

They spread their wings and ascended. A flock of featherless reptiles flew from the tube of methane and circled overhead, intercepting the Iashen coming down for them. Deka stood in attack stance on one side of the Togi. He turned to Sonjaa.

"Now!"

She shivered, turning to Deka and then to Kiyi. The Togi's limbs moved in random directions as he shouted words in multiple languages. Sonjaa backed up a step.

Above her, the Iashen from the column fought the reverted reptiles. They collided in midair, smacked one another with their beaks, struggled, threw each other off, and then separated. Some flew upwards, made a loop and then approached for another attack. Kylac took position on the other side of the Togi, looking up.

An Iash broke through the flock above, sailing for Deka. The raptor darted out of the way and squared off with him when the Iash landed. He charged Deka. The raptor charged back, going for the throat. Deka clamped down, but the Iash stabbed him in the shoulder, and Deka stumbled back. The Iash chased him and Deka ran backwards to stay out of reach.

He called to his mate. "Sonjaa, there's your fox! You can bring him back!"

Sonjaa turned to Kiyi as he flailed on the ground, mind leaking into the Lake, memories spreading out, slowly going insane. He looked exactly like the people on Neben as they died, sounded exactly how Sonjaa imagined she would have if someone could have heard her as she fell deeper and deeper into the Lake.

Two Iashen had landed and Kylac was fighting both of them off. They behaved like reverted foxes, not flying reptiles. The same thing could have happened on Neben had the antifox figured this out sooner.

Kiyi lay in place, convulsing and shouting gibberish. Sonjaa heard herself. The sight of it made her feel like the universe buckled under the weight of her thoughts and at any moment she would break through and fall out of it. She took another involuntary step backwards.

Kiyi screamed. Sonjaa caught a glimpse of his eyes as he thrashed. They weren't empty yet, but he was draining.

Deka stomped and flashed his claws in all directions, keeping six Iashen away from the fallen Archeon. Kylac held three a few paces away as they clapped their beaks at him.

Deka had been pushing her to face this feeling for multiple planets. Pushing her and Kylac to talk about the

Lake. Kylac knew it as a concept, but she had been there. Kylac wanted to know, but thinking about it still filled her with a special kind of dread, and Deka had forced her to think about it over and over, each time letting her mind sink further and further.

She felt the pulling desire to help a fox in need, but the repulsion and fear of watching someone fall to where she had been—into the pit she had only escaped by luck and never wanted to go near again—held her in place.

The fight had drawn other Iashen from the third layer. Now the reverted ones outnumbered the unaffected, and the fight wasn't so easy. One of the Iashen broke through the cloud of fighting reptiles and swooped straight for Sonjaa. Kylac leaped into her and pulled her down to the ground. Deka jumped to Sonjaa's other side and fought off two reptiles.

Sonjaa felt her mind falling away again at the mere sight of Kiyi. His garbled voice took her further and further away with every syllable. She had been alone since the disaster, longing for someone to comfort and nurture. She imagined Rupi lying like this, mind draining away, about to revert.

She unfolded herself and stood up. She took a step toward Kiyi. He screamed again. Sonjaa winced. Her mind disconnected from her body for half a breath, and then fell back into place. It felt the same as what Deka had been pushing her to face. She should have been used to it by now, but it was no less scary than the first time.

She ran to Kiyi before she could give in to the fear. She lay on top of him and held his muzzle still, forcing him to look straight up at her.

"Kiyi! Ignore everything else and concentrate on me! Your mind is draining out of the universe! If you don't hold yourself together, you will spread out so thin there will be nothing left of you! I was where you were, and I came back!

The Lake will pull you apart, but you can hold yourself together!"

She realized talking would not be enough. As she spoke, she understood what Deka wanted her to do.

Her stomach heaved just thinking about it, and this time without a way to pull herself back. The longer she held him, the stronger the instinct to help a reverted fox became. For the first time since she had lost her fox to the disaster, the one that had destroyed Rel and pulled Sonjaa outside the universe, she knew she could do something about this. She panted as she allowed her mind to become heavy.

Deka slashed and cut the wings of an Iash swooping for Sonjaa. Kylac landed on the back of another, and brought her to the ground. Two unreverted Iashen dove down and took over for the fox, holding the reverted one down until she suffocated. Kylac turned his muzzle up and observed the fight happening above. It was getting larger.

7

Stephen and Norh couldn't find any more Iashen to abduct, so they swooped down into the first layer and observed. It was disgusting, watching these people fight like foxes and die for lack of proper instincts in their brains.

They wondered if they were right. If there was no hope for them. They did not want to think they had just sent hundreds of people to die. The logic was sound, and it matched with their observations from the past, but a part of them doubted the conclusion. One could have all the evidence in the world for something to be true and still be wrong.

They wondered where this doubt came from. It was on the tip of their tongue. And then they realized it was coming from Stephen. A memory he had not shared yet.

The gap in their knowledge of each other separated them. Norh now became aware of Stephen filling the left side of their body. Stephen was aware of Norh on the right.

"That was amazing," Stephen said.

"Why do you doubt?"

"Because it happens all the time! You're sure you know something, you bet money on it, and you're still wrong because of one thing you didn't know. Happened to me every time I stood up to a master sergeant, or my boss, or my parents. Teachers. So sure I knew something and then they prove me wrong."

"Doubt. It's a crippling feeling. Humbling. Submissive. Sometimes too much knowledge can have the same effect."

"How so?"

"I will share everything with you as soon as this threat has passed. The Krone are not familiar with lack of knowledge as the cause of sorrow and humiliation."

"Not many people know too much either."

"I am eager to understand."

The Iashen and the Yil brawled in the air. Both sides forgot they couldn't breathe in this level of the atmosphere, and they began to drop.

"I know the evidence," Stephen said, "but a part of me still wonders if we're missing something. If they really are gone. I feel guilty for causing this. Please tell me these are just zombies."

"I am sure of it. They are animal instincts separated from the body they were intended for, infecting another body."

"Keep telling me that. Please."

Norh spread their wings and lifted them off. "It's time to handle the Togi."

"What makes you so confident in yourself?"

"You already know. Think about it."

Stephen did. He went over the evidence again and again in his mind. He synchronized with Norh, and they controlled their body together as they dove for a reverted Togi. Her eyes were empty, her mind full of scent anxiety.

8

Sonjaa felt her mind falling through the universe. It wasn't as terrifying as it had been. Deka had pushed her to let her mind fall deeper into the Lake, further from her body. Just when she thought she had reached her limit—as soon as she thought her mind could not move further away from her body without breaking apart—Deka urged her to endure it longer, again and again, on every world since Fusina.

Though her eyes still saw reality, her mind became aware of something underneath it. A place where only thought existed and where the mind had no physical container to keep it from flying apart. Her mind sank into this place, and she allowed it to slip away. She became aware of Kiyi. She felt where his mind leaked into the Lake, and where it was going.

Reality fell away. Sonjaa had never gone this far before, but Kiyi's screams of agony both in the universe and outside it made her want to dive in no matter how deep he had gone. She recognized Kiyi here. Particles that reminded her of other Togi, other Yil, and other Iashen surrounded him, spread out far enough to be aware of themselves but too far to hold themselves together.

Their efforts to comprehend where they were would only spread them out faster. Sonjaa didn't blame Kiyi for believing they weren't dead. Out here, Sonjaa felt them all, and many had not died yet. She still felt individual particles that seemed connected, but some had been scrambled.

Eventually they would lose their identities and become background noise.

Sonjaa's mind pulled away from her body and descended further into the Lake, following Kiyi's agony. She remembered how she had once moved out here. She exerted force on other particles and crossed the barrier. The memories were clear now, and they seemed less intimidating now. She found particles that felt like Kiyi. She held them. Back in reality, she became aware of a change in the Togi. He saw her.

She felt him think it before he spoke. "Sonjaa? Is that you?"

She ignored the sickening disconnect between her mind and her body. She collected herself and followed Kiyi's particles. The nausea and anxiety increased as she chased him, but the further away she spread herself, the more distant the feeling became.

She found the leading edge of Kiyi's mind. She exerted force and began pushing it back toward the hole in the Lake from which his mind still leaked. Somehow Sonjaa perceived reality and the Lake at the same time. Kiyi was holding her.

"This... How are... you...?"

Sonjaa did not trust herself to speak. She spread part of herself out farther, collecting more particles of Kiyi and pushing them back to him. She felt a few particles that did not belong to him, and she extended herself over the leading edge and ejected those. She found one that seemed familiar and left it alone, though it did not feel like the right species.

Back in the familiar universe, reptiles dropped from the sky left and right. The Iashen who were not reverted went back to the column to breathe once in a while, but the reverted ones lacked such an impulse. They began falling. Deka and Kylac had fewer of them to keep away from Sonjaa, but the new arrivals still had full bones, and they attacked with all the strength a fox's scent anxiety provided. Blood was everywhere. It had landed on Sonjaa, but she did not feel it.

Finally, the last reverted Iash dropped dead. The flock landed around Sonjaa straddling their Togi Archeon. They formed a tight circle around them. Kiyi was still shaking. Deka stood with his flank against hers.

Sonjaa felt Deka touching her real body, but it had become so distant she comprehended the sensation as the idea of touch, not something happening right now. Particles of consciousness that comprised Kiyi felt more real. She concentrated. Her perception expanded to include billions of particles around her—random particles from random people who had been scrambled long ago. Her perception suddenly included the universe as it moved across the Lake, and it began to fill her with images and sounds and scents happening everywhere at once.

She remembered the practice sessions Deka had forced her to endure and shut out the extra information. She focused on Kiyi. She had pushed most of his mind back into the container in the real universe that was his brain. Only a little more remained. She continued exerting force on the particles, surrounding them, containing them for Kiyi.

Moments later, she found the crack in the barrier that separated the Lake from the universe. She did not know how to heal the crack, so she sent him the thought: now that he knew how it felt to go into and out of the Lake, it was up to him to keep his mind contained inside his body. Sonjaa felt him understand, and she pushed the last of his conscious mind back into its container. In the real universe, he settled, blinked, and breathed normally, still holding her by the neck.

She considered following it through, but that was not how she would have to return. She felt her real body in this universe. She felt herself in the Lake. Sonjaa had gone so far out she wondered if a connection even existed anymore. This is what she had been afraid of. Descending into this place, being unable to come back, accidentally escaping her container. She floated in both places for a moment, body still sick and threatening to vomit.

She felt Deka's touch. She inhaled his scent. She found the exact place in the Lake where those sensations caused particles in reality to interact, and she gathered around them. The nauseating feeling of her mind falling through reality enveloped her. It didn't feel terrifying anymore. She had been so afraid of this before because it had nearly ripped her apart, but Deka was right. She could control it, and it would not destroy her. She found where the nearly-empty container touched the Lake. It also had a crack in it, and she moved into it. Deka's touch and scent existed in the Lake and in reality. Her duel perception of them phased into a single sensation, and her conscious mind snapped into her body.

She rolled off him to keep from crushing him under her weight. She lay on her side, panting, gripping the soil, licking it to make sure she was here. Deka stood over her, taking her hand and rubbed her claws.

The reptiles took flight and circled them in celebration. Somehow not a single bird touched as they flew in opposing rings around and above them. They retreated to the methane column and settled down to breathe.

Kiyi rolled to his feet. Kylac scented him. As soon as the Togi was on his feet, he hobbled over to Sonjaa and held her around the muzzle, the short spines on his back rising and falling in joy. He was trying to speak, but words failed him.

Sonjaa touched Kiyi on the snout. Her hand wandered down to under his forelegs and pulled him close. The Togi rolled with it. Sonjaa pulled him down and curled up next to him. He lay still in the theropod's embrace.

"Sonjaa! I can feel him! Seeg! He's... He's..."

She answered distantly. "He was out there. He found you. Probably tried to collect around you. I thought you'd want to have it. It was all I could save."

She felt his spines rise in laughter and gratitude and then fall in grief. After many breaths, he spoke again.

"How did you know to do that?"

Sonjaa curled up with him tighter. "Please. Just be my fox for a little while. Please."

Kiyi lay still. Sonjaa lay with him and growled. Deka nuzzled her. She rubbed her muzzle against his.

"Deka, what's happening to me?"

He sat beside her with his hands together, rubbing his claws. Kylac sat next to him, tail twitching.

9

The few remaining reverted ones now found themselves outnumbered and overwhelmed. Norh and Stephen showed them how to confront the empty shells of their former companions and stop those bodies from harming anyone else.

Kiyi was opening the portals to the rest of the columns around the globe and the hub as well. The three species were coming back together, comforting one another through the columns of rising and falling atmospheres. The hub was returning to normal. Animals were out again, no longer afraid of the reverted Togi, Yil, and Iashen.

The Relians and Norh lay in the hub. In the distance, the people buried the bodies of the fallen. Family grieved for other family. Mated pairs, separated when the portals went out, reunited.

Sonjaa had new determination in her posture. Determination had replaced dread, which was exactly what Deka wanted. All that remained was Kylac

The canine was about to unlock the last part of his mind. The part that would fill his consciousness with the scents of everyone in the universe at once and trigger his instincts in a way Deka could not relieve. They were almost ready for the Lake.

"Everyone..." Stephen said. All eyes turned to him. "I want to tell you it's been wonderful knowing all of you. Deka, Kylac, thank you for letting me come with you. Sonjaa, working with you on teaching the Relians all the languages of Earth was some of the best months of my life on Earth. I'd say goodbye to Rive and all the Relians if I could."

"You two are finally going to merge?" Kylac said, pushing aside his worry.

Norh took over their voice. "Not merge. Synchronize. We will agree on what to say, and we will speak it at the same time. We will agree on what to do, and we will do it at the same time. No more switching back and forth. No more separate personalities."

Deka clicked claws with Sonjaa. "I'll miss the two of you. When will you do this?"

"Right now," Stephen said. "I can't think of a better place. Well, I can; I know almost all the planets by now, but you know what I mean."

Norh took control of their mouth: "We are so far along now we can't stop it. It may as well happen here, willingly, instead of catching us by surprise again."

"What should we call you?" Sonjaa said.

"I was thinking a new name should combine our names," said Norh. "Sorven."

"Are you sure?" Stephen said. "It's not a very equal combination."

"It's better than Snorh," he replied.

"I'm happy for you," Kylac said, wagging his tail as he looked at the Krone. "I want to enjoy this place, too. Soon I won't enjoy anything."

Norh spread their wings and took off. The others watched them fly to the oxygen column in the second layer by the mountains. Deka leaned on his fox. Kylac leaned back, taking in as much of his scent as possible. They watched the three sentient species of this planet come back together and grieve for the ones they had lost.

10

Norh and Stephen flew through the barrier and landed in the column of falling oxygen. Stephen took control of their neck and turned it upwards. They stood beneath a slow motion waterfall of blue air. Ribbons of color cut through it, changing from purple to blue as they passed from nitrogen to oxygen.

Nobody else was here right now, all busy cleaning up the mess Friend's old ways had left, burying their dead and identifying people they knew. They had the entire column to themselves.

Stephen knew Norh did not find this interesting at all. These columns were simply examples of density interactions forming systems to redistribute gases in high concentration out to areas of lower concentration, chemicals organizing themselves over time according to natural laws.

Norh knew that Stephen thought it was still astonishing to be able to stand here at all and witness something so unimaginable. Just a few reaches from their face was an atmosphere of nitrogen and certain death, but under this tube of oxygen made by plants and animals who breathed methane, they were safe, and there was something about being surrounded by death and yet being untouched by it that he found so engaging.

"So this is it," Stephen said. "The last block of memories I have that I can still point to and say those are me. I did those things and you did not."

"I have my last memories as well. I feel bad for what I'm about to do."

"I've lived with you this long. I'm sure I can handle everything else. I've done some shit I'm not proud of, too."

They lay under the falling oxygen, looking out at the landscape of nitrogen, and the animals that behaved like plants. They observed a Yil buzzing around, then landing in the soil and taking root.

"I'm ready for this," Stephen said.

"So am I."

"Count from ten. On zero, we give each other our blocks."

"Agreed. You count."

"No... You count."

Norh lay their head down on the ground. "I think you should."

Stephen sighed. "All right. How 'bout we both count?"

"Sure. When do we start?"

Stephen unfolded their wings. "I'm starting to think I've influenced you too much."

Norh reached up, felt Stephen's side of their muzzle with his fingers. "You are exactly what I have needed for centuries. Where have you been all my life?"

"Not even born yet."

"I would still be in my cave if not for you. I'm about to show you why."

"Norh, you gave me what I always wanted. A chance to get out of my damn job and experience things I never could. Even if you failed big time getting me killed on a planet that didn't exist, it still worked out."

Now North spread their wings. "This is about to become easier. I think I will miss the disagreements and explaining things to you."

"I will miss listening to you. Synchronizing felt so good. Just being so in tune with you. I can't think of anybody I'd rather spend the rest of my life with. Hell, I can't think of anybody I'd rather become."

"I liked your scent the day I met you. I knew we would get along. I am so glad it worked out for the better, even if you had to die for it to happen. I have lived a lifetime I never could through you, and I am so grateful you have influenced me."

"Damn it, Norh, I wish I could hug you right now."

"Ten. Nine."

"Eight. Seven." Stephen stood on the ladder facing a nearly empty shelf in the library of his mind. A few dozen books remained, and they were his alone. The last pieces of himself the dragon at the base of the ladder had not eaten. He gathered them up and held them over the dragon's open maw.

"Six. Five. Four." Norh thought about the last planets he had yet to share with Stephen. One of them was especially important because it was the one planet he did not want Stephen to know about: the last world he had visited before retreating to his cave for good. One of the last pieces of himself he still called his own. He did not want it, but he did not want to force it on someone else either, and yet the human wanted it anyway.

"Three."

Each knew what the other's sense of timing was, and when the next count would be. They synchronized.

"Two. One. Now."

Stephen jumped from the ladder into the dragon's mouth.

Norh leaped up to meet him, but instead of eating him, he embraced him so hard they fell into one another.

Stephen remembered some eighty-four worlds at the same time, both in the contacted universe and outside it. One world outside the contacted universe stood out. It had no name. By the time Norh visited it, he was furious. He had witnessed civilization fall dozens of times despite his best efforts to steer lone species away from those ends. He knew he was wiser than they were. He was smarter. They should listen to him. This time he tried something new.

He destroyed the entire population—all eight million bipedal crocodiles. He had hunted them down and devoured them one by one. Those he could not eat, he crushed their bones under his feet. He had slaughtered the entire civilization except for fourteen individuals.

He started their civilization over, with himself as the beginning. He declared they could live as they pleased, so long as they made sure to please him first. He announced ridiculous rituals they would have to perform, sacrifices they would have to make to keep him happy, all of it unnecessary; he did not care what they burned or what time of year they burned it. The goal was to keep them so busy performing pointless tasks and appeasing an external force they had no time to bicker among themselves.

It worked. He remade their civilization. Generations passed. Their god was visible, and the people feared him and they taught their children how to fear and please him so Norh would not destroy everything again. Seeing them in harmony made Norh happy for a time, until he realized what he had become.

He could save any species this way, traveling from planet to planet, maintaining civilizations across the universe, being god to all of them, making sure they stayed in line, but it required being an object of hatred. It required manipulating their fear of and helplessness in their environment, becoming the very thing the Lost had loathed.

He was superior to them. He was smarter, wiser, bigger, stronger than anyone in the universe, contacted or not. He could make them obey. He could make everyone obey.

But that wasn't what he wanted to be. Since he hatched, he had imagined what having a companion species must be like. Two species so deeply connected from learning how to understand one another they became one culture as equals. The best Norh could do was acquire a flock of timid worshipers. He didn't want to be feared. He wanted the people to understand. He wanted them to be a companion species, but the Krone had killed off its companion race centuries ago, so now the Krone were alone with their mistake, condemned to sit in their caves imagining what the rest of the contacted universe enjoyed.

In his anger, Norh had swept over the land and killed them all. He slaughtered and devoured everyone as they performed one of the rituals he had ordered them to do. There were no consequences for doing so. No witnesses. He could do this everywhere, and nobody could stop him. It wasn't the answer he wanted, but it was an answer—something to give his long life some sort of meaning. It would give the Krone a place. It would give them a purpose. It would give them what they so desperately craved. He was exactly what the Krone's extinct companion species feared, and no matter how hard he tried, he would never be anything else.

He retreated to Kronia and hid in his cave so he would not be tempted to subject another species to that again. No longer was he a happy youth. He was now an adult.

...

Stephen remembered being in the grocery store with his wife. He saw another man walk by her and touch her ass. He ran up to that man and punched him in the face. It was an emotion Stephen never knew he had, but he was capable of much worse.

Stephen was in basic training. There was this guy. Really annoying kid. Talked with a lisp, had the most annoying voice and rattled on about the most inane subjects. One time he spent an hour talking about all the cats his family had on the farm. Talking to nobody and yet to everybody. Despite everyone telling him to shut up, the kid just didn't get it.

Stephen got several guys together, they wore bags over their heads, yanked the kid out of bed while he was sleeping, and broke one of his legs with a fire extinguisher. There had been an investigation, but the drill sergeants were not unhappy to see him gone either, so the grilling had not been too serious. Still, nobody suspected Stephen Penarrow, the quiet, Asian kid from California, had been the leader.

Recently, in the factory, Stephen had had a flashback. There was another kid at the die press. Absolute idiot. Wouldn't stop talking about himself. Thought he knew everything. Stephen tried telling him he didn't know as much as he thought he did, but the kid would not be quiet and do his job. He kept insisting he could do it better than Stephen, and no matter how many times he messed up he still kept spreading that story around. Stephen cleaned up the messes he made, and yet the kid kept telling his bosses Stephen was making mistakes, wasting parts.

Stephen was showing him how to remove a part that became stuck in the machine. While the kid's arm was inside, Stephen cycled it and crushed the kid's arm. OSHA investigated, but even on camera it looked like an accident. The kid was gone for over a month, and when he came back, he was a changed man. That one incident was all he needed to grow up. Stephen felt bad for robbing him of forty percent of motor functions in his hand, but at the same time, it felt so good to do something about a problem nobody else had the guts to deal with.

Jealous, vindictive, cruel... Stephen was not raised to be any of those things, so where had they come from? What was he supposed to do instead? Let those people walk on him? Tolerate them while they made everyone around them miserable? Weren't smart people supposed to take action and get things done? Wasn't that a virtue? Wasn't that a leadership quality?

Stephen did not feel bad about taking someone else down, and that's what scared him. He was capable of it, and if he ever got to be the boss, he would probably be free to inflict it on even more people. People like him deserved to be in a dead-end job, alone, because nobody would have suspected him.

Brenda never knew. He had planned to take those secrets to the grave so she would never know she had married someone who could, at any time, become a monster. Some days Stephen felt on the brink of letting go. One bad day away from pulling out the stops.

Suddenly Stephen felt alone in their body. So did Norh. Every memory of both lives was now his and complete. They knew each other so well they thought the same thoughts at the same time, and now nothing differentiated between the two of them.

"So what are we now?" they said.

They looked back on their lives, all the different experiences mixed together. The good and the bad. The happy times and the miserable ones. The hope and the disappointment. The pain and the joy. The determination and the self pity. They felt all of them at the same time. A few breaths under the oxygenfall, and one set of emotions rose above the others.

They stood up, spread their wings, and soared up through the column. They burst through the third layer and flew to the mountaintop. They sat on the summit looking down over the valley through the three layers of atmosphere.

"We can't change them," they said, their voice laughably high-pitched. "We are superior! We can do anything we want! So let's be useful out here! Every species is our companion! All of you!"

It felt so good to believe in something and be able to act on it they opened their mouth and let out a triumphant roar. It sounded like a mousy squeal in the methane atmosphere. They laughed and squealed again. Their voice would strike terror into no one, but that was just fine with them. They squealed again and again, flapping their wings, laughing at themselves until they were out of breath.

Sorven leaped off the summit and glided down to the first layer.

Tavax

I

After ten hours at the factory, plus half an hour of commuting each way, Malcolm wished he hadn't taken that extra shift tomorrow. His usual relief on Friday now felt like bitter disappointment. As he pulled into the apartment complex, he sighed. He'd had plenty of time at work to ponder the idea that he was part of history. The interview had been last week, and it had taken all this time for it to hit him: he would forever be remembered for what he had said in the interview. He could have said anything, but future generations would know him as the guy who talked about raptor cock in his ass while fox dick was in his mouth. Replaying it in his mind, he felt satisfied.

It didn't feel like the truth until he had to speak it out loud, but that was him, it was on tape, so he felt proud. If nothing else, his interview would stand out a hundred years from now.

He pulled into his parking space and stepped outside. It was cold and yet Malcolm was not wearing a jacket. Ratash had been teaching him techniques to control his metabolism, and to his surprise, they seemed to be working. The cold affected him a lot less now.

He walked up to the door. It wasn't locked, and he stepped inside. As soon as it latched, a pair of furry hands threw him against the door. Ratash was in his face, claws slashing his shirt downward and to the side. His foot rose and a killing claw tore his pants. A few slashes later, Ratash yanked the ribbons that used to be his shirt off his torso. Irus was at his waist, chewing through his slacks. He tore the waist apart, and the pants fell. The force of his clothes being ripped off sent him to his knees.

"Guys, wait, wait! I'm not ready!"

An orange muzzle bent low to his face. "Come on!"

Irus was pulling him up by his arm, and Malcolm rose to his feet. Ratash turned and ran across the apartment to the bedroom. Irus led him there and held him in the door-frame. Ratash threw open the closet door. Malcolm couldn't close his mouth.

A sphere occupied the entire closet. It led to some-place with green grass, so at first it looked like Earth, but then a two-legged creature twice his size with scales, feath-ers, and fur walked by, a bovine with translucent skin be-side it.

"Is that...?"

"It's our own personal portal to Tavax," Irus said.

Ratash ran into the sphere. He appeared inside it but Malcolm saw a distorted image of him projected around the sphere turning his head and looking over his shoulder at them, waiting.

Irus nudged him. Malcolm walked up to the sphere. He had only seen one in person once before, at the conven-tion, when the Archeons brought freshly-slaughtered bulls into the convention center. It had turned Malcolm's stom-ach at the time, but watching how they ate had been a cul-tural experience unlike any other.

Malcolm ducked his head and walked through. The air on the other side smelled different, tasted different. Gravity felt slightly higher, and the light from the sun in the sky was green instead of yellow. Malcolm turned to it, and it did not hurt his eyes. Irus followed him a second later.

Ratash dashed to the right. Malcolm and Irus ran after him. More portals hovered here, arranged on either side of a wide path. Judging by the worn dirt, there had once been many more spheres. They passed one hovering globe every ten strides or so. Malcolm turned to Irus.

"Where are we? Where are we going?"

"You'll see. It was hard for him to wait until you came home. He's been pacing the house for hours."

Ratash turned and dove into a portal. Malcolm and Irus veered toward that sphere and ran through it as well. Malcolm guessed this was the same planet, as the gravity and sunlight felt the same. The land reminded Malcolm of drawings of what prehistoric Earth looked like: long stretches of bare dirt, large leafy ferns everywhere, giant mammals gathered in herds.

Ratash was already fifty yards ahead of them, and Irus led Malcolm to follow. The human had a difficult time keeping up with them; the fox tail was pulling farther ahead.

He and Irus were keeping pace with a herd of mammoth-like things. The resemblance ended at the thick fur coat and elephant-like feet. Their faces were more like a cat's, and they had no tusks. Malcolm wished he could stop and look at them, but Ratash had veered into the herd.

The cat-mammoths stampeded forward. Irus stopped and held his arm out. Malcolm halted behind it. Between the moving legs of the mammoths that ran in front of him, Malcolm saw Ratash climbing up the flank of a young calf and then clamping his jaws over the back of its neck as the calf screamed. The herd stomped past them. Malcolm looked upstream, and the line of cat-mammoths stretched as far as he could see up the prehistoric landscape.

The calf fell. The herd now ran around the other side of the raptor and the calf, so Malcolm had an unobscured view of them. The incredible amount of dust the herd kicked up drifted upstream.

The migrating herd veered so far around the kill it created a new line that ran to the horizon parallel to the one that had existed prior. Malcolm wondered if they would meet in the same place.

The herd migrated far enough away from Ratash that the dust blew away entirely. Ratash stood on top of it, holding its neck as the calf breathed its last. The thing was easily five times the size of the raptor and still young.

"Holy shit."

Irus turned to him, his wagging tail brushing Malcolm's crotch. "Yep, this is what's been living in your house for the last year."

"I knew he was a predator, but wow."

"Don't be afraid of him. Nothing has changed."

"I'm not afraid."

"You just pissed on your feet."

"I did?" Now he felt warm liquid covering his toes. "Oh, shit. I didn't even feel..."

Irus turned to him, his muzzle right next to Malcolm's ear. "You've never been afraid before, have you?"

"Yeah... I've been scared."

"When you lose control of yourself, that's real fear."

He took Malcolm's hand and led him to the kill. The calf was still not dead. Malcolm thought he wasn't afraid, but the closer they got to Ratash, the faster his heart raced. By the time they were ten yards away, he was sweating.

"Okay, you're right. That was terrifying. I've never seen him do this before."

"Everybody feels this. Especially prey species. They all learn to take control of their instincts. You will, too."

The calf finally stopped moving. Ratash leaped down and sliced open the abdomen, standing fast against the torrent of blood that washed over him. Ratash grabbed a hunk of something inside and gulped it down. Lube dripped from his slit like he was pissing. Irus must have recognized the hesitation in Malcolm's step.

"Hormones surge during a kill. It's normal."

"Jesus!"

"This is what he always was. It's a lot different now, isn't it?"

"Fuck yeah!" He watched Ratash eat for a few seconds, then turned to Irus. "So what about you? Am I going to see what you look like during a hunt?"

Irus wagged his tail. "Ah, immature species. A little bit of fear rises up, and the brain shuts off. I don't hunt. I can't."

"Oh yeah, you said you reverted, didn't you?"

Irus stopped them five yards away while Ratash gulped down another mouthful of internal organs.

"I reverted a few times when I was young. Ratash kept me stable. We still haven't found a trigger for me. It happens at random. One time I reverted in front of several hundred people. Ratash brought me back."

"Shit..."

"I can feel it wiggling in the back of my mind. Like my sanity can come loose at any moment. It still does. Ratash was afraid for a long time he caused it when we decided to start fucking around with each other. My sanity just started slipping out after that. We're sure it was coincidence. Ratash always puts it back. I hope you never see me like that. It's why I need him. He keeps me from becoming that. Just in case, he hunts the meat. I don't."

Ratash swallowed one last mouthful of organs. He visibly relaxed. He raised his foot and carved open the skin and fur of one of the legs and ripped out a chunk of meat.

He turned to Malcolm and Irus. At the sight of his blood-spattered face and arms, Malcolm stumbled a few steps backwards. Ratash walked toward him. Malcolm almost took another step, but he caught the fox's eye and planted his feet as the raptor neared.

Ratash stood before him, still holding the hunk of leg muscle. Malcolm wasn't sure what made him do it, but he held out his hands. Ratash dropped the meat in his hands. He then stretched his neck and nudged his cheek with his muzzle.

"Holy fucking shit, that felt good! I thought I forgot how to hunt! Eat!"

Malcolm looked down at it. It was so warm it felt like it just came off a grill.

"Are you sure I can eat this?"

Ratash bumped noses with him. "It's only dangerous when it starts to rot. You're getting it so fresh it's almost alive."

Malcolm looked at it. He looked at Ratash. He raised the meat to his mouth and took a bite. It was surprisingly soft and hot, and it tasted like rare hamburger.

Ratash danced from foot to foot, nudging Malcolm on the shoulder with his snout, and then ran back to the kill. Irus followed him up to the calf. Malcolm held his steak and took another bite. He had already forgotten how unusual this was.

2

The mammoth-like creature fell to the dirt. Six predators piled on top of it, including Vae and another Relian theropod. The other four predators Lucy did not recognize. One was a quadruped, and the others seemed to be something in between.

Lucy stood off to the side with the onlooking foxes, jaw hanging open. Tema had her arm around her, never allowing her to forget this wasn't a dream. The predators cheered and howled in victory. The migrating herd gave the kill site a wide berth, and the dust quickly blew away in the warm breeze. The six predators began carving into the kill. Vae was slicing open the abdomen, tearing off pieces of its lungs and swallowing them whole.

Lucy was shaking, terrified but still in awe.

Tema nuzzled her cheek. "If it helps, just imagine all of them as lawyers."

That was surprisingly easy to do. She imagined every one of these hunters in tailored suits and ties tearing at the prey, taking whatever they could from it, and yet nobody fought over the kill. Everyone took it down, everyone shared it. They were actually more civilized than the usual company she kept.

Vae turned to them. The other raptor leaped from the kill and faced his fox. Tema rose, leading Lucy to her feet. The other fox approached the kill. Lucy watched his raptor pull a piece from the kill and feed it to him. Tema walked up to Vae, leading Lucy at arm's length. Vae ripped a hunk of meat from the kill and fed it to Tema. She bit into it, chewed, swallowed.

Vae pulled a piece of muscle from the kill and held it out to Lucy in her jaws. Lucy reached out and pulled the meat from her mouth. Lucy held Vae's gaze as she took a bite. Vae nuzzled her neck and then reached for another piece.

Lucy felt a little self-conscious eating from a kill she did not make, but nobody stopped the foxes, so it must have been polite. Lucy finished the meat. She ignored the blood dripping from herself, though she felt like a cavewoman. Somehow Vae knew how much she would eat and stopped carving pieces off for her. Tema had her fill at about the same time, and then Vae left the kill. The other predators were still busy stripping it. One of them was chewing on a rib bone, and Lucy stared.

She felt Tema next to her. "He is a Tava, one of the native species of this world. Believe it or not, they don't eat meat. They eat bone."

"Wow."

The Tava opened his jaws and snapped off another rib that was twice as thick as Lucy's arm. He chewed it like cereal. His jaw muscles were enormous, and his teeth looked disproportionately thick compared to his skull.

Lucy felt Vae standing on her other side. "I speak his language. Go and meet him."

"Is it safe? It's not rude?"

"He won't bite," Vae said, holding her claws together. "And he's actually just as curious about you. You're a new species, and he saw me feeding you, so he's wondering what you are, too."

Lucy took a step forward. "Hi."

Vae said something in a language made entirely of throaty growls. The Tava set the rib down and approached her. He was a quadruped about four times the size of a Golden Retriever, covered in black and green fur. He stood chest-high to Lucy at the shoulder.

Lucy just now realized why this planet looked so familiar. It resembled those depictions of prehistoric Earth, with woolly mammoths and saber-toothed cats roaming the land. The Tava were more like thick-toothed dogs. Everything on this planet was a giant mammal.

The Tava scented her. He made a few throaty growls.

"He wants to know if you've ever been offworld before."

"I haven't."

Vae translated. The Tava spoke again. Vae clicked her claws.

"He wants to try a language exchange. He's never heard English before. He's going to say a sentence in his language. Try to imitate him. He will try to imitate whatever you say. Ready?"

Lucy nodded.

The Tava made a couple growls. Lucy did her best to repeat them. It wasn't unlike making fun of the neighbor's dogs when they barked and growled at her, but this was not just noise. Even Lucy could tell it had structure.

"You just said 'I walk home' with an accent he has never heard before. Your turn. Make the sentence simple."

Lucy said the first thing that came to mind. "What big teeth you have."

The Tava imitated her. "Ut ig geeth oo ave." He tried again, this time moving his lips. "Wha ig eeth you ave. Wha bi-ig keeth you have."

Lucy smiled. She hoped she could learn just as quickly.

3

The Tava were enormous pack animals the size of tigers. They looked like dogs, but they had claws like a cat and they did not eat the meat. They were grinding solid bone. Ratash told Malcolm they were scavengers, and they once lived a life following predators from kill to kill, eating what they left behind. The saber-teeth were actually for mating display, and they considered large teeth to be beautiful.

Since they discovered their companion species, and portal physics, they opened this continent as hunting grounds. Now they did not need to trail the predators of their world, waiting for them to make a kill. They ate with the offworld predators who took down prey.

Malcolm sat at the hub of this world with Ratash and Irus. He had just watched a small pack of Tava consume an entire skeleton. The predators here knew to leave the bones for the locals, and Ratash was happy to, as the skeleton did not interest him in the slightest.

The hub wasn't as busy as usual. It was pretty much just the Tava and the Savex here, but some offworlders wandered about as well. Three Tava and six Savex walked along the hub, and they looked comical together. The Savex were the Tava's companion race, and they looked like feathery kangaroos. Ratash had told him they were not marsupials, but Malcolm couldn't help but see them as the lovechild of a parakeet and a macropod that hunted small mammals. Malcolm had a hard time believing there were small mammals on this world.

"How long has it been?" said the human.

Ratash was sitting next to him. "Six hours."

"Oh God, I need to get to bed. I got... I got work in the morning."

"It's Saturday," said Irus, sitting on his other side, munching on some kind of plant with thick leaves that grew in roughly spherical shapes.

"I took an extra shift. I told you last week."

Ratash nuzzled under his arm and sniffed his pit. "You don't need that fucking job now. You're coming with us."

"I am?"

"That's what this is all about. That's why we're here. We were never going to stay on Earth. We were looking for people who could come with us."

Malcolm stared at him. He stammered. "I... I... How? Jesus, it's like being a caveman. I can't live like this. I need a shower—how the hell does that work?"

"I smelled the substance you use to clean your skin," said Irus. "It's made of fatty oils and abrasive metal. You are not the only species that needs to clean its skin. There are metallic lakes you can bathe in and various plant oils you can rub. Some species have saliva and abrasive tongues that will work."

Malcolm laughed. "You want me to get a tonguebath from an alien?"

"Anything you need, it's out there."

"Humans," Ratash continued, "are not the only species that has to keep things clean. Don't worry about your teeth. There are soaps that will work on those, too. Reeds and insects can get between them. Plenty of species eat hair; they'll be happy to trim you."

"Well... What about the bathroom? How is that done? What about cleaning up after sex? Hell, what about preparing for it? It takes enough effort at home—I can't even think about how we'd do it here. "

"We'll show you how it's all done," said the fox. "Every planet has its own rules. Every species does things differently. Raptors only eat once every two or three days. Us omnivores need to know what plants we can eat. I'll show you. Here, try this."

He handed Malcolm a branch from the plant he had been eating. Malcolm took it, sniffed it, bit into one of the leaves. It tasted like rosemary and a chili pepper had crossbred. He swallowed.

"What is it?"

Ratash rubbed his claws. "In about two hours, it'll clear you out. Then I can fuck you all night. Lots of plants on other worlds have this effect."

Malcolm laughed and turned to the raptor. "That's not fair. What do you eat when I need to fuck you?"

"You'll know when I'm ready 'cause I'll be covered in blood."

"Um..."

Ratash swiped him down the arm lightly with his claws. "It's how my metabolism works. Everything is tied to the hunt. I wish you could experience it like I do. Hormones pump through my body even more than usual. Raptors often fuck over a kill we just made."

"That sounds freaky."

He reached over, fondled Malcolm's balls. Numerous people walked by, and they did not seem to notice. "You'll love it when it happens to you."

"You've been living this whole time without hunting..."

"That portal offworld was exactly what I needed."

Irus ribbed Malcolm. "He's trying to tell you he clogged the toilet again."

"Bastard."

Ratash released Malcolm's junk and faced the hub.

"We call it *killsex*. It's not a good translation, but it's about the only way to describe it. A special kind of sex Relian reptiles share. It's kinda the reason we take mates, so we can have someone to share it with. There's nothing like fucking while hormones are high after making a kill. Lots of mates meet up for that, spend a day or two together, then part ways, find each other again for another kill."

Malcolm laughed. "I was wondering how marriage worked with Relians."

"It's a bond only they understand," Irus said. "Many predators have something similar, but our raptors have it particularly strong. They might live for it if not for foxes pulling them in other directions. We help them as much as they help us."

Malcolm sat up and spread his arms across both of their shoulders. "So... So what are we going to do out here?"

Irus peeked from his sheath from being touched. "Explore. Learn. Meet people. Broaden your mind. All the things you couldn't do before while you were an automaton at the factory."

"No TV. No music. No beer. What's to do?"

"You have lot to unlearn," Ratash said, "and since the day I met you, I wanted to help you unlearn it."

"Once you start exploring, you won't need to be entertained. You will live it yourself."

"You'd have it better than a movie star. You'd actually be on another planet teaching aliens how to love. Or being taught."

He clicked his claws. The human smiled as he stared at the feathery kangaroos talking to the thick-toothed dogs.

4

Lucy heard some strange sounds from behind her and turned to look. A Tava was leading a furred biped along the hub. Lucy did not recognize the young one.

"She is caring for a Mezel child," Vae said.

The two walked past them. Lucy followed them with her eyes and started walking again.

Tema spoke now. "Mezel infants make loud sounds that adults of the species find annoying. They're genetically wired to react that way so they'll want to care for the infant. It's not uncommon for them to let others raise their children during this part of their lives. The Tava actually find the sounds melodic."

The Mezel biped opened its mouth and made a screeching sound. It pierced Lucy's ears and went straight to her toes, curling them backwards.

"Humans have a similar love-hate relationship with their own offspring," Vae continued. "I think some other species will enjoy the squall human babies make. They know what mammals need."

"This place is unbelievable," Lucy gasped.

"It's only the beginning," Tema replied.

Lucy was walking down the hub, Vae on her right, Tema on her left. Giant dogs and birdlike kangaroos passed them, as well as other offworlders. Many stopped to sniff her. A few spoke English, which stunned her. She wondered why they learned English when so few people spoke it. Tema told her that's what happens when people are free: they can pursue what interests them instead of only whatever earns money.

"I made a list of places I want to take you right away," Vae said. "I have a couple worlds I like to visit when I'm in the mood for tracking but not for a fight afterward. I know a species whose females lay a clutch of eggs every couple of weeks, whether they're fertilized or not. When they joined the contacted universe, they designated an island for themselves to leave their eggs. An entire island full of clutches to find. Some of the most satisfying scents to track, and I'd love for you to come with me."

"To eat raw eggs?"

"Your body can handle them. It can handle a lot more than what you've been led to believe."

"Vae, we should get something *fresh*!"

The raptor clicked her claws. "Even better. We'll take you to meet a species with males who lay eggs."

"They what?"

"The female lays the real ones," Tema said, "and the male lays a decoy clutch for predators to find. Their eggs are delicious."

"You've had them?" Lucy asked.

Vae clicked her claws. "We convinced a few to drop some into our mouths. That's a hunting experience unlike any other."

Tema's tail was wagging. "Evolution crafted the male's eggs to be tastier. They're the only intelligent species who does this, and they are proud of what their bodies do. Some of them love showing off, especially in front of predators."

Lucy giggled, felt the fur on Tema's back. "That would be weird."

"Once we figure out how to make up for your lack of fur," Vae continued, "we can go anywhere."

"And eat eggs? Go hunting? Doesn't anyone have to make a living out here?"

Vae bumped noses with her. "In the contacted universe, there are no shareholders who expect a return, no executives who demand enormous salaries, no rent or debts to force you to keep going somewhere you don't want to be to do something you don't want to do."

Tema finished the thought: "You'll be surprised how little you have to work when you're not required to hunt for someone else all your life."

Vae: "You became a lawyer because you were pressured to go into something that would make money. When you were a child, what did you want to be?"

Lucy blinked a few times as she struggled to comprehend all the people in sight. "I never really had an answer to that. One time I told the teacher I just wanted to be myself when I grew up. All the kids laughed at me."

"Now you can do that," Tema said. "You can just be yourself. Oh, look who else is here."

Lucy saw someone so out of place here it made her aware of how much she stood out.

"Malcolm!"

He was walking through the hub in the opposite direction with a raptor and a fox of his own. He zeroed in on the English and waved to her.

"Lucy!"

He ran down the hub against traffic. He hugged her. She hugged him back, though it felt odd without clothes. They separated and looked one another over. An orange raptor stood next to Malcolm, facing Lucy. Malcolm had new scars on his body where claws had been, which made Lucy smirk.

"Oh my God, I haven't seen you since the convention! You're here, too?"

Lucy smiled. "I never thought I'd see you again. Ratash hasn't broken you?"

"I'm tougher than a marine, remember?"

"You weren't kidding. Sorry I didn't call. It's been a busy year."

"Are you leaving Earth, too?"

Lucy looked around. "Do you have to ask?"

They held one another and laughed.

Washington D. C.

I

CJ sat alone in her office, the door shut to keep the world out. It was the first time since she took this job that she had ever wanted to do that.

Rive had been gone for two months. CJ figured that was more than enough time to open a portal into every household in the country that had a pair of Relians in it. She expected him back by now, but then she remembered households in other nations also needed spheres.

She always knew that raptor made her job easy, but of course she didn't know how easy until he was gone. Now she had to drive everywhere, appoint local police officers to perform tasks, and delegate to people she didn't trust. If this kept up, she feared she would have to hire staff and turn this department into a bureaucracy.

Relian Relations was becoming a government job. She had to work through others instead of taking care of matters personally. The president had loved this cabinet position because it had such a small budget in relation to the work it did. Now people were starting to ask questions.

Rive's absence was getting harder to cover for. People noticed her expenses rising, and pretty soon someone would deduce it meant Rive wasn't transporting her from site to site.

For the last month and a half, things had balanced out. There had been a sharp decrease in Relian Relations incidents since Rive left Earth. The remaining instances meant she had to fly places and stay in hotels, which had kept her expenses about where they had been before, but as they added up, her expenses exceeded her usual compared to the number of incidents she responded to.

The whole time she traveled the country, she pondered that it was pointless. The Relians were leaving with their humans, and she was not part of it. She had a brief glimpse of an alien planet and multiple alien species, and then she had to return. Nobody noticed her absence, nobody asked questions, but she knew the questions would come.

She had just returned from a drive to Delaware. It was only a couple hours away from DC, and she had to see for herself if it was true. She had knocked on Lucy Schrifton's door. No answer. To her surprise, the front door was unlocked. Inside she had found a pile of clothing. Business attire. Lucy searched the house and found a sphere in the spare bedroom. People were visible on it. Some of the species she recognized but most she did not. When she saw an unclothed human woman walk by, flanked by a pair of Relians, she turned around and walked out the door, locking it behind her.

Before she left Delaware, she drove up to the law firm where Lucy worked and asked about her. Lucy was still showing up to work as usual, as were Vae and Tema. CJ figured all the people were still going about their routines, weaning themselves off human civilization. She could only imagine what this transition was like.

The drive back to DC had been lonely and depressing. Now it was well past business hours, and CJ sat at her desk staring at the filing cabinet, the one that was still empty be-

cause her department had yet to generate enough paper-
work to fill it.

She kept replaying the interviews over and over in her
mind. She had even played some of the tapes to be sure she
remembered correctly. She welcomed the new year by listening to the first interview. She tried to imagine herself as
a scholar a hundred years from now attempting to understand this moment in history.

When she had recorded the interview, she did it under
the assumption that the Relians would be here for that
long. Now she listened to it from a new point of view, and it
was so obvious what the raptors and foxes were doing she
wondered why she hadn't noticed. The raptors had taken
the humans under their wing, so to speak. The people had
become part of the Relian pair.

She had spent much of her time preparing the attorneys for the case that would not happen. She flew across
the country to settle minor disputes that she knew meant
nothing in the long run. All she was doing was buying time
for their eventual departure. It had been eating away at CJ
for weeks, and now it was mid-January and she was still
coming to grips with it.

The aliens were leaving. The most important moment
in human history, and they were just going to leave. All CJ
had done was keep the peace while the Relians decided
that their humans could adapt to their way of life. She still
wasn't sure if she felt proud of that or depressed.

She rose from her chair and walked to the filing cabinet. She quietly opened the top drawer. A sphere the size
of her fist, just large enough to slip a note through, rested in
the back. Once in a while she saw Rive through it, but right
now all she saw was bare dirt and blue sky enclosing a landscape that reminded her of images from the last ice age. She
shut the drawer, silently latching it, then held the filing cabinet and sighed.

They were leaving. Right now. The process had started, and it had been long enough for Rive to open ways across the country. He was probably visiting Relian households all over the world by now, leading those people to whatever planet that was. In just a few weeks, she would not have a job, and it would be up to her to explain it. She wasn't sure what she wanted to tell the president, let alone the nation.

The phone on her desk rang. It didn't startle her, though it was an intrusion into her thoughts. She turned around and picked up the receiver.

"Secretary Rhine."

She recognized the voice of the secretary of state telling her to turn on the news. She already knew what she would see.

2

A man in a ski mask pointed behind himself at the fox in the cage, who was soaked in blood, snarling and screaming like a dog with rabies. The angle of the camera meant the audience could not see the bottom of the cage and all the dead dogs that lined it.

"One day she was coherent and friendly," he was saying. "Now look at her. Do you want this living in your neighborhood? Do you want it near your children? Do you want it serving your food, or working in your office?"

The fox in the background clawed the air through the bars, screaming at the top of her lungs.

"We're sending these tapes to every news outlet in the country. Someone will report it. Someone will show the world the truth of what we've let into our homes! You can't hide the truth forever!"

The tape paused, and the reporter's voice played over it. "NBC news has learned that this was recorded late last year, and that the people responsible for this dramatic video are now dead, killed by the very fox you see."

The screen changed to a shot of the reporter in Portland, just outside the police station. "Authorities tell us the tape was not released to the public because it was evidence in a pending self-defense lawsuit involving a pair of Relians. The state is prosecuting."

CJ changed the channel to CBS. A pie graph showing the latest survey results took up most of the screen. The question at the top read *Do you feel the Relians are dangerous?* The anchor was narrating over it.

"...latest poll showing over seventy percent of people surveyed are concerned that the Relians might in fact be a danger to them and their community. This poll was conducted just after news of the tape began to spread."

She changed the channel to ABC. The anchor was on camera, talking into it. The graphic next to him was a still shot from the tape, the snarling fox reaching for the camera.

"...continuing coverage on this breaking story. The leaked tape showing a reverted fox. Is the government doing enough to protect you and your loved ones? We are receiving reports of people everywhere clamoring for the federal government to take a more active role. Our cameras are on the ground capturing footage of protests that have sprung up around the nation. Throngs of people clamoring for someone to do something to protect the American people. Numerous senators and members of the house of representatives have come forward with proposals for new legislation. These proposals range from mandatory muzzling in public, to defanging and declawing. Our latest ABC news poll shows public opinion shifting away from a favorable view of the Relians."

The screen changed to a bar graph. Four answers were possible, and the bar on the far right had ninety-six percent.

"The question that was asked was whether or not it was fair that Relians are receiving food stamps regardless of their income, and as you can see, ninety-six percent of our poll shows an unfavorable opinion of this."

CJ's heart sank. The news had only just now broke about this tape. There had been no time for public opinion to change, and yet the press claimed that it had. She wondered how many people had been part of this survey, and when it had been conducted.

"As a follow-up, respondents in and around areas that had Relian visitors were asked just how safe they felt in their community."

The bar chart showed an overwhelming majority answered *very unsafe*.

"And finally we asked if they would be in favor of state or federal laws mandating some sort of precautions to protect innocent lives and children around the Relians..."

The chart showed almost a hundred percent in favor of it. CJ looked down at the floor, rubbing her forehead. The phone rang again. CJ did not want to answer it, but she picked it up.

3

The news reports never stopped. The more the press reported on it, the stronger public opinion became. The press ran hour-long segments talking to people about this revelation. All the clips showed people who were scared and uncomfortable around the Relians.

Over the next week, CJ saw coverage of protests in every major city around the nation. Protesters carrying signs reading "end the fear" and "dinosaurs go home" and "Foxes are around: hide the children." Lots and lots of interviews with the people on the ground. CJ had seen other protests before, and the police broke them up within an hour. Not these. They persisted for weeks.

Politicians announced joint legislation proposals, and these merged into a single proposal: Relian Rights Act. It had nothing to do with anyone's rights and everything to do with ending the food stamp program, requiring the Relians to get jobs and abide by all applicable laws and guidelines set forth by the employer, upon punishment by prison time, and requiring raptors and foxes to attend empathy courses and wear special gloves and muzzles in public that had yet to be invented.

The press reported on people clamoring for the law to require defanging and declawing, and the people began calling for just that.

The press reported that people were afraid of the Relians, and people became afraid.

The press reported that the foxes were unstable and could not be trusted, and the people started repeating it. The press reported people repeating it, and people repeated it even more.

CJ had given interview after interview, telling the whole story about the tape and the circumstances under which it was made. Some news networks aired those clips but immediately afterward put on an expert who refuted every word CJ said. She felt like a rowboat caught in a hurricane, and no matter how many times she repeated the entire story, the press focused on the violence, the fear, and the blood.

The speed at which they reacted to the news should have been enough to convince anyone that something was amiss. Politicians never reacted quickly to anything unless something else was going on.

Now CJ wished she had people to answer all the questions coming her way. She felt there was no harm discussing the pending lawsuit now that the key piece of evidence was public. CJ was working with the legal team to make other pieces of evidence public as well, such as the photographs of the crime scene, the identities of the kidnappers, and the taped interview with Veronica and the Relians. Lawyers were worried it would compromise the case. CJ declared the case already compromised, so they had to shift public opinion the other way.

The evidence was released. The press presented it, and then each outlet interviewed experts who dismissed it as circumstantial. CJ was watching one on NBC right now. He was old and white, and had *Dr.* in front of his name.

"While I agree we need to consider all circumstances surrounding this, I think the fact remains that this is possible. It is possible for a fox to become this monster. If it can happen in Portland, it can happen anywhere. What if a fox becomes angry at his boss? Will that trigger a reaction like this? What if it happens around a small child? How are we going to protect ourselves?"

She muted the television and tried to concentrate on jumping through the hoops to make as much evidence public as possible. She hoped Rive was right, that the truth would survive and the right people would react with their brains instead of their emotions.

The one question on CJ's mind was why now. The press had those tapes months ago, so why not broadcast them then? CJ suspected someone had given them permission to go against the president's request for restraint, but she could not prove it.

The phone rang. CJ picked it up. It was another reporter asking her if the rumors were true and people were disappearing all over the country. It caught CJ off guard. For weeks it had been the same questions over and over, but this was different.

"I have heard no such rumor."

"What about the rumor that the Relians are abducting innocent people and taking them to unknown locations?"

"I know of no such rumor."

"Can you tell us anything about the reports that the Relians all over the country are nowhere to be found?"

"I have not heard—" Her phone beeped. A call on the other line. "That is all I have to say. Goodbye." She hung up, waited a moment, and then picked up the other line.

"Secretary Rhine."

"CJ!" It was Mildred, one of the attorneys she had been preparing for the Portland case. "We have a problem. They're gone!"

"Gone?"

"Ekal, Nipe, and Veronica. Police searched their apartment and nobody's there. They found a note written in Veronica's handwriting. It said 'gone fishing'."

CJ stared into space for a moment. Then she snapped out of it. "I'll call you back."

She hung up, pulled out her day planner, and looked up the numbers she needed to dial to reach the Minister of Relian Relations in England.

4

CJ thought the media had been in a frenzy before, but now the coverage was nonstop. When nothing new happened, they got experts on camera to argue all the angles. Cable and network news became a shouting match of opinion and analysis, and sandwiched in between all of that—gasping for air—was actual journalism.

Endless photos and videos of empty apartments and houses. Shots of the notes the people left behind. They ranged from the cryptic "gone fishing" to heartfelt goodbye letters.

CJ had managed to get a look at one of those notes and read the entire thing. The woman had written the whole truth about where she was going, and what the Relians had done for her, and that she had been accepted as part of the Relian pair to live offworld as one of them. The media never read that part, only the emotional highlights where people said goodbye to friends and family, making sure they knew it was permanent.

They released polls that showed people were terrified of being abducted. Almost overnight, commercials began to appear advertising lead-lined "safe rooms" and bomb shelters guaranteed to prevent abduction.

The press gave lots of air time to experts who engaged in speculation as to the motive behind these abductions. Opinions ranged from an elaborate hunting scheme, to finding human livestock for breeding on another planet, to brainwashing. *To Serve Man* became a popular graphic and refrain on cable and network news.

CJ dodged the press. She even hired an intern to field the calls so she could get in touch with the local police departments to find out exactly what they had found. She drove back to Delaware and was escorted around Lucy's house. The portal was gone. So were the people. They had taken nothing with them. At the police station, CJ read Lucy's handwritten note.

Dear everyone,

I am leaving Earth now with my raptor, Vae, and my fox, Tema. They offered to make me part of their group and to teach me how to live in the contacted universe. How can I say no? They have done so much for me in the short time they've been here, and I trust them. What little I've seen of life outside society leads me to believe there is no reason to stay. Life on Earth is stress, worry and pointless work that forces me to be a hypocrite until I the day I die. Vae and

Tema showed me a life of exploration and wonder. A life in which the pursuit of knowledge and understanding and personal fulfillment is the goal, instead of staying ahead of the bills. I will not miss it on Earth, but there are some people I will miss. I wish I could take you with me, but one human is all a raptor and a fox can handle.

She concluded with personal messages to friends and family and coworkers. The press reported on this note a few days later, and they only read the emotional farewells at the end, nothing from the beginning. She returned to her office, checked the filing cabinet. The portal was still there. She considered writing a note of her own and sending it off-world, but she could not think of anything to write.

CJ found herself locked in meeting rooms answering the same questions to different officials. She denied everything. It seemed like the right thing to do until she got a grip on what was happening.

Then she received a call from someone at CNN for a sit-down interview. She sat in her office with the phone to her ear. Finally she realized there was nothing left to fight for except the truth. She agreed to the interview.

5

CJ sat in a studio newsroom in CNN's Washington headquarters. Anita Jones, the anchor, sat opposite her, hair styled to frame her face. CJ never realized how unnatural it looked in person until now.

"Good evening," said the anchorwoman. "We've all heard the rumors, we've heard the reports circulating over the past few weeks, but so far the official word from Washington has been mum. Joining me in the studio tonight is White House Secretary of Relian Relations CJ Rhine." She turned partway to CJ. "Thank you for joining us, Madame

Secretary. I understand you wish to clear up all the rumors that have been flying about recently?"

"That's right. I want to tell the American people exactly what happened and why."

"I'd like to start with the question that is most on America's mind. Just how in danger are ordinary Americans of being abducted by predatory Relians?"

CJ had resolved to keep her composure no matter what the press threw at her. She managed to resist punching this woman.

"If I may start at the beginning, and then I will answer specific questions."

Jones nodded and crossed her legs. CJ faced the camera. One of the men behind the camera gestured for her to address her words to the interviewer, but CJ ignored him.

"As most of you know, I have been working very closely with the Relians for the last year, since before the position of Relian Relations was created. The Archeon Rive in particular."

"The one who was made of metal?" said the anchorwoman, trying to bring CJ's attention back to her.

"He was not made of metal. His body had been destroyed during the disaster and then partially reconstructed out of a sentient species of metal. It is just this kind of oversimplification I am here to address. I will be to the point. Nobody is in danger of being abducted. The Relians were never dangerous. The Relians never even intended to remain on Earth."

The anchorwoman was about to speak. CJ cut her off.

"The Relians are gone. They found what they were looking for, which was people they could take with them. The people left Earth entirely by their own will because they were the right kind of people to live in the contacted universe. Raptors and foxes were not hunting those people, or searching for livestock, or anything like that. As for the danger Relians posed, let me reiterate that the Relians were never dangerous. The fox in that video had been abducted, separated from her raptor, subjected to torture, and forced to fight feral dogs to the death. Those men made her revert to her old ways. Would any of us do better under such circumstances?"

"Secretary—Secretary—we have heard from experts—perhaps you are unaware—who agree that regardless of circumstances, the fact that it happened shows that there is risk—"

"As for the rumor that Relians are harvesting the planet for human livestock, or finding people to breed for human cattle, it's absurd. They spent months learning our languages, lived among us, went to work with us. A whole year of that just to harvest us? That doesn't make any sense. They have no interest in doing that. There are plenty of things to eat on other planets. I have seen it myself. They don't want us for livestock. They wanted to rescue those people."

"If I may, Ms. Rhine, rescue them from what?"

CJ now faced Anita Jones. The cameras on set adjusted to her new position. "From human society. There's a lot more to it than that, but I think we can all agree the stress and worry of everyday life is something we'd all like to get away from. We're so used to it we don't think to ask. Why is there stress and worry? It's because we live in a Darwinian culture. As advanced as we are, as far as we've come, we still live in a survival-of-the-fittest environment. Aliens have learned how to move on from that, and they wanted to take us with them. It was a surprise to them that they could. They did not expect to find anyone who could adapt to a new way of life."

"What evidence do you have of their intentions?"

"I have seen another planet. Rive told me everything they were doing, and why they were really here. I only learned about it a few months ago. Until then, I was under the impression that this was going to be a long-term arrangement."

"So you have only his word to go on?"

"His and the word of every human being I've interviewed over the last few months."

"So again, testimony? No hard evidence of their intentions?"

CJ smiled. "With respect, nobody in the media has hard evidence of their intentions either, and yet the press is reporting on it anyway."

"You have to admit the evidence we do have is compelling. People going missing just as it comes out how dangerous the Relians are."

"If you put a human being in that same situation and forced her to fight for her life, she would be just as dangerous. We've known from the beginning that foxes have an animal nature, and might revert to it. They told us that when they first arrived. Now that we've seen it, it shows just what a fox is without her raptor."

"Admittedly, and surely even you must concede, Secretary Rhine, the fact that it happened at all is cause for concern. Are you asking the American people to take the government's word for it that we have seen the last of the Relians? That there is no danger to any man, woman, or child on this planet of being abducted for some unknown purpose?"

"I am announcing what I have known for some time. Nobody was afraid of the Relians until the press began telling people to be afraid."

"We are reporting the facts as they happen, Madame Secretary."

"Then why have you not told viewers Nipe was kidnapped and tortured? Why have you not reported the contents of the goodbye notes on air? They say a whole lot more than just gone fishing; they explain why they're leaving, what the Relians are doing for them, and where they're going."

"Where they believe they are going, we can be sure, but how do they know? You only know what you saw, but clearly the Archeons are capable of much more than they let on."

A man offstage was making a hand gesture. Anita Jones turned to the camera.

"We'll be right back with more of this extraordinary interview with White House Secretary of Relian Relations CJ Rhine."

The cameras turned off. Makeup people rushed in and touched up both CJ's and the Anita's face. They still had two more segments to go. CJ hoped this one-on-one exposé would be able to cut through the noise.

Her phone rang. CJ reached into her pocket and extended the antenna.

"CJ. Make it quick. I'm in an interview."

"I'm still in the White House," Mildred whispered. "They're about to indict you on criminal charges, CJ."

"No kidding?"

"You just admitted you knew about their plan. You didn't tell anyone here about it. They're using the T-word."

"Crap."

"They're going to confiscate everything in your office, everything in your house. They're already building a case against you."

Her first instinct was to run, but the men behind the camera were gesturing she had one minute left before they went back on. She remained in her seat.

"Do me a favor. Make sure they don't shut me out of my office yet. There's something in there I need to get."

"I'll get it for you. What is it?"

"Just squat there. They can't take anything until formal charges are made. I have to tell the people what's going on no matter what it does to me."

"Good luck. Don't take too long."

CJ closed the phone and composed herself for the second segment.

"Welcome back," said Anita Jones. "I'm here with White House Secretary of Relian Relations CJ Rhine, who has quite a story to tell about where the Relians went and why they were here. Would you care to elaborate more on why, in your view, the American people have nothing to fear from further abductions, or a pending invasion?"

CJ had a feeling her body was burning a ridiculous amount of calories from the act of not strangling her.

6

CJ opened the door to her office. Nobody was here, but it didn't look like anything was missing either, so she was not too late. Quickly she ran to her desk and grabbed a pen and the sticky-note pad.

Rive, they are investigating me for high treason. Everything I have done will be confiscated. I will have to testify. I will tell them everything. I already have, in public. I could use your help. —CJ

She reached into filing cabinet and dropped the entire pad into the tiny portal, hoping it would not blow away in the wind. She withdrew her hand and waited. Nobody was on the other side. The pad was still beside the portal, gently fluttering in the breeze. She closed the cabinet and walked out the door. Tomorrow she expected to be under house arrest, and then it would be real.

Labccr

I

The large sphere remained open behind them as they stood underneath a gas giant. It reminded them of Lesa, but Labccr was actually a moon of the gas giant nestled inside its ring system. Several hundred bright fragments glinted in the sky. The moon's orbit was slightly faster than the ring system itself, so these fragments would either be deflected by the moon's gravity or drawn into it.

The sky was black. The moon had enough atmosphere to support life, but the distant star was so far away it did not light or heat this moon. Light came from the ring fragments and from the gentle glow of the gas giant itself. Heat came from the giant's gravity stretching and twisting this moon's shape as it completed its elliptical orbit around the planet.

The hub here only consisted of spheres that led around the moon, vital to the survival of the people. Without warning, the ground on Labccr could start shaking, and sometimes it would swirl and become molten. The locals remained vigilant about the condition of the soil and the position of the planet in the sky. They had developed special instincts that could predict when the next quake would hit, and when to run for the nearest portal. Entire hemispheres often remained molten for years at a time.

They had already verified the hub from the other side to make sure it was still on solid ground. Now they stood on warm soil beholding the planet that filled the sky.

Friend's face appeared superimposed over the gas giant. "It's still here."

"Where?" Deka said. "Why is it here?"

"I don't know. Perhaps it wants to see the sights. Right now it's on the other side of the moon, swimming in the lava."

"Maybe it finally figured out the laws of physics don't apply to it anymore," said the Krone.

"Are the people here all right?" Sonjaa said.

"Everyone is fine." The gas giant itself seemed to be speaking to them. "It seems to be avoiding the people. I'm not sure if it knows they are there. It must, and yet it is leaving them alone."

"It is where people are not," Kylac muttered. "That's what a fox's instincts leads him to seek. Or create. No scents for half a planet. No wonder it came here."

"Nobody else even knows they're here," Friend said. "Hopefully it will stay that way."

"The best thing to do is evacuate these people," Sorven said.

"Yes," said Deka, "let's find them."

Deka began walking through the hub, checking the different portals. Gravity on this planet was weak compared to what they were used to, so Deka bounded along easily. So far they didn't see anyone. The only sign of life here was the tiny trees.

They resembled bonsai trees and shrubs, and everyone walked carefully around the ankle-high plants. This was as high as they would ever grow due to the lack of light. They did not absorb light from the distant star but from the ringshine. The soil was also unstable and prone to becoming molten, so their roots were shallow, and everything on the plants was retractable. When the temperature became too hot, the plants folded into tiny, rocklike balls capable of surviving the molten soil indefinitely until it hardened again. When the ground cooled, they unfolded and took root. These plants covered much of the planet, making it look like a vast bonsai garden.

Friend descended from the sky and joined them at the hub, fur absorbing most of the dim light that reached this moon, making him appear much darker than the surrounding landscape.

"This wouldn't be a good planet to try to trap them on. Its orbit will decay in only a hundred years. It will break up before it reaches the planet's atmosphere, become part of the rings, and its biological components will impact another moon and eventually give rise to new life there."

"You say that about every planet we visit," said Kylac. "No world is good enough."

"Because you can't trap them anywhere forever. You are not thinking about this in the long term."

Sonjaa stopped at a portal. "Maybe you should hurry up and make your own universe so you can take your old ways with you." She stuck her head through and scented the other side.

"Yes," Deka said, "shouldn't you have figured out where you are by now? Why haven't you? Hasn't it been long enough?"

Friend remained impassive as he wandered the hub with them. Each person saw Friend as facing them personally. "I've never stopped working on it, but it eludes me still. I would like nothing more than to understand exactly what the Lake is and how it works."

"You can't do it," said Deka. "Even after all this time, you still can't. It's as if something is holding you back."

"Perhaps something is."

"You're so smart. What is it you don't understand?"

"If I knew that, we wouldn't be talking."

"What makes you so confident Kylac will be able to make more sense of it?"

"I already told you that."

Deka began walking, circling Friend. The projected fox didn't have to turn around to remain facing him.

"You once said your old ways kept you from perceiving the Lake. You separated from them, but you're still here. Is it really that simple?"

Deka locked eyes with Friend as he circled the fox. Friend did not answer. Deka continued.

"The antifox hasn't destroyed a planet yet, but we've seen it is capable. It always disappears after it causes damage, but it never sticks around to kill everyone. That is what it wants to do, isn't it?"

Deka had made a complete loop around Friend. Neither had blinked.

"Found them," Kylac said.

Everyone turned to the portal on the far side of the hub. Kylac was standing next to it.

"I can see them through another portal on the other side. They're at an impact site."

"An actual impact?" said Sonjaa, approaching.

"They were in the mood for something cooked," Sorven said, wings spreading at his own joke and then sagging at the size of the portal. "I'll keep this portal open for everyone. If you need me, I'll be here."

He lay down and observed the planet that filled the sky.

The Relians hopped through the portal one at a time. This new location was flatter, and the ground was warmer. Their sense of electromagnetic fields was scrambled on this world thanks to the gas giant, which made it difficult to tell where they were on the moon. Deka and Kylac were aware of more subtle changes in the atmosphere and ground density and orbital location, so they quickly figured out exactly where they were.

The sphere just fifteen paces away opened to another region, also uniformly flat and covered in tiny plants. Friend was already on the other side, waiting for them. They filed through and joined the feast.

Thirty-seven quadrupeds had gathered inside a large impact crater. Half of them resembled a cross between an elephant and a cheetah, but only a third of Kylac's height. The Mipor. The other half of the people resembled Earth camels crossed with horses, and they, too, were only a fraction of the size. The Hadane.

Each person licked a chunk of meteorite like ice cream. Their saliva was highly acidic, and it visibly wore down the metal and rock, breaking it open and exposing the tasty nutrients within.

Unlike on every other planet, the plant life on this world was devoid of nutrition. The animals instead evolved to take the nutrients from another source: the ring fragments that frequently pelted this planet. They suspected Labccr used to be much farther out in orbit, and other life had once existed, but as its orbit decayed and was then caught up in the ring system, everything died out except those that started examining the collision sites. The particles were frozen packages containing amino acids, nutrients, useful metals their body needed, and water. The chunks of rock and ice that made up the rings were likely the remains of another habitable planet that had long ago shattered to pieces.

The Mipor and the Hadane once roamed the moon, following the collisions, each adapted in a special way to cope with the scarce food. The Mipor were small and fast, able to speed across the land to find new impact sites. Their feet were sensitive to vibrations, able to detect a tremor, and if the ground would become molten.

The Hadane, however, were slow-moving. They used as little energy as possible and survived months without food, storing up the excess in their humps for later. Their hooves were not sensitive to vibration, but to heat. They reacted to temperature differences and would move when the ground became too warm.

Both races had been in constant motion around the moon to stay ahead of the ground when it became molten, and when moving between impact sites. Now they used portals to bring pieces of orbiting ring debris to themselves. They had ways open across the whole planet so they did not have to be on the move all the time. When the ground became molten, they took a sphere to safety.

They estimated this moon's orbit would eventually decay far enough that it would either crash into the gas giant, or become ripped apart and scattered throughout the ring system. The moon may only last another century, so they had already found substitutes offworld.

Offworlders came here to experience a landscape in constant change. The ground would not be the same from week to week, or month to month, which projected a sense of danger like no other world.

Friend stood on the rim of the small crater, making sure the Relians could tell just how impatient he was.

One of the camel/horse-like creatures rose to his padded hooves. The Hadane approached them, leaving his fragment of meteorite behind. Nobody else made a move for it. Their instincts compelled them to, but there had been no need to fight over food since they had discovered portal physics.

"Is something wrong?" said the Hadane.

"Hello, Lakan," Kylac said. "We're here because you have a visitor."

"Are they here? Nobody's seen them. I closed the off-world portals so I wouldn't fall unconscious in another disaster."

The other Hadane and Mipor rose to their feet. The Mipor all used their trunks to hold their piece of rock.

"We're told they are on the molten side of the moon," said Deka. "Everyone should evacuate just in case. Where is everyone else?"

"At another meteorite."

"Get them," Deka said. "There's an offworld portal at the hub. It leads to Onoic. You can take another way from there to find things to eat."

The Mipor gathered their fragments in their trunks and jogged to the portal. The Hadane held their rocks in their teeth and galloped through as well. Friend now sat on the crater edge, feet dangling.

"I'll find the others," Lakan said. "We'll meet at the hub." He slipped through the way and ran through the second portal along with the others.

Friend kicked his legs on the edge of the crater a couple paces above them. "In a few billion years, these people will cease to exist. This moon will be long gone. The star in this system will burn out, the planets will fly out of orbit, this gas giant will fall into the orbit of another star in eighteen billion years and crash into it. Pointless. An objective waste of precious time."

"If it's all so pointless," Deka said, "why do you still pretend to care? Why not merge with your old ways and end all life anyway? What would be the consequences? You'd be able to work on the solution uninhibited."

"Because I'm not a monster, and I'm smart enough to know I will go insane without things I can't predict."

"Part of you is both insane and a monster."

"Kylac has a monster inside himself, too. He will have to face it sooner or later."

Deka huffed at him and walked through the portal. He carefully avoided the tiny trees and shrubs as he approached the other sphere that led back to the hub. Kylac joined him at his side.

"Why are you provoking him?"

Deka looked at him. He hoped Kylac could tell what he was thinking. He was almost sure Friend could.

They walked into the portal that led to the hub. Hadanes and Mipora poured from the other spheres, gathering around the waiting Krone. Sorven lay still with outstretched wings. These were not scent-based creatures, so his scent did not affect them at all. They were mostly touch-based, so his scales fascinated them endlessly, and everyone was rubbing against him with their hooves and trunks and paws. He looked like a mother bird sheltering her chicks.

Friend was among them, a giant compared to the creatures and plants. He was not solid at the moment, so the people ran right through him and into the offworld portal.

The sound of the galloping footsteps was incredible. The total population of both species combined was only eight thousand, and most of them had gathered right here at the hub, filing into the portal in an orderly manner.

Lakan emerged from one of them and galloped against the crowd toward the Relians. He stood beside them, watching everyone go. Many carried pieces of rock in their trunk or cheek. Lakan's scent reeked of worry.

"Why did they come here?" he said.

"We don't know why they go anywhere," Sonjaa replied.

"I hope it doesn't destroy the moon or the rings. There's nothing else like it in the universe. We can survive on outcroppings of metal and drink from mineral lakes on other worlds, but nothing tastes better than a freshly fallen meteorite."

"I wish I knew," Sonjaa said, rubbing her claws.

The Mipora and Hadanes had no instinct to feed on plants or hunt other creatures. Their instinct was to eat rocks, which was rare in the contacted universe.

More than half the people had walked through the portal. The spheres to the other locations around the planet were now empty. Sorven stood and watched them file into his sphere.

The antifox appeared in the center of the population. The Relians froze. Sorven froze. The Mipora and Hadanes had no fear instinct stemming from other creatures, only from their environment, so they stared at the apparition.

The antifox spun in all directions, soundlessly made gestures and screaming at them to move away. It then launched an antisphere at the nearest Mipor. The sphere sailed straight through her, and it grew from the size of her hoof to the size of her body as it traveled. It engulfed half her body and continued bowling through the crowd, cutting through people as easily as it once used its claws.

It turned and threw another antisphere from the center of its head, carving a tunnel through the people that surrounded it. It sliced them in half, limbs fell to the ground, heads rolled, entrails spilled freely.

The Mipora and Hadanes began running to the off-world portal. Sorven unfolded his wings and stood between the portal and the antifox. The people of Labccr ran around and underneath him and dove in. There were still so many people here.

The antifox turned in tight circles where it stood. Kylac shivered. Deka watched, snarling. Sonjaa also snarled at it. Lakan was not sure how to react, so he simply observed it, his scent now the same as if he had been caught on ground turning molten.

It turned. It saw them. Deka expected it to attack, but it did not move for them. It had obviously learned it did not need to use its claws anymore and that its body was lethal to anything it touched. Now it had learned to open anti-spheres. The Relians were ready to dive out of the way, but the antifox merely stood still and stared at them.

A sphere began to open halfway between them. It was white hot and dense: a piece of the star's core.

"Get to the portals!" Sonjaa screamed.

The sphere expanded. Deka picked up Lakan in his jaws and carried him into the sphere that led back to the other region. Sonjaa and Kylac bounded up to the portal right behind them.

The Mipora and Hadanes leaped for any sphere they could reach. Some made it to the offworld portal. Others happened to be near a way that led elsewhere on Labccr. Most were caught too far away and were out in the open.

Sorven leaped away from the offworld portal, landed with his back to the emerging sphere and slid into a group of Mipora and Hadanes. He cradled a couple dozen people against his underbelly as his wings wrapped around them. The Relians tumbled through the sphere and lay on the other side. They righted themselves so they could see the portal.

The antifox's sphere closed. The chunk of core did not remain still for even a breath. Without the gravity of an entire star holding it together, it exploded.

The light burned. The sound traveled through the entire planet. The tiny plants felt the heat and retracted their foliage and roots. Most were too late and were blown away as the nuclear blast ripped them out of the soil and vaporized them. The wind from the blast blew through the portal, but the portal itself absorbed the radiation.

The wave passed. The charred ground was all that remained. Even Sorven was gone, and in the distance they saw him sailing across the moon, still balled up. He landed eighteen breaths later about five hundred paces away, boring a path through the dirt as he slowed to a stop.

The antifox stood in place, surveying the area. Apparently it was satisfied at the lack of people in its territory. It folded into itself and vanished. No one else remained at the blast site.

The wind blew the other direction, and now the explosion soared upwards in an enormous fireball. The Relians saw the mushroom cloud just over the horizon. The wind did not reach them this far, but the sound still did.

2

The rumbling along the ground ceased. The blistering heat on his back faded, though he still felt the absorbed radiation along his spine. It was more than he had been exposed to in centuries.

Sorven uncurled his neck and looked back. The mushroom cloud had dissipated into an ordinary cloud. He calculated it would start raining fallout within four days, and it would spread across the land. The good part was this world frequently became molten, so within a lunar year all the radioactive particles would be gone.

He uncurled his body and unfolded his wings from his abdomen. Thirty-two Mipora and Hadanes spilled away from his abdomen, shaken but alive.

"Everyone all right?"

They looked at him, and then around, too shaken to respond. Sorven was relieved they weren't deaf. His body must have muffled the sound well enough. The longer he was alive, the more impressed he was by what his body could do.

Sorven turned and looked at the mushroom cloud. The soil underneath had been scorched. Some of the plants at the epicenter had managed to curl up into magma-resistant stones. They would survive. The portals were still open. Sorven saw faces through them, surveying the damage from safety. He stood up and lowered his head among the group he had saved from the blast.

"Walk the other way. Don't stop until you are over the horizon. I will have to clear the contaminated soil before I can bring anyone else to safety. I will return for you shortly."

As a group, they solemnly nodded and rose to their feet. They began walking away from the blast site. Sorven turned and galloped in the other direction. The low gravity allowed him to bound faster than he normally could, and he crossed the distance in only forty-six strides. The blast had thrown him over a mile away.

He slowed when he reached the offworld portal. Faces of all kinds looked in, and they rose to attention when Sorven neared. He regarded the people on the other side. His wings sagged. The people cried.

The Krone walked to the portal where the Relians had pushed Lakan. They were huddled around the sphere as well. They backed away and made room for him, and Sorven stuck his head through the sphere.

Deka and Sonjaa held their hands low. Kylac sat off to the side with his back to the portal, whimpering. Lakan's scent was both angry and sad at the same time. Nobody spoke for a few breaths. Finally, Sonjaa broke the silence.

"Are you all right?"

"I used to wait in long lines for rides like that," said the Krone.

Nobody laughed.

"Sorry... Over eight hundred people were vaporized. I saved thirty-two. The others made it through portals and are waiting to leave. I believe we still have more than a thousand people to evacuate."

Friend appeared sitting atop Sorven's head. "It was because you decided to evacuate those people the antifox showed up. It was attracted to the vibrations."

Laken could not see Friend, and addressed Sorven. "Forget the evacuation. We'll never get everyone off in time. We'll have to lie low and hope it leaves without incident."

"No," Kylac said.

All eyes turned to him. He was still sitting on a clump of tiny trees, scent giving off waves of anxiety and fear.

"It ends here. Too many people are dying."

"Good idea," said Friend. "Do you remember what I told you about how to separate your higher mind from your old ways?"

Kylac turned around and screamed at him. "I will not go to the Lake! We trap the old ways here! I can open an antisphere to send them farther out into the Lake. Maybe I can spread them out!"

"It won't work," Friend said, kicking his paws in the Krone's face.

Deka turned to him. "You keep insisting there is only one way out of this, and yet you still don't understand where you are or how this works! You are not qualified to tell us what works and what won't!"

"Are you conscious of the entire universe at once? I know more than you ever will."

"They always show up when you're in a group. Why? You can be in all places at once; how do we know they're not following you around on other worlds, too?"

Friend held Deka's stare again. Neither blinked. Deka continued.

"And they always hurt a group of people, always in front of Kylac. You said you separated your old ways, but how far were you able to send them? Why do they follow you at all? Are they really separated?"

"I could make this moon disappear," said the fox perched on the Krone's head. "You saved enough people to continue the species, not that it matters. The problem is solved until my instincts show up on the next world. Evacuating people just wastes time."

"No more death!" Kylac shouted. "I will do it here! Get those people offworld fast so I don't hurt them!"

"It will take me some time to clear the soil," Sorven said. "Keep the portals open, Lakan."

He retracted his head. Friend disappeared just before he touched the sphere. Sorven shoved his hands into the soil and dug up a semi-truck's-worth of dirt and balled-up plant life. He spread his wings and flapped high into the sky. He scanned the ground for a good disposal site. He looked up at the gas giant. It was like Jupiter, but even more beautiful because it was blue and green as well, with multiple hurricanes swirling around it. Labccr was close enough to see the clouds moving in real time. The last time he had been on this moon, none of these storms existed.

He turned his attention to the ground again. A crater just ahead looked like a good enough place to leave the radioactive soil for the time being. He banked, dove down, and dropped the dirt inside. He corkscrewed and soared into the air again. At this rate it would only take an hour. He hoped Kylac would be all right until then.

It had been wearing on all of them, the pressure, the helplessness. Deka had been even more abrasive than usual toward Friend lately. Sorven wanted to ask him about it, but Friend would hear anything he said. The older fox already knew Sorven's thoughts, so Friend probably suspected Deka had figured it out, too.

Sorven returned to the hub. He used all four feet to dig a trench and lifted another load of topsoil off the ground. He flapped and carried it just a few paces into the air, picking up more speed. He reached the disposal site in a few breaths, unloaded, and then returned to the hub.

He didn't want to think about what would happen if they succeeded in trapping the antifox here. It had figured out how to use their universe against them. It had figured out the laws of physics did not apply to it anymore. It was free to satisfy its needs in new and bigger ways. Kylac knew this much, but he had not smelled right in multiple worlds. Every planet he had resolved to open his mind and remember the Lake in detail, and every time he had stopped short.

Deka had been pushing him, but not as hard as he had pushed Sonjaa. He had prompted his mate not only to remember the Lake, but to let her mind fall back into it again and again. For some reason, her mind had become prone to slipping out of her body since she had returned, and Deka wanted her to control it instead of hide from it. Since Mero, she had been less afraid of it. She had even begun to play with it on her own, without Deka. She had faced her fear. Kylac had not.

Sorven dumped the soil, spun around, and returned for another armful. His scales began to itch.

Kylac's mind had been cloudy. His scent did not indicate he was becoming more aware, but sinking further into misery. Sorven had done all he could to comfort him, but for these last few planets he had been beyond help. Sorven remembered fucking around with him almost every night when he was human. That was the Kylac he wanted to remember. Friend had destroyed that fox, and Sorven wanted to be there when Kylac destroyed Friend.

Armful after armful, he removed the topsoil from the hub around the portals down to five paces. His scales itched more and more. The hub became a crater, and all the portals floated five paces in the air. He stood in the crater and looked up. His scales itched so badly he roared. He addressed everyone looking in, voice strained with discomfort.

"My scales are shedding! I will build ramps when I return! Sit tight!"

He rose from the crater and flew out about a dozen paces. He gritted his teeth and pushed through the pain until he sensed he was in an area with minimal contamination. He landed, lay on his stomach, and screamed as the top layer of scales separated from his body. Sorven felt every single scale pop loose from his tail up his spine and then down each wing.

The Krone only shed once every few centuries, or after an event such as being at the epicenter of nuclear blast. Normally it was not this uncomfortable, and it certainly was never painful, but he had absorbed more radiation over the last couple of hours than he had over his entire life thus far, so his body knew it needed to decontaminate in a hurry —just another stimulus the Krone had evolved to survive.

The scales popped loose and formed a thick sheet that unzipped from his body. It ran down each leg. Without thinking, he stood up, and the scales separated from his abdomen. He felt scales wiggling and popping free all the way down to his slit. Sorven screamed as the scales down his face and eyelids separated and fell away in a thick sheet of sandy-yellow.

His skull fell away. His legs separated. His stomach fell off. The sheet of scales settled on the ground, and Sorven stood in a pile of his own skin. He sensed the radiation clinging to them. He flapped his wings and lifted out of the pile of skin. It was still attached to him by the feet, and Sorven flapped in place for a few beats while those scales separated, too. Moments later, the empty hide fell to the ground and settled in the low gravity.

His body was a vibrant yellow and black again, and now as he looked down at himself, he saw his black scales were actually dark green, now free of radiation. He sighed in relief as he banked right and flew back to the hub. He soared into the crater and stood on all four feet.

Two of the portals were now at the new ground level, no faces behind them. A dirt ramp led up to the offworld sphere, and elephant-cheetahs and horse-camels walked up the ramp into the Krone-sized sphere. Lakan stamped his hoof at Sorven, their smiling gesture. The Krone lay still and spread his wings.

3

The tower of equations had been churning away this whole time, but Kylac had kept it under control. It was the other part of the tower he still had walled off. Now he was staring at it. To others, he stared into empty space.

The universe was said to be made of variables, but if Kylac zoomed out far enough, he noticed the variables changed in predictable ways. If he held enough of those patterns in his mind at once, the variables became constants, and the constants made everything predictable, including life.

Life was wonderful and fascinating. To reduce it to a series of equations was to render it nothing more than math. To be so aware of life was to be aware of the presence of every creature in the universe at once.

Now he stared at the tower of equations in his mind, partially blocked off to keep him from remembering that. He tore down the last barrier and forced himself to behold reality.

The universe was not real. Nothing in it was real. He knew it in his mind, but his instincts still reacted to the knowledge of all those people the only way they knew how. He shivered as he pondered them. His mind ran the numbers. As an Archeon, he had learned how to predict orbits with such precision he could pinpoint an atom on the other side of the universe. Now he calculated the movement of the people within the universe with accurate precision as well.

Their thoughts. Their actions. Their hopes and dreams. Their words. All of it calculable, and the implications stretched along the future path of the universe like beams of light.

Millions of them.

Billions.

Septillions.

Billions of septillions.

Past, present, and the calculated future. Every person carved a little path through the universe as it drifted through the Lake. They all had a voice. A name. A scent.

Kylac's heart raced. Deka and Sonjaa were near, but a raptor's scent could not calm anxiety that extended this far. The entire universe was now his territory, and he knew every single life form within it. Now he confirmed Friend was right. Sonjaa and Deka did not have paths cutting through the time dimension—the only two people in the entire universe he could not calculate.

He saw another hole on the far side of this planet, still swimming through the lava. Apparently, it enjoyed being able to do this.

Kylac became aware of the people walking up the ramps and into the offworld sphere. He could easily open spheres over every single person and kill them right now, but he remembered Friend. He remembered what Friend had smelled like before he died on Reyno, how his fur had been saturated in blood. Kylac was better than this, and he would prove it by waiting until everyone was gone.

Killing them would not relieve his scent anxiety. His scenting distance encompassed the entire universe now, and he was capable of destroying them all. He shivered. He couldn't breathe correctly. Deka and Sonjaa had sat down on either side of him, bodies touching the canine. Friend was right that they were the most fascinating things in the universe—everything else blended together into predictable variables and became constants, but not them.

"Speak to me," he said. "Keep my mind busy."

"Remember when you took us to Cadmaw?" said the theropod.

Kylac remembered. His memory was even better than before. He despised having such a perfect memory of every person and life form in the universe—of their paths through the universe, and then not being surprised when they ended up exactly where he had calculated they would be. But Deka's words were new. Special. He did not know what he would say next. Kylac rocked back and forth and tried to breathe normally. His fur brushed reptile scales. His nose was aware of their scents, but they seemed less real than the calculated awareness of everyone else. Kylac thought he might be happy killing everyone in the universe except these two. It would relieve his old ways, and he would have company—the best of both.

"You... wanted to see the ice falls," said the fox.

Sonjaa spoke to the void Kylac stared into. "Is that the world where ice forms in the searing heat?"

"You've never been there?" Deka asked.

"I've met people from that world, but no, I haven't."

"Bacteria live in the water. They turn it to solid blocks of ice no matter what the temperature is. Warm ice is bizarre, and to watch it flow like a paste is even more exotic. We can't drink the water, but touching it is an experience like nowhere else in the universe."

"You never told me you two were there."

"We weren't even apprentices yet. We went walking on the ice as it flowed over the river. It's solid, but it still moves, and it's one single piece. It doesn't break off the way normal ice does. Fascinating planet. And then I accidentally pissed in it."

Sonjaa turned to him, clicking her claws. "How? What happened?"

"I slipped and got scared. As soon as it hit the block, the entire sheet opened up and swallowed us."

Sonjaa clicked louder. "I heard the water is a superorganism."

"The bacteria form a colony that encompasses the water across much of the planet. The ocean is a giant trap catching any wildlife that falls in. It opens entire oceans to allow populations of fish to come back, and then it moves in and harvests those places. I had just given the water stimulus."

Kylac's tail twitched. He knew what happened, but hearing Deka and Sonjaa talk about it was more precious than life itself, which scared Kylac even more. Deka held onto him tighter.

"People saw us," Deka continued, now looking out over the moonscape covered in miniature shrubbery. "They knew how to manipulate the ice and brought us out. They had to give us a tongue bath to wash all the digestive enzymes off."

"The bacteria on that planet are an invasive species," Sonjaa said.

"They decontaminated us until we were sick of that world. We only went there once more as adults. This time we heeded the warning not to touch the water."

Kylac closed his eyes. "I'm in control. The people of Labccr have been evacuated. They're still not safe from me, but they are safe from whatever happens here. Deka, I meant what I said on Mero. I want to be happy again. No matter what happens, you'll have to kill me because there's no way back. I can see the Lake now, and I can't forget it. I thought I could move on, but I can't go on like this. We had a wonderful life together. Now I'm beyond help. Sonjaa, I want you to know I liked having you here, too. You never took Deka away from me, and I hope you two can make a wonderful life together when I'm gone. Without foxes, maybe you can find each other. First I will finish this. What happens to me after... I don't care anymore. If I can never be the person I once was, I want to be happy one last time, and letting my old ways take me is the only chance I have to get a small piece of joy back in my life. Just before the end. This is the end. I'm ready."

Kylac stood up. He was aware of the antifox on the other side of the moon. It was of the Lake, and yet it had numbers, so Kylac could calculate what it would do no matter what he threw at it. This surprised Kylac, as anything in the Lake should not have numbers.

The fox reached forward with his mind and plugged all the exits. Every point in spacetime around Labccr became part of Kylac's consciousness, and nothing could touch any of them without him knowing. Leaving this universe required passing through spacetime, and Kylac now controlled all of it around this moon. The old ways were trapped here.

The antifox noticed. It tried to fold into itself and emerge in a different part of this planet, but Kylac blocked it. Kylac calculated it was thrashing in the lava right now, and it had become aware of the scents of everyone on this moon. It had to destroy those scents. It dove through the lava, eating a hole straight through the crust. The lava rushed in and filled the gap.

"It's coming."

"Scramble it!" Deka snarled.

Kylac was already working on it. He calculated where the old ways would be, and began opening a series of anti-spheres that would send the antifox to a six billion places across the Lake, hopefully far enough apart they could never recollect.

The antispheres opened on top of the antifox. Kylac sensed holes opening in the antifox, and yet it still came. Moments later it burst up through the crust. Lava gushed out of the hole the antifox made in the soil, and the plants curled up into tiny balls and floated away on it.

The antifox stood in the emerging lava. It was indeed full of holes where Kylac's antispheres had been, and those holes were filling in. It tried to throw an antisphere in their direction, and it seemed surprised when nothing happened. Kylac tried to open new ways over the antifox, and he sensed the antifox was also trying to open ways on top of him.

"It didn't work!"

"Why?!" Sonjaa shouted.

"I don't know! I'm blocking its antispheres! It still has numbers—I can still predict what it's going to do, but it's pointless now! I can't hurt it! It has no choice but to attack us with claws and teeth now!"

The antifox grew longer legs and sped across the bonsai land. As it neared, its claws grew. It raised an arm and swiped down. Deka dove out of the way. The claws sank into the ground with seemingly no resistance, making five thin slices through it.

It noticed Sonjaa, screamed at her, and dashed. She snarled at it as she backed away. It swiped its claws at her horizontally. She jumped over them, sailing higher in the weak gravity, and landed behind it.

Kylac stood off to the side, concentrating. Suddenly, the antifox's numbers vanished from this universe, which left Kylac feeling furless in the snow.

He thought back to Deka's words since Fusina. The questions he had been asking Friend, the answers Friend had given. They added up to something, but Kylac had been so preoccupied with dread and the looming tower of numbers in his mind he hadn't noticed.

Kylac examined the old ways closer as they swiped and lunged at Deka and Sonjaa. He found it. A piece of spacetime he did not control, so small he did not notice because something else was already there. A thin thread cut through this point in spacetime and connected the antifox to the Lake. Kylac followed the thread with his mind. It led to the spot where Friend was.

The antifox wasn't here. It was a projection, too.

Deka leaped to the side. The antifox swiped upwards. It moved mass to form a third limb with an extended claw. It slammed its limb down and cut through Deka's shoulder. Deka's arm fell off and bounced on the miniature plants.

The antifox smelled the blood and turned to Sonjaa. It shifted mass into its claws, making them as long as a shadow at dusk. Four claws extended twenty-two paces across the moonscape and into Sonjaa's skull. She hung still for a moment, and then the antifox withdrew its claws. It turned to Kylac, limbs retracting to normal proportions.

Friend manifested next to the younger fox.

"It can't be done, can it?" Kylac said. "You can't separate your old ways. Sorven was right."

"It *can* be done," Friend whispered as Deka and Sonjaa screamed. "The equation I gave you was complete, but it's impossible to send them away. This is what they do when I'm holding them back with my higher mind."

He now manifested at his other ear and whispered in it. "Imagine what they would do if I severed them entirely."

Deka had risen to his feet, blood running down his shoulder. Sonjaa lay on the ground, twitching, breathing erratically. Deka glared at both of them, then turned and stumbled to his mate. He knelt over her.

"Sonjaa..."

He smelled no fear in her scent. She reached up with a weak hand and touched Deka's claws. "I'll catch you when you fall."

Her mind drained from her, leaving her eyes empty, but her heart still beating. Deka felt light in the head. The blood had clotted, but he was still in bad need of water. He rose to full height and faced the three foxes. Friend now stood next to the antifox, just a claw's reach away from touching it.

"I'm not the monster," Friend said. He appeared to be facing both Deka and Kylac at the same time. He gestured toward his instincts. "*That's* the monster. The same thing is in you, Kylac. I can't defeat it. I can sever it, but it finds me again, and if it doesn't, it finds the universe and destroys everything it touches! That's why it took me so long to come to you! That's what I was doing in the Lake after you killed me! I couldn't learn about my environment with this *thing* reminding me everything in the universe is in scenting distance! The best I could do was keep it on a leash and let it play on a few isolated planets! It won't leave me alone! Kylac, you are better at handling your instincts than I am! You can destroy it, but you can't do that from here!"

"You can stay up there for eternity," Kylac said, ear folded back, stepping away. "I won't go there. I won't help you."

"I've been keeping them on a short leash since you killed me! I can send them to a million planets at once! They're not satisfied unless they kill everything on those worlds! They won't be happy until they destroy everything in this universe, and any other universe I visit! I'm giving you a chance to destroy your instincts, too! We're both getting what we want! They will kill everything if you don't help me stop them, and I can't leave this universe until you do!"

Kylac panted again. He was losing control. Portals opened up around them. Dozens. Hundreds. He enclosed them in a dome of boiling spheres and antispheres opening and closing every few breaths. Spheres to every planet in the universe. Antispheres to random places in the Lake.

"Kill my old ways!" Friend screamed. "Kill them so I can leave, and you will never hear from me again! That's all I want!"

The antifox still stood in attack stance, and now the bind between them became visible: a cord of consciousness connecting it to Friend, thin but obvious.

"To get away from everyone—it's the only thing I've *ever* wanted for myself! It should be easy, but it's always just out of reach! You can come back to your fake reality if you want, but kill this thing for me! Help me! Please!"

Kylac looked at Deka. The raptor's body stance told him Friend was still not telling him everything. Kylac wished he knew what Deka knew. Kylac thought of the thousands of lives they had lost to come this far only for it to be a dead end. He knew no way to win except in the Lake.

Kylac halted the chaotic portals around them and focused his energy on leaving the universe. He ran the equations. His mind drifted from his body. The universe became skewed. It bled away. It was disorienting, and he knew it was a trick of perspective. He adjusted his thoughts to comprehend reality as it was, not reality as he was used to. He became aware of his body falling to a heap on Labccr not unlike the piece of dead skin Sorven had left behind.

He had no body out here. He was consciousness. There was no light. Nothing had a form. He was simply aware of things. The universe was the only thing that had a physical form. He could still see it, but not with light. He was everywhere at once, aware of everything happening at once.

The scent anxiety took hold even faster and stronger outside the universe. The universe was as small as the distance he could reach with his arms now. There was so much life in it, and it would only take a single thought to wipe it all out and calm his anxiety.

Quickly he executed the equation to separate his instincts from his higher mind. He became aware of a piece of himself dividing from him. He sent it away. Further and further. He wasn't sure if he should let the single connection snap or not. Friend told him it was pointless, so he considered leaving it on a leash for now until he dealt with Friend's old ways.

He sensed a presence. Friend himself. The conscious part, not his animal side, metaphorically wagging his tail. He severed the cord holding Kylac's old ways to his higher mind, and just like that, Kylac was free of his animal impulses. He had never experienced such relief in his life, even with a raptor. Raptor scent merely kept the animal down; it never got rid of it entirely. The Lake began to take on some kind of form. He wasn't sure what it was, but he suspected if he stared at it long enough, he would understand.

Friend was moving into him. He had severed his own instincts and was now embracing Kylac.

Not embracing.

Engulfing.

Kylac's memories began falling into Friend. He wasn't sure how to move out here, but Friend knew. Kylac caught a glimpse of the older fox's intent. He was taking over.

Kylac could only think of one thing to do. He opened an antisphere on Labccr. Instantly, he became aware of Deka running through it. He sensed another presence surrounding the new conscious mind that entered the Lake. Sonjaa.

Kylac cried out for help.

4

The dome of bubbling spheres came down. Kylac's body lay lifeless on the ground. Deka was missing an arm, and he stood over a motionless Sonjaa. Sorven growled, wishing he hadn't been right and hoping Deka had reached the same conclusion he had. Less than a breath after Kylac fell, an antisphere opened, and Deka jumped through. The sphere closed. All was still.

Sorven walked up to the site. It had taken him far too long to fly here, but he had arrived just in time to see the last moments. He approached Sonjaa's lifeless body and scented her. The body was still alive, but she was gone. He walked up to Kylac. His body was also alive, but the mind had also been vacated. He walked around and found Deka's severed arm.

He lay facing where the antisphere had been and waited under the gentle glow of the gas giant and the glinting chunks of ice rock high above as lava bubbled and flowed around him.

Washington D. C.

CJ Rhine walked into the senate hearing chambers. The members of the committee had already gathered, all nine of them, and sitting at the head was Senator Sattle of Massachusetts. Secret service men escorted CJ to her chair at the center of the long table. She pulled out the chair and took a seat. She sat alone.

CJ had not been allowed to speak to the press since the Justice Department placed her under house arrest last month, but she had been following the news. Despite, or perhaps because of her interview, the rumors had only become bigger.

Cable and network programs reported endlessly on people gone missing, and allegations that alien abduction was to blame. The cable channels devoted entire days to commentary and speculation. According to the press, Relians were around every corner, waiting for mothers to leave their children alone. They watched through a network of surveillance portals, looking for the right people to pick off. Some speculated Earth was being turned into their new hunting grounds, and the Archeons would let loose a raptor or fox to hunt down an unsuspecting human at a moment's notice.

Gun sales skyrocketed. Movie ticket sales dropped. A lot of people were afraid to leave their homes. The press made sure people were afraid of that, too, by saying people at home were not safe from an intrusive portal.

Crude, computer-generated animations illustrated what a Relian home invasion might look like, and how to be prepared. Experts recommended placing weapons in key points of the home, and they had opinions for what to do if ambushed on the street.

To watch the news, one would think the entire nation had huddled under their blankets with flashlights waiting for Armageddon, but CJ had been allowed out of the house for basic errands as long as she wore her ankle monitor, and she had seen the reality on the ground. People went to the grocery store. People went to the movies. People ate out. Most of the people she overheard on the street were not talking about Relian invasions. The few that did merely repeated what the press said. CJ wanted to tell those people the truth, but it didn't matter anymore. Too much fear drowned it out.

She had been waiting for the ax to drop, and she was surprised when she learned this would be a public hearing. She shouldn't have been surprised; the press was looking for someone to blame, and the finger often pointed straight at her. How much did she know? When did she know it? Did she knowingly and willingly help the Relians invade the planet? Did she betray the United States of America by going along with the plan to place aliens in people's homes? Was that part of the plan to test humanity for weaknesses? How did the initial disappearances factor in to their larger plan?

CJ was ready for these questions. She was used to staying on point despite the opposition trying to throw her off. All she worried about was that even this would not make a difference. She had accepted she would be found guilty regardless of the truth; the press was clamoring for someone to be punished, and it happened to be her. Maybe she would be allowed to write a book in prison.

She was sworn in, the deputy called the hearing to order, and the panel of old white men was prepared to receive CJ's official testimony. They noted in the minutes that she was providing her own legal representation, and with the formalities out of the way, Senator Sattle leaned up to the microphone.

"Madame Secretary Crystal Jessica Rhine, did you ever think you would end up here?"

"Not as an alleged criminal, Mr. Senator."

"You've been an upstanding member of congress for years. I am sorry it has come to this. Do you have a statement for this committee?"

"I do."

"You may read it now for the record."

CJ had spent her time at home memorizing it. She hoped it would take care of all the major points right away.

"I stand accused of the highest crime in the country. I choose to represent myself in defense, as there is no person better qualified than I to state the truth of what happened. There have been a lot of rumors circulating in the press since the tape showing a reverted fox was broadcast on the national news. Let the record show the fox in question was kidnapped and forced to fight dogs to the death in order to induce reversion in her. The fact that the Relians and their human companions disappeared at around the same time is, I assure you, coincidence. The Relians were here to identify people they could take with them to live offworld, and they were here only for those people. They are not planning an invasion. Neither are they coming to abduct people from their homes. Those people were chosen because they were capable of living off planet Earth and joining the contacted universe, and they are leaving on their own volition. We should count them lucky. I did not know of this plan until the day the Archeon Rive disappeared, and I fully admit to not disclosing this information as soon as I learned it. I believed doing so without more information would have incited panic, as it has now, and interfered with their good intentions. I submit this does not constitute treason, as it has not betrayed the interests of the United States in the slightest, neither has it compromised national security, and I am prepared to defend my actions."

Senator Sattle cleared his throat. "Thank you for that statement, Madame Secretary. I'd like to begin with this committee's investigation into the incident in Portland. Considering the defendants are unaccounted for and presumed not to be on this planet anymore, it seems appropriate to provide the victims some closure here."

CJ tried to keep a straight face.

"Seven deaths, incredible damage to property. One victim was brutally stabbed through the eye and later died of his injuries. I've spoken to family members of the deceased. They find it hard to believe a fox caused all that damage. What do you have to say to that?"

"As I have stated before, the so-called victims were actually the perpetrators of a kidnapping. They forced that fox to fight savage dogs to the death. She reverted because they separated her from her raptor. The fox defended herself from the worst humanity has to offer."

"So you agree foxes presented a threat to human life, as did the raptors?"

"That is a loaded question, Mr. Senator."

"Please answer it."

"If you are trying to corner me into saying something on record for the media to take out of context, I will not. The Relians were upstanding citizens while they were here. It was only when human beings attacked them that they had to fight back. Everyone in Washington expected the raptors to go on a killing rampage, but it never happened."

Mr. Sattle huffed. "I beg to differ on the upstanding citizen statement. I have numerous reports from all over the world that the Relians were unreliable. Some of them did seek employment, and their employers found them to be unreasonable. The raptors were uncooperative and insubordinate. The foxes refused to work unless their raptor was also there. Most, it would seem, preferred to live off entitlements, which were only meant to be temporary to help them adjust to life in this nation."

"With respect, Senator Sattle, it had only been a year since they were settled. They were used to hunting for themselves and being able to go anywhere they wanted at any time. They were not used to a hierarchy, or being employed, or submitting to authority. Given enough time, I believe they might have learned, but we will never know now."

"That remains to be seen. There is still the possibility that they could come back. Would you agree it is possible?"

"No, sir."

"What makes you confident in that?"

"Because Rive told me why they were here. They got it, and now they are gone. They are not interested in anyone else."

"Did he tell you why those people were chosen?"

"Yes."

"What was the reason he gave?"

"The Relians wanted people who could survive offworld. People willing to adapt to a different way of life."

"So defenseless, unassertive, obedient people?"

"People who would not be afraid of those who are different from themselves, Mr. Sattle."

"Those same people could also have been selected as a slave race, or perhaps hunting stock. People who won't stand up for themselves or ask questions about where they are."

"Sir, I have personally conducted interviews with ten households that had Relians. I have been all over the country resolving disputes between Relians and humans. From my personal observations, I promise you the Relians helped those people for the better. One raptor helped a man quit smoking. Another pushed the human host into a better job. It's all on tape, Mr. Sattle."

"I have reviewed some of those tapes. I found what the raptors were doing to those people disturbing. In every case, the raptor treated the human like a fox, someone to be ordered around. A pet. The evidence is clear. The raptors were here to find a new race of people to enslave, denying them freedom of choice. Do you recall the taped interview with the human who stated her raptor told her not to become pregnant by a certain man?"

"I recall that interview."

"Then you will recall it is exactly what the raptors do to their foxes. The foxes have no freedom. They are entirely submissive to the reptiles."

"Sir, the interviewee in question also admitted she was in a bad relationship, and the raptor helped her see that. If a fox is separated from his or her raptor, the result is what you saw on the tape of Nipe, the reverted fox. The raptors are helping the foxes become more than animals. In that manner, I believe they have given freedom to the humans."

"By making them subservient? Madame Secretary, that is no less than admitting to being an accomplice to handing over United States citizens to an aggressive foreign power. You knew about this, and you complied with it."

CJ took a drink of water. She hadn't realized how dry her throat was. She set the cup down as she met Sattle's hard stare.

"Mr. Senator, the raptors came here to find out if the humans stimulated the same inborn response they feel for foxes. They help their foxes become more than animals, and they wished to help those people become more than what society would allow them to be."

"By oppressing them."

"By showing them a new way to live."

"A life of enslavement and obedience for God knows what purpose. You have only the Archeon Rive's word on all of this. You complied on his word alone, potentially compromising the interests of the United States and condemning hundreds of people around the world to an unknown fate."

"The interviews I recorded speak for themselves. I have also spoken to my counterparts in China, Germany, Japan, Laos, Botswana, Australia, and Chile. It is the same story again and again. The raptors helped them become better people, the same as they helped their foxes."

"You approve of people being subjugated in this manner?"

"If I believed the Archeons were conspiring to enslave us, I would have told the president himself immediately. Those people testified that the Relians were the best thing to ever happen to them, and I witnessed it myself."

"Do you know what Stockholm Syndrome is?"

"I do."

"Would you agree there is a possibility that you were seeing that?"

"No."

"It sure looks like it to me. If a person is subjected to control for long enough, he will eventually become convinced it's a good thing. Every interview is full of it. The incident in Portland represents what happens when noble Americans attempt to reveal the visitors for what they truly are. You dishonor them and their family members in your defense."

"Do you consider people who ran a dogfighting operation noble, Mr. Sattle?"

"I will ask the questions, Ms. Rhine, or you will be in contempt of these proceedings. I wish to open the floor for others to put questions to the defendant."

"I do not believe you consider them noble Americans, but I speculate you consider the people who funded the making of that tape as such."

"Ms. Rhine—"

"I have looked into those protests that seem to have popped up around the country. The press frames them as spontaneous grassroots movements but all of them received funding from offshore corporations registered in tax havens. One of them funded your election campaign, Mr. Sattle, so I conclude they are the same people who funded the creation of that tape, as well as the elections of many, if not all of the people on this committee."

"You are in contempt of these proceedings—"

CJ talked over him. "The protests are fake. The public outcry is fake. A tiny group of wealthy businessmen is magnifying a minority of voices to make it seem like everyone is scared, and because it's being shown on television, people are afraid. These businessmen own a controlling interest in the media and the corporations who were trying to exploit the Relians for personal gain. The turn in—"

"—the committee will weigh the evidence and decide your fate in good time. You are to be held in custody until sentence is delivered. The committee is asked to consider precedent regarding cases of high treason. Capital punishment is not out of the question, however, if mitigating evidence of genuine ignorance or negligence can be found, this committee is encouraged to show mercy."

Men had already begun to vacate the room. CJ hoped the cameras picked her up words as Mr. Sattle tried to drown her out.

"—public opinion happens to coincide with the revelation that the Archeons could not be coerced to help their business interests. Once they decided the Relians could not be used, they told the people it was time to be afraid of them, and that is exactly what's happening. Nobody was afraid until now. Nobody is afraid, but people are seeing protests, so now everyone thinks they should be."

A spacetime sphere opened next to CJ. She turned and stood up. The grey and tan raptor emerged from it. The chamber rose in an uproar. Some members of the committee began moving to the door. Members of the press scattered snapped photographs from every angle they could. The sphere closed behind Rive, and he turned and faced the committee, picking up the nearest microphone.

"Gentlemen, if you please. I would like to say a few words for the record."

Senator Sattle was still seated. "This hearing does not recognize an enemy of the United States."

"You don't have to listen, but I will speak."

CJ leaned close to his ear. "I thought you left for good."

He turned his muzzle slightly to her. "That was the plan, but I couldn't go through with it."

Many members of the committee and the press had left the room. Some of the observers were also missing. Police stood at every entrance, guns drawn and ready. Rive held the microphone up to his mouth.

"You want to know why we were here, but you won't listen to one of your own, so I will tell you exactly what we have done, and why. The basic structure of human society fits the general profile of most primates. One person rises up to dominate the others and control reproduction in some way. In your case, it's the male who rises up, claims the females as his own, and keeps competition down so no others can challenge him. As long as he is dominant, others do things for him to remain in good standing in the group, lest they be ousted from the territory. Their lives depend on it, or they risk being alone and vulnerable. Over time, these favors evolved into organized tasks which you now call work.

"To varying degrees, every oppressed human feels compelled to rise up and challenge the alpha to become alpha himself so he will mate, can enjoy the comfort of knowing others will not challenge him, and will be the recipient of the others' work. It is the foundation of your mentality. On a subconscious level, all behavior serves it, and it leaves most people frustrated and unfulfilled for their entire lives.

"A mature society would recognize this primitive urge and channel it into something beneficial for all. Many societies over the course of your history did recognize it, and they used it to help their fellow humans rise higher, but your impulses to cooperate and care for one another are falling to an exaggerated instinct to dominate. Cultures that emphasized empathy are being driven into extinction by the more aggressive societies which live by their drive to suppress and exploit other human beings. Because you are a lone species, you have allowed this behavior to grow out of control, and society is becoming little more than males struggling for dominance of the group, controlling resources to keep the other males down on a global scale.

"The raptors discovered they can be that dominant person, and humans will submit to them, but instead of oppressing you, we will use this position to allow you to become whatever you wish to be. That's who we were looking for. The oppressed. The ones whose drive to nurture outweighed their drive to dominate, and wanted to become more than what their superiors would allow them to be. As for the alphas, we cannot help you. Your uncontrolled urge to control others and use them for your own benefit keeps you from becoming part of the contacted universe."

The room buzzed with chatter. Senator Sattle's voice pierced the confusion.

"Then you admit you wish to enslave us."

"My point is that those people were already enslaved. Most humans are to some degree. Freedom is an illusion imposed on lesser humans by the men who control their reality. The humans who are not dominating others are dominated by someone who has taken away their free will. The raptors seek to fill this role."

"This is outrageous. You have taken our people. You are going to turn them into an obedient slave race."

CJ laughed. "Is that really all you got out of watching the interviews I did? Encouraging someone to get out of a bad relationship is equal to servitude? Helping someone quit smoking is a bad thing?"

Rive continued as the chatter in the room rose in volume. "Those people will not have to give up their free will any more than they already gave it up to a stoplight, or a police officer, or their boss. Please allow me to ask a lofty question. What does it mean to be human? It seems to be a great, unanswerable riddle to you, but the answer is simple. To be human is to submit to authority or rebel against it. Everything you do is one or the other. Every action in your history is human beings fighting to break out of the control of other human beings, or people trying to control others for their own gain. It is the only kind of society a species with untamed base instincts such as yours can yield. It's obvious to anyone on the outside of your society looking in that your civilization is primate instinct expressing itself on bigger and broader scales. Believe it or not, there are species who do not think this way. It would never occur to them to take charge of others.

"Every problem in your society stems from this carnal drive—either exerting control or resisting it. The very reason you spread out across the globe, leaving the comfort of the environment for which you adapted, can be traced back to it. This drive has been unchecked for thousands of years. Even your culture's concept of original sin is in fact disobedience. This shows what kind of people you are, and you have never met anybody who can show you things could be different. Until now.

"In your particular culture, you want to believe anyone can rise up and improve their status with enough work and determination, but at the same time you also understand that society still works the way primate society does: whoever kisses up to the alpha best gets a higher status. Those who do work are used for the alpha's gain and remain where they are, but those who help the alpha use others, move up. You have not learned to use this instinct for the better of your fellow man. In fact, you fear any culture which does. On a subconscious level, you see them as a threat to your dominance, and by extension a threat to your chance at reproduction. That's what this is all about. Your entire civilization is built to protect the dominant male's reproductive rights within the primate group. Society appears complex and advanced, but it is little more than males living to satisfy their most aggressive reproductive instincts. That is why we cannot stay, and why you cannot be allowed to leave this planet unsupervised. We, the Relians, will be the ones to do what you have not and make this instinctual behavior useful instead of oppressive."

"I would have you arrested if I believed you could be," Sattle said over the murmur. "I wish to be on record that I condemn every word you have said. It should not be tolerated. We allowed you into our homes, but your true goal was to capture our most vulnerable citizens and enslave them. Do you intend to come back and take others? What assurance do we have that you will not?"

CJ did not even blink. "You really can't comprehend it. I thought you were putting on a show for the cameras, but no, this really is how you see things. The raptors want to help us without exploiting us. You watched my interviews, and you think *that* is oppression but creating fake protests to deceive the American people is not."

Rive picked up the thought. "We will not enslave the people who came with us. Instead of giving their free will to a human who wants to control them, those people have given it to someone who will help them become everything they are capable of, as we have done for our foxes."

Sattle was fuming, but he was trying to sound calm. "And does this entail treating human beings the way you treat foxes? Telling them who they can be intimate with, what to eat, where to go, forbidding them from being their own person?"

"The instinct to dominate others is strong even in the oppressed. I expect humans will remain part of the Relian grouping to keep this instinct tamed, just as foxes do because they know what they are without their raptors. You seem obsessed with the idea that we are denying them freedom, but the only people concerned with losing their autonomy are the alphas of the human world. They are, after all, the only ones with true freedom. Nobody has been forced to do anything. The people we took simply realized submitting to a raptor was better than submitting to a human because we are not using them. We are bringing them higher. The humans on this world who live by their exaggerated instinct to dominate are free to fight it out on Earth. The raptors have chosen a few omegas to take to the stars. We are only asking them to give to us the same freedom they had already given up to their superiors."

Sattle shook his head. "The raptors have turned foxes into docile, helpless creatures who can think of nothing but sex, leaving themselves in power. I see no other end for those people. I knew Relians were judgmental hypocrites, but I didn't realize it was this severe."

CJ laughed. "Whoever paid for your last campaign is afraid of the Relians because they can't control them.

They're afraid of someone doing to them what they're doing to everyone else. People are not afraid of the Relians! Nobody is but you and your—!"

Sattle leaned forward and shouted over her. "Secretary Rhine, your actions today confirm what we already knew! That you conspired with an aggressive foreign power to turn our most vulnerable citizens over as a subservient race! This committee will not show compassion or mercy. It will look at the facts as presented here today, and I suspect it will find you—"

"—donors! This hearing is designed to make people even more afraid but it's manipulation! You can fund protests all you want, but when this is over, people will ask questions. That's what you're really afraid of! That other people will want to leave. Where would your rich donors be if there were no people to do the work? What if everyone decided to leave? They're terrified of that! If the people left the planet, your sponsors would have no money. They'd have to do their own work. The world doesn't have to be this way, but that's the kind of world you want."

"—guilty on all counts. You are clearly without remorse and I recommend the maximum scrutiny and sentencing. You will go down in history as a traitor of the United States, and perhaps the planet."

A spacetime sphere opened next to Rive. All members of the press, and some men in the seats, stood up and took pictures.

Rive spoke as it opened. "Madame Secretary CJ Rhine assisted us in determining if part of humanity can be saved from itself. Eventually the animal drive to rebel against control will outpace your donors' ability to constrain the people, and it will tear society apart. Take comfort knowing something of humanity will survive offworld, and it does not threaten your chance at reproduction at all. You won't meet us again."

Rive set the microphone down as he turned to CJ. He held out his hand. She looked at him and took it. Rive walked through the portal. CJ followed him through as pandemonium erupted. Reporters shouted questions, police rushed for her. The way closed as soon as she had stepped through.

CJ stood still and glared at the raptor. He turned to her, still holding her hand. She stared at him for half a minute, waiting for him to say something. He only looked at her. Finally she lunged forward and embraced him. Rive wrapped his neck around her.

"Rive... Your metal. It's warm."

Rive held her tighter. "I've had time to talk to my metal a little more. It's learning."

He radiated heat now, and it was an improvement. It was such a relief to touch someone else after being isolated for so long. She separated from him, looked him in the eye.

"Where are we?"

"Mexico."

"That's not far enough! They're going to convict me! They'll send people to kill me!"

Rive nuzzled her nose. "We can live anywhere."

"Offworld?"

"If you wish. We don't have to leave. There must be many things you want to do here. Truthfully, I feel bad that our presence is going to make life worse for so many people. It is why we never visit uncontacted planets. Especially lone species. The dominant males who own this world have told everyone to be afraid of us, and now people are. It will be used to justify all sorts of atrocities, and it will not end. I am sorry for that."

Rive's hand trembled as he reached down and touched her fingers.

"CJ... Crystal... I can go anywhere in the universe, but on Tavax I realized... All I wanted was to be where you are.

I enjoyed working with you all these months. On your days off, I was at the White House waiting for you. I was lost without you. I... have not felt like this for anyone before. Not even my fox. I do not want it to end. I will stay on Earth for you. I will take you anywhere you want to go, anywhere you need to be, and they will not find you."

CJ smiled. She felt his claws. She leaned into his muzzle and pressed her lips to his. Rive embraced her even tighter.

The Lake

The universe swirled around Deka and fell into him. He could not look away, as his vision encompassed all directions. The universe seemed to exist all at once now. Past and present eclipsed one another, as if the entire universe had been compressed into a single panoramic image that surrounded Deka, and layered on top of that was the next fraction of a second, and the next, and the next. Projected onto that was the future, everything in front of him, moving constantly, testing the limits of his mind. His body did not exist, so he presumed the antisphere had separated his mind from his body without scattering it.

He became aware of someone touching him, not a body, but another conscious presence, and it had surrounded him. He recognized it as Sonjaa. There was no language here. No touch. No sensations perceptible as Deka once knew. Only the mind without the body existed here. He became aware of Sonjaa's mind. She was talking to him. She knew he would come, and she had caught him.

Deka thought of something in English. It was the only language in the universe that had the words to express what Deka was feeling. Holy fucking shit!

Sonjaa told him to get a grip on himself. She was holding him together right now, but he had to learn how to hold himself.

Deka felt Sonjaa moving away from him, and he felt a lurch. The universe seemed to speed up slightly. Deka realized what was happening. He remembered what Sonjaa had said, about how she held herself together. He needed an anchor, a focal point. Deka chose Sonjaa's touch, focused on that and nothing else. His mind took in the rest of the information around him, but comprehending it was dangerous.

Sonjaa still enveloped him, and she began moving. Deka was not sure how to move out here, so he settled for being moved, not in the sense he was used to, but through the spaces between the real universe, aware of the reality he had left behind all around him, but out of reach.

The more he comprehended the space between the universe, the more he perceived the things inside it. Other things touched him, but they did not seem to be made of anything.

Sonjaa sent him direct vibrations through their particles. She asked him how long he had known what was happening to her.

Deka took comfort as she contained him. He told her he suspected the Lake had torn down her subconscious, and the shock had been too large for her to rebuild a new one. She had become an Archeon, but not in the usual way. He realized back on Neben if they were to survive this, she needed to face the Lake again, and he had to prepare her for it. Sonjaa sent him warm vibrations in reply.

Other vibrations came from somewhere out there. Deka understood them as a sense of sight and traced the waves to the source. Two conscious minds wrestled in the distance. Two more waves hovered a little distance from both of them. The vibrations on the left were Kylac, and the ones on the right belonged to Friend. Some distance away, their old ways vibrated, moving closer, trying to join back up with them.

Kylac was screaming.

Deka shouted back, which sent vibrations through the particles of consciousness and reached both foxes. Friend had been lying to them even on Labccr. He didn't want Kylac to kill his old ways, and he never expected Kylac to kill his own. Severing his old ways was possible, but it did not solve the real problem, which was that Friend had animal instincts, and he was not strong enough to handle them.

Kylac was just learning how to move out here, and he swam away from Friend. The equations had told him how to hold himself together, so that was not a problem. Deka felt the vibrations coming closer. He and Sonjaa were almost there, and Friend was in pursuit.

Deka shouted out to Kylac that he had figured out what Friend was trying to do a long time ago, but he could not tell him about it for fear Friend would change tactics. Friend wanted to absorb Kylac's higher mind to gain his self-control. The reason he had not succeeded in understanding the Lake was because his old ways were holding his mind back, and he needed Kylac to tame those instincts for him. The antifox had been a show purely to convince Kylac coming to the Lake was the only solution. If not for this possible way to gain control of his animal side, Friend would have destroyed everyone long ago.

Friend thought back as he pursued Kylac. Thoughts and communication produced equally strong vibrations through the medium in which they swam. He said it was essential to being free of the universe. Every species has an animal nature, and he believed a species' animal side prevented it from perceiving the real universe, thus leaving it and beginning a new one.

Sonjaa swam faster, still holding Deka together as he tried to perceive everything around him, following the nonlinear vectors of the vibrations of Friend pursuing Kylac, both their old ways also in pursuit.

Friend continued that he had run the clock forward in his mind, perceived everyone who will ever live and die in the universe, and he had calculated nobody will come into contact with the Lake. The universe was doomed to die, forgotten and isolated; nobody will leave it except Friend, and yet he could not perceive what the Lake actually was. He didn't come all this way just to find out it's impossible for him to cross the last threshold. He won't let all those people die for nothing. The universe will mature, and it will start with himself and Kylac.

Kylac expressed disgust merging minds with him.

Friend replied that it was actually Stephen and Norh who inspired the idea. Knowing how they did it gave him the idea to do it, but he could not force Kylac to merge until his old ways were separated. Merging minds might mean their instincts would not recognize them or seek them out and reconnect. They would destroy all life in the universe in time, free to wander about as they pleased, but that would not matter once Friend learned how to explore the Lake. Even if they did reconnect, Friend was confident they would be strong enough together to resist them, so there was no way to lose.

The reptiles swam faster. Sonjaa flowed around Deka, exposing one side of him. Deka felt himself spreading out again. Perceiving the universe complete and whole was so new and exciting he wanted to take it all in. He felt the pace of the universe slowing down, and he took that as a sign it was time to pull himself together. He exerted something similar to gravity on his own particles to keep them from drifting apart. He would have become scrambled out here long before he realized this without Sonjaa holding him.

Deka and Sonjaa caught up to the vibrations that felt like Friend. They gripped it. Deka had no hands, and the only way to exert force here was to extend his personal gravity. A piece of Friend became trapped in Deka's field.

Sonjaa exerted attractive force on Friend as well. Kylac swam farther away, and floated at some distance.

Deka snarled at Friend.

The older fox laughed. There was no way to harm anything out here; he had no claws or teeth, and no way to consume anything.

Deka threatened to absorb him.

Friend warned Deka not to hold him too long. His old ways were catching up, and if he still valued the people in the universe, he would not allow them to touch him.

The entire universe flashed around and through them —every planet, every person, every molecule visible at once, within their perception, flashing and flickering. The present. They were moving with the universe as it traveled through the Lake. The future was obvious, and the past lingered some distance behind its nonlinear motion.

Cutting through it, catching up to the universe, swam two antifoxes.

Friend laughed again. Consumption did not work the way it did in the familiar universe. Deka could begin to absorb Friend, but Friend was confident he had way more experience out here, and he would dominate Deka. He wasn't interested in Deka. He only wanted Kylac.

Deka thought he knew how to speak without sending waves through the entire Lake. He sent Kylac an idea.

Kylac sent a narrow wave to Deka, full of fear—Deka had not seen what was beyond the universe, and if he thought reality was scary like this, he was in for a shock at what lay beyond.

Deka replied that he had no other ideas.

Sonjaa had been getting these thoughts directly by touch with Deka. She agreed, and she was ready.

The antifoxes swam up to their respective foxes. Friend pulled in Deka's grip, but the raptor's gravity was apparently stronger than Friend's. The older fox was snarling. He was so close to understanding. Together, he and Kylac could figure it out. He was sure of it.

Deka sent Kylac another narrow wave. He trusted Kylac's self control with the fate of the universe.

Friend's antifox slammed into him. Deka and Sonjaa held him by the tail. Friend screamed. It sent shockwaves across the Lake, and people in the real universe perceived it as a disembodied sound.

Kylac's old ways slammed into him a moment later. Kylac also screamed, but unlike Friend, he had experience stopping himself from destroying all life in the universe. He swam over to Friend.

The other fox writhed, casting out waves of panic and undiluted scent anxiety. Waves appeared all around him, and the Archeons recognized they were portals into the real universe. He was trying to kill the scents. There was nothing to stop him now. He didn't need Kylac on his side, so there was no harm in destroying everything, except that it would not help him perceive the Lake. His old ways would still be there, holding him back, but now he would be alone with them, a fate worse than death, but the animal nature only knew urges, and satisfied them.

Deka moved his conscious mind around Friend, blocking the ways from reaching the universe. Friend thrashed. Kylac swam up to them and enclosed Friend the rest of the way, encasing the reverted fox completely inside three conscious minds, held in place by the willpower that kept their essence from flying apart in the Lake.

The fox snarled and thrashed and shot millions of portals in all directions. None found the real universe. The vibrations Friend sent were gibberish, the screams of the antifox. He was trying to separate his old ways from his higher mind, but the gravity of the other Relians prevented his substance from going anywhere.

Deka announced all together.

They halted.

The universe froze in place. Deka recognized what it was doing. This was a moment in the past. The universe had sped on without them, leaving them here, inside the impression it had left in the Lake.

Deka nudged them to the side. The past moved around them for a time, and then they left the outline of the universe. Before them was the snapshot of the universe as it had been at that instant. Another universe lay behind and overlapping it, the same one, just an impression of where it had been in the past.

They could now see the waves in the Lake where their universe had been. An infinite number of impressions it had made as it traveled through this place, all at slightly different time intervals. They adjusted their perception and focused on the path it had taken forward. The universe had moved on without them, leaving a wake that was the past. The universe was gone, and they now drifted away from it.

The fox enclosed within them like a nucleus had calmed down, but he was still reverted. Still thrashing. Still trying to lash out at them, but he had no claws or teeth, and their will to resist being consumed was stronger than his will to snuff out their scents. He huddled into himself and panicked silently.

Kylac's old ways had calmed as well, but he was still consciously reverted. The other Relians had no scent out here, but Kylac was aware of their presence, which his instincts interpreted as scent, which was a danger. It took effort not to lash out at them, too.

Sonjaa perceived the line of travel that marked their universe getting further and further away. The vibrations the universe generated through the lake became weaker and weaker. The distance became palpable, and she gravitated herself against Deka harder.

Deka held each of them tightly. He felt particles that comprised the Lake washing around him, but no mind behind any of them. These were pieces of lost minds, scrambled and flying about at random, and it was all he could perceive in every direction.

They clung to one another's thoughts as they drifted into the void.

About the Author

James L. Steele has had the idea for the Archeon series in his head since the mid-1990s.

He has been published in various anthologies and magazines, including: *The Furry MEGAPACK®*, *Zooscape*, *Tall Tales with Short Cocks V.2*, *The Reclamation Project*, *Claw the Way to Victory*, and *Shark Week*.

His sci-fi novel *Huvek* is published through Argyll Productions.

He lives in Ohio, where he pursues his hobby of becoming a wine connoisseur while having several simultaneous existential crises per day.

Blog: DaydreamingInText.blogspot.com

Twitter: @JLSteeleAuthor